CIRCLE OF LIES

CIRCLE OF LIES

DOUGLAS ALAN

A TOM DOHERTY ASSOCIATES BOOK
NEW YORK

This is a work of fiction. All of the characters, organizations, and events portrayed in this novel are either products of the author's imagination or are used fictitiously.

CIRCLE OF LIES

A Forge Book
Published by Tom Doherty Associates, LLC
175 Fifth Avenue
New York, NY 10010

www.tor-forge.com

Forge® is a registered trademark of Tom Doherty Associates, LLC.

ISBN 978-0-7653-2246-3

First Edition: December 2010

Printed in the United States of America

0 9 8 7 6 5 4 3 2 1

ACKNOWLEDGMENTS

ADVICE TO ASPIRING WRITERS

Listen to your editors. You will come to learn that they are part friend, part psychologist, part counselor, part complaint department, and the lions at the gate. My sincere thanks goes to Claire Eddy, Kristin Sevick, Tom Doherty, and the wonderful people at Tor for their constant support, suggestions, and their ability to make a writer in a solitary profession feel like part of the family.

CIRCLE OF LIES

PROLOGUE

THE sound of a branch snapping pulled the woman's head around. She stopped walking and peered into the woods where the noise had come from. There was nothing. The forest surrounding Atlanta's Stone Mountain was not dangerous. It was probably just a small animal, she decided. The park was full of them. She shrugged and resumed her walk.

A network of paths and nature trails crisscrossed the acreage. Some had little signs indentifying the kind of plant or tree visitors might be looking at. A haven twenty miles from the city, Stone Mountain was a good place to pass a few hours. The air had a clean feel to it that she liked.

In recent weeks life had become increasingly complicated and Charlotte wasn't sure how to deal with the situation. Some quiet and a little time to think was what she needed now. She was still young and there were options. Her face had few lines and her figure still drew looks from the men in her office . . . which was precisely the problem. Recently, two coworkers had begun to show more than just passing interest in her. Both men were nice and both had been generous. Unfortunately, both were married. The last thing she needed was an office intrigue. Such relationships usually ended badly with someone either losing their job or leaving. It was all very confusing.

Thanksgiving would arrive in another week, bringing her children home from college. It would give them a chance to talk. They were a close family and she needed someone to confide in. Her job was important and she didn't relish the prospect of starting over again.

Despite a chill in the air, fall was her favorite season. Charlotte pulled her sweater tighter. It had been getting dark a little earlier each day. Dry leaves crunched beneath her feet as she went, their colors still vivid, but fading now. For some reason, the farther up the path she went the more she became afraid. It was nothing she could put her finger on. Annoyed, she chided herself and kept going.

Fifty yards ahead, where the trail turned, two men stood in the shadows watching her. One was Hispanic and barely in his twenties, the other perhaps fifty. The younger man's hands were shaking and there were beads of sweat on his forehead. Though tough and street-smart, he had never been involved in anything like this. He swallowed several times. His companion, on the other hand, seemed at completely ease. He was dressed in a pair of worn Eddie Bauer slacks, a conservative plaid shirt, a dark green windbreaker and Timberland loafers. When the younger man started forward he placed a hand on his shoulder.

"Not yet," he said quietly.

"She's almost here."

The older man nodded and kept his eyes fixed on the woman. "Wait until she passes."

On the opposite side of the path a third man also watched as the woman approached. He cast a questioning look at the leader, but the other motioned for him to stay put. The third man understood and scratched the stubble on his chin. His body was thick and his hands large and calloused. On his right forearm was the faded tattoo of a swastika. There was another with two lightning bolts on the side of his neck. When you came right down to it, he decided, women were all the same. They only wanted a man for what they could get. This one was probably like all the rest.

Preoccupied with her problems the woman walked past them. She didn't hear them coming until it was too late. At a signal from the leader the two men started forward. The older man watched the unfolding scene with an unchanging expression. When it was over he glanced over his shoulder at a fourth man who had also been observing what transpired from behind some boulders. It was obvious they knew each other.

THE following morning two teenage boys walking a dog noticed a woman's naked leg sticking out from under a bush fifteen yards off the path and ran for help. They found a maintenance worker who returned with them, saw what happened, and promptly summoned the police. A detective and a crime-scene photographer arrived thirty minutes later and cordoned off the area with yellow tape.

It was the first rape-murder anyone could remember in Stone Mountain for a long, long time.

ONE

Atlanta, Georgia
November 2008

Y defining moment as an attorney didn't come in court. It happened outside it in the lobby of the Fulton County Judicial Building. Theodore Jordan could have asked a dozen lawyers to represent him. He didn't . . . he asked me.

We had grown up together, and as his friend I suppose my first inclination was to believe he was innocent.

What occured at the courthouse changed all that. It brought my religion into sharp focus. Not the kind you practice in church, or in a synagogue, or even in a mosque. The faces in the crowd are what did it for me.

I stood off to one side watching people nod in agreement as the district attorney laid out his case during an "impromptu" press conference. For them the battle was over before it had begun. Ted Jordan was guilty. Simple. The cops had found his fingerprints at the murdered man's home. And they traced money stolen from his law firm to his bank account. What more did anyone need?

"We hope to dispose of this case quickly," the DA said, pitching his voice to carry to the farthest corners of the lobby.

More people nodded.

News of Theodore Jordan's arrest for murder and embezzlement had made the front page of *The Atlanta Journal-Constitution*. It carried a wow factor of ten on the Richter scale. Before you could say due process, the national press picked up the story. The courthouse became a media circus with Ted Jordan and myself at center stage. Like everyone else, I'd read about the grizzly murder of Sanford Hamilton in the papers, but never expected my friend to be arrested in connection with it. His call from the jail came in at 2:00 A.M.

As Thornton Schiff fed more details to the crowd, people in the lobby exchanged knowing glances. Not that you could blame them. It was like watching the Jerry Springer show or a bad accident. The facts were mesmerizing, something a canny politician recognizes out of instinct. I'd met Schiff on a number of occasions and always considered him an insufferable prick. In fact I might have said that to his face at a bar luncheon several years earlier, so there was no love lost between us.

A podium with the State Seal of Georgia had been hurriedly set up under Robert Fulton's portrait, our county's namesake. In front of it were a half-dozen microphones. Behind Schiff stood the director of the Georgia Bureau of Investigation, Bennett Lange. To Lange's right was a woman I knew by sight, but not personally. Her name was Rena Bailey. She was an assistant DA. Judging from past experience, there was a good chance she would handle the majority of the trial with Schiff coming in for the kill once it was a lock. There's nothing like a high profile case to get a faltering election campaign back on the right track. Mr. Schiff needed a winner and this was it. His recent downslide in the polls made this opportunity doubly attractive. The last man on the podium I also didn't know, but everything about him said cop.

The dog and pony show continued as paralegals from Schiff's office moved through the crowd passing out copies of a prepared statement to the press corps and anyone else who was interested. I took one and glanced through it.

A slender woman with the Channel 2 Action News Team held a copy in one hand and a microphone in the other. She reminded me of Joan Rivers. She shouted questions along with a score of other reporters.

"Mr. Schiff, is the state confident of a conviction?"

The DA's head swiveled in her direction. He paused for effect. "Jean, nothing in the law is certain, but I'll tell you this, our investigators have done a fine job pulling this case together. At this point we don't know what evidence will be admitted until Judge McKenzie rules, so I can't get into much detail at this time, but the answer to your question is 'yes.' I'm reasonably certain the people will have a conviction once the dust settles."

"Are you seeking the death penalty?" a reporter from WKZT called out.

The din of voices immediately dropped to hear Schiff's answer.

"Good morning, Jack. Normally, we reserve decisions like that until all the facts are in, but I'm going to break precedent and say that we *will* be asking for the death penalty in this case. Sanford Hamilton was tortured and left to die in a burning inferno. In addition to the other charges, Ms. Bailey will be adding arson to the indictment."

Big surprise there since my handout contained a section entitled, "Victim Torture and Arson." There wasn't time to read all the details, nor was it necessary. Thornton Schiff was doing that for me.

The questions lasted five minutes. Those the DA didn't want to, or couldn't answer, he simply sidestepped. More reporters crowded into the lobby along with a number of lawyers who happened to be there by chance. They were curious to see what all the commotion was about.

"Jesus, they're crucifying the guy," said a familiar voice next to me.

I glanced to my right and recognized an old friend. Like myself, Jimmy d'Taglia was a transplanted New Yorker and at one time a lawyer in my wife's firm. He had since moved on and was now an assistant U.S. Attorney.

I nodded slowly. They were crucifying Ted.

"Sightseeing?" he asked.

"Not today."

There was a pause.

"Tell me you're kidding," Jimmy said.

"Wish I could."

"Won't your school mind? You haven't been teaching there that long."

"I know."

"It sounds like this guy's in a world of shit. Do you have a defense?"

"I hate seeing people build a gallows before the trial starts. Puts a damper on things."

"Jesus," Jimmy said. "You're walking into a buzz saw."

And I nodded again. The people around me nodded. But our reasons were different. To this day I don't know what made me do it. One minute I was standing there with Jimmy and the rest of the crowd listening to Schiff's spiel and the next I began to applaud. Heads turned in my direction.

I announced, "Well, I think he's guilty. By a show of hands, who else here thinks Ted Jordan is guilty?"

Incredibly, several people raised their hands.

"C'mon, the rest of you, don't hold back. He sounds guilty as hell to me. Why don't we skip the bond hearing and go straight to conviction?"

A moment of shocked silence followed. People weren't sure what to make of the interruption. I wasn't sure—it was just coming out.

"Doesn't he need a trial?" asked a woman at the back of the room.

"What for? I say go for the death penalty right now."

A number of spectators exchanged confused glances and the cop on the podium started toward me. He stopped at a slight head shake from Schiff. A paternal smile appeared on the DA's face.

"If the gentleman would please restrain himself," he said, holding a hand above his eyes and squinting into the lights. "This is an emotional time for all of us. We're trying to conduct a press conference." It was obvious he couldn't see my face yet.

"If I restrain myself, I'll be the only one doing it."

"Excuse me?"

"No, I don't think I will. I was under the impression a lawyer can't seek publicity to gain an advantage at trial, but I guess that doesn't apply here."

Schiff's smile slowly dissolved. "Who the hell do you think you are?"

"I know who I am. The question is, who are you? And what right do you have to bend the law?"

The color in the Schiff's face rose by at least two shades. Keeping his eyes fixed on me he said to the cop, "I've had enough of this idiot, Burt. Get him out of here."

The investigator nodded to two sheriff's deputies who were leaning against the far wall observing the proceedings. They began to push their way toward me.

"Unless you want a lawsuit for violating Theodore Jordan's civil rights, I'd tell your men to back off."

The cameras immediately swung around focusing their black

lenses on me. Through the lights I saw Rena Bailey take a step toward the rear of the podium.

Schiff shielded his eyes and finally recognized my face. "Ah, Mr. Delaney. My job is to see everyone gets a fair trial. You'd do well to remember that. I was elected to protect the people of this county from predators and that's what I intend to do."

Spoken like a true politician. "Then do it in court and not out here."

"Listen you smug, son-of-a—"

"My client wants the same rights as everyone in this lobby—the right to a trial not poisoned by publicity and political grandstanding."

"Your client?"

"That's right, Mr. Schiff."

A buzz circulated throughout the crowd as eight or ten microphones were shoved under my nose. Katherine is fond of saying there's nothing like making an entrance. Reporters started shouting questions from all sides. I held up my hand for silence.

"Ladies and gentlemen, I'm appalled by what's happening here. We're better than this. Ted Jordan has been a respected member of this community for years. His children go to school here. His job is here. So are his friends. He didn't steal any money from his law firm and he sure as hell didn't murder anyone. I promise you these charges will be contested with every ounce of our strength.

"Theodore Jordan is an innocent man. In case any of you missed that, I'll repeat it. The word is *innocent* and we're going to prove it. Only we won't do so here in the lobby. We'll do it in a courtroom where cases are tried. You can take that to the bank."

The last part was for effect. It was something Donald Trump might have said and he generally comes off as credible, except maybe for the hair. A number of reporters wrote down my words verbatim. I hoped they wouldn't come back to haunt me. *As Theodore Jordan was led to the gallows this reporter was reminded that his lawyer once said . . .*

More questions were shouted, but with a little help from Jimmy we managed to push our way through the crowd and onto the elevator. That's the way it goes with religion. You might say it was an epiphany of sorts. Friend or not, Ted Jordan wasn't there to speak for himself. I was.

TWO

THE ride to Judge Dan McKenzie's court didn't take long. Several out-of-breath reporters began arriving by way of the stairs and the other elevators. Their questions started the moment they saw us. I ignored them and entered the court. Most of the benches were already filled. Ted's wife, Maureen, a pretty blonde he had married thirteen years earlier, was sitting in the third row. Next to her was Charles Evans, senior partner of Ted's law firm and its founding member. That was a good sign. Evans had been Ted's mentor and a second father to him since law school. Maureen waved when she saw me. Evans made eye contact and nodded.

The sole issue that morning was whether bond would be set. This meant the people packed into the courtroom weren't there as witnesses or even connected with the case for that matter. They were merely curious. Not that I blamed them. As I scanned the room my eyes settled on an attractive dark-haired woman in a navy blue dress seated in the last row. Lawyers are good at recognizing one of their own. Sort of like sharks. I'm no different. My impression was that she was simply another spectator, but there was something in the way she returned my gaze. I looked away before she did.

Since the news of Sanford Hamilton's murder had hit the papers several months ago, the DA's office had managed to leak a steady stream of details about the case to the media—the more sensational ones. When an arrest was finally made, the result was a mêlée. I was still in the dark about many of the details. Most of what I knew came from CNN, Fox News, and my passing conversations with Ted on the subject. There was no sign of my client in the room, which meant the sheriff's deputies hadn't brought him up from the holding cells yet.

"Mind if I hang around?" Jimmy asked, pulling my attention back to the moment.

"What?"

"I said do you mind if I hang around? I was down here to file some papers and got sidetracked by the commotion. I'm curious to see how this turns out."

The former cop in me noticed he wasn't carrying a briefcase or any files, but I didn't comment. There was no harm in Jimmy being present. Even if I did mind there was nothing I could do about it.

I said, "You were just down here by coincidence?"

Jimmy didn't answer immediately. He glanced out the window at a red-and-white news helicopter hovering above the street.

"Okay, what gives?" I prompted.

"John, all I can tell you is our office has an interest in this case. How about if we grab a cup of coffee when you're through?"

For the life of me I couldn't figure out why the feds cared about what was happening here. Murder cases, even spectacular ones, are strictly state affairs. Unfortunately I didn't have time for guessing games.

"Suit yourself."

I left Jimmy and made my way down the center aisle to the defendant's table. An identical version with four chairs was situated opposite it on the other side.

EARLIER that year, Judge Dan McKenzie had announced his intention to retire from public service. This was to be his last case. His opinions were legend in Atlanta's legal circles. Some were longer than those the Court of Appeals handed down. Over the last thirty-three years he'd rarely been reversed. According to a colleague who had tried several cases in front of him, he was irascible and had little tolerance for incompetence. If you showed up unprepared in his court you could expect a public tongue-lashing or worse. The operative words here are *his court*. I knew of one instance where he had actually put a lawyer in jail for three hours because he came in five minutes late for a hearing. Since moving to Atlanta I'd heard a number of "McKenzie stories," none of which increased my comfort level at the moment.

As I was getting my papers organized, Thornton Schiff, Rena

Bailey, and their entourage entered the courtroom. Schiff paused to shake hands with several people, leaving Rena Bailey to continue on alone. I half-expected him to do one of those Pope-on-the-balcony waves. He settled for a sneer in my general direction. The cop and the GBI director took seats in the row behind Jimmy. Rena walked down the aisle and directly up to me. For the first time, I noticed she was pregnant. I thought she was somewhere in her early thirties. Except for a touch of lipstick she wasn't wearing any makeup.

"Hi, I'm Rena Bailey," she said, holding out her hand. "Looks like we're working together."

"Looks like it." I said, getting to my feet. We shook.

"Do you have a minute to discuss the case?" she asked.

"Sure, but I think the judge is about to come out."

Rena glanced at the bailiff and motioned to attract his attention. Using hand signals, she got her message across. The bailiff nodded and stepped inside the judge's chambers.

She informed me, "We'll be fine. Let's use the jury room. It's a little more private."

Impressive. Whenever I motion to a bailiff all they do is stare back at me. Once we were inside she closed the door, walked up to the thermostat, and frowned at it.

"Do you mind if I turn this down? I'm boiling."

"Be my guest. How much longer do you have?" I asked, indicating her belly with my chin.

"Four months," Rena replied, slowly easing herself into a chair. "He kicks like a son-of-a-bitch."

"You already know it's a boy?"

"An educated guess. Only guys give you this much trouble." She patted her stomach. "I'll make him pay when he's out."

I smiled politely.

"Mr. Delaney, I thought we should talk before you make your motion."

"You can call me, John."

"Only in private. I assume you're asking for bond. Right?"

"And I assume you're here to oppose it."

"Truly, Thornton doesn't like you very much at the moment."

"The feeling's mutual."

Rena laughed silently. "I never saw him react like that. As soon as we were alone he went off like a Roman candle."

"Probably due to my pleasing personality."

Rena shifted her weight in the chair to a more comfortable position. "So what are you looking for, John?"

"How about a release on his own recognizance?"

At least she was polite enough not to laugh.

"Even if I did agree, there's no way McKenzie will go for it. We're dealing with a murder compounded by aggravation and a half-million-dollar theft, not to mention the arson charge. We also have the attention of the free world focused on us. It ain't gonna happen. We both know that."

"Ted Jordan isn't a flight risk. He has no record and he's a member of the bar with substantial ties to the community. I've known this man for years and I'm telling you he didn't kill Sanford Hamilton. They were partners."

Rena stared at me for a moment. She appeared to be struggling with something. Eventually, she reached into her briefcase, retrieved a file folder, and slid it across the table to me.

"I've met Jordan, too, and I agree he doesn't seem the type. To be honest, a lot of things don't add up in this case. When we took your client's statement he said he had never been to Hamilton's home. Unfortunately, we found his fingerprints there. We also turned up a credit card receipt showing he purchased two five-gallon containers of gas the night of the fire. That's not good."

The fingerprints and arson charges I'd heard about in the lobby, so this wasn't news to me. The gasoline purchase was. It took every ounce of effort I could muster to keep the surprise off my face. In theory, nothing is supposed to take a defense lawyer unaware. Theories however, tend to work better in classrooms than in real life. The revelation was jolting. Thus far, my only opportunity to speak with Ted had been at 2:00 A.M. during our call. The phones in the jail are supposed to be secure, but you can't be certain. I took a mental breath and fell back on that time-honored response of all lawyers.

"Everyone's entitled to bail," I insisted.

"Everyone who hasn't become a public figure overnight," Rena said. "Give me something to work with and I'll go to bat for you."

"On the level?"

"Scout's honor," she said, holding up her right hand.

"What about your boss?"

"Thornton will scream his head off, but I think he'll go along with my recommendation—*provided* I bring him something reasonable. I don't have carte blanche here."

"Do you have anything specific in mind?"

"A good place to start might be returning the stolen money we found in your client's bank account."

I opened my mouth to respond, but Rena anticipated my objection and held up her hand. "*Alleged* stolen money," she added.

I nodded. "I'll need to talk with Ted Jordan. Until then, I'm not sure what I can agree to and what I can't."

The assistant DA considered this for a moment then heaved herself up out of the chair. "How long will you need?" she asked, scratching her stomach.

"At least an hour."

"Fine, I'll square it with the judge. Jesus, I hope they have the air conditioning working in the courtroom. It's hot as hell out there, don't you think?"

"You're incubating for two," I pointed out.

"There's the truth."

I liked Rena. She might be acting, but I didn't think so. Call it male intuition. We shook hands again and I followed her out the door.

THREE

ONCE inside the courtroom, Rena went to speak with the bailiff while I approached Maureen Jordan and Charles Evans. It occurred to me the situation must have hit Evans pretty hard because it was his partner who had been killed and his law firm that had been robbed. The fact that he was sitting with Ted's wife was a show of support. Hopefully, the press and jury would see it the same way. I slid onto the bench next to them.

Maureen was wearing a white dress with a floral print. The neckline was cut low and showed off her cleavage. Attractive, but not exactly court attire. I made a note to speak with her later. Once the public forms an impression it's hell trying to change it.

I informed them, "I'm heading downstairs to see Ted in a moment, but I wanted to speak with you first."

"John, this is terrible," Maureen said. "Do you think they'll let him out today?"

"It depends on how high the bond is and whether we can meet it."

"I'll do anything. I'll sell the house and my jewelry if I have to."

"Let's hope that won't be necessary. I spoke with the assistant DA a few minutes ago and she said if Ted voluntarily turns over the money in his account, she won't oppose a bond. I don't know what his position is yet, but I'm going to recommend it."

Evans nodded his agreement. "Do you have any idea how much they'll be asking for?"

"No, we've just started talking."

"Delaney, I'm in a funny position here. Sandy Hamilton was my partner and my friend. I don't believe that boy killed anyone. But my partners don't share this view. They're out for blood. I can't afford an open break right now. Any help I give will have to be private."

I understood. I also had less than an hour to get my client's side of the story. I thanked them and excused myself.

GETTING to the basement of the Fulton County Courthouse is easier said than done. I was forced to weave my way through a throng of reporters who started shouting questions the moment they saw me. I gave them my best presidential wave and kept going. A second before the elevator doors closed, a slender female hand slipped between them and hit the open bar.

It took a second before I realized the hand belonged to the dark-haired woman I'd seen at the back of the courtroom. I gave her a tight-lipped smile. For the second time in the last fifteen minutes I had to struggle to keep the surprise off my face when she asked, "May I have a word with you, Professor?"

Her English and pronunciation were excellent, but I could detect a slight accent—French I thought.

"I'm somewhat pressed for time right now. Is this in connection with the case?"

"It is."

"In what way?"

"I'm a friend of Theo."

"Theo? I'm sorry, I—"

"Theodore Jordan. You and your friends call him Ted. Personally, I prefer Theo. It's so much nicer, don't you think?"

"Immensely. Unfortunately, I can't discuss anything without my client' . . . uh, Theo's permission. I'm not trying to be rude, but—"

"The attorney-client privilege. Yes, I know. We have the same thing in France."

"Oh, are you a lawyer, Ms.? . . ."

"Severin, Professor. And to answer your question . . . yes, I am a lawyer. But I'm here in the capacity of a friend."

Ms. Severin was a handsome woman. Her eyes were green and she had an athletic figure. There was an air of confidence in the way she carried herself. Her height was about 5'8". In heels she nearly came up to my eye level and I'm 6'1". I liked the way she looked straight at you when she spoke.

"That's wonderful," I said. "At the moment Ted needs all the

friends he can get. Actually, I'm on my way to see him now. Perhaps
we can talk later."

"Perhaps."

"May I ask how you know him?"

"We met on a business trip several months ago."

"I see."

The elevator arrived at the basement and we got off together. It
was a bleak place lit with fluorescent lights. The floors were cement
and painted gray; the walls olive green. From time to time I've
mused the same person must design basements around the world.
Just being there is depressing. You get a sense the building is press-
ing down on you. Opposite us was an incongruous poster of a mountain sunset and a blue lake. The slogan beneath it read: THE CHOICES
WE MAKE IN LIFE DETERMINE OUR DESTINY. Alongside the poster was
another that bore the sheriff's seal and the motto: SERVICE & EXCEL-
LENCE. WE'RE HERE TO HELP.

My new companion handed me her business card. There were
two phone numbers written on the back of it.

"Are you leaving, Ms. Severin?"

"In a few minutes. And please call me Gabriele."

"John," I replied, extending a hand to her.

She shook it. Her grip was firm and dry. "Do you think there will
be a problem with Theo's bond?"

"A *problem* is a rather mild way of putting it. Theo is being charged
with murder, torture, embezzlement, and arson. Under the best circumstances it would be difficult to convince any judge to release
him. All the publicity just makes matters worse."

"But there *is* a chance."

"Yes, there's a chance. Assuming we can get a bond set, the amount
is likely to be very—"

"Agree to whatever they ask for. I'll have the money transferred to
your trust account as soon as you let me know how much it is."

Her statement brought me to a halt. "That's a very nice thing for
a friend to do, Ms. . . . uh, Gabriele."

She didn't reply immediately. She simply held eye contact with
me. That was when it entered my mind Ted and Gabriele might be
more than just friends. Ted and I had known each other forever and

I'd never heard him mention her name before. Understandable, since most people are reluctant to advertise infidelity. I thought of Maureen waiting upstairs and wasn't sure what to make of the situation.

"Why don't you just hang around and hear the result for yourself?" I said.

"I've already taken a chance in coming here. It's not safe for me to stay."

Gabriele glanced over her shoulder and checked the corridor. There were people at the opposite end, but no one was paying us any attention. Turning back to me, she said, "Please call me once the hearing is over."

"At one of these numbers on the back?"

"The first one."

"Where are you staying?"

"At the Four Seasons Hotel."

"I see. What is this second number?"

"It's to a man named Marc Honoré. Marc is my banker in Paris with Crédit Lyonnais. I'm sure you've heard of them. I spoke with him earlier and he's waiting for your call. Feel free to check my references, if you wish. I know this is confusing, John, but if you truly are Theo's friend you'll help us. He has no place else to turn."

Her reference to "us" wasn't lost on me, but it was neither the time nor the place to get into the specifics of their love life. Conceivably the lady standing in front of me was nothing more than a concerned girlfriend trying to help. At the same time I also remembered Ted Jordan was being charged with embezzling a great deal of money. I took Ms. Severin under the elbow and guided her to the side of the hallway. We had to wait for two people to pass us, before I spoke again.

"Gabriele, I'm an attorney, not a spy. If the judge decides to set bond it will be high—really high, so I need to know this is on the level. Forgive my being blunt, but using stolen money to post bond is frowned on by most courts."

Gabriele looked down at the floor for a moment then smiled. I noticed lighter streaks of brown in her hair.

"The funds are from my personal estate. My family is quite wealthy."

I started to speak, but she continued.

"I know what you are thinking and your concern is natural. Make whatever inquiries you need to."

"I will."

"There is only one stipulation. My name must be kept entirely out of these proceedings. May I rely on your discretion in this?"

I studied her for a moment and read nothing in her face. My gut told me she was being honest. At least that's what I wanted to believe. Her eyes were vaguely almond shaped and her hair came down to her shoulders. The impression she conveyed was one of class without trying. It was an attractive combination, but I recalled the Sirens who lured Ulysses to the rocks were also attractive.

"If that's the way you want it. I'm sure Ted will appreciate your offer. Assuming he gives me permission, I'll call and let you know how much to send. This is a very odd situation. I probably need to have my head examined."

Gabriele's smile faded slightly. "You don't," she said. "There is one other thing I must mention. If anyone from the Tissinger Corporation approaches you, please be extremely careful and trust nothing they say."

"Tissinger? The drug company? What do they have to do—"

"That's all I can tell you right now. Theo will fill in the rest." She glanced down the corridor again then back at me, gave my hand a quick squeeze, then turned and walked away.

It was the second time that morning someone told me that was all they could say.

FOUR

TED Jordan and I grew up in the same neighborhood. When we were in college we talked about climbing the Alps and hiking across Europe. Life got in the way. I became a cop and he went to law school. In recent years Ted's climbing had been confined to rock walls in upscale gymnasiums or weekend getaways. Mine consisted of trudging up tenement staircases to interview Manhattan's crime victims.

The practice of law came later to me than to him. My first career ended abruptly when a robbery suspect put three bullets in my chest. That was seventeen years ago. As a result I retired on a medical pension and went to law school at night.

We had each moved to Atlanta for different reasons. Ted was hired by one of the city's leading law firms. I relocated to be with Katherine. Once I settled here, I accepted a position at Emory where I teach courses in forensics and evidence.

Ted is your prototypical urban professional. He coaches little league soccer and belongs to a pricey country club that hosts a professional golf tournament every year. Katherine and I had socialized with Maureen and him a number of times and their marriage always seemed solid enough to me.

I shook my head as I watched Gabriele disappear around the corner. You never know. When she was gone I glanced at the poster on the wall again and read its slogan. THE CHOICES WE MAKE IN LIFE DETERMINE OUR DESTINY. Words to live by. I started down the hall toward the holding cells.

A deputy sheriff led me to a conference room. Ted was brought in a minute later. He was in handcuffs, leg restraints, and generally looked like hell. The only plus was that he had changed into the suit

Maureen had sent him. The shackles weren't necessary for our meeting so I asked the guard to remove them.

"Sorry, counselor—Mr. Schiff's orders. They have to stay on until he gets upstairs."

I thought the restraints were a bullshit thing to do. But there was no point in arguing because the guard wasn't likely to change his mind and the clock was ticking. The door closed after him with a thud, followed by the sound of a lock snapping into place. I'd seen prosecutors pull this sort of stunt in the past if they were trying to make a point. Sometimes it was effective, but it was still a bullshit thing to do.

I asked Ted, "Are you okay?"

He shrugged. "They woke me up at four a.m. to tell me they were adding arson to the other charges."

"I heard. So what did Sanford Hamilton do to piss you off?"

My question earned me a flat look. "I didn't kill anyone, John."

"I know."

"I swear to God. I—"

"Ted . . . I *know*."

He took a deep breath and relaxed. "Sorry. I think I'm losing it."

"Unlikely. Right now now we need to work as a team. We only have about forty minutes before they bring you upstairs. Take another breath and let's talk."

Ted closed his eyes, composed himself, and then opened them. "Go ahead," he said.

"Good. Tell me why the DA thinks you killed Hamilton."

"Because I've been set up to make it look that way. If the situation were reversed I'd probably think the same thing."

"Set up? By whom and why?"

Ted glanced at a security camera in the corner of the room. I followed his gaze.

He then lowered his voice and informed me, "It's better if we speak once I'm out. I don't want to talk in here. This whole thing is like a bad dream."

I stared at him for a long moment. "You're kidding? I'm your lawyer, remember? How can I defend you if I don't have the facts?"

Another glance at the security camera. "John, I've stumbled onto something I shouldn't have a couple of weeks ago. It involves the Tissinger Corporation. I need you to trust me. I'll fill you in on everything, but this isn't the place."

I knew the look, and I knew better than to push him, so I tried a different approach. "All right, tell me about Sanford Hamilton."

"Sandy is, or I should say was, our managing partner."

"I already know that. Any idea why your fingerprints were at his home?"

"None at all. I've never been there."

"You worked together for seventeen years and never visited him once in all that time?"

"Of course I did, but it was at his old house. Sandy moved into a new place about six months ago. He talked about inviting everyone out for a barbecue, but the idea never got off the ground."

I made note of that on my legal pad, then took out the copy of the indictment Rena Bailey had given me.

"It says Hamilton was murdered on April twelfth, 2008 as a result of a gunshot wound to the head. Following his death his house was set on fire. Any idea where you were then?"

"Any idea where you were?"

"No, but I'm not charged with murder. I don't have to account for my time. You do."

"John, I don't even know what day of the week April twelfth was."

Unlike many of my colleagues, I haven't bought a fancy PDA yet. I use a little notebook with a calendar on the back, a carry over from the old days. Katherine tried to convert me, but it hasn't taken. She finally gave up, grumbling something about me being a dinosaur in the twenty-first century. Whatever. The notebook doesn't need batteries and you can read it in sunlight.

"April twelfth was a Saturday. Does that help?" I asked.

"I don't know. I was probably at home, unless the kids had a game. I'd have to check my computer. I keep their soccer schedule on it."

"Can anyone verify that?"

"Sure, Maureen."

"Maybe you went shopping? Is that possible?"

"I suppose. Why?"

"Because if you did and you made any purchases with a credit card, we might be able to establish an alibi."

Ted wasn't much help here either, nor did I expect him to be under the circumstances. I withheld the obvious question about him buying two containers of gasoline the night of the fire. Instead, I tore a sheet of paper off my pad and drew up a release authorizing me to get his bank records. I had to place it under his hand so he could sign it. This wasn't easy because of the cuffs that were attached to a belt around his waist.

I asked, "When did you last see Hamilton alive?"

"About a week before he was killed. I got back on a Sunday afternoon from an out-of-town trip and went to the office to drop some papers off. He was in good health when I left."

"And the money?"

"You mean the funds I'm supposed to have embezzled?"

"The same."

"Total horseshit. There's no truth in it whatsoever."

"Then how did a half-million bucks get into your bank account?"

"In the first place, I didn't even know the account existed."

My eyebrows lifted.

"I know it's supposed to be in my name, but that's the goddamn truth. The first time I even heard of it was when Schiff and his goons questioned me. I told them exactly what I'm telling you. The bank is located forty miles away."

The distance meant nothing. If I had decided to steal a bunch of money I sure as hell wouldn't deposit it next door to where I lived. It was obvious Ted's nerves were frayed. His eyes were bloodshot and he needed a shave. I didn't press the point.

"You never saw any statements or deposit receipts from the bank?"

"Never. The whole thing was a complete surprise to me."

"What about Maureen?"

"The same. She asked the same questions you did."

"Do you have *any* idea why someone would open an account in your name and put a half-million dollars in it?"

"I do, and it all goes back to Tissinger. I'd have to be insane to do that." Ted leaned forward as far as his restraints would allow. "I told you I don't trust this place. Just get me out of here as quickly as you can."

I stared at him.

"John, I swear on my mother's soul I'm being straight with you."

Since my conversations with Jimmy and Gabriele, an uneasy feeling had been slowly creeping up on me. To begin with, we weren't dealing with a garden-variety murder, assuming there is such a thing. One of Atlanta's leading citizens had been killed in a pretty gruesome manner. Ted's story about a drug company wanting to frame him for killing a man he had no motive to kill only made sense in the movies. In the cold light of day it didn't hold.

In law school they tell you not to judge your client. You accept their position and advocate it to the best of your ability. That's another theory that works better in academia than in real life.

The man sitting across from me had been my friend for over forty years and I wanted to believe him. But before becoming a lawyer I'd spent a long time dealing with New York's criminal element as a cop. Contrary to what some people think, a realistic view of the world isn't bad. Something didn't jive from the mystery lady I'd met earlier to Ted's reluctance to speak now. Theatrical? Yes. Practical? No. Not when you're staring at the electric chair.

FIVE

I INFORMED Ted, "The assistant DA is a lady named Rena Bailey. We only talked for a few minutes. The bottom line is she wants the money in that account returned. Schiff's office is probably under some pressure from your partners to get it. If we relinquish our claim to the funds and turn them over voluntarily, it might go a long way toward getting a bond set."

"Fine with me."

I sat back in my seat and stared at him. No argument. No counterproposal. Good. I told him I'd see to the details.

Ted asked, "What do you think the judge will do?"

"If this case was just about embezzlement, bond wouldn't be a problem. Unfortunately, the crime-scene photos of Hamilton's body, or what was left of it, have been circulating through every tabloid in the country."

"And I'm supposed to be a mad killer, right?"

"That's how the DA sees it. Tell me about Gabriele Severin"

The question brought Ted to a halt and he leaned back in his chair. Several seconds ticked by while he looked at his feet. Eventually his head came up.

"She's a woman I'm in love with, John."

"Interesting. And how does Maureen feel about that?"

"I don't know and I don't care. I met Gabriele in France five months ago. Charlie sent me there to negotiate some contracts for one of our clients. She's an attorney."

With our ability today to fax and e-mail documents, I couldn't imagine why a lawyer needed to make a trip to France, nevertheless I motioned for him to continue.

"I made a total of three trips," he said. Tissinger is actually

Gabriele's client. They're the parent company. We represent the American division. The contract involved a huge amount of money. Each time we met we got a little closer and I don't mean legally. Our final meeting lasted maybe two hours and we followed it with a working lunch. By the time we got back to the office, I think we both knew we were going to be more than friends.

"On my second trip to Paris I received a call from a man named Mac Mercer, a private investigator I hired.

"For the past year, I've suspected Maureen has been fooling around with someone. Mac confirmed it. He has a stack of photographs of her and some asshole named Frank Nardelli."

"Who's he?"

"A tile man who's been working at our house. We're redoing the kitchen and bathrooms."

"Tile?"

Ted frowned and thought for a second. "Yeah. The son of a bitch has been on the job forever. We have a shitload of tile."

I remarked, "Gives a whole new meaning to customer service. Sorry, buddy."

"I'm not. I was going to leave her anyway. The boys are my main concern. I need to make sure they're taken care of. We can go over the details once you get me out."

"Assuming I can."

"Just give it your best shot. That's all I'm asking."

"I will."

"You should probably talk to Charlie Evans and my other partners when you get a chance. They don't believe I killed anyone."

This wasn't exactly what Evans had said. In the end, what anyone except twelve jurors thought didn't matter. It would all come down to what the State could prove and what it couldn't. I promised to speak with them and then returned to a previous topic.

"I need to know about Tissinger. You can't expect me to operate in the dark. If there's a legitimate defense, let's have it."

"John—"

"We're safe enough in here. Tell me why a major drug company is trying to frame you for murder and embezzlement."

"But—"

"*Now.*"

Ted took a breath. "You've never been particularly patient."

"The quality is overrated. I'm capable of it, but not at this moment."

Ted angled his body so his head was facing away from the security camera. I turned as well, if only to increase his comfort level.

He began. "Tissinger is about to introduce a new drug that's supposed to revolutionize the treatment of depression. It's called Torapam II. They've invested millions in research and ten times that in an advertising campaign waiting in the wings."

"Doesn't it work?" I asked.

"It works just fine if you don't mind an occasional suicide every now and then. There were four in their original test group, which the company conveniently forgot to mention to the FDA. If that information comes out it would delay the release of the drug for years."

"And you know this how?"

"Part of the information came through Gabriele. Her father was Tissinger's head of research for nearly twenty years. When he found out the data had been withheld he complained to his superiors and they fired him."

"Is that it?"

"No, there's more and it involves Stevie."

"Your son?"

"Right."

The last I heard Steve Jordan was a junior at the University of Georgia. He was studying economics or accounting. I couldn't remember which.

"Explain."

"Shortly before I left for France on my second trip I received a call from their security office asking why I had requested copies of their old test data on the Torapam trials. Not Torapam II, but the original medication that came out in 1988.

"I told him one of my boys was writing a school paper on the new depression drugs and I was trying to help him out. It never occurred to me anyone would care, because the first trials took place in the early 1980s and the information's a matter of public record. Our firm handled the FDA application back then so I figured I could save Stevie some time."

"And?"

"And nothing."

"Nothing?"

"Right. The man told me it was just a routine inquiry and I could expect a package from them with the information in a couple of days. There was nothing the least bit unusual about our conversation."

"Did you tell anyone else about the call?"

"I mentioned it to Charlie but he didn't care one way or the other. A few days later I received the package and passed it along to Stevie."

I made a note of that and asked, "So how does this translate to Tissinger being after you?"

"I'm getting to it. A week later Stevie called to ask if I had sent him everything. He thought a page was missing from the materials. Rather than bother the company again, I decided to look in our closed files."

"You keep client files from the eighties?"

"Normally, no. The bar only requires us to maintain them for seven years, but there have been a number of lawsuits involving Torapam. None of them ever amounted to anything, but each time one came up we had to produce the company's basic research in discovery."

"So, did you find anything was missing?"

"Not really. Our file contained the same number of pages as the one Tissinger had sent."

"Then what made Steve think something was wrong?"

"He and his roommate were fooling with the data from Torapam's test results. The roommate's from India and he's a math major. I guess they do that to amuse themselves. According to the boys, the report's conclusions were fine, but they weren't possible based on the calculations. That's why the kids thought there had to be another set of numbers someplace."

"Which represent what?" I asked.

"The figures are from two control groups the medication had been tested on. The researchers stated no clinical problems were uncovered during a two-year period. Apparently everyone accepted this at face value because it was such great news, including the FDA. There was no reason not to. The missing pages are just column after column of numbers. Nobody ever bothers reading them except—"

"Statistics majors."

"Right."

"Go on," I said.

"So the FDA gave their blessing and Torapam hit the market in record time. I think everyone *wanted* to believe the drug worked, considering how many people suffer from depression. At the time it was considered a breakthrough and the company made a fortune."

I was incredulous. "The FDA wouldn't approve a drug that kills people. That doesn't make sense."

"You're right, *assuming* they had all the information. They didn't. Tissinger withheld the suicide data from the final study."

I folded my arms across my chest. "How could you know that the information was withheld from the final report?"

"That's where Gabriele comes in. On my third trip to France we were having dinner and I casually mentioned what the boys had found. It was just a chance remark, but she got a funny look on her face. After some pushing she gave in and told me about her father being fired and the suicide information being left out of the FDA application. The same number of suicides showed up again in the Torapam II tests. They were left out as well."

I asked, "Did you share this with anyone?"

"Sandy Hamilton. I placed a phone call to him from Paris and asked if he knew anything about pages being edited out of the Torapam applications. Sandy had been lead counsel. He said he didn't, but would check into it.

"After that, I put it on the back burner. When I returned, I ran into him in the hallway and he assured me he was on it. He was murdered three days later.

"At his funeral two men approached me and asked if we could speak. One was from the NSA; the other was from Tissinger's security. They were interested in my conversation with Sandy and wanted to know if I had mentioned the missing data to anyone else. I decided to keep Gabriele's name out of it and told them the only reason I asked was because of my son's school project. At the time I thought they were investigating Sandy's death."

"That's not unreasonable. Is that it?"

"Pretty much, except for five dead members of Tissinger's Torapam's research team."

SIX

THE rest of our conversation was interrupted by a knock at the door. Three deputies had arrived to escort Ted upstairs. One was a sergeant. The other two were corporals.

I asked the sergeant. "Do you mind if I ride with you?"

"No problem, counselor," he said.

He stepped aside to allow his men to enter the room. One was a black man, about Ted's height. The other was white and slightly shorter, but powerfully built.

The sergeant watched while one of the deputies undid the arm restraints anchored to the chair. Once Ted was free he was escorted out of the room. I followed. Both men took up positions on either side of him and we started down the hallway toward the elevators. Each of the deputies were armed.

After we all got on the elevator the black deputy turned to Ted. "Hey, Jordan, you really cut that guy's fingers off and torch his place?"

"Wilson," the sergeant said.

"What? I can ask. He's already been given his rights. No one says he has to answer. He even got his lawyer here. That was some cold-blooded shit." He turned back to Ted. "How 'bout it, Jordan? You do your partner, then burn him up?"

The sergeant said, "Knock it off. He ain't gonna talk to you."

"I'm telling you, that was the coldest thing I ever heard of. You know they found the man's fingers at his home? Come on, Jordan, just between us."

The sergeant shook his head and looked up at the elevator's indicator lights. It wasn't necessary for me to say anything. Ted was too smart to be baited, or so I thought.

What happened next surprised me. The deputy, seemed to be enjoying the taunts, and escalated the situation by thumping Ted with his shoulder to prompt an answer. Ted's eyes suddenly grew intense and he slowly turned to face the man. He leaned forward until his face was only a few inches from the other's. The sergeant noticed what was happening and tugged on Ted's arm, trying to put some distance between the two. Deputy Wilson's smile evaporated and he took a half step backward. I had known Ted Jordan since we were six and this was the first time I'd seen this side of him.

The elevator finally came to a halt at the seventeenth floor and the sergeant pulled on Ted's arm again to get his attention.

"Let's go, we're here," I said.

Ted was still glaring at Wilson as they led him off the elevator.

SEVEN

JUDGE Dan McKenzie stared at me over the top of his glasses. He was a short man with thinning gray hair, angular features, and a prominent forehead.

He inquired, "Tell me why should I go along with your request for bail counselor? Does your client have a million dollars to put up?"

"He does, your honor. The amount's been agreed to by all parties."

"I'm delighted Mr. Schiff, Ms. Hailey and you all get along so well, but I'm not bound by any agreements you've made."

"*Bailey*, your honor," Rena said, correcting him.

"Whatever."

She responded with a pleasant smile. "Mr. Delaney's client is also willing to relinquish any claim to the money we've located."

McKenzie folded his hands across his stomach and leaned back in his seat. "Has he now?"

"Yes, sir. Arrangements will be made to have the funds transferred into the court's registry today. In return we've agreed there will be no evidentiary presumption against Mr. Jordan. His position is he knew nothing of the account's existence."

Thornton Schiff chose that moment to put his two cents in. "Your honor, given the nature of the offenses, I'd like to point out—"

"I didn't get an answer to my earlier question, Mr. Schiff. And don't interrupt me again," McKenzie said. He turned back to me and raised his eyebrows.

"Judge, the constitution gives everyone the right to reasonable bail."

"The constitution? Do you have some authority to cite, counselor?"

Normally a statement like this is so obvious no lawyer would consider bringing cases with them to court. It's something they teach in seventh grade social studies. Fortunately, a friend of mine had warned me what to expect from the Honorable Dan McKenzie. He enjoyed making lawyers look foolish when they couldn't produce. Some judges think trials are about them. Before leaving for court that morning, I had downloaded a half-dozen cases on point as a precaution.

I replied, "I believe the Eighth Amendment covers this. I took the liberty of making copies of several decisions for your edification."

I pulled the cases out of my briefcase and carefully laid them on McKenzie's desk.

He didn't bother to glance down. "Actually, the constitution says *excessive bail* shall not be required, nor excessive fines imposed, nor cruel and unusual punishments inflicted."

"Yes, sir."

McKenzie kept his eyes fixed on mine. I returned the stare. Eventually a smile appeared on his face.

"Ladies and gentlemen, we have a three-ring circus outside and I don't need more excitement in my life. Personally, I'm not convinced a million dollars is enough to ensure Mr. Jordan's appearance in light of the circumstances."

I countered, "Your honor, I've known Ted Jordan since we were boys and I consider him above reproach. Would it help if I personally guaranteed he'll show up for trial?"

"And if he doesn't? Do I put you in jail in his place?"

"Hopefully not. I have a condominium in New York I own free and clear. It's worth considerably more than a million dollars. I'll put that up as collateral if the court will accept it."

Schiff immediately pointed out, "Judge, we have no way of knowing—"

"Mr. Schiff, I've already told you not to interrupt me. If I require your opinion I assure you I'll ask for it. Mr. Delaney is a member of the bar and if he's willing to affirm the value of his property in an affidavit that will be good enough for me. I'm setting bond at two million dollars. One half is to be paid in cash and the other can be posted as property.

"My secretary will draw up the ruling. I'm also imposing a gag order on each of you. This means you are neither to discuss the merits of this case with the press nor to make any public statement regarding it. Do I make myself clear?"

It was clear to everyone, except to Thornton Schiff, who opened his mouth to speak again, but never got the chance.

"Yes, Thornton," McKenzie went on, "Mr. Delaney will issue a statement retracting what he said in the lobby earlier." He smiled to himself and then turned to me. "You're to do that before you leave the courthouse, counselor.

"When this is over you can beat the crap out of each other for all I care, but I'll have no more bickering outside my courtroom while the matter is pending. I expect each of you to behave in a dignified and professional manner. That'll be all."

After leaving the judge's chambers I went directly to the lawyers' lounge and placed a call to Gabriele Severin. She answered on the second ring. I informed her that bond had been set and how much it was. She didn't hesitate at all, though she seemed surprised when I said I'd be putting up my home as collateral.

"Are you sure you want to do that? I can handle the entire amount," she said.

I was about to make a joke that French lawyers had to be earning more money than their American counterparts but decided against it. An image of Ted Jordan carrying my six-year-old son out of Van Courtland Park Lake stopped me. Sixteen years earlier, our families had gone there for a picnic. My son slipped off the dock trying to catch his model airplane. I was in the parking lot at the time getting a cooler out of the car. My wife had her back turned and didn't see what happened. Maybe it wasn't the most heroic act of all time, but it was enough. Ted jumped in after him and I've never forgotten that. Friendship doesn't come and go with changing circumstances. Either it exists or it doesn't. In June I would attend Doug's graduation from Penn State thanks to Ted. Sometimes you have to step up to the plate. He did and it was my turn now.

I told her, "Let's leave things the way they are."

My next call was to Gabriele's banker in Paris. I decided not to rely on the number she had provided. Instead, I called international directory assistance and confirmed it with their records. After that I phoned the bank directly. A little caution can go a long way. Her banker's English was excellent and he assured me the funds were available and quite legitimate. He promised to wire them to my trust account within the hour.

So far so good.

JIMMY d'Taglia was still waiting for me in the court. Rather than keep him hanging on, I agreed to meet him at a neighborhood pub later that afternoon. He said that was fine, though I got the impression he wasn't happy at being put off.

"Did the judge agree to set bond?" he asked.

I nodded.

"How much?"

"Two million dollars, cash and property."

Jimmy whistled through his teeth. "That's a lot of money. See you later."

On his way out, I noticed him acknowledge a blond-haired gentleman in a gray suit seated in the last row. The man had been watching us since I got there. He stood, glanced at me, then followed Jimmy out.

There may have been some meaning in his look but I couldn't tell what it was.

EIGHT

THE last people I spoke with before leaving the courtroom were Maureen Jordan and Charles Evans. I told them bond had been set and how much it was. When Maureen heard the amount she gasped and put a hand over her mouth. Before I could explain it would be paid later that morning, Evans leaned closer and lowered his voice.

"Call me when you're free and we'll figure out what to do. You've just gotten involved in this case, right?"

"Last night."

"I understand. When we meet, I'll bring you up to speed as best I can."

"Ten a.m. at your office tomorrow?" I asked.

Evans nodded and rose to his feet. He gave Maureen an affectionate squeeze on the shoulder then left us alone to talk.

There were still a few people in court, many of whom were reporters, and it was obvious we were the center of attention. I motioned for her to join me at the far end of the bench.

Our conversation this time was a bit different from our first one. The supportive wife I met earlier was replaced by something else. In light of what Ted had revealed, I wasn't completely taken aback.

"Two million dollars!" she whispered, gripping my arm. "John, we don't have that kind of money. Can't you go back and talk to the judge? This is so unfair."

On impulse I decided not to tell her about the arrangements. Instead, I asked, "How much can you come up with?"

"I don't know. We have some money in savings and some in stocks and bonds, but I can't go down to zero. I have to consider the boys. We'd be destitute."

"I understand. The decision is up to you, of course."

"I mean, I will. It's just that . . ."

"How much can you raise?"

"I'll call our broker today and let you know. Normally Ted takes care of these things."

"Just a ballpark figure will be fine," I said.

"Maybe $250,000, but that's just a guess. You understand it's all the money we have?"

"How much is your house worth?" I asked, taking out my notebook.

"We don't have much equity yet. We've only been there five years."

"The court didn't say anything about equity. They're only interested in its present market value."

Maureen went silent for a moment. I knew my statement wasn't accurate. I was simply curious to see how she would respond.

"John, what happens if Ted runs away? I know he won't, but what if he doesn't show up for trial?"

"Technically, the State could seize the property and sell it."

A short distance away a swarthy-looking fellow in an Armani suit slid closer to us. He was doing his best not to listen to our conversation. He wore a silk scarf around his neck as opposed to a tie. It was very continental. Unfortunately, this wasn't the continent. We were in an Atlanta court. Without being told, I knew it was Frank, the tile man.

"I need to give this some thought," Maureen said, pulling my attention back.

"I understand."

"I know you think I'm being horrible, but this is a big decision. We're talking about our children's home."

"Of course."

I glanced at Frank again, who had moved a little closer. He quickly averted his eyes and went back to pretending to read the fire marshal's notice about how to evacuate the building in case of an emergency. Fascinating stuff.

Maureen followed my glance. "That's Frank Nardelli," she said, "a friend of ours. I was so nervous I asked him to drive me here today. His company's been retiling our kitchen. Would you like to meet him?"

"I have enough tile."

"Frank can do a lot of things. He's extremely talented. You'd like him."

"I'm sure I would." *Only I don't need the services he's providing for you.*

Maureen exhaled a long breath. "Can I call you later?"

"Absolutely."

"What happens next?"

"I need to talk to the press before I leave. The judge wants me to tell them Thornton Schiff isn't quite as big an asshole as I made him out to be. After that I'll start preparing our pretrial motions."

"Don't get yourself in trouble, John. We need you."

We hugged and Maureen headed toward the elevators followed by Frank, who had a smug look on his face. He turned and glanced back at me. Just before the doors closed I winked at him.

NINE

I took a little under an hour for the money to reach my account. After filling out surety papers for Ted's bond and depositing the funds with the clerk's office, I made my way uptown to Colony Square. I had been unable to reach Gabriele by phone again and decided to leave a note at the hotel. I wanted to know if she shared Ted's view about his being set up. I also wanted more details on the research team deaths Ted had mentioned.

I found a parking lot near the Four Seasons and was about a half block away when Gabriele came down the steps. She didn't see me. She turned right and began walking north along 14th Street. My curiosity was peaked.

I stayed well back and lost her several times. When she reached Piedmont Road she turned left. I kept to the opposite side of the street. Ahead, three teenage boys were practicing skateboard acrobatics on the stoop of an old apartment building.

"How much for that hat?" I asked the closest one.

"Excuse me?"

"I'd like to buy your hat. Do you want to sell it?"

"This hat?" he asked, taking off his Atlanta Braves cap and looking at it.

"The same."

"Why do you want to buy my hat, mister?"

"Because I'm a big fan of the Braves and I'll die without it."

"Yeah, right."

"So, how about it?" I said.

The boy shrugged and said, "Ten dollars?"

"Deal."

I took my wallet out and saw that I only had twenties. "Your lucky day," I said, handing him a bill.

"Whoa."

His companion asked, "Hey, you want to buy my jacket? I'll sell it for twenty bucks."

My new friends obviously grasped the concept of capitalism quickly. The jacket was made of gray cloth and looked like it hadn't been washed in a year. Nevertheless, I forked over another twenty and put it on. John Delaney, master of disguise.

Gabriele was well ahead of me and walking with a purpose. I had a good idea where she was going. The entrance to Atlanta's Botanical Garden lay just ahead. I didn't think she was sightseeing. She had changed into jeans and sneakers and was wearing a pullover brown sweatshirt. Her outfit was out of place with the Louis Vuitton handbag she was carrying.

The garden has a small café across from the gift shop. Gabriele went in and took a seat at the far corner. I paid the admission and followed. A large fountain surrounded around the base by hydrangeas afforded sufficient cover for me to observe her. At a table near Gabriele were an elderly man and woman. Both had a glass of wine in front of them. The man was reading a newspaper and didn't look up when Gabriele entered. The woman appeared to be in her early sixties. She was dressed in a conservative business suit and was typing something on her cell phone.

Gabriele set her purse on the floor and picked up a menu. A minute later a waitress came by and took her order. I noticed the man and woman also had plates of food; neither of which appeared to have been touched. Due to the distance and spraying water it was difficult to see clearly, but I could tell there was a conversation going on between the women. The man's head was still buried in his newspaper. On the floor by the elderly woman was a handbag, a twin of the one Gabriele was carrying.

The couple stayed a few minutes longer then called for their bill. The man paid in cash. He put a hand on Gabriele's shoulder before he left and followed the woman out. The meeting would have been innocuous except for the fact the woman took Gabriele's handbag when she exited the café.

TEN

ARRIVED at Winston's Pub a little before six o'clock. It's nothing fancy, just a quiet comfortable bar. The wood is dark and they have sawdust on the floors. Their food is decent and goes down easily. Most of the staff knows me by sight. A chunky waitress named Karen came over and brought me a Heineken without my having to ask for it. I told her I was waiting for a friend and ordered a corned beef sandwich with a side of fries. The cold beer tasted good.

Jimmy arrived fifteen minutes later and slid into the booth across from me.

"Nice job today," he said. "I didn't think McKenzie would go along with a bond."

"We got lucky," I answered, through a mouthful of sandwich.

"How's the food here?"

"They make a good stew every Thursday and the chicken's safe if it's not overcooked."

"It's not Thursday," Jimmy pointed out.

"And you didn't come here to eat."

Jimmy smiled.

"Tell me why the U.S. Attorney is interested in a local murder case," I said.

"I can't go into detail, but this is one situation you might want to stay away from. I'm telling you this as a friend."

"And as a friend I appreciate it. You want half my sandwich?"

"I'm not kidding, John."

"Neither am I. The corned beef is actually pretty good today."

"That's not what I'm talking about and you know it. There are other agencies interested in this case beside our office."

"What other agencies and why?"

"I really can't—"

"That fellow at the back of the courtroom who followed you out, is he one of them?"

Jimmy paused and took a breath. "The man you're referring to is with the NSA and yes, they're one of the agencies monitoring this situation."

"What in the world does the NSA have to do with a local murder? This isn't a matter of national security."

"That's all I can say and I shouldn't have said that much."

"And you're here out of friendship . . . with no prompting from Ray Rosen's office? That's real decent of you, Jimmy."

"I do consider you my friend and I didn't say who sent me."

"Then stop dancing around and tell me what's really going on."

Karen returned with my desert, a piece of apple pie topped with a scoop of chocolate ice cream. Jimmy made a face when he saw it.

"You actually going to eat that?" he said.

I glanced up at Karen. She shrugged and headed back to the bar.

"The color combination appeals to me."

"Apple pie and chocolate ice cream? It's gross."

"Been eating it since I was a kid."

"Then I'm surprised you've made it this far. You can practically hear your arteries snapping shut."

"Are you going to order something or just sit there and issue cryptic warnings?"

"I'll take a beer," Jimmy said.

I caught Karen's eye and held up my glass, pointing at Jimmy. She nodded in reply. Turning back to my friend, I said, "Frankly, I was surprised you took an administrative position with Rosen's office. I thought you were hot to be a litigator."

Jimmy nodded. "I miss it sometimes. You get a different perspective from the administrative side."

I asked, "Are you really here as a friend or is this an official visit?"

"Maybe a little of both. Rosen and I did discuss Ted Jordan yesterday and he thought it would be a good idea for us to talk."

By way of history, Ray Rosen had been Katherine's boss when she was a prosecutor. I'd met him a few times but didn't know him well.

From what she told me he was volatile, brilliant, and considered an excellent trial lawyer. She also said he was a straight shooter.

"Okay, I'm listening."

The waitress returned with Jimmy's beer. He paused until she left.

"Jordan posted a million dollars in cash, right? The rest was property. That's a lot of money for a guy on salary to come up with."

"Yes, it is," I agreed.

"His home doesn't have that kind of equity. I checked."

"No, it doesn't. I put my condo up as collateral."

Jimmy shook his head. "That was stupid. Where will you be if he skips?"

"His wife asked me the same question earlier. Let's hope he doesn't."

Jimmy took a sip of his beer. "Why stick your neck out like that?"

"It's personal."

"Can you tell me where the cash came from?"

"Privileged. Any idea when you'll be coming to the point? It's been a long day."

"I think you should consider backing off the case."

"Give me a reason."

"It's just something I was asked to pass along."

"By whom? Rosen?"

"I told you, I can't—"

I pushed my plate away. "Look Jimmy, you were someone I could trust. What does Rosen care if I represent Ted Jordan? If I don't take the case, some other lawyer will. It doesn't make sense."

"All I can tell you is there are people watching what happens here and they don't fuck around. I'm concerned about you."

I thought of my conversation with Gabriele and how she kept checking over her shoulder to see if we were being watched. "What sort of people?" I asked.

Jimmy took a sip of his beer and stayed silent for several seconds. When our eyes met I could feel a wall going up between us.

"I didn't want to do this, but I've delivered the message. Stick to teaching, John. Do yourself a favor and let this one go."

"And if I can't?"

Seconds passed.

"You're right," Jimmy said. "It's been a long day. I'd better get moving."

We shook hands and I watched him walk out the front door. His car pulled out of the lot a minute later.

When my attention returned to the apple pie I found the ice cream had melted . . . along with my appetite.

ELEVEN

WHEN I got home, I found a note from Katherine saying she would be late. She was meeting Alley at Perimeter Mall for a drink. After graduating law school, Alley had joined her mother's firm.

I changed into a pair of worn blue chinos, pulled a t-shirt over my head, and headed for our garden at the rear of the house. The rake was where I had left it. I keep a small weatherproof CD player on the patio so I can listen to music while I work. I hit the PLAY button and Astrud Gilberto came on singing "The Girl from Ipanema." Stan Getz accompanied her on sax, or maybe it was the other way around.

A brick path leads to a sundial. I bought it a few months earlier at a flea market in Jonesboro. The sales lady tried to convince me it was an antique. Though I'm far from an expert, I've hung around my wife long enough to know what's junk and what isn't. Antiques are one of her passions. This one was merely old. The metal was rusted and its base was chipped. The imperfections didn't bother me. It was a nice focal point and twenty-five bucks was a reasonable price. To the left of the sundial is a wildflower garden I started a year ago. The other side is "under construction," due to a giant oak stump that sits squarely in the middle of it. I've been fighting that stump since I moved in.

On the patio Getz produced notes that floated effortlessly on the air. I worked for half an hour before the music got to me. My feet began to move in time with the rhythm. For some reason, an old black-and-white movie where Fred Astaire danced with a coatrack popped into my head. I picked up the rake and imitated him. Astaire made the coatrack look good. My rake was probably embarrassed. Getting Ted out of jail made me feel good in a way I hadn't for a long time. The rake would get over it.

I might have continued my impromptu routine, but the sound of clapping stopped me. I turned to see Katherine standing there.

"I had no idea you were so talented, Professor."

I was grateful it was dark, because the color of my face probably went up by a shade or two.

I replied, "Yeah, the garden's coming along pretty well."

"No, I meant your . . ." Katherine raised an arm above her head and pirouetted to illustrate.

"Well . . . I've got a good partner," I said.

Katherine giggled. She was still in her work clothes, that is to say a designer business suit. Dior, I thought. Scary thing is I was beginning to tell them apart, along with who made which handbag. There's something inherently wrong if a man knows who Jimmy Choo is.

"Ready for a break?" Katherine asked.

"Sure."

I followed her into the living room and poured us both a drink. White wine for her, a scotch and soda for me. Our cat Peeka was stretched out in the middle of the couch. He opened one eye, satisfied himself there were no treats forthcoming and promptly went back to sleep.

Katherine said, "I caught some of the news on the way home. It sounds like you had an exciting day."

I told her about my meetings with Ted, Jimmy, and Gabriele.

While she listened Katherine reached out and gently scratched Peeka's neck. He began purring.

She asked, "Do you believe Ted . . . about the conspiracy?"

"I don't know. I need more information on the research team members. One or two deaths I might accept. Five is hard to pass off as coincidence."

"What about his girlfriend? Clandestine meetings and switching purses in restaurants sounds pretty sketchy to me."

"Not if she's in fear of her life. I'd love to know what was in that purse."

"So, what's your plan?" Katherine asked.

"I'll meet with Charlie Evans in the morning and get his take on the conspiracy. In the meantime I've asked Luther and Nikko to keep an eye on Ted and Gabriele."

"Luther will stand out like a sore thumb. A six-foot-five black man with dreadlocks loitering around the Four Seasons lobby will probably get the police called."

"Luther knows how to handle himself," I said.

I took one of Katherine's feet and began gently massaging it. She tilted her head back and made a little noise that sounded like our cat. At fourteen pounds, Peeka took up most of the couch's middle section. He looked mildly annoyed at the invasion of his space.

The massage moved from foot to calf and then to her thigh. Katherine's eyes were half closed. I loved her eyes. They were blue with flecks of gray and could draw you right in.

"Would you like another drink?" I asked. I leaned forward and kissed the nape of her neck, then her jawline.

"No," she said, pulling me to her.

TWELVE

AT 10:00 A.M. I headed downtown for my meeting with Charles Evans. According to the radio, I-75 was a mess again, so I took the streets. Used to be if you picked your battles carefully you could negotiate your way through Atlanta's traffic. Over the last few years the situation's gone from bad to worse. The trip from Marietta took nearly an hour.

Evans, Stanley, Doster & Young occupies three floors in Peachtree Center and looks out over Five Points, Atlanta's downtown hub. You enter the office through a pair of glass doors. I announced myself to the receptionist, who said she would let Mr. Evans know I had arrived. She then pointed me to a comfortable-looking couch at the far side of the room. While I was waiting I picked up a copy of *The Economist* from an end table and began to leaf through it. The first article was by a dour-looking fellow at the Fed complaining that Americans' "irrational exuberance" for high-tech stocks was dangerous. Another story talked about the worldwide market drug companies were discovering for their new AIDS medications. It took all of twenty seconds to finish the magazine. The only other reading material I could find was a leather-bound self-published book containing photos and biographies of the law firm's partners and their associates. I flipped to Ted's page and studied his picture. It's surprising how time can get away from you. A younger, smiling Ted Jordan looked back at me. His hair was darker and the deep lines around his mouth and eyes weren't as obvious as they were now.

I glanced at my own reflection in the mirror for a moment, pursed my lips, and closed the book.

"Mr. Delaney?"

The voice belonged to an attractive woman in her early thirties.

"Yes," I replied, getting to my feet.

"Mr. Evans will see you now. I'm Martha Ludlow, his personal assistant. If you'll come this way."

I followed Martha down a wide hallway, past paintings of pastoral scenes with cows standing in the woods and portraits of people I didn't know. The walls were covered in expensive grass cloth. The ceilings all had intricate crown moldings. At the end of the corridor sat a Biedermeier secretary that probably cost a third of my year's salary.

Most of the attorneys were dressed in standard blue or gray pin-stripes. The more laid back ones had taken off their jackets and wore white shirts with suspenders. Big wow. I was wearing a brown tweed sport jacket and felt slightly shabby. We turned right at the Bieder-meier and headed down another hallway, equally as long. A small brass plaque on the third door bore the name THEODORE JORDAN.

Martha didn't comment as we walked. She was, by the way, very good at walking . . . one foot in front of the other, the way runway models do. It created a distinct hip sway. Women have radar about these things and any man who thinks they don't know when they're being watched is kidding himself. I concentrated on the cow paint-ings.

Charlie Evans's office was about the size of my garage, maybe a little larger. A picture window behind his desk gave an excellent view of the downtown area. Either way, the panorama from the forty-second floor was impressive. Two flat-screen television sets mounted on the wall across from his desk were both on, though the volume had been turned down. One had the latest CNN headlines; the other was a financial network with a ticker tape streaming across the bottom of the screen.

Of Evans there was no sign.

Martha invited me to have a seat and departed, her hips working synchronously. For a moment I wondered if "personal assistant" might mean something more than "secretary who doesn't type."

I glanced around the office. There were photos of Charlie Evans with the last three governors, Evans with Atlanta's mayor, and Evans with a nationally syndicated talk-show host, whose name I couldn't recall. A moment later I heard the sound of a toilet flushing and the man in the photograph emerged through a door at the far end of the room.

"Sorry I couldn't see you sooner, Delaney. With Ted out of commission and Sandy gone, I'm up to my ass in alligators."

He had to lean across his desk to shake my hand.

"I understand."

Evans motioned for me to sit again. While we were shaking hands he used his free one to turn a thick packet of papers face down. I caught the name *Tissinger*. Apart from dancing with rakes, another talent I'd developed over the years is the ability to read documents upside down, a holdover from my police days. His action didn't strike me as odd. Lawyers are obligated to protect their client's privacy.

"What can I do for you?" Evans said. "Good looking sport jacket, by the way."

Charles was somewhere in his midsixties, though he could easily have passed for a man ten years younger. His face was smooth with only a few lines. There was a treadmill in the corner of the room, so his condition might have been the result of exercise, or possibly Botox.

"I'd like to talk to you about this mess Ted is in."

"I'll tell you what I know, but shouldn't we be concentrating on getting him out of jail first? Two million dollars is a helluva nut to crack. Maureen called me last night hysterical. She can't raise that kind of money. She's afraid she and the boys will be left destitute. Tell you the truth, I wasn't real thrilled by her attitude. You'd think a wife might be a little more supportive."

"Ted's already out," I said. "He was released yesterday. I thought you knew. It was on the news."

Evans blinked and sat back in his seat. "No I didn't. I was involved in meetings until late. How did he manage it?"

"I put up my condo as collateral for half his bond. The rest was in cash."

"You loaned him a million dollars?"

"No, that came from another source."

Evans digested this for a moment. "Mind if I ask who it was?"

"I can't tell you that, Charlie. It would be violating a confidence."

"I see. Well, I suppose that constitutes good news. I called my stockbroker this morning and told him we'd have to liquidate a bunch of securities. He wasn't in favor of it given the market, but I meant it when I said I would help."

"Ted's lucky to have a friend like you."

Evans waved the comment away. "At least we have one hurdle out of the way. What do you need to know?"

"Were you aware of any bad blood between Ted and Sanford Hamilton?"

He shook his head. "Absolutely not. Sandy could be abrasive at times, but I never heard of him and Ted having problems with each other."

"According to the newspapers they were seen arguing in your conference room a week before Hamilton was killed."

"I don't put any stock in that," Evans said, making a dismissive gesture. "If Sandy got on his high horse about something, he'd jump on anyone around him. He was our managing partner."

Charlie might not put any stock in it, but the district attorney did, and so would a jury.

"Any idea what they were arguing about?"

"Not a clue. I read the same thing you did. Honestly, I didn't even know they had an argument."

"Fair enough. How did the DA's office decide Ted embezzled money from the law firm?"

"That came afterward. One of their investigators showed up here out of the blue and started asking questions about whether we were missing money or valuable papers. I had no idea what the man was talking about. All he would say was that it was a routine inquiry, which is complete bullshit. Schiff's office doesn't make routine inquiries of law firms. It was obvious someone had contacted them, but he wouldn't say who. We cooperated, of course."

"What happened?"

"Nothing. I told him we weren't having any problems and he left. Later that night I got to thinking what a strange conversation it was, so I placed a call to Bill Doster. Bill's not only a partner, he's a CPA. I asked him to make sure our trust account was in order and report back to me. You can imagine our shock when we came up $500,000 short."

"And you concluded that Ted took the money?"

"It was pretty obvious. And that's the part that doesn't make any sense. Ted's a smart man and this was dumb on a level I can't begin to comprehend. After Bill started his reconciliation he came up with a missing item, a disbursement that was supposed to have gone to one of Ted's clients. Try as we might, we couldn't locate the canceled check and Ted wasn't here to help because he was out of the country. Eventually we called the bank and asked them to send us the paperwork. Until then we thought it was just a clerical error of some kind. We were stunned to find out the money had been wired to Ted's personal account."

"How did you know it was him? Couldn't an employee, say a bookkeeper or someone—"

Evans shook his head. "No, the order came directly from Ted. All our partners have individual codes they enter before the bank will honor a request like that. There's just no question about it. At that point we had no alternative but to notify the State bar. My partners and I made up the shortfall from our own pockets."

"But now the money's been returned, you'll be reimbursed, right?"

"Sure, and that's wonderful. Unfortunately, there aren't a whole lot of warm feelings around here for Ted now." Evans leaned forward and pressed the intercom button on his phone. "Martha, would you ask Bill Doster to step into my office?"

THIRTEEN

BILL Doster was a big fellow with a body that might have been athletic in his youth, but had long since gone to fat. Charlie introduced us and we shook hands. He took a chair opposite me.

"Bill, Professor Delaney is representing Ted Jordan. I invited him because he has some questions. He tells me Ted was released on bail yesterday."

"That's too bad," Doster said. "I was hoping the son of a bitch rots for what he did."

"I understand how you feel," I said. "You've lost a partner and a friend. I've spoken to Ted and he insists he's innocent. I was hoping you'd give him the benefit of the doubt until that's proved otherwise."

Doster responded with a derisive noise.

"I told the professor we'd cooperate," Evans said, "and I'd appreciate it if you'd back me up. The money is one issue. We've discussed that already and you know my feelings on the subject. I can't see Ted Jordan doing those horrible things and I don't believe you do either. The sheer magnitude of it defies the imagination. I mean we've worked with the man for eighteen years."

Doster paused for a long beat. "What is it you want?" he said, turning to me.

"I was asking Charlie if it's possible an employee might have transferred the funds to Ted's account without his knowing it."

"Absolutely not."

"But supposing someone got hold of his password?"

"It's not as simple as that. In the first place, we don't rely on a password alone for security. We have almost seventy lawyers here and the amount of money flowing through this office is staggering. That's why we have multiple safeguards in place. They're designed to prevent a situation like this from occurring. Clerical mistakes happen even in the best of companies. We know that. Three separate things have to take place *in sequence* or the transaction won't go through."

"Would you explain how that works?"

Doster glanced at Evans for confirmation. Evans nodded.

"Each partner is assigned something called a site key. They use it to enter the bank's Web site whenever a wire transfer is involved. The key is just a little thumbnail photo. It can be a picture of Venice, a bluebird, or whatever. It doesn't matter. None of the partners give them out. Ever.

"That key has to match the password, which is also secret. If it doesn't, that's as far as you go. Three wrong attempts and the user gets locked out of the system.

"Finally, we require a paper trail on any amount over $5,000.00. In other words, you need a partner's signature."

"I see."

"I hope so. All three have to be in place *before* the funds are dispersed, then there's a fourth. We put it in about six months ago. We now require that someone from the bank call the partner directly and verify a transfer should be made.

"There's no way Ted Jordan was unaware that money went into his account. I believe Sandy Hamilton found out what was happening, confronted him, and Jordan killed him to keep it quiet. I hope they fry the miserable bastard."

"Thank you. That was very helpful," I said.

"Is there anything else you want?"

"No, I appreciate you coming in."

This time Doster didn't bother to shake hands. He got up, nodded to me, and left the room without shutting the door.

Evans looked embarrassed and stared down at his hands for a moment. "I'm sorry. He and Sandy were close."

FOURTEEN

MY discussion with Charlie Evans was helpful on several levels.
Not only did it give me a perspective on how Ted viewed his situation, I got to learn first hand what his partners thought of him.
The two were not in concert. According to Ted, none of them believed he was responsible for the crimes. Obviously, this was not the
case with Bill Doster and I was willing to bet he wasn't alone. The
biggest surprise, however, was yet to come.

I asked Evans, "Did you ever notice any displays of temper on
Ted's part, or violent outbursts?"

Evans rubbed the back of his neck and thought for a moment.
"Can't say I did. I mean he could get hot under the collar like anyone else, but I never saw him lose it. Why?"

"Because the indictment says that Hamilton was burned to death.
According to the Medical Examiner, before that happened three of
his fingers had been severed. A man would have to be pretty angry
to do something like that."

"How do you know it was a man?"

It was my turn to shrug. "Instinct, plus a line of psychological studies that go back fifty years. A woman could have done it, but I've
never heard of one who'd fit the profile."

Evans snapped his fingers. "I remember now. You were a detective
with the NYPD before you became a lawyer, weren't you? Ted mentioned that to me when you moved here."

"Good memory."

"So what made you get out of police work and into lawyering?"

"Well, three bullets in the chest had a lot to do with it."

"*Jesus*," Evans said, rocking back in his chair. "How the hell did
that happen? You piss off someone's husband?"

"Not exactly," I smiled. "My partner and I were questioning a robbery suspect when he pulled a gun and started shooting. I forgot to duck. The department paid for me to go to night school while I was recuperating."

"So you changed professions and now you're in Atlanta, Georgia."

"Now I'm here."

You couldn't help but like Charlie Evans. He was personable and made conversation easily without putting on airs. In view of what had happened to his partner, his attitude interested me because it's not the way human nature works. Despite the Southern cornpone, I knew Evans was no fool. No one who had risen to his position could be. He was also astute enough to pick up on what I was thinking.

"Something wrong, Professor?"

"No, I was just reflecting on how well you're taking all this. If I were in your place I don't think I would be as charitably disposed."

Evans laughed to himself then reached over to a polished wooden box sitting on the corner of his desk. He took out a cigar and offered me one out of courtesy. I declined and waited while he clipped off the end with a cutter. He then took a long match out of his pocket and slowly rotated it around the tip until it glowed red.

"I don't know what happened with Ted and the escrow account, but the client's been paid and we're getting our money back. That will help of course. As to the rest, I've been going round and round with it in my mind and the only explanation I can come up with is maybe Ted has a mental problem and went off the deep end."

"Are you saying he killed Hamilton?"

"I'm saying I don't know," Evans replied, shaking his head. Until a couple of days ago I would have said, no way. All Ted would have done is talk the man to death if they had an issue with one another.

"I knew Sandy Hamilton for over thirty years and he didn't have an enemy in the world." Evans got up, crossed the room, and shut the door. "I want the sonofabitch who killed him, but between you and me, I'm afraid where the investigation will lead."

"Ted thinks he's being set up. What's your reaction to that? Can you think of any candidates?"

Evans eyebrows went up, and he started to reply, then thought

better of it and closed his mouth again. It was obvious he didn't believe it. I admired his loyalty.

"No . . . no candidates," he finally said, taking a seat near me.

"How about the Tissinger Corporation?"

"Tissinger?" Evans said, surprised. "Why?"

"Ted told me he stumbled across a document indicating they deliberately held back information about suicides from the FDA."

Evans was quiet for a long time. He seemed to be struggling to
find the right words.

"Delaney, let me be straight with you. For the last two days I haven't
slept very well. I lay awake at night trying to make some sense of what
happened, and I can't. This whole business is awful, just awful.

"Do I think Tissinger or someone set Ted Jordan up by murdering my partner and sticking $500,000 in his account? No. I wish to
hell I did. Do I think he's caught in a nightmare? Yes. Have you considered having him evaluated by a psychiatrist?"

"You think he's crazy?"

"I don't know, maybe. But an insanity plea shouldn't be discounted
as a defense. I'm not saying he is mind you, but it's something you
might want to keep in the back of your mind."

It was more than in the back of my mind. If Ted's staunchest sup-
porter harbored these doubts, that didn't bode well. The conversation was becoming depressing.

"Thanks, I'll certainly think about it," I told him.

"That family's had more than their share of problems. If it
weren't for bad luck, they wouldn't have any luck at all," Evans said
quietly. "First the daddy falls off a roof like a fool and gets himself
killed, then his mother went before her time, and now Ted. I don't
get it. Were you close with them?"

"Yes."

"I knew his mama, too. Damn fine woman. She was the one who
got him his clerkship here."

Evans shook his head sadly and sent a stream of blue smoke into
the air. He contemplated at the end of his cigar for a long moment.

"Ted mentioned he'd been going back and forth to Europe for
Tissinger. Is that true?" I said.

"It is. Between you and me, I don't know the first thing about any suicides and we've represented that company for twenty years. But I'll check. If there's anything to it, I'll let you know. Is that going to be his defense?"

"So far," I said.

It's never been in my best interest to reveal everything I know and I decided to keep the information about the five deaths on the research team to myself for the moment.

Evans informed me, "We're going to have to cut this short. With one partner dead and one out of commission we're scrambling like mad just to keep our heads above water. I've got people lined up all day. We can meet later in the week if you like, but I'm slammed at the moment."

"I understand. I was almost done anyway. I'll call if I have more questions."

What happened next surprised me further. Charlie Evans reached into his desk drawer, pulled out a check, and pushed it across the desk. It was made out to me in the amount of $50,000.

"What's this for?"

"Like I said in court, I want to help, but I can't do it publicly. It's none of my business how much Ted is paying you, but we both know litigation ain't cheap."

"That's very generous, Charlie. But I can't take this. Ted and I haven't even discussed money yet."

"Then hang onto it for expenses. I've got a feeling you're going to need it before too long. If you don't use it all, return whatever's left."

"Charlie—"

"I'm serious. Tuck it away for emergencies. I've been doing this for a long time and I can tell you problems come at you out of nowhere. Trust me."

"Thanks, Charlie," I said, folding the check and putting it in my breast pocket. "Do you have time for one more question?"

"Shoot."

"Can you think of any reason why the feds might be interested in this case?"

"The feds? No. This is strictly a local matter. Why would they stick their nose in where it doesn't belong?"

"I have no idea, but yesterday a friend suggested I drop the case."

"Why?"

"Let's just say he was offering unsolicited advice."

Evans stared at me for several seconds. "It's a mystery to me. I'll start asking around—discreetly, of course. You've got me spooked now."

There was another pause before he continued.

"Let me be honest with you, Delaney, you're a decent fellow to jump into this situation the way you did. I want to believe Ted Jordan is innocent and I think you do, too. Unfortunately, we're about the only people in Atlanta who feel that way. Right now Ted is in a shitload of trouble. The DA's already stuck his neck out with the press and he's not gonna let this one go without a fight. Our escrow money aside, the police found Ted's fingerprints at Hamilton's house after he told them he'd never been there. How the hell do you explain that away? Schiff's also got credit card receipts showing he bought ten gallons of gas the night of the fire and two cans to put it in."

I started to speak, but Evans held up a hand to stop me.

"Relax. I spoke with Rena Bailey this morning. That's how I know about the gasoline and the fingerprints."

"I see."

"I don't know if you do. There are some cases that can drag down a law career along with the client. I suspect that's what your friend was trying to tell you.

"I know Schiff said he was going for the death penalty and I'm not telling you how to practice law. But you might want to consider working out some type of plea bargain. I'll speak with Thornton privately if you like."

"Thank you, Charlie. I appreciate your candor."

"All I'm saying is, if the handwriting is on the wall, you might want to give some thought to your own interests. Law schools generally don't like their professors getting involved with high profile criminal cases, particularly unpopular ones. Your friend, and don't tell me who he is 'cause I don't want to know, might have a point."

Everyone seemed to have a point and the point was look out for yourself.

FIFTEEN

No one was waiting to escort me out, so I started down the hall alone. When I reached Ted's office I noticed his door was now ajar. Inside the room I could hear the voices of two men. It was obvious they were trying to keep their conversation down. More interesting was the sound of furniture being moved and drawers being opened and shut. I stopped and pushed the door open.

Both men had their backs to me. There was a third man present but he was looking out the window at the street below. I recognized Bill Doster. The man next to him was younger, slightly shorter, and in better shape. He was bald and wore an expensive-looking suit. The third man still had his back to me.

"It's not here," baldy said.

Doster replied. "It has to be. Keep looking. We need to—"

"I think you'll find the lobby is in the other direction, Professor," a female voice said behind me.

I glanced over my shoulder to see Evans's personal assistant, Martha, standing there. The men in the room immediately stopped what they were doing and straightened up. The third man finally turned around to face me. His action was unhurried and if there was any surprise on his face, he didn't show it. Doster closed the drawer he was rummaging through and stared at me.

"Sorry. I lost my way," I said. "I was wondering if I could ask you gentlemen a few questions." I made a point of looking at Ted's name on the door. "This is Ted Jordan's office, isn't it?"

Baldy took a step toward me, but stopped when man by the window shook his head.

"Ms. Ludlow why don't you show Mr. Delaney the way out?" Doster said.

"Honest fellas, it will only take a second. I just want to—"

Doster crossed the room and slammed the door in my face.

Martha escorted me to the elevator. She departed with a tight-lipped smile that had about as much warmth as an air-conditioning unit. I pressed the DOWN button and waited. A few seconds later, two of the men from Ted's office emerged through the lobby doors.

"Professor Delaney, do you have a minute?" the bald man asked.

"Sure."

"I'm Stan Coleman. I work with the Tissinger Corporation in their security division here in the states and this is Brad Britton with your NSA."

"That's nice. When did it become my NSA?"

Neither reacted to my joke, which is puzzling because I've got a great sense of humor. They both produced their IDs.

Coleman replied, "It's just an expression. When it comes right down to it, we're all on the same team, aren't we?"

"That depends on your perspective. If the team specializes in searching the offices of private citizens without a warrant, and I assume you didn't have one, count me out."

Coleman informed me, "We weren't searching anything. We were merely acting as observers while Mr. Doster looked for property belonging to his law firm. I think you'll find that's quite legal. Perhaps we could go back to the conference room and chat for a moment. It's a bit more private there."

"Perhaps you can say what you want out here."

Coleman added, "We would consider it a personal favor."

There was no reason not to, so I shrugged and walked back inside.

This time the man from the NSA began the conversation. He was tanned, blond, fit-looking, and reminded me of a tennis instructor in a suit. "We understand you represent Theodore Jordan," he said. "We also know your job is to inquire into the facts surrounding his case. That's your right, of course."

"Of course."

"A few weeks ago it came to our attention that Mr. Jordan was making inquiries into private matters involving the Tissinger Corporation. These inquiries went far beyond the scope of his representation of them as a lawyer. May I ask why?"

"You can ask, but it's none of your business. My client likes to keep some things private. You know, attorney-client privilege and all that."

Britton waited a beat before he replied. "Professor Delaney, I know that you were in law enforcement at one time, so I'll be straight with you. The government has a number of relationships with Tissinger that are very important to it. We're trying to avoid any . . . *misguided actions* on your part which could generate unwanted publicity for them.

"Mr. Jordan apparently believes Tissinger is somehow at the bottom of a conspiracy to get him, and I'm here to tell you it's bullshit."

In the past, when a federal agent said he was going to be straight with me, I usually reached for my wallet to make sure it was still there.

"Now how would you know what my client thinks, Agent Britton?"

"Call me, Brad. Let's just say a little birdie told us. The bottom line is, whatever Jordan has conjured up to save himself is pure fantasy. It's easy to put two and two together and come up with five, particularly with what he's facing. If my butt was on the line I'd probably do the same thing."

"It's real decent of you to come all the way from Washington to fill me in on the situation, Brad. Correct me if I'm wrong, but that was you in the court yesterday, wasn't it. You left with Jimmy d'Taglia."

He gave me a good-natured smile and I smiled back, then he turned to his partner who smiled, too. We were all getting to be great friends.

"You're right. That was me. Good eyes."

I asked, "Which office did you say you were out of?"

"I didn't, but since you ask, it's the New York office. I recently transferred there from Dallas. For the last two years I was part of an antiterrorist task force."

"Oh, then you probably know Mike Franklin?"

He thought for a second. "Franklin? Yeah, I think so. We're weren't bosom buddies, but we've met. Like I said, I've only been there a couple of months."

"Isn't Atlanta a little out your way?"

"Definitely. Unfortunately, I'm not at liberty to discuss the details of my assignment. You understand."

Mr. Coleman added, "Perhaps I can answer that question, Professor. The NSA is involved because Tissinger has a number of projects here in the States the government considers critical to its interests. Right now, we're in the middle of a drug-testing program in several countries around the globe. Some of these countries are predominantly Muslim, where our government's image is not the best. So the balance is a delicate one. Pulling Tissinger into your lawsuit will only upset the apple cart. Do you see what I'm getting at? Jordan's allegations are completely baseless."

"What allegations would those be?"

"That Tissinger has somehow set Mr. Jordan up to take a fall."

"And why would they do that?"

Coleman shrugged. "Who the hell knows? But doesn't it make great press to finger an evil drug company as the real villain?"

"I suppose it does. Are you asking me to drop Ted's case?"

More smiles all around.

"Of course not," Coleman replied. "By all means, represent him. We wish you well. If you get him off, great. I'll come and talk to you about my brother-in-law. He's going through a nasty divorce and could use a good lawyer. We're only asking that you go about your job in a responsible way and not damage innocent parties."

I looked from one to the other and they seemed genuinely amused.

"I'll certainly give it some thought. I haven't gotten into the bones of Ted's defense yet."

"We know." My new friend gave my shoulder an affectionate squeeze. He was a wide guy, built like a linebacker. "I told Brad we could count on you."

"Exactly what do you mean, 'you'll give it some thought?'" Britton asked.

"Just that. I'm a very deep thinker."

The smile faded a little. "Maybe I didn't make myself clear. If you attempt to shift blame for Sanford Hamilton's murder to the Tissinger Corporation you'll be exposing yourself to considerable liability. I'm sure you're aware there are criminal penalties for making false claims in a court of law. Shall we say . . . that sort of thing wouldn't advance your career."

"Shall we say, I'll do whatever I have to do to protect my client?"

A muscle in Agent Britton's jaw clenched. Understandable, because

I can be very annoying. Fortunately, he kept control. I've also played good cop—bad cop before, so I wasn't surprised when his partner took over.

Coleman informed me, "Look, there's no need for anyone to get hot under the collar. Believe it or not we're trying to help. I like you, Delaney."

"Well, I like you, too, Stan."

"Then we can count on your cooperation?"

"You can count on me to defend my client."

Coleman's partner let out a long breath and helped himself to a cup of water from a stainless steel pitcher on the conference table. "John, did you ever wonder why Ted Jordan picked you to defend him?"

I raised my eyebrows, inviting him to continue.

"Would you say you've handled a lot of criminal cases in your time?"

I made no reply.

Britton continued. "In the last five years you've represented three clients. One was a student of yours arrested for DUI, another was a neighbor charged with date rape. You want me to go on?"

I remained silent.

"Your last case involved defending an acquaintance of your wife who was facing a shoplifting charge. I believe you pled him out.

"It's an impressive track record—real major crimes," he said. "Jordan could have picked any hotshot defense lawyer in the city, yet he comes to you. Smarten up, Pal—you're being played."

"Thanks for the insight, Brad."

This time it was Coleman's turn. "Your former captain told us you were a good cop. That's why we decided to speak with you. Put whatever spin on this you want, but you're about to get yourself in a world of shit. We're only telling you to think before you act."

"Okay, you've told me. So take a hike."

Coleman's color deepened, and he started to say something but decided against it. We wound up doing the eye-to-eye thing for several seconds, before he shook his head.

He said to Britton, "You were right. There are some people you can't talk to. We'll see you around, Delaney."

SIXTEEN

Luther and Nikko were waiting in my office. Nikko was stretched out on my couch, ankles crossed, eyes closed, and listening to his iPod. The only indication he was awake was his head moving slightly in time to whatever was playing.

Luther was reading an article in *Newsweek*, his large frame all but obscuring the chair he was sitting in. I placed a bag of doughnuts I was carrying on the desk and poured myself a cup of coffee from a pot on top of my filing cabinet. As soon as I tasted it my eyebrows went up. I held the cup under my nose and breathed in the aroma. It clearly wasn't my usual blend.

"Good," I said, nodding to him. "What is it?"

"Blue Mountain. Grandma Hannah sent it. Couldn't stand that swill you drink no more."

"Thank her for me."

Luther inclined his head.

"What are you drinking?" I asked, frowning at the purple concoction in his mug.

"Mango and acai berry juice. Been tryin' to get Nikko on it. Make a man of him."

Nikko opened one eye and gave him a sour look.

The two were a study in contrast. Nikko was maybe 5'7" on a good day, sharp-featured and slender. His movements were always exact. Luther, on the other hand, was raw-boned and huge. It looked like his chest and arms were straining to break out of his shirt.

I offered the bag of doughnuts to them. Nikko swiveled upright and took one.

"From Katherine?" he asked.

"Baked fresh this morning."

He nodded and took a bite. Luther declined.

"My body's a temple," he said. "No offense to your thoughtful lady. Beautiful, too."

"I'll tell her."

"She already know."

"Did anything happen last night?" I asked.

Luther said, "Quiet on my end. The French woman stayed in and ordered room service. Nikko's the man to talk to."

I turned to Nikko. "What happened?"

Nikko held up a hand for me to wait as a piece of doughnut made its way down his esophagus.

"So I'm outside the jail waiting for Jordan, like you said, only he don't come out the front. They let him out a side entrance, probably because of all the reporters. Anyway, I spot him jumping into a cab and I follow."

"Anyone else tailing him besides you?"

"No one I saw. I wasn't worried about losing him 'cause I had the home address you gave me and I figure that's where he is going. But I was wrong, see? The cab drops him off at a townhome in Morningside Heights. Two story job—nice place. New-looking."

"Really?" I said.

"Yeah. I watched him take some mail out of the box and go inside. After that I parked halfway down the street. An hour later the garage door opens and your guy drives out. He's wearing shades now and a black windbreaker. It was nearly dark by this time, but I kept him in sight. Silver Audis ain't hard to spot. I ran the plate this morning and it's registered to him."

Nikko paused to take another bite of doughnut.

"We drive for like twenty minutes, and all of a sudden he pulls into a gas station. The problem is he don't want any gas. He stays at the pump pretending to pump it, but what he's really doing is checking to see if anyone's tailing him."

"Understood," I said. "Did he spot you?"

I got an are-you-kidding-me look for an answer.

"Sorry."

"Eventually we start moving again and I find myself on Bankhead

Highway. A few more turns and we're in the garden spot of Atlanta. Most of the buildings are either abandoned, burnt out, or just plain falling down. You know where the old Hotel Roxy used to be?"

"No."

"Well, it's west of there, but that don't matter. Jordan parks his car and gets out. I get out, too, feeling like an albino at the Apollo, if you know what I mean."

Nikko glanced at Luther, who flashed him a brilliant smile.

"Anyway, there's another car waiting for him with three people of, uh . . . Hispanic descent in it. The driver gets out and Jordan tosses him an envelope. Driver then hands it to someone in the backseat, who opens it and counts out a bunch of bills. I guess the price was right, because they tossed him a piece and a box of ammunition.

"After that he drives back to the Four Seasons and spends the rest of the evening with Frenchie. I kept Luther company until this morning. Junior is watching them now."

I looked at Luther.

"Maybe it's time you have a talk with your man," he said.

SEVENTEEN

WILL Ted be all right?" Katherine asked.

It had started raining late that afternoon, a cold blowing rain that seemed harder because of the wind. Katherine was sitting on the bed watching me make a Bloody Mary. The secret is in the amount of Tabasco sauce you add.

"I think so. It's too early to say yet."

There being no celery around to stir, I improvised with my finger and licked it off. Katherine crinkled her nose, but didn't comment.

"His behavior bothers you, doesn't it?" she asked.

"Yes it does. I can understand buying a gun for protection. I can understand him finding companionship elsewhere if Maureen was cheating. But what he did on the elevator was out of character. Maybe it was the stress."

"Is that what they call it . . . companionship?" Katherine asked.

I took a sip of my drink. Perfect.

"K.J. You know what I'm saying,"

"I suppose so. Did he tell you he moved out of his home or that he bought the gun?"

"No to both," I said.

"According to Nikko, the home looked like it was furnished. Right?"

"Right."

"That's quick work for a man who just got out of jail twenty-four hours ago."

"It is," I agreed. "I'll reserve judgment until we meet tomorrow. Neither of those facts are essential to my defending him. He might just be trying to keep some things private."

"Hmph," Katherine said. "I don't know if I buy the conspiracy theory, but he can definitely do better than Maureen with her dyed blonde hair and boob job. Regardless, he needs to tell her he has a girlfriend."

Now I could have pointed out that Maureen was also cheating, but there was no profit in going down that road. Though she was a divorce lawyer and probably heard this ten times a day, Katherine's personal views on the subject of marital infidelity are decidedly conservative.

"Maureen had a boob job?" I asked.

My wife let out a long-suffering sigh. "John, it's so obvious. They stand straight out. You can rest a book on them. Don't men notice anything?"

Apparently not. As a rule women pick up on anatomical enhancements faster than we do. Maybe it's their attention to detail. We're just happy they have breasts, real or fake. When you think about it, we're really quite democratic in that regard. Over the years I've found my female acquaintances are usually happy, if not anxious, to pass along their knowledge about which are genuine and which aren't. Katherine is no exception.

"I'll mention about telling her when we meet," I said.

Katherine gave me an emphatic nod, stood, and removed her jacket. She laid it on the bed and then opened her armoire to pick a more casual outfit for dinner. I watched her.

"What?"

"Nothing. I just like watching you. Would you rather I leave?"

"No, but I'll try some of your drink. Ted and Maureen both sound like a mess you know," she said, unzipping the side of her skirt.

"I know. I handed her the drink and went to make myself another.

"If you ever cheated on me I'd have to kill you," Katherine said, opening a drawer.

"That seems excessive."

"I'm not as forgiving as you are. It's a character flaw."

She removed her panty hose and placed them on the dresser. A gray cashmere pullover followed. Bra and panties were La Perla, and matched, as they always did. I came up behind her and cupped her breasts. She responded by pushing backward with her hips.

"John . . . don't let friendship mar your professional judgment," Katherine said, looking over her shoulder at me.

"Good point," I said, kissing the nape of her neck. I slid my hands down to her waist and across her stomach. "I was just . . . thinking—"

"What were you thinking?" Katherine asked, turning around to face me.

"That dinner can wait."

EIGHTEEN

THE following morning, I was in the kitchen sipping a cappuccino when Katherine came in wearing the top half of my pajamas. It was cute and sexy at the same time.

"Ted's on the phone," she said, deftly avoiding my grab for her waist. She stuck out her tongue, put the phone on the table, then disappeared down the hallway. I watched her for a moment. She could look spectacular in a gunnysack.

"Good morning," I said.

"You awake?"

"Obviously. How does it feel to be a free man?"

My friend let out an audible breath. "I never want to go through that again."

"I don't blame you. That was only round one."

"Have you seen today's papers?"

"Not really. What's up?"

" 'Judge frees accused murderer.' There's a smaller headline underneath it that says, 'Jordan's lawyer apologizes to DA.' They have a picture of you."

"How do I look?"

"Like a deer caught in the headlights. Why the apology?"

"It wasn't an apology. The judge wanted me to tell everyone Thornton Schiff wasn't a complete asshole."

"But he is."

"I know. It was part of the deal to get you out. I didn't mind eating a little crow."

"Do you have some time today? I'd like to get together."

"I don't have to teach until later this afternoon. Is something wrong?"

"We need to talk about Maureen. I didn't go home last night."

"Is that so?"

"Yes."

I asked, "Why don't you come out to the school around five p.m.? I'll be done with my classes by then and we can meet in—"

"I've moved out of my house, John, and I'm not going back."

"I understand. I'm sorry to hear that. Do you need a place to stay?"

"No. I rented a condo not far from our home. Let's meet there. It's close to the university."

So far so good. I was beginning to feel like a man who catches a fleeting image in the fog. You're sure something is there, but you can't tell what it is.

NINETEEN

ED'S condo was located in an old neighborhood. The land had become worth more than the homes, many of which had been built in the early fifties. He was just turning into the driveway as I pulled up. He waved when he saw me. He was wearing a baseball cap and a pair of dark sunglasses. I thought he looked thinner than usual.

"What's with the disguise?" I asked.

"Every place I go, it feels like people are staring at me."

"That's just your imagination."

"Maybe, but it sure feels that way. I was at *St. Mary's* earlier and people were definitely staring at me."

"The cap might have had something to do with it," I pointed out. "How come you went to church?"

"Today is my mother's birthday," he said. "I light a candle for her every year."

I nodded. "Ninety-eight percent of the population are too worried about their own problems to be dwelling on yours. Forget it."

Ted appeared unconvinced. "Let's go inside," he said.

The house was already furnished just as Nikko had informed me. Ted noticed my expression and explained.

"I've had this place for six months now. It's rented under the name of Phillip Jordan."

Really? "I was under the impression your father's been dead for twenty years. When did he start doing business again?"

"This isn't funny, John. I set it up when I found out Maureen was screwing around."

"No, it isn't funny. How come you never mentioned it to me?"

"Because it's none of your business."

I turned around to face him. "It's my business to withdraw from a case if I think my client is full of shit."

His color immediately rose. "I didn't kill anybody and I didn't steal anything and you goddamn well know that. One thing has nothing to do with the other."

"Let's hope not."

My friend let out a breath and relaxed. "Go sit down," he said. "You want a beer?"

"No, thanks."

"How about a Coke?"

"Do you have any mango iced tea?"

"Mango *what*?"

"Iced tea. I tried some at school the other day," I said. "Forget it. How about Perrier?"

"That I can do. The living room's through that doorway," he said, pointing. "Make yourself comfortable."

It didn't take more than a glance to tell that a woman had put the room together. I'm not saying men can't arrange furniture, but the little touches, like doilies and silver picture frames, all but shouted a woman's presence. An Oushak rug with muted colors dominated the center and contrasted with the dark parquet floor. The couch was French, as was an antique coffee table in front of it. All of the windows had wooden shutters and yellow panel drapery. I'd been to Ted and Maureen's home a number of times and the furniture there was modern, so this was a change. I'm strictly a traditional type. The rest of the pieces in the room were eclectic, but worked well together, particularly a large English wingback chair near the fireplace. I sat down in it and waited for my Perrier.

On the coffee table, I noticed a copy of Tissinger's stockholder report. I picked it up and glanced through it. There was nothing even mildly suspicious, not that I expected there to be. It would be pretty dumb to outline your murder plans in a stockholders report. I set it down when Ted returned. He was carrying a packet of photos he dropped onto my lap.

"What's this?"

"See for yourself."

I opened the package. Inside were a series of eight-by-ten shots. I took them out and began flipping through them. The pictures were taken at night with high-speed film and showed two people in a hot tub. The woman was clearly naked. Another shot had them getting into their robes.

"Frank and Maureen?" I asked.

Ted nodded. "Mac Mercer took them. He's the private investigator I mentioned to you yesterday. The situation at home hasn't been good for a while. We're barely been speaking. I hired Mac before I went to Europe.

"He called me in Paris to let me know I was right about Maureen cheating. I wasn't gone more than four hours before Frank moved in. I guess I should have been shocked, only I wasn't."

"What made you think Maureen was seeing someone?"

"We were having our kitchen remodeled and it was taking forever to finish the job. She began spending more and more time out of the house with him, supposedly to pick out tile. I had Mac follow them. Turns out she's known this guy since high school. They've dated and broken up several times, but sooner or later they always seem to get back together."

I turned over the next three photos and stopped short. They showed Maureen giving Frank a blow job in the front seat of his truck.

"Jeez."

"Yeah, Jeez," Ted repeated. "When I returned to the States, I began making plans to move out. I found this place. Gabriele's been here a few times. She's the one who helped set it up."

"Sorry, man."

"I'm not. Gabriele's the best thing that's ever happened to me."

I nodded.

"I want you to represent me in the divorce, John."

"I don't practice that kind of law. Besides, I know you both. You're better off with an expert."

"If it looks like we're going to court, I'll get one. Would you at least meet with Maureen and see if we can work things out quietly?"

"I'll have to give it some thought. I'm not glossing over the situation, but right now we need to put it on the back burner. There are more important matters to discuss."

"But—"

"But nothing. You're being charged with murder and you've asked me to represent you. I can't do that unless I have all the facts."

"John, I really want to talk—"

"About Maureen and Frank and your sons and getting divorced. I know. We'll get to that, I promise." I leaned closer to Ted and gripped his knee. "Thornton Schiff is seeking the death penalty which makes this situation about as serious as it gets. Discussing your divorce won't do you much good if you're dead. Understand?"

The message finally got through. Ted nodded. "What do you want to know?"

"Let's start with the missing suicides."

Instead of answering, Ted stood up, crossed the room and turned on his stereo system, then went to the window and checked the street. I raised my eyebrows in a question.

He said, "We're dealing with an incredibly ruthless group of people, John. I probably didn't do you a favor by getting you involved."

"I'll deal with it. In addition to the papers your son stumbled across, you told me Gabriele confirmed their omission from the reports independently."

"Right. Our job was to draw up contracts transferring ownership from the parent company in France to their division here in Georgia.

"While we were hammering out the details, I mentioned about putting a clause in the contract saying that all known test data on the drug had been disclosed. Language like that is pretty boilerplate, yet she reacted oddly. She told me she would check with management and get back to me.

"I didn't push the issue because there really wasn't one.

"Over lunch one day, I think it was on my third or fourth trip, I asked her why she had acted so strangely when I mentioned the disclosure clause. That was when she told me her father had been Tissinger's lead scientist on the Torapam project. The company knew something was wrong with the medication just like they did with the original formula. They culled the suicides out of both applications."

I inquired, "At the jail you said Gabriele was aware of the missing data."

Ted nodded soberly. "Her father told her."

"And they fired him?"

"Not right away. When he found out he raised a stink and was told to shut up. He didn't. He lives in a small town outside of Paris now. In fact . . ."

Ted's voice trailed away as a white Dodge van slowly drove past his home. He stepped away from the window and quickly drew the curtains.

"What's wrong?" I asked.

"That's the third time that van has been past this house. I saw them earlier today as I was leaving."

I got up and went to the window, moving the curtains aside to see what he was looking at. The van came to a halt at the end of the block and pulled over to the curb.

"Did you see who was driving?"

"No. They're too far away. What do they want from me?"

Ted's reaction could have been the result of frayed nerves or an overactive imagination, but he genuinely looked upset. If there was truth in what he was saying, this was a good time to find out.

"I don't know," I said. "Let's go ask them."

TWENTY

IFTY yards from the vehicle, I knew it wasn't Ted's imagination. Brad Britton stepped out of the van with a friendly wave.

"Good morning, Professor. Didn't think I'd be seeing you so soon. Having an nice visit with your client?"

"That's right. What are you doing here?"

"My job."

"Does that involve electronic surveillance?" I asked, gesturing to the van.

Britton smiled and shook his head. "Not at the moment. You've been watching too many movies."

I returned the smile. "And I have your word on that as a gentleman?"

"It's exactly the way I told you at Mr. Jordan's office. For the moment, we're only interested in who's been coming and going here. So far it's been pretty dull. We were about to pack it in and grab a bite to eat. Care to join us?"

"Thanks, I'll pass."

Coleman stepped out of the van, too, but stayed by the passenger door. He gave me a small salute.

Britton shrugged. "We ran across a great little pub near your house. Good atmosphere; decent food. The name's Winston's, ever hear of it?"

I didn't respond. This was where Jimmy and I had met yesterday.

He went on. "You should definitely try it sometime."

Obviously, this was his way of letting me know they were keeping tabs on me as well, which was fine. As long as he didn't interfere with the case or harass my client they could follow me until the cows came home. I'd have to let Luther and Nikko know we had company. Ted wouldn't like it, but he would have to get used to being under the microscope for a while.

Britton continued. "Has your client been telling you about the big bad conspiracy to get him?"

"My discussions with Ted Jordan are private."

"Don't be a chump, Delaney. Maybe we came on a little strong the other day, but Jordan and his girlfriend are using you. That's what we were trying to tell you at the office. Don't get sucked in by their bullshit."

Britton must have picked up on my expression, because he added. "That's right, we know all about Gabriele Severin, too. She's using him and they're using you. It's a mutual admiration society. They feed off each other. Ms. Severin has had it in for Tissinger ever since they let her old man go. He's a complete nut case."

"Is that so?"

Coleman finally walked over to join his partner. He informed me, "It was Noel Severin who screwed up the calculations. When he realized what happened he wanted the company to rerun their tests. That would have cost a fortune, but they were willing to do it. As a precaution they went to the other members of his team to get their take. They all knew what was going on and said Severin was trying to cover his ass. When he found out he went crazy and attacked one of them in the office. Management had no choice but to let him go.

"We're not the bad guys, Delaney," he added.

"And you're telling me this, why?"

"Because, despite the hard case act, I don't think you're a bad guy either. I don't want to see you get sucked in, or our government hurt," Britton said. "I apologize for being an ass the other day. You do what you have to do. I just thought you should have the facts."

Agent Britton stuck out his hand. So did Coleman. I hesitated for a moment then shook with them. Then I headed back to Ted's house to hear the rest of his story.

TWENTY-ONE

I RELATED my conversation to Ted and told him about Doster searching his office. He didn't appear surprised.

"Are you really serious about a divorce?" I asked.

"I am. The marriage is beyond saving. I don't give a damn about the house. Maureen can have it and all of the furniture. My main concern is the boys. I want to be a part of their lives—that's important to me and it's nonnegotiable. I won't be a father who sees them every other weekend and on holidays. I coach Scott's baseball team, for chrissake."

I took out my legal pad and made a few notes. "What about custody?"

"Joint. I'll give in on everything else, but not that, and not on alimony. She doesn't get a dime. I'm willing to pay reasonable child support and set up an education fund to them see both through graduate school. Either a bank or you can administer it. I don't want her touching their money."

"Understood."

"If it's possible I'd like to part on good terms."

"If you were on good terms you wouldn't be getting a divorce."

"True."

I told him, "You need to let Maureen know. I'll speak with her, too. But if it looks like it can't be settled, you'll have to retain someone else . . . Katherine, maybe. This is her field."

"All right."

"Let's get back to the important stuff now. What about this argument you're supposed to have had with Hamilton?"

"It wasn't an argument. Sandy was bitching about the attorneys not billing their clients for photocopies and faxes. He always talks at the top of his lungs. I guess I should say, 'talked.' We made him office manager because no one else wanted the job."

"That's it?"

"As far as I know. I saw Bill Doster's quote in the papers about Sandy investigating a discrepancy in the firm's trust account. I don't know where that came from."

"Any idea why Doster would make a statement like that?"

"None, except he's a loudmouth and a drunk and we've never gotten along. Speak to Charlie. He'll give you the straight story."

"I did speak with him and he confirmed there was a discrepancy in the trust account. I also met with Doster. He sat down and explained the security procedures your firm uses to make wire transfers. The bottom line is, they both think you took the money."

"*What?*" Ted's mouth dropped open in shock. "That's not possible. Charlie knows me better than anyone. You must have misunderstood."

"No, he was pretty clear. He told me all the partners have to enter a personal code before the bank will authorize a wire transfer. When they couldn't locate a disbursement for one of your clients, they called Doster and asked him to check into it. You were in France at the time."

"Oh, that's just fuckin' wonderful," he said, grabbing the phone from the end table. "I'd like to hear Charlie say that to my face."

Ted started to punch in what I assumed was his office number. His indignation seemed genuine enough, but it was inappropriate.

"Put the phone down."

"No way. I want to talk—"

"I said *put the phone down.* I don't need you flying off the handle and getting charged with witness tampering, so put it down now. We need to get to the bottom of this. Assuming you didn't kill Sanford Hamilton, someone else did."

"I know. I know. I'm just stunned about Charlie. I can't believe he—"

"Charlie Evans is in our corner, but it was clear he has doubts and I honestly don't blame him. He gave me a check for $50,000 to defray your legal expenses on the condition I keep his name private. According to Charlie, now that the money's been returned, your firm won't prosecute."

"It won't make any difference, the State Bar will still go after my license."

I pointed out, "That's the least of our worries at the moment."

I expected more argument and was a little surprised when I didn't get one. Ted went quiet and leaned back in his seat. He swirled the contents of his coffee around in the mug, then stared out the window.

"This Starbucks stuff is better than the supermarket brand," he commented absently.

While my friend was lost in his reverie, I turned my attention back to the photographs and came to a halt at the last one. It was taken with a telephoto lens and showed Maureen and Frank coming out of a building. She was wearing a burgundy dress and Frank had on the same Armani outfit I'd seen in court, though without the scarf.

I inquired, "Why is this important?"

"That's the Southern Federal Bank in Decatur. Mac cut off the top, but you can make out the bottom of the letters above their heads."

I felt my pulse quicken. This was the bank where Ted had supposedly opened his secret account.

"Where were you when this picture was taken?"

"At the Hotel Maurice in Paris. They have a record of it. I met with three different people during the trip."

"Do you happen to know what day the account was opened?"

He didn't have to answer the question. The Cheshire Cat smile on his face was answer enough.

TWENTY-TWO

THE bottle of Perrier paused halfway to my lips and I put it down. "You're kidding?"

Ted slowly shook his head. "I called the bank this morning to verify it."

"But you need ID to open an account. How could she—"

"Actually, you don't. These days you can do it over the Internet. Maureen has access to all my personal information—credit cards, driver's license, social security number, you name it."

"You're saying *she's* the one who set you up? That doesn't make any sense. Why?"

"I don't know why, but Maureen's definitely involved. Somehow she and Tissinger are in bed together—you should pardon the expression."

I was incredulous. Maybe a psychiatric evaluation, as Charlie had suggested, was a good idea. "Maureen and Tissinger want to frame you? To what end?"

"Let me show you something."

Ted stood up and I followed him into his office. The place was cluttered with papers and envelopes. On the desk was a framed photo of his two sons. In the opposite corner was another showing him and Gabriele. He was sitting on a park bench and she was standing behind him, her arms around his chest. The photographer had caught them laughing. They looked natural and at ease with one another.

A set of law books lined the shelves to the left of his desk. On the credenza behind him were two texts I was familiar with because he had borrowed both of them from me several months ago. One was on forensic techniques; the other was on DNA.

"Still boning up on your science?"

He shrugged. "Just something to keep me busy."

He took a seat in front of the computer monitor and started typing.

"Take a look at this," he said. "This is Southern Federal's home page on the Web. "If you want to open an account, you just click on their link and you're off and running."

Before I could respond my cell phone went off. I looked at the caller ID and recognized Ted's home number.

"Maureen," I mouthed to him.

He nodded.

"Delaney speaking."

"Hi, John. It's Maureen. I wanted to get back with you. I don't know if you're aware of it, but Ted didn't come home last night. He must have borrowed the money for his bond."

"Yes, he did. We spoke on the phone earlier. I'm sorry."

"So am I. I'm not sure what he's told you, but things haven't been right between us for a while. I've tried my best, John, honestly I have. I guess he needs some time by himself."

"I'm sure that's it. If there's anything I can do to help . . ."

Out of the corner of my eye I caught a glimpse of Ted's face. It had gone to stone.

"I know you'll think I'm terrible but I've been thinking about what we discussed yesterday, about putting the house up for Ted's legal expenses, and I just can't do it."

No, you and your boyfriend might need it to live in, but you'll have all the tile anyone could ask for. I informed her, "I don't think you're terrible, Maureen. Besides, Ted's out of jail, so the point is moot."

"But he'll need more money, won't he?"

"Probably."

"This whole business is terrifying."

"How so?"

I found it interesting that Maureen wasn't overwhelmed with curiosity about how her husband had gotten the funds to post his bond. She probably figured they had come from me since I had put up my condo as collateral. That made it somebody else's problem, which most people are happy to ignore.

She continued, "Ted's a different person from the man I married. I don't want to get into details, but I went to see a lawyer today."

Now I knew where the conversation was going. I pressed a button on my cell phone to put it on speaker.

"Why is that?" I asked.

"I'm filing for divorce, John. I have to look out for my children."

I glanced at Ted, who stuck his lower lip out and nodded.

"Are you afraid he might hurt them?"

"I honestly don't know. Ted's changed. He's been like a complete stranger to me over the last few months."

"It sounds like you've had a pretty rough time."

"I have. I know you're friends and I don't want to tell you what to do, but you really need to look out for yourself. You have a lot to lose now."

"I will. Thanks for the advice. May I ask the name of your lawyer?"

"Joe Edward Fanning. His office is at the IBM building."

Ted glanced at me and shrugged and I shrugged back.

TWENTY-THREE

We were sitting in my car across from Luther's favorite restaurant, Beneath D Island Moon. It's a scruffy dive that specializes in Caribbean food. Luther was eating jerk chicken salad from a take-out bowl. I was working my way through a bowl of conch chowder that was so spicy it made my eyes water. Nikko had somehow convinced the chef to make him a hamburger with fries.

"It's good your man leveled with you about the gun," Luther said. "Not so good him carrying it, though. The feds have two different teams watching him. One is driving a white van. The other is in a black Chrysler 300. Got the plate numbers here." He slid a piece of paper toward me.

"I've met one half of them," I said.

"That so?"

"Yeah, they tried to convince me Gabriele is using Ted to get back at the company because they fired her father."

"Were they successful?" Luther asked.

"Not quite. It's hard to explain the five dead research team members."

"So you believe Jordan's story about being set up?" Nikko asked.

"Let's say I'm keeping an open mind," I said. "Right now it's the only game in town."

"But what about the gas he purchased the night of the fire?" Nikko said.

"Anyone with access to his credit cards could have done that."

"Right. And his fingerprints at Hamilton's house when he swore he was never there?"

"It's possible to lift a fingerprint and replace it elsewhere. Has anyone ever told you you're a very skeptical person?" I said.

Nikko shrugged. "Part of my nature. The question is why aren't you? And why go out on a limb like this?"

"Delaney live on that limb," Luther said.

"How come?" Nikko asked.

"I don't know. How come?" Luther said, turning to me.

"We've got history together," I said.

Luther nodded as if that explained it. Nikko shrugged and took another bite of his burger.

"Well, I think the guy's hinky," Nikko said. "If it were me, I'd leave skid marks."

"Let's discuss me later," I said. "In the meantime, I want to check out the research team. Each of the deaths is listed as either accidental or the result of natural causes. They're a good place to start."

I took a note I had made out of my coat pocket and put it on the table.

"Isao Tikumi," Luther read. "French national. Died of anaphylactic shock due to bee sting."

"What the fuck does that mean?" Nikko asked.

"The man got stung by a bee and had an allergic reaction to it," Luther said.

Nikko was puzzled. "And that can cause you to die?"

"It can," I said.

"So what are we supposed to do, interview the fuckin' bee?" Nikko said.

"Just poke around and see what you can find," I said.

"Why us?"

"Because we subtle and inscrutable," Luther said.

"There's one thing I don't get," Nikko said.

"Just one?" Luther asked.

Nikko ignored him. "How can this guy be French with a name like that?"

"It's possible for Asians to immigrate to other countries," Luther said.

"Yeah? I thought only Americans had that kind of stuff."

"What stuff you talking about?" Luther said.

"You know like, African-Americans or American-Indians. Who ever heard of French-Asians?"

"You learn something new every day," I said.

"And what will you be doing?" Nikko asked.

"I've got calls in to Phil Thurman and Maury Katz. Katz is listed as agent-in-charge now. I want to have a look at the murder scene myself."

"And Thurman?" Nikko said.

"I'm going to ask him for help with the heart attack victim."

"Too late to help that man," Luther pointed out.

"It's never too late," I said.

" 'Course not," he said.

TWENTY-FOUR

PHIL Thurman hadn't changed much in the last five years. He still reminded me of a drill sergeant in a suit. We had worked together several times in the past and butted heads once or twice, but he was someone I trusted. As agent-in-charge of the FBI's Atlanta office there wasn't much he didn't know about in the southeast where crime was concerned. His private office was neither large nor opulently furnished, merely lean and efficient like the man who occupied it.

"I was a little surprised to hear from you," he said. "What's it been, two years now?"

"Sounds right."

"And Mrs. Delaney?"

"She fine, except she kept her maiden name."

"They call it a birth name these days. Otherwise you're a sexist," he said.

"Taking sensitivity courses?"

Thurman picked up a memo sitting on the corner of his desk. "This is from the new administration. Everybody's more sensitive now. Did you happen to catch the president's press conference last week?"

"Not really."

"A fly was buzzing around annoying Obama, so he brushes it away a couple of times. Unfortunately, the fly didn't get the message, so he swatted it."

"The Secret Service is never around when you need them," I said.

"Exactly. Now here's the good part. Some jerkoff from PETA sees it and takes offense. They issued a statement saying the president should have treated the fly more *humanely*. Let me repeat that for you: They want the Commander-in-Chief of the United States to treat flies humanely. They even sent him some kind of contraption that catches flies live so he can release them into the wild."

"Don't they carry malaria?" I asked.

"I think that's mosquitoes."

"Got it. So what does PETA stand for?"

"Who the fuck knows . . . people who eat tasty animals or something like that," Thurman said.

I looked at the memo on Thurman's desk and read aloud: *"People for the Ethical Treatment of Animals."*

"Whatever. I hope you have something better for me."

"Phil, you think I'm here because I want something. I'm deeply hurt."

Thurman turned his palms up and waited.

"Well, there might be one thing," I said.

"Let me save you some time," Thurman told me. "We don't get involved in local murder cases. It's against our federal mandate."

"How about a drug company that's conspired to frame an innocent man and is in the process of releasing a drug on the market they know will induce some people to commit suicide?"

The smile faded from Thurman's face. "That would fall under RICO and as a law enforcement officer I'd take a dim view of such conduct. Is this on the level?"

"I can't be certain yet, but I think there's a good chance I'm onto something. I need a little help pulling the information together."

"Tell me more."

I told him.

When I was finished, Thurman swung around to his computer console and punched a few buttons.

"You're certain this fellow Britton is with the NSA?"

"According to his ID."

"And he's working with a security officer from the Tissinger Company?"

"That's their story," I said.

Thurman frowned. "That doesn't make sense. They'd need to let me know if they were running an operation here."

"One would assume."

"So you've come to me out of patriotism?"

"I'm here because I don't like seeing the little guy get screwed, particularly if that guy's a friend. The larger issue is if Tissinger is putting out something that kills people, that's not right."

Thurman was silent for a moment. "No, it's not," he said. "What do you need?"

"One of the scientists who died originally worked at Tissinger's Atlanta plant. After Noel Severin blew the whistle and was fired, this man also complained to his superiors about the missing test data."

"And they fired him, too?"

"No, he became ill and was hospitalized. He was treated at Piedmont Hospital, but no dice. His family flew his body back to Miami for burial. The official diagnosis lists his cause of death as pulmonary edema. The man was forty-eight."

"Jeez."

"According to what I was told he worked out regularly, wasn't overweight, and had no prior history of heart problems."

"Thurman asked, "Was an autopsy done?"

"Nope and that's where you come in."

"Why am I not surprised?"

TWENTY-FIVE

I PHONED Katherine as I was pulling into the faculty parking lot. The receptionist was a voice I didn't know and asked me to wait while she found Katherine's secretary. Across from the school two men were changing an ad on a billboard. It was for a local airline. The scene showed a couple walking along a deserted white beach. I was mentally inserting Katherine and myself there when her secretary came on the line.

I've always liked Galena Olivares. She's a bright, personable woman who pulled herself up by her own bootstraps. Fifteen years earlier she emigrated (legally) from Honduras and managed to learn English on her own. She enrolled in night school, took classes in typing and shorthand while supporting a young son. Heroes come in all shapes and sizes.

"How are you, John?"

"Never better. You?"

"Getting along."

"And Danny?"

"He's almost as big as I am. Can you imagine that?"

"Not really. Time flies, doesn't it?"

I remembered when Galena used to bring her son to the office. She couldn't afford a babysitter then, so the other secretaries took turns watching him when she was tied up. Katherine had put Galena's ex in jail at least four times for failure to pay child support. It was probably up to five now.

"I'll have to drop by and see him sometime."

"He still talks about how you used to pull money out of his ear with your magic tricks."

I smiled at the memory. "Is the boss in?"

"Just a second."

Katherine came on the line a moment later.

"How's it going?" she asked.

"Slowly. I was hoping for a piece of advice on how to handle something that's come up. It looks like Ted and Maureen are headed for a divorce."

"Divorce would seem to be the least of his problems."

"True."

"What sort of advice?"

"Do you know a lawyer named Joe Fanning?"

"Joe Edward Fanning?"

"I think so."

"He's a typical divorce gunner and a real s.o.b. I've tried a few cases with him. You'll have to verify everything he tells you."

"That bad, huh?"

"Joe Edward can milk a case better than anyone I've ever met and he doesn't believe in settling until his fee is well into the five-figure range."

"Marvelous."

"Why do you ask?"

I told her. "Can you give me any pointers on how to handle him?"

"You're not representing Ted in the divorce are you?"

"No. If it looks like they're headed for court I'll turn the case over to you or someone in your office. Right now all I want is to set up a meeting and see if we can work matters out privately."

"Good luck. Fanning will go straight for the jugular. And he'll do it with as much fanfare as possible. Joe Edward is the best self-promoter in Atlanta."

"Better than Thornton Schiff?"

"All right, second-best. But you're wasting your time with him."

"You're probably right. I've got some pictures that might help the negotiations though."

"Ooh, what kind of pictures?" Katherine asked.

"If you have some time later and you're willing to dispense a little more advice, I might show them to you."

"How about six o'clock at Ouzo Blue? You can buy me dinner in exchange for my services."

"Bribery?"

"Absolutely."

"Sounds good, K.J. See you then."

I glanced up at the billboard again with its turquoise water, white sand, and palm trees. *Utopia is just a short ride away.* I read the words aloud as I locked the car door. It would be nice if everyone could catch that flight.

TWENTY-SIX

At a quarter to three I packed my books and notes and headed down the hall to my classroom. Along the way I passed Harriet Grabowski's office and saw her sitting at her desk. We waved to each other. Harriet has been with the school for nearly twenty years and once gave me a good piece of advice at a cocktail party.

"Don't let 'em get ahead of you, John. Law students are famous for trying to trip up the teacher. Year after year, it never fails. If they smell blood, they'll go straight for the throat."

Her words were still fresh in my mind. As a result, I'd spent the last hour going over the cases we were to cover that day. Conversations dropped when I entered the classroom and headed for the lectern.

"Good afternoon, everyone. Today we'll be reviewing the fascinating case of *Palzgraf v. The Long Island Railroad,* one of the seminal decisions in the area of negligence and forseeability. When the *Palzgraf* decision was handed down it literally caused a split in courts throughout the nation."

Following the time-honored principle of law professors everywhere, I asked for a volunteer to brief the case, and was met with thirty blank looks.

For over a hundred years, ninety percent of our law schools have used the case study method to teach. A student is selected, or victimized, depending on your point of view, and asked to recite the facts and legal issues involved.

Palzgraf was decided in 1928, and it is a law professor's dream because there are so many points to deal with. Therefore I was confused when no one raised their hand. In every class I'd ever taught there was no shortage of students wanting to impress. After a moment, I turned my palms up in a silent question and looked around the room.

"Professor Delaney," a voice in the back row called out, "I read in the papers you were on the *Ocean Majestic* when it sank. Is that true?"

I turned to identify the speaker, a slender young man with spiky hair, and stared at him for a moment before answering, "Yes, I was on the ship."

"Was it horrible?" a wide-eyed girl in the front row asked.

"It wasn't as much fun as you'd imagine. Listen people, we've got a lot of ground to cover today, so—"

"They said over two thousand people drowned," a girl with thick glasses in the second row blurted out.

"It wasn't two thousand. The figure was closer to nine hundred, but that was high enough."

"And you and another lawyer helped catch the people responsible, isn't that right, Professor?" she continued.

"The lawyer's name is Katherine Adams, and she did most of the work. I just tagged along. Now, why don't we—"

"Did a terrorist really try to kill you?" the spiky-haired boy asked.

I looked down at my hands for a moment then slowly surveyed the room. I realized this session was going nowhere until I answered their questions. To the students I was something of an anomaly. I knew that. Now with the newspapers dredging up what had happened on the *Ocean Majestic*, that perception was only enhanced. Three years earlier the tragedy had captured the world's attention, thrusting Katherine and me into the limelight. We were both grateful when the furor finally died down. Most of those memories were bitter and painful. Unfortunately, the newspapers had resurrected them again.

I informed the class, "Yes, one of them did try."

"It said in the papers you killed him," the girl with glasses said.

"Not exactly. The man's name was Umar Maharan and he had connections to several Middle Eastern organizations. He was actually on the *Majestic* to steal a genetics formula."

A murmur went around the classroom.

"Did you shoot him?" the girl asked.

"No. We were fighting and he went over a balcony. His neck was broken in the fall."

"Whoa," the boy with spiky hair exclaimed, his mouth dropping open.

Another student wanted to know, "How come you were fighting, Professor?"

"Because he failed to recite the *Palzgraf* case when I asked for it."

I followed this with what I thought was a feral smile. Several people in the first row actually moved their chairs back an inch or two. Then the laughter started. It was slow at first, but increased as my students picked up on the joke. More questions came at me and I let them go on for several minutes. I even answered a few about Ted's case before we got back to business. As rumor mills go, law schools are notorious. I figured the best way to deal with them was head on.

A COUPLE of glances were directed my way as the students filed out. Some of them probably expected me to grow another head. I was able to joke about what happened, but at the time the situation was far from humorous. Umar's face and his dead eyes still show up in my dreams every now and then.

When I was alone, I took a deep breath and sat at my desk to make some notes as students from the next class began filtering in.

A tap at the door caused me to look up.

Ben Chambers, the school's dean, was standing in the hallway along with Paul Mendoza, a colleague from my department.

"Hello, Ben. What brings you to this neck of the woods?"

"Got a moment, John?"

"Sure. But we're about to begin."

"Paul will cover for you. Let's take a walk."

My eyes narrowed and I didn't get up. I glanced at Paul, who nodded a greeting and immediately averted his eyes. It didn't take a genius to put two and two together.

"Am I being fired?"

Chambers smiled. "No, no, nothing like that," he said. "Let's go outside, where we can speak more freely."

Ben Chambers is your typical Southern gentleman: tall, slender, and always immaculately groomed. That afternoon he was dressed in a tan suit, white shirt, and a red bowtie. For the past fifteen years he had managed to walk a delicate line between administration, faculty, our students, and the general public without becoming entangled in any one group's agenda.

My first inclination was to tell him what he could do with his job, but that would have embarrassed everyone present, plus it was bad form. It also wouldn't have done any good. Ben could be as tough as nails if the situation warranted and he'd do it in the most genteel way. Everyone who knew him regarded him as a straight shooter. With some gentle pushing from Katherine he was largely responsible for my teaching position at Emory, so I held my tongue, got up, and started walking.

"Hell of a mess, this Jordan situation," Ben said, after a moment.

"Seems that way."

"I only know what I read in the papers, John, but it looks like your client is in some pretty hot water."

"That would be a mild way of putting it."

"The news about him mutilating his partner was very distressing."

"Particularly to Sanford Hamilton," I said.

Ben glanced at me and kept walking. "I was listening to the radio earlier and they said the police recovered the murder weapon last night, a handgun registered to your client."

And the hits just keep on coming. I shook my head and remained silent.

Ben continued, "Last night and this morning I've received calls from several of the school's trustees."

"I hope they were pleasant."

"A number expressed strong sentiments about letting you go. This is a conservative institution and John, we're not used to controversy involving one of our professors, particularly one who hasn't achieved tenure yet."

"I see. So, what's the bottom line, Ben?"

"The consensus is for you to take a leave of absence while your trial is pending. That way you'll be free to devote your time to Mr. Jordan's defense. It looks like he's going to need it. Your position will still be here when you get back, unless of course . . ."

"I withdraw from representing him," I said.

"I'm not suggesting that. That's something you'll have to decide on your own."

"But you think I should."

"Officially, I have no position on the subject," Ben said.

"And unofficially?"

"As your friend . . . I'd drop him like a hot potato. To put it bluntly, the board is concerned about your judgment in the matter. Our teachers teach, they do research, they lecture. They don't represent—"

"Criminals?"

Ben continued unruffled. "That's for a court to decide. In the past twenty-four hours I've also received letters from parents, calls from talk shows hosts, and a half-dozen tabloids wanting to know what Emory's involvement is."

"I see."

He stopped walking and faced me. "I hope you do, because I busted my butt to keep you here. As an institution we'll have no comment and let the situation die down. Your leave will be without pay since you'll be taking it voluntarily."

"And if I refuse?

"Don't."

It was a simple choice really. Take a hike, or get the axe. For a fleeting moment I considered caving in and telling Ben I'd withdraw from the case, but I owed Ted Jordan and I was raised to believe you pay your debts. Friends don't abandon friends when the waters get rough. Some things I could do, and some things I couldn't.

"When does my leave of absence begin?"

Ben informed me, "Immediately. We'll make the announcement later today."

TWENTY-SEVEN

Ouzo Blue is nothing special, just a nondescript little restaurant on Marietta's town square. Nevertheless, they serve some of the best Greek food around. After moving to Georgia I found 90 percent of Southern towns seem to have a square. Don't ask me why—they just do. This is usually where the sheriff's office, police station, and courthouse are located. In bigger cities, like Atlanta and Savannah, the squares have given way to skyscrapers and parking decks. I'm not sure if that constitutes progress, but it's a reflection of the changing times.

Though Marietta's population is probably close to 600,000, locals still think of it as a small town. In the summer they hold concerts in a white wooden gazebo, and a couple times a year the city hosts local craft fairs. Because the population has steadily been creeping upward for twenty years, it's become increasingly difficult to find a parking spot near your final destination. The situation is worse when courts are in session. I left Emory shortly after four-thirty and the drive took me almost an hour. Atlanta's metro traffic screws everyone with democratic impartiality.

I finally located a parking spot five blocks from the restaurant and began walking. On the corner I stopped at a drug store and picked up a copy of the *Marietta Daily Journal*. The front-page headline read:

Police Recover Hamilton Murder Weapon

Directly under it was a picture of Sanford Hamilton with the caption, "Victim." Next to him was a mug shot of Ted Jordan taken when he was arrested and the words, "Accused in Slaying." There was also a photo of me announcing to the world, "I guarantee my client is innocent."

I thought Ted looked better than I did.

I was halfway across the room before I saw my wife. She was sitting in a booth at the back of the restaurant. She smiled and I waved. I liked that she still wore her hair long. It fell softly on her shoulders and framed a perfect face. Her cheekbones were high, like her mother's.

"You look good," I said.

"So do you," she said. A bare foot rode up my pant leg as soon as I sat down. "Did you have a good day?"

"It's getting better by the moment. Can I get you a . . . oh, I see you already have one," I said. "What is that?"

"A mojito."

"How did your deposition go?" I asked.

"The doctor forgot to mention the apartment he was leasing with his partner."

"Is that bad?" I asked.

"It is when you swear under oath that you've listed all your assets on the disclosure statement."

"What's wrong with having an apartment?"

"Nothing, as long as you stay there. This one is occupied by two strippers from the Gold Club. It's a live-in bordello."

"Ah . . . patients?"

Katherine gave me a flat look. "Hardly. His wife, who happens to be my client by the way, knew nothing about it. She kneed him in the groin on the way out."

"Ouch."

The waiter appeared and took my drink order. I decided to try a mojito as well. The limes looked refreshing. I wasn't just making conversation when I said Katherine looked good. She did. A mutual friend once remarked she had a dancer's body.

"How is Ted's case going?"

"They might wait on building the gallows yet. I'll be leaving for Miami in two days."

"Why?"

"You remember Phil Thurman?"

"Of course."

"He's arranging for an autopsy on one of the scientists who died."

"That makes sense. At least you'll know if the conspiracy is real or it's just in Ted's mind." Katherine leaned forward and put her elbows on the table. "So . . . if he didn't kill Hamilton, who did?"

I shook my head. "I don't know, but I'll have plenty of time to find out. Ben Chambers informed me I was on leave of absence as of today."

Katherine's mouth opened in shock. "Oh, John, I'm so sorry. Is there anything I can do? Do you want me to call Ben?"

"No, it's probably for the best. Ted deserves a full-time lawyer right now."

"But it's unfair."

"Life isn't fair, K.J."

A long moment passed before she said anything. "Are you sure there's nothing I can do?"

"A little coaching on how to handle Fanning would be helpful."

"All right," Katherine said letting out a long breath "Ted believes Maureen and her boyfriend set him up when he was out of the country. Is that right?"

"It is."

She suggested, "Is it possible Maureen has an account there?"

"Ted told me he checked and she doesn't. I'll verify that, of course. There could be a legitimate reason for her being at the bank, but it's a hell of a coincidence."

Katherine commented further on the subject. "But why sell him out? Ted's her security—unless she's cut a better deal with someone else. I don't think the tile guy makes what patent lawyers do, no matter how good his business is. Her actions don't make any sense."

"My thought as well."

I took out the packet of photos Ted had given me from my briefcase and slid them across the table. My wife arched one eyebrow and flipped through them quickly.

"Tacky," was her only comment. "How do you plan to handle this?"

"Like you said, the divorce is the least of Ted's worries right now. I have no idea if a settlement is possible. If there's a chance I'd like to get it over quickly. I understand about Fanning trying to milk the case, but I really want to see Maureen's reaction when the bank account question comes up. I also want to know what she and Frank were doing there."

"Reasonable."

"Good, then I'll call Fanning and try to set up a meeting."

After a moment of silence, Katherine informed me, "It won't work."

"Why not?"

"No offense, but you're a paper tiger. Fanning will know that right away. He'll also know you can't stay on the case because you have a conflict of interest. A court will disqualify you without a second thought."

"Any suggestions?" I asked.

"How about if I come on board? I've only met Maureen once and I never really liked her."

"Twice."

Katherine shrugged. "Whatever. The point is, if my firm is counsel of record, Joe Edward will know he's in for a fight. Besides, I'd love to be there when you pull out those photos. We can do good cop–bad cop."

"I can't ask that of you, K.J."

"You've asked more in the past," she said rubbing my leg again with her foot. "I may owe you one . . . maybe two."

"Can I collect later?"

"Absolutely," she said, moving her foot higher.

It's a good thing the restaurant had long tablecloths. Some of my drink promptly went down the wrong way. Katherine solicitously patted me on the back. She had a mischievous look on her face. The waiter appeared and began telling us about the daily specials. They sounded like the same ones I'd heard a year ago. Ouzo's needed to invest in new menus.

By the end of the meal I was feeling more relaxed. Maybe it was the mojito. It had been a long day and I wanted to be home in bed with my wife. The rain had finally stopped, leaving a chill in the air. The clouds had also moved on. The result was a clear night sky behind them. I took off my coat and put it around Katherine's shoulders as we walked her to her car. The gesture was automatic. We kissed good-bye and I promised to meet her at the house. Once her taillights had disappeared around the corner I started back across the square.

Most of the businesses were closed for the evening. I paused at Eddie's Trick Shop to see if there was anything new in the window. The extent of my magical repertoire consists of two sleight-of-hand moves and a plastic thumb Eddie sold me a few years ago. You fit it over your own finger and hide a tiny silk scarf in it. Katherine's young nephews and Galena's son were always amazed. Personally, I harbored a secret desire to use it in court one day. I just haven't figured out how yet.

Other than my car, the only other vehicle on the street was a black Chrysler parked at the end of the block. A cigarette glow from inside the darkened interior brought me up short. Whoever was sitting behind the wheel had a clear view of the restaurant.

The old saying goes . . . it ain't paranoia if someone's really watching you.

TWENTY-EIGHT

THE following morning, I awoke to find a note on the nightstand from Katherine saying she had to leave early for a meeting with her client. She informed me there were fresh bagels in the kitchen. The note was signed with a smiley face and a few x's and o's.

While the coffee was going, I stood in our bay window placed a phone call to Ted. I got his answer machine and left a message about trying to set up a meeting with Maureen's lawyer. Outside the wind whipped leaves around in a circle. My next call was to Joe Edward Fanning. I got his paralegal. She informed me Mr. Fanning would be tied up in court for the next two days and promised to tell him I had called.

Until someone proved me wrong, I would continue building Ted's defense. The bottom line is, you have to assume your client is telling the truth. It makes no sense to lie to your attorney. Doctors bury their mistakes; lawyers . . . well, you get the picture.

My next call was to Maury Katz. Maury was a thirty-year veteran with homicide who had a good eye for details. We'd met a few times and had even socialized. Though he came across as low key, I knew he had a sharp mind and the best conviction record on the force. Other detectives thought of him as a plodder. But I'll put my money on a plodder any day of the week when it comes to police work. In real life, cases aren't solved by those flashes of insight television detectives get each week. It comes down to hard work and following each loose end.

The first time Maury and I had met was in Katherine's office. She was handling his son's divorce and he was there waiting to review his deposition. I was just waiting. We began talking and the subject of my background came up. Apart from police work, we learned that we both had a passion for forensics. In the last two years he had come to the school several times for a second opinion on different crime scenes or a piece of evidence. I considered him one of the good guys.

Cops have a tendency to stick with their own. Still, a New York Irish Catholic and a Southern Jew aren't your typical combination. Years earlier, Maury and his wife had retained Katherine's services because they wanted to make sure their grandson would receive a Hebrew education and be Bar Mitzvahed. His son's wife wasn't Jewish and had been leveraging her permission to get more alimony. It was a scummy thing to do and I felt for them because the ceremony was obviously important in their faith.

Katherine and I attended their synagogue a few times as their guests. Maury and his wife Emma reciprocated by visiting our church.

My call was returned within ten minutes. We agreed to meet at Hamilton's house, or what was left of it.

Maury was already there when I pulled up. Yellow tape had been strung around the perimeter of the home, declaring it a crime scene. The color was incongruous against the fescue and flowerbeds. Beyond that stood a shell of brick, its roof collapsed. Through shattered windows I could make out parts of the wooden frame. Most of it had been charred black.

"Hello, young man," Maury said.

"How have you been?" I said, shaking his hand.

"A little older, a little stiffer."

"Viagra can work miracles."

He looked slightly offended and informed me, "Emma is a very happy woman. She has no complaints . . . well, not many."

I smiled. "And Clifford?" I asked, remembering his grandson's name.

Maury's face lit up. "A good boy, a lovely boy. He's a real *mensch.* You know what that means?"

"No."

"If you're a *mensch,* then you're a person—a human being. It's a Yiddish expression."

"*Mensch,*" I repeated. "And your son?"

He made a dismissive gesture. "Better not to ask."

I'd heard rumors about Maury's son moving to Miami and going into the charter fishing business with some woman he'd met in a bar, so I dropped the subject.

"What's it like inside?" I asked, motioning toward the house.

"Not pretty. The fire did its job. Fortunately, it didn't get everything. You want a look?"

We walked across the lawn, ducked under the tape, and pushed the front door open. It wasn't locked because there was no need to. I stepped around a pile of rubble in the foyer and followed Maury into the study. A distinct mildew smell hung in the air. The home's interior must have been elegant at one time. Most of the wood paneling and crown moldings were still intact along with remnants of heavy velvet drapes. On the floor in front of a mahogany desk was the chalk outline of a body, a grim reminder of what had happened there.

I said, "According to the newspaper, you just recovered the murder weapon, is that true?"

"We found a gun, yes."

"Where was it?"

"In the bushes near the swimming pool."

Maury pointed to the spot through a set of bay windows. Outside was a patio surrounded by a twenty-foot-high privacy hedge. The water had been drained out of the pool and the bottom was covered in leaves and debris. At the far end of the hedge was a gate. From what I could see it appeared to be the only way in or out with the exception of the house itself.

I asked, "Was the gate open the night Hamilton was killed?"

Maury shook his head indicating it wasn't.

I let that process for a moment. "He shoots him in here . . . then goes outside to ditch the murder weapon. A little odd, wouldn't you say?"

"It wasn't a terribly smart thing to do, particularly for a lawyer who graduated fourth in his class, but people do strange things under stress."

We held each other's eyes for a moment.

I asked, "Why go outside at all? Why not leave through the front door? It doesn't follow."

Maury shrugged for a reply.

"I'm not buying it," I said.

"And I'm not selling, John. That's the DA's job. Me . . . I'm just here to look. Like you, I only got this case a few days ago."

I shook my head. "Something's wrong."

"Maybe yes, maybe no," Maury said. "There's certainly an unusual element—several actually, as you point out."

"You said you just took this case over?"

"It was originally assigned to Baxley and Eberhart. They were working out of the North Precinct at the time."

I took out my notebook and made note of their names.

"Who wrote the original incident report?"

"Eberhart. Baxley signed off. Eberhart left the department shortly thereafter. He's doing security work for a private company now. Baxley transferred to robbery."

There are times you have to read between the lines. Officially, the department had done its job. A murder was committed, investigated, and an arrest was made. Once that was finished—game over. The ball gets handed off to the prosecutor.

I inquired, "So how did you get involved? This appears to be a done deal."

This time Maury's shrug was more elaborate. "Actually, my captain received a call from a nice young lady in the DA's office—Rena Bailey. He asked if I would take a second look, so here I am."

"And what are you looking at?"

"Everything. It never hurts to have a fresh pair of eyes. You know what I'm saying?"

"I do."

I was aware Maury had sidestepped my earlier question about their finding the murder weapon so I raised the point again. "Tell me about the gun."

"It's a SIG nine-millimeter semiautomatic, fired one time according to forensics."

"The shoot was clean?"

"In a manner of speaking."

I took a deep breath and let it out. "Why don't we cut to the chase and you tell me what I'm missing?"

In all of our previous encounters Maury had always been straight-forward, so his reticence now surprised me. I waited for him to continue.

"Let me show you some photos and maybe you can tell me. You're the professor."

TWENTY-NINE

I FOLLOWED Maury out to his car. On the front seat was a thick loose-leaf binder. In one form or another, most detectives put together a file documenting each step of their investigation. Sometimes they do this in book form. Maury picked up the loose-leaf and handed it to me, then strolled over to a small wrought-iron bench and sat down. He took out a pack of Turkish cigarettes and lit one. Their pungent smell reached me fifteen feet away.

"Emma doesn't let me smoke in the house," he said.

I nodded and turned my attention to the book. The crime scene photographs were in clear plastic holders. In my years as a cop I'd seen more corpses than I cared to remember. Sooner or later you think you'll become jaded. You don't. The sight still comes as a shock—even when it's just pictures. The photographer had done his job well.

Sandy Hamilton's dead face stared back at me. His body had been badly burned, but large sections of it were untouched by the fire. Pieces of clothing were visible—gray trousers, a white long-sleeve shirt and loafers. Hamilton lay on his right side, his knees slightly pulled up toward his chest. The worst part was his eyes. They were horrible to look at. The mixture of terror and agony went straight to my gut. I fought down a rising feeling of nausea when I saw that three of his fingers had been cut off. This man had died in terrible pain.

The next two photographs were close-ups. I took a deep breath and examined the wounds to Hamilton's fingers. Each had been inflicted with a sharp object. In other words, there was no tearing or serrations present. A glance at the ME's report confirmed this. The newspapers and television had made a great deal over the missing body parts which were found in Ted's basement. Again, this made no sense for someone as bright as Ted.

An insane murderer takes the victim's fingers for souvenirs, hides them in the basement, but conveniently leaves his gun lying around to be discovered? He might as well have drawn a map for the cops.

The moment I saw the entry wound beneath Hamilton's right eye my antennae went up. The fire's heat had blistered his skin, but for the most part his face was untouched. The area around the bullet's point of entry was blackened, indicating the gun had been fired at close range, perhaps even pressed against Hamilton's face. To the right of the wound and just underneath it, between his eye socket and his nose, was a purple crescent-shaped bruise where the blood had pooled.

In gunshots of this type the trauma radiates outward from the bullet's point of impact. There was nothing like this here. I glanced over my shoulder at Maury, who was now wreathed in a cloud of blue smoke. He motioned for me to continue. To me it indicated the bullet had been fired *after* Hamilton was dead, hence the pooling.

The last four photos had been taken by the medical examiner. They showed Hamilton in the morgue on an operating table. He was lying on his back with his eyes open, staring at nothing. Someone had the decency to drape a towel over his genitals, preserving a small shred of dignity in death.

I studied the first two carefully and saw nothing unusual.

The third photo was of Hamilton on his stomach. My eyes scanned the length of his body searching for anything out of the ordinary. I found what I was looking for a second later. At the back of his head was a darkened area that could have only been dried blood. But according to Maury, Ted's gun had only been fired once.

I flipped back to the ME's report again and went straight to the section dealing with the cause of death.

A wound approximately four inches in depth was observed at the back of the victim's skull. Entrance is at the dorsal portion of the occipital area, continuing downward on a curved path well into the cerebellum almost to the point where it meets the Medulla oblongata. A number of serrations from this wound are noted. As a result of blunt trauma the victim went into shock, complicated by massive internal tissue damage and bleeding.

The murder weapon cannot be determined at this time based upon a physical examination of the wound, other than to say it was square at the top and tapered to a point at the bottom. The entry point into the skull is one inch on all sides.

"The gunshot's a phony," I informed him.

"No, the gunshot is quite real," a voice behind me said.

I was concentrating on the photos so intently I hadn't heard Rena Bailey drive up.

"You know what I mean," I said, turning to her. "That gunshot didn't kill Sanford Hamilton and neither did Ted Jordan."

"We're still on the fence about that," Maury said. He pushed himself up from the bench and came over to join us, waving at the air to clear the smoke away.

"Thank you," Rena said.

He smiled and patted her on the stomach. "The world should be filled with children and laughter." Then he turned to me. "As I mentioned earlier, Mr. Jordan is a clever man. I think no one would disagree on this point. It doesn't strain the imagination to conceive of him planting a series of false clues designed to deflect the blame."

"Bullshit. Why drop yourself into a meat grinder like this? Why not just kill the man and have done with it?"

Rena massaged the small of her back and leaned against the hood of her car.

She said, "We don't know the answer to that, John. As Jordan's attorney you have a right to see these files. Sooner or later you'd have made a discovery motion, so I called Maury and we decided to show them to you now. He reached the same conclusion you did about the head shot. Something isn't right. We're just not sure what it is or why."

I inquired, "Does your boss know about this?"

"Not yet. I'll tell him, of course, but I wanted to speak with you first. We have a solid case against Ted Jordan—a very solid one, even with the anomalies. His prints place him at the crime scene and he lied to the investigators. Hamilton's fingers were found his house and now we have a weapon registered to him."

"But it's not the murder weapon," I said.

"Agreed. The point is none of these things make him look good, particularly when you add embezzlement and his argument with Hamilton. Do you see where I'm going with this?"

I saw. Inconsistencies aside, Ted was still the prime suspect and there were no other candidates in second place.

"So what is it you want me to do?"

"Give us a reason to keep Ted Jordan out of the electric chair."

I looked from Rena to Maury and back again. Neither had the slightest trace of humor on their face.

THIRTY

AFTER leaving the house I headed for the public library. I needed to understand what kind of man Sanford Hamilton was. Generally, you don't kill someone over an argument about whether to charge clients for photocopies. It was clear both Rena and Maury had problems with the case. But having problems was a long way from getting Ted off the hook.

Shortly after exiting I-75 at Williams Street, I became aware that I was being followed. A burgundy SUV had been with me since I left Cobb County. Rather than turn onto Forsyth Street, as I normally would have, I kept on going and pulled into a parking garage across from Woodruff Park. I waited to see if the SUV would appear.

Calling Woodruff a "park" is a misnomer, unless your tastes run to concrete. It has an enormous fountain with water that cascades down a series of granite steps into a retaining pool. Near the fountain on a pedestal is a large bronze statue of a woman holding a bird by the legs, its wings stretched out above her head—Atlanta rising from the ashes. The bird is supposed to be a phoenix, or at least the artist's conception of what one might look like if they actually existed. Personally, it reminds me of a stealth fighter with feet.

A few years ago the city decided to plant some trees and bushes around the fountain to enhance the "park-like feeling." Great idea, but it didn't work. All in all it's not a bad place to sit and look at the signs advertising "Atlanta's new aquarium." As far as I knew Atlanta had never had an old one. Most of the funds to build it had come from a private individual and if he wanted to call it "new," I guess the city council figured, who were they to argue?

The burgundy SUV pulled into the lot shortly after I did. Whoever was tailing me would have no trouble spotting my car. I was driving

Mr. Jag, my old SK-150 convertible. There aren't many of these around anymore. A man got out of the SUV and scanned the area. I made no attempt to conceal myself. I simply stood in front of the fountain watching the water. At the same time I was also watching him out of the corner of my eye. I thought there was a good chance it was either Agent Britton or one of his pals. Satisfied he had seen me, I started walking.

At the corner I turned and went down another block. My companion followed, keeping a safe distance. Two more turns headed us back toward the fountain. Out of curiosity I decided to pick up my pace and see what he would do. It had been a long time since I'd carried a gun and I was feeling exposed now without one. My pulse began to quicken. I had to assume whoever was tailing me was armed. There aren't a lot of weapons one can lay their hands on in the middle of downtown Atlanta, so surprise would be my best ally. The entrance to Woodruff Park was fifty feet away and my pursuer was starting to close the distance between us.

As soon as I passed the entrance, I stepped inside the park flattening myself against the nearest wall. A store window across the way gave me a clear view of the street. The man rounded the corner and stopped for a second trying to figure out which way I had gone. Then he began jogging. A hundred feet. Fifty feet. Twenty.

I stepped out from behind the wall, grabbed him by the front of his shirt, and using his own momentum, swung him toward the fountain. The man let out a startled yelp as his shins hit the granite lip. He went sprawling into the water face first.

The last person I expected to see was Frank the tile-man.

Two women coming up the street from the opposite direction saw the exchange and promptly crossed to the other side without a word.

"*Motherfucker*. Are you, nuts?" Frank said, sitting up in the water.

I rested my foot on the fountain's lip. "Hello, Frank."

"You threw me in the fuckin' water. This is a silk shirt, asshole."

"Very attractive. Why you were following me?"

"And these shoes cost more than you make in a week." He got to his feet. "I'm gonna kick your ass."

We were both spared the experience by the appearance of an

Atlanta police officer. The man was large and could easily have passed for a Falcons defensive lineman.

"What's going on here?" he asked.

"This cocksucker just threw me in the water. I want him arrested."

The officer's eyebrows rose. "You threw him in the water?"

"He assaulted me," Frank shouted. "Arrest him."

The officer said, "Sir, please step out of there and let me ask the questions." He reached out, took Frank under the elbow, and helped him over the granite lip.

"Well," he asked, turning back to me.

"My name's John Delaney. I'm an ex-homicide detective with the NYPD. I teach law at Emory University now."

"So what? This man says you threw him in the fountain."

"I've just come from a meeting with Detective Maury Katz, and Rena Bailey, an assistant DA. This gentleman has been following me since then. A moment ago he rounded the corner and came at me in an aggressive manner. I felt I had no choice but to react defensively."

"What a fuckin liar!" Frank yelled.

The officer digested this for a moment. According to his nametag he was Sergeant R. H. Malcolm.

"Please keep your voice down," Malcolm said to Frank. "This is a public street. Let me see some ID—the both of you."

I took my wallet out and flipped it open, displaying my gold shield. It bore the word "retired" underneath. Opposite it was my Georgia bar card. Malcolm examined them for a moment and nodded.

"What about you?" he asked Frank.

"I left my wallet in my car. It's parked in that garage up the street. I can get it if you want. Hey wait, I've got a business card. Will that do?"

Frank fished around in his back pocket and came up with a soggy business card. He handed it to Malcolm, who used his thumb and forefinger to examine it.

"Nardelli," he said, repeating Frank's name. "Mr. Delaney says you were following him."

Frank bent down to wring some water out of his pants cuff. "I wasn't following anybody. Jesus, look at these fuckin' pants, would you? They're ruined."

Malcolm glanced at them and then at me. I raised my shoulders in an it-beats-me gesture.

"What's your business here today, Mr. Nardelli?" Malcolm asked.

"Business?"

"Yes, sir . . . business. Why are you in the city?"

"I'm a tile contractor, like it says on the card. My company's in Marietta, but we got customers all over. If you ever need some tile give me a call at that number on the bottom and I'll fix you up. That's my personal line."

Whatever else might be said of Frank he was clearly a great little capitalist. Unfortunately, it's not a good idea to try and bribe a policeman with witnesses present.

"Thank you, but I don't need any tile, sir," Malcolm answered. "Now I'll ask you again. Why are you here?"

"I got a right to be wherever the hell I want. He's the one you should be questioning. He threw me in a *fucking fountain* in case you haven't noticed."

Malcolm's brows came together in a scowl. A second later he took out his cuffs, grabbed Frank and spun him around, yanking both arms behind his back.

"You're arresting *me?*" Frank shouted. "I can't fuckin' believe this. He attacked me. Are you nuts?"

Malcolm replied, "Mr. Nardelli, you're under arrest for trespass, disturbing the peace, and using profane language in public. You have the right to remain silent, and I wish to hell you would. Mr. Delaney, you're free to go. Thank you."

Then turning back to Frank he continued. "Where was I? Oh, yeah, anything you say can be used against you in a court of law . . ."

We exchanged nods and I headed down the street toward the library. Sometimes I regret not being a detective anymore. It's a close-knit fraternity and the feeling of having someone watching your back makes it easier to sleep at night. Practicing law isn't quite the same. But you take what you can and pick your battles.

My assumption was that Maureen had put Frank up to following me because I was helping Ted with the divorce. Their conversation later would be interesting.

THIRTY-ONE

I<small>T</small> might have been petty, but I was feeling good after my encounter with Frank, so I decided to treat myself to a latte before the library. On the next street was a coffee bar called TJ's. A teenage girl behind the counter took my order and asked if I would prefer a "grande or a venti."

"No, just a medium cup will be fine."

"The venti is our large; the grande is our medium." She selected two cups off a stack to illustrate.

"Then I guess I'll take the grandee. Why don't you just call them small, medium, and large? It would be a lot easier."

"Because we don't have a small size."

"Really? What's that little one over there?"

"That's a 'tall.' What kind of milk do you prefer?"

"Uh, the normal stuff I suppose."

"We have one percent, two percent, skim, soy, and whole."

I took a deep breath. Life was a lot simpler when I was young. Back then all we had was the moo-cow stuff and no one complained. Now you needed a nutrition degree to place an order. I didn't want to think about where soy milk came from. The concept is revolting. I settled on whole milk, left a tip in the jar, and proceeded down the street.

In the lobby of Atlanta's Central Library I located a building directory that informed me the reference area was on the second floor. I took the stairs instead of the elevator. A woman in her early forties with her hair tucked into a bun watched me as I approached the desk.

I smiled. She didn't.

"Sir, you can't bring that in here," she said, pointing to the cup in my hand.

"Oh, sorry."

I looked around for a trash can and didn't see any.

"I'll take it for you. You can pick it up when you're through.

"Great. Thank you very much," I said, watching my grandee disappear over the top of the counter. "Where can I look up information about a person?"

"What sort of information? If you need a biography, they're located on the fourth floor."

"No, this is more along the line of newspaper articles."

"All our periodicals are stored on microfiche. If you go to that second desk over there and turn left you'll see a room directly in front of you. That's where the readers are."

"Readers?"

"Microfiche readers," she explained. "They let you look at what's on the fiche."

I read the name tag on her dress—Ms. Cheryl Detmer.

"If you're not too busy, I might need a little help getting started."

I received a thin-lipped smile in return. "Of course. Follow me."

A sign in front of the PERIODICAL ARCHIVE CENTER warned people against bringing food or drinks into the room. I eyed it without comment and followed Ms. Detmer inside.

"With this terminal you can do a keyword search for any relevant articles," she explained. "It's tied in to both the internet and the library's own database. Unless the name is very specific you should consider using Boolean connectors. They'll help a great deal."

I stared at her without comprehending.

"You really haven't done this very often have you?"

"I haven't done it at all."

Another tight-lipped smile. She'd probably heard the same thing several times a day. Ms. Detmer sat down at the console. "What name are we looking for?"

"Sanford Hamilton."

Her hands paused over the keyboard momentarily and she glanced up at me. It was obvious she had just made the connection, but she didn't inquire further. Our first effort brought up page after page of articles in which the names "Sanford" and "Hamilton" appeared together. Most of them were completely unrelated.

"Hmm," she said, frowning at the screen, "we'd better put the name in quotes and do a phrase search."

This time the list was pared down to thirty-eight hits. I was beginning to miss my latte. It was going to be a long morning.

Ms. Detmer explained, "In case you're interested, the word 'or' is one of the Boolean connectors I just mentioned. Use it when you want to expand your search."

"Isn't there a button I can press or something?"

She was polite enough not to laugh. "Not really. If you decide to do any other searches just type in 'Sanford or Sandy' Hamilton. That will bring up every instance where his name is mentioned in an article. If you need to be more specific use the word 'and.' For example, 'Sanford Hamilton and murder.'"

When I didn't respond she twisted around in her seat and looked up at me. "We've received a lot of requests for that name lately. I thought I recognized you when you came in. You're the lawyer from TV, aren't you?"

"Not intentionally. I was just in the wrong place at the wrong time."

"I'm usually good with faces."

"So I see. How can I view the actual article?"

"These numbers on the right signify where the fiche is located. If you fill out a green form at the help desk, the attendant will pull them out for you. Do you think you'll need assistance in working the reader?"

I gave her a weak smile. After five minutes of instruction I found myself staring at a photo of Sanford Hamilton's face. It was not the grotesque thing I had seen earlier, but a distinguished-looking healthy man in his mid sixties. Most of the articles were innocuous and there was little to be learned from them. They talked about Hamilton being a decorated war hero and his receiving an honor of some sort from the bar association. There was also an announcement regarding the birth of his granddaughter, and a variety of other things that did nothing to advance my understanding of the man.

The second fiche was more useful.

I found articles and photos of Hamilton, including one that mentioned he was a pallbearer at Charlotte Jordan's funeral. The article was nearly twenty years old and it stopped me cold. All the painful memories of her death came flooding back. Eventually, I moved on. For the next hour, I slowly made my way down the list of articles, skimming some and reading others in detail. As the process wore on I began to lose hope of finding anything useful . . . until I was nearly finished. The twenty-first article had appeared in the business section of the *Atlanta Journal* some fifteen years ago. It contained a reference to Hamilton filing a permit request on behalf of Tissinger Pharmaceuticals.

My curiosity peaked, I typed in "Sanford Hamilton *and* Tissinger." The hard drive whirred for a few seconds before five separate entries appeared on the screen. Apparently Hamilton had sued one of Tissinger's competitors for patent infringement. The second article quoted him as telling *The New England Journal of Medicine* that Torapam would change the way the medical community treated depression and panic attacks. The last articles were just clippings that listed Hamilton as a participant in a Pro-Am golf tournament Tissinger had sponsored. I moved on.

In his younger days Sandy Hamilton had been an active member on Atlanta's social scene. He and his wife attended various charity functions and fundraisers for the Republican Party, the Save the Children Federation, and the drive to redo the state capitol's gold dome. I learned that he became partially paralyzed in an automobile accident eight years earlier. Following this Hamilton appeared to have curtailed many of his charitable activities. From time to time I saw references to Charlie Evans and some of the law firm's other partners. None of them were particularly interesting and there were no red flags.

When I finally looked up from the screen I was surprised to see it was nearly dark outside. Two stories below, traffic inched its way up Peachtree Street. Six hours had passed since I sat down at the terminal and my back was stiff.

Practicing law and police work are similar in that you have to decide which facts are relevant to your case and which aren't. The best attorneys, like Katherine, do this without thinking. Training and experience help, of course, but I've found it comes down to instinct in the end. You see a piece of the puzzle here, a piece there, and a picture begins to form in your mind. Something had finally clicked in mine.

I felt anxious as I turned back to the computer screen. There are coincidences and there are coincidences. I typed in Ted Jordan's name, added Tissinger to the search, then hit the ENTER button. Three results appeared a moment later.

I jotted down the reference numbers and asked the librarian to pull the microfiche for me.

"We'll be closing in a half hour, sir," she said.

"Thanks."

I went back to the reader and sat down. By this time I was practically an expert in using the machine and I found the articles I was looking for quickly. Amazing the amount of information they can get onto those little plastic sheets. The first one was written less than a year ago.

French Pharmaceutical Giant Tissinger
to Build Plant in Woodstock

Attorney Theodore Jordan filed an application three days ago with the Woodstock Zoning Board on behalf of the Tissinger Corporation for a variance at the intersection of Stellmach Road and Hwy 5.

According to Mr. Jordan, the plant will bring nearly eight hundred jobs to the community and well over a million dollars in tax revenue.

Environmentalist and animal rights activist Anna Slatter-Jeffries promptly announced her opposition to the project.

Ms. Slatter-Jeffries said, "Until Tissinger renounces its policy of testing products on defenseless animals we will do everything in our power to keep them out of the State of Georgia."

Slater-Jeffries went on to say that she intends to organize rallies in the upcoming weeks and submit "thousands of petitions to the zoning board expressing our outrage over the application."

Speaking on behalf of his client, Mr. Jordan said he hoped any differences between the parties could be worked out.

With respect to the issue of animal testing, Mr. Jordan commented, "We work with animals because few congressmen and senators are willing to offer themselves up as test subjects.

"The important thing to keep in mind is whether the medications will benefit people."

Other clippings chronicled Ted's progress in the zoning hearing, where he was ultimately successful. Construction of the plant, despite Ms. Slater-Jeffries promise to "lay down in front of the bulldozers," was set to begin in early April of next year. The article also spoke of a second, larger facility in North Carolina, under construction at the time, which was to be associated with Duke University's Medical School.

THIRTY-TWO

AFTER the library, I tried Ted's home phone again. He still was out, so I left a message on his answering machine. The cell phone was in my hand when it rang.

"John Delaney?" asked an unfamiliar voice.

"Yes."

"This is Joe Edward Fanning. I'm returning your call. I understand we have a case together."

"Possibly. Ted Jordan asked me to see if I could help him and his wife work out their differences. I'm acquainted with both parties, Mr. Fanning, so I'm in an awkward position."

"Call me Joe Edward—everybody does. Do you have authority to speak on Ted's behalf?"

"I believe I do."

"Well, that's fine. I always say if you can settle a problem without going to court it's in everyone's best interests. You do much domestic work, John?"

"Not really."

Joe Edward chuckled. "That doesn't matter. I'll be happy to show you the ropes. What did you have in mind?"

I had a good idea around whose neck those ropes would go, but said, "I thought if you and I talked we might resolve some of the issues."

"That sounds reasonable. How about if we meet up at my office, say around one o'clock tomorrow. Would that suit you?"

"Suits me fine, Joe Edward. I'll see you then."

"All right, I'll pencil in the time. This might be short notice, but if your boy can get his hands on his tax returns and bank statements for the last five years it would be real helpful to me. I'd also like to see his credit card records and a profit and loss statement if he has one."

"I thought we were just going to talk."

Another chuckle. "We are. Unfortunately, I can't advise my client on how much alimony and child support to expect until I have some idea of his income. Tell you what, John, I'll have my secretary put together a few standard discovery requests. You can pick them up when you come in. Okay?"

"That'll be fine."

I was about to hang up when I remembered Katherine's advice about Ted paying Joe Edward's fee. According to her, his motivation to settle a case was directly related to how much money he would make.

"I probably don't need to mention this, but I advised Ted it's typical for a husband to pay for the wife's attorney fees, so he's prepared for that."

"John, I can see you're going to be a pleasure to work with. When you raise that subject it's like waving a red flag at a bull for a lot of husbands. I'll try to hold the expenses down as best I can."

He was still chuckling when I clicked off. I tried Katherine at her office again.

She said, "One o'clock works for me. I'll have to move some appointments around, but I can make it."

"Sorry, honey, I should have checked with you first."

"It's not a problem."

I glanced down at my phone and saw that a text message from Luther had just come in.

"Thanks. I'll be home late. Luther just sent a note asking me to meet him at the gym in an hour. I'd like to see what he came up with."

Doc's Gymnasium is located on Ponce de Leon Avenue in Virginia-Highlands. The Highlands is a trendy section of Atlanta that's been enjoying a resurgence in recent years. It was originally formed by a streetcar company, which began selling off pieces of land to the public in the late 1920s. A number of businesses have banners outside proudly announcing they are part of a "carbon neutral zone." There were no more plants or trees that I could see, and the street was still just as crowded with cars.

If there was anything trendy about Doc's I missed that as well. I spotted Luther doing pull-ups on a wide curved bar. The knots of muscles in his back were obvious even from the doorway. Nikko was seated on a couch so old and faded its color was nearly back in style. His eyes were closed and he was listening to music.

I went into the locker room and changed to my workout clothes. Luther was still doing pull-ups when I came out. He made them look effortless, as he did most things. The only sign he was working was a sheen of sweat on his face and shoulders.

He saw me and moved aside. I managed three sets without embarrassing myself. Not bad for a fifty-year-old.

"We gonna make a man of you yet," he said, flashing me a smile.

"What have you got?" I asked.

"What makes you think I got anything? My call could have been a clever ploy to get your sorry white ass back in the gym."

"Or into a carbon-free environment."

"Carbon-neutral," Luther said.

"What the difference?"

Luther pondered that for a moment, then yelled across the room to a man seated at the welcome desk. "Doc, what's the difference between carbon free and carbon neutral?"

"How the fuck do I know?" Doc yelled back. "I think we use eco-friendly chemicals to clean the machines and recycled toilet paper or some shit like that."

"There's such a thing as too much information," I pointed out. "Is Doc in a bad mood?"

"Doc always in a bad mood. Been that way since I was with the Jets."

I nodded and waved at Doc, who shook his head and went back to reading his newspaper. We moved over to the leg-press machine. It's not one of my favorites, but I completed two sets with four plates on each side. When I was through Luther added four more forty-five-pound plates to the rack, bringing the total up to twelve, and began pushing out reps. It was annoying not to see him gasping for air. In all likelihood he could have asked Nikko to sit on top of the rack and it would have made no difference.

"Met with that Martine Tikumi, like you asked," he said.

"Wife?"

"Daughter. She and her brother here in town to wrap up the father's estate. They sellin' the house in Brookhaven. She's maybe twenty years old. She and Nikko got along real good."

"He likes them young," I commented. "Why are they selling?"

"Daddy's dead; she lives in San Francisco. Brother lives in Ohio. Guess they thought it was time. There were moving boxes in the foyer and in the living room. Same with the rest of the house."

"I see."

"We explained we was helping you do some investigating on your man's case so she invited us in. Nikko even apologized for interrupting her."

"He's a charmer."

Luther chuckled.

"We asked if she could tell us about how her daddy died."

Luther pulled a piece of paper from his pocket and unfolded it.

My father died of anaphylactic shock after being stung by a bee. He was extremely allergic to them. There was nothing the paramedics could do by the time they reached him.

"We already knew that, so I asked her if an autopsy was done," Nikko said, from behind me.

I hadn't heard him approach.

"She told us the county did one and that everyone at the company was real upset by what happened. She said Tissinger paid for the entire funeral and flew the whole family out for it."

"Generous," I said.

"The girl's daddy was a biochemist at the research plant in North Atlanta," Luther added. "Then Nikko here sweet-talked her into giving us a copy of the autopsy."

I looked at Nikko.

"I have my moments," he said, handing me an envelope.

I opened it and removed a three-page report prepared by the Fulton County Medical Examiner. Both of them waited as I began to read.

According to the narrative, Isao Tikumi, a white male, sixty-three years of age, was found at the side of a jogging path in Piedmont Park just after 10:00 P.M. by a couple walking their dog. They immediately called the police, who dispatched an ambulance. Tikumi was dressed in a warm-up suit and was wearing running shoes.

Paramedics arrived on scene within fifteen minutes and attempted to resuscitate him, but without success. The victim was then transported to Grady Hospital's emergency room where doctors worked on him with the same result. According to the EMT's report, Tikumi was initially thought to have suffered a heart attack, because he was blue around the lips, ears, and fingers. Eventually, a second doctor noticed his airway passage was swollen and immediately called for a breathing tube to get some oxygen his lungs. Tikumi's blood pressure continued to drop and he was pronounced dead twenty minutes after his arrival.

In accordance with state law, the county medical examiner was called in. The ME confirmed the emergency room doctor's findings and ordered that a toxicology report be done after noting what appeared to be three bee stings at the back of the victim's neck. A blood test showed the presence of insect antibodies.

The following morning, Harry Eberhart, a detective assigned to the case, located a self-injecting syringe of epinephrine a short distance from where Tikumi had been found. As a result, it was concluded the cause of death was a probable-anaphylactic reaction due to bee stings. It was thought the victim either dropped his medication and was unable to recover it in the dark or lost consciousness while attempting to administer himself an injection. And so on.

In short, there was nothing to indicate Tikumi's death was anything other than an unfortunate accident—until my eye trailed down to the section listed as "Supplemental."

The deceased's personal effects, consisting of his clothing—a pair of runner's shorts, one T-shirt, a pair of socks, one pair of athletic shoes, and a man's Timex watch—were signed for and returned to Michael Tikumi, the deceased's son. A copy of a receipt for the same is attached hereto as exhibit "A."

Nikko noticed what I was reading and explained. "Luther asked her if her father wore one of those medical alert bracelets about his condition. She said he did and that her mother was always fussing at him to make sure he had it on him. Then she got a funny look on her face."

"In what way?" I asked.

"Her voice trailed off and she looked around the room with a puzzled expression, then says it was funny she hadn't come across it yet."

THIRTY-THREE

KATHERINE was in the family room doing stretching exercises on her ballet bar when I got home. I stood in the doorway watching.

"Anything new?" she asked.

"Luther and Nikko did a good job. They interviewed the daughter of one of the research team members. He died from bee stings. Turns out he wasn't wearing his alert bracelet at the time of the accident and it wasn't at his home. The cops didn't find one at the scene either."

"That's odd," Katherine said. She bent from the waist, touching her nose to her knee.

"Yes, it is, particularly since his daughter says he always wore it."

"Odder still. So what's next?"

"I'll meet with Ted early tomorrow morning, then with you and Fanning. I want to get more details on that husband and wife who died in an auto accident. They were also part of Tissinger's bioresearch team."

"You're staying with the case, then?"

"Until there's a reason not to," I said.

Katherine nodded and draped a towel around her shoulders. She came over to kiss me. "Have you eaten?" she asked.

"I grabbed a burger on the way home."

"John, you should really eat more salads. They're better for you."

"I'll try."

"Promise?"

"Promise."

She reached up and brushed a lock of hair off my forehead. "I want you to live a long time. I have some edamame, if you'd like a snack."

"Eda-what?"

"Edamame. They're really healthy," Katherine said, pointing to a bowl of odd-looking green beans on the coffee table.

"It'll feel like a long time if I have to eat that."

Katherine made a face and pushed me away. "What would you like to drink?"

"A scotch and soda would be nice. Use The Macallan. It's healthier than the Balvenie."

This time I got an arched eyebrow and decided to change the subject. "How was your day?"

"Busy. I received a call from Eleanor McMichael, with the Daughters of the South. They want to know if I'd be interested in running for state senate."

"Wow. That's wonderful, K.J. You'd make a great senator."

"Earlier in the week Miranda Kaufman from B'nai Torah called and asked me the same question."

"What do B'Nai Torah and the Daughters of the South have in common?"

"Excellent taste in women. How do you feel about it?"

I thought I had just answered that question, but with women you can't be certain. They always want to know what you're feeling. At the moment I was feeling like I wanted my drink, which Katherine was still holding.

"Honey," I said, "I don't want to share you with the world, but if it's something that would make you happy, I'm behind it. As long as you don't have to compromise your integrity with scumballs."

Katherine finally released the scotch. She had forgotten the soda. I didn't care. I finished it in one gulp and we adjourned to the living room. The drink warmed as it went down. Outside the wind had begun blowing again. The rain was back, too, moving through the trees and splattering large drops against the glass. We sat on the couch and were joined by Peeka, who wedged in between us and put his head on Katherine's lap. She reached down and scratched him behind the ears. After a few seconds his eyes closed and he began purring loudly. Even though we'd seen him do this a hundred times before, we looked at each other and smiled.

The room was dark, illuminated only by the embers from a dying fire. This was where I wanted to be.

"I met a friend of yours today," Katherine said.

"Who was that?"

"Stan."

"Who?"

"Stan Coleman. He came by with a friend for some legal advice. His brother-in-law is going though a bad divorce."

I felt an icy tug in the middle of my stomach and sat up straighter. Peeka opened one eye and looked at me for a moment. There being no cat treat forthcoming and nothing of any real interest he closed it again.

"Is something wrong?" Katherine asked.

"Yes."

"What?"

"Describe Stan's friend for me."

"Well, he was tall, blond, and well-dressed . . . an attractive man. I think his name was Brad something. He smiled a lot but didn't say much during the interview."

"No."

"What's the matter?"

"His last name is Britton. He and Coleman were the ones I met at Charlie Evans's office. Britton is with the NSA and Coleman is Tissinger's head of security."

Katherine was silent for a while. "I see." She paused again, longer this time. "Why did they make up a story?"

"Intimidation."

"They want to intimidate me?"

"Me. Did they make a return appointment?" I asked.

"No. Stan said he hoped that wouldn't be necessary. He wanted to see how the situation would develop. I feel like a fool, now," Katherine said.

"Don't."

"Well, I do. Obviously, they wanted you to know they were there."

I nodded slowly. "Would it cause you a problem if I have Luther hang around for a while?"

"No, I like Luther. But I really don't think it's necessary."

"I do. Humor me. I have that trip to Miami and it would make me feel better."

"All right," Katherine said. "When are you leaving?"

"Phil Thurman called earlier and let me know the autopsy has been set up. He sends his regards, by the way."

"Thank you. Why are these men trying to intimidate you? Won't some other lawyer take the case if you quit?"

It was a great question and one to which I didn't have an answer.

THIRTY-FOUR

LUTHER showed up at our house at six-thirty in the morning. Nikko was with him. The previous evening we spoke on the phone and I told them about Katherine's meeting.

"Feds be flexing their muscles," Luther said.

"Yes," I said.

Nikko nodded his agreement.

"Maybe they not tryin' to run you off so much as slow you down," Luther said. "You stay here to protect Katherine, you won't be doin' your work for Jordan."

"I thought of that. I just don't know why yet."

"But you're not gonna let it go, right?" Nikko said.

"Delaney don't let nothing go," Luther said.

"Why not?" Nikko said.

"How long you know the man?" Luther asked him.

"Long time," Nikko said with a shrug.

"It's just the way some people be."

"Maybe we should get him into counseling. I know a guy."

"Maybe we can discuss someone else," I said. "K.J. will be down in a minute. I want you both to stay close to her . . . within the bounds of discretion."

Luther smiled broadly. "We nothin' if not discreet."

"I really do know a guy," Nikko said, as he walked out the door. He went to the passenger side of Luther's Mercedes and got in. Luther joined him.

Katherine came into the kitchen, looking splendid in a tailored blue suit. She had added one of those Miriam Haskell pins she loves so much. After a good-bye kiss, she filled a traveling mug with coffee and headed for the garage. Her last words to me were not to worry. They didn't help.

For the next hour I occupied myself with computer research on Tissinger. They were tied into everything from the World Health Organization to colleges and universities around the globe. Newspapers seemed to announce a new drug testing program, internship, or research grant the company was sponsoring every other week. According to a *Time* article, they were constructing new laboratories in at least fifteen different countries. Reports in medical journals called their new depression medication "a breakthrough."

The doorbell interrupted me.

Ted looked a bit more like his old self. The deer-in-the-headlights expression was gone and he seemed more confident. He was carrying a bag of bagels and two cups of coffee. He took a seat at our patio table while I found some plates.

I inquired, "How are you doing?"

"Better. You want plain cream cheese or vegetable? I bought both."

"Plain."

"I got us some coffee, too," he said, holding up the two cardboard cups. "They only had the medium size."

"Those are grandees."

Ted frowned at the cups. "Yeah?"

"Katherine and I are meeting Joe Fanning at one o'clock to discuss your case. I assume you're okay with her being there."

"Sure."

"Let's talk about the Tissinger Corporation," I said.

"What do you want to know?"

"What was Sanford Hamilton's involvement with them?"

Ted shrugged. "A number of people in our firm have worked on their file . . . me, Sandy, Charlie Evans, Jack Tatum, Elaine Verdugo to name a few."

"What about Bill Doster?"

Ted's brows came together and he thought for a second. "Bill? No, I don't think so. He generally stays in commercial real estate."

"Any idea what he was looking for in your office the other day?"

"I imagine it was the Torapam data. They don't want news of the cover-up getting out."

"The agents I spoke with said Gabriele has had a personal vendetta against the company ever since they let her father go."

"They're full of crap. Her father was the one who blew the whistle on the project."

I informed him, "Maybe I don't need to spell this out, but I'll do it anyway. Your conspiracy idea is intriguing and it may work. I've already made some progress on it. But right now most of what we have is conjecture. If we don't show the jury something tangible there's no point risking it. The second they think we're trying to put something over on them, they'll shut down."

Ted pondered this for a moment, then asked, "Want to take a ride? There's something I'd like to show you."

THIRTY-FIVE

OFFICIALLY, Lake Sidney Lanier is not a lake at all. It's a sprawling reservoir northwest of Atlanta with over six hundred miles of shoreline. A little over fifty years ago the Army Corps of Engineers completed the last pour of concrete on Buford Dam and closed its massive control gates. Within minutes torrents of water from the Chattahoochee and Chestatee Rivers began flooding the valley basin. As the water level rose it engulfed homes, neighborhoods, farms, banks, streets, roads, and whatever else had not been removed from the valley. A colleague in the geoscience department at our school once showed me a number of sonar images he had taken of the lake's floor. The only word I could come up with at the time was *surreal*. The street signs and buildings still lay sleeping beneath a thousand feet of water.

Ted pulled off the main road and parked his car in front of a metal barricade. A sign informed visitors this was as far as they could go. Beyond the barricade was a single one-lane road that disappeared around a corner. It reemerged again and continued across the top of the dam. A security gate consisting of a single long metal tube with a counter weight on one end, like you see at border crossings in Europe, extended across the entrance blocking public access. A padlock attached to a steel stanchion secured the gate.

Ted shut the car's engine and got out.

He began, "Approximately thirteen months ago, a lady named Savine Boudreau left a Christmas party hosted by Tissinger at their plant. You can just see the building on the opposite side of the lake. It's that two-story cream-colored one next to the cell phone tower."

I followed where Ted was pointing and nodded for him to continue.

"The most recent tests on Torapam II had just been completed, so there was double reason to celebrate because the results were positive and they were ahead of schedule. Everyone was happy. Savine and her husband owned a home in Lawrenceville in a little development called Rolling Hills. It's about fifteen miles south of here. According to witnesses, they stayed about an hour before leaving. At least ten people acknowledged seeing them take a few drinks, but no one thought either was drunk or incapable of driving.

"At some point, maybe a thirty minutes later, Savine and her husband, Charles, found themselves on the road we were just on. It was dark, visibility was poor, and it was raining. The rain was mixed with sleet. For the first time anyone in the Army Corp of Engineers could remember, the gate was unlocked and it was up. The Corp maintains the dam, by the way.

"The next morning a detective assigned to the accident scoured the area with four officers for the missing padlock and couldn't find it. They concluded kids or vandals must have taken it."

I made a mental note to get the accident report. "Go on," I told him.

"For whatever reason, Savine's husband left the main road and turned onto this service road. He lost control of his vehicle about a quarter mile from here. The car made it halfway down the dam before it exploded. The medical examiner said Savine had approximately fifteen percent alcohol content in her blood and Charles would have qualified point twenty-three percent."

I arched one eyebrow.

Ted continued, "Exactly. It's contrary to what all the witnesses stated."

"How long did this lady and her husband work for Tissinger?"

"Eighteen years. They were part of the original research team as well as the Torapam II project. They also signed a letter of protest when Gabriele's father was canned."

I folded my arms across my chest and stared across the lake at Tissinger's building, then glanced up at the sun, noting its position in the sky. It was still early in the morning and the sun was low on the horizon, northeast of where we were standing.

"You said the Boudreaus lived south of here?"

"Right."

I glanced south toward Lawrenceville, then back at the Tissinger building, trying to reconstruct their route in my mind. The bridge that crossed Lake Lanier was about eight miles north of us, which meant Savine and her husband had been driving *away* from their home. They were also going to the opposite side of the lake. Drunk or not, that made no sense.

ON the way to my meeting with Joe Edward Fanning, I placed a call to Maury Katz. He agreed to cut the red tape and fax the accident report on the Boudreaus to me in the morning. I also told him what Luther and Nikko had learned from Tikumi's daughter and about the feds trying to lean on me through Katherine.

"We should get together when you're back in town," he said. "I'm becoming intrigued by this."

"Has anyone ever told you you have a flair for understatement?"

"Actually, several people."

"Who said I was going out of town?"

"My colleagues in the law enforcement community and I are very close. You should call Phil Thurman and tell him what you've found."

"Have you worked out who'll get credit for the collar yet?"

"Assuming there is one. Right now all we have are possibilities," Maury informed me.

"It's more than Ted Jordan had a few days ago."

"True. By the way, there's nice restaurant in Miami Beach you should try when you're down there. The deli melts in your mouth. The name is Mo's."

"You sure about that?"

"Am I Jewish?"

"You are."

"Jews know good deli. It's genetic."

I smiled. "I'll remember that."

"And if you're not terribly busy, you might even bring back a half-dozen potato knishes," Maury said. "Mo freezes them and they're to die for."

I took a breath. "How many does Thurman want?"

"Six."

THIRTY-SIX

I ARRIVED at Joe Fanning's building ten minutes early and went to a little café at the far side of the lobby to wait for Katherine. Someone had left a newspaper on one of the tables. The front-page headline was about Iraq again. Apparently, their latest government had approved another constitution for the people. Of course, the terrorists, or insurgents as the press had taken to calling them, were vowing to continue their holy war and kill any official who voted for it. I concluded the concept of democracy was still escaping them and flipped the page. Attributing a political agenda, as our media often does to people who murder women and children, raises them to a level of legitimacy they don't deserve. Our preoccupation with political correctness plays directly into their bloodstained hands. If ever a newspaper comes out and calls them a bunch of murdering bastards, sign me up for a subscription.

On page three, I glanced at a side story and came to an abrupt halt. The headline read:

Jordan Attorney Suspended From Teaching Post
Emory Asks Delaney to Step Aside

I had to read it again. The reporter was a fellow named Guy Sellers. I remembered him from Thornton Schiff's press conference as the one asking all the prearranged questions. I pulled out my cell phone and called Ben Chambers.

"I didn't say that," Ben announced, before I had a chance to speak.

"Then where the hell did he get it, Ben?"

"I don't know. The school's president and our attorney have both fired off letters to the *Fulton Report* this morning. I also called Sellers and spoke with him directly. All he would say was, his information came from a confidential source. If you read the article, near the bottom it states, 'officially, Emory lists Professor Delaney as having taken a leave of absence to devote his time to Theodore Jordan's defense.' That's exactly what I told him. I don't know who else he might have spoken to, but we've demanded a retraction."

"Which will appear on page fifty-three a week from now."

"Probably. I'm sorry, John. You don't deserve this."

"Great, I'll sleep much better tonight knowing that."

"The *Fulton Report* isn't exactly the pinnacle of journalism," he said.

"Wonderful."

"John, I *am* sorry,"

I asked, "What do you know about the reporter?"

"A typical brown-noser. He's been Thornton Schiff's point man for years. It's a safe bet that's where his marching orders came from. We'll do our best to clarify the situation. You have my word on it. If there's anything I can do personally—"

"Sure. I'll be in touch."

I was so angry when we hung up I crumpled the newspaper into a ball and threw it at a trash can. It bounced off the rim and fell to the floor. A female hand reached down and picked it up.

Katherine said, "You white guys can't play basketball at all. I'm so sorry, John."

She was holding another newspaper under her arm. Everyone was sorry that afternoon. I took a deep breath to calm myself and stood up.

"This story only goes out to the legal community," she informed me, dropping her paper in the trash.

"There's a relief. Now, just my colleagues will know I've been fired."

"You weren't fired. You took a leave of absence. Everyone knows the paper is a fish wrapper," she insisted. "If people read the article, they can clearly see the headline's misleading . . ."

Katherine's voice trailed off and she gave me a weak smile. "Do you want me to find Sellers and kick him in the balls?"

I laughed in spite of myself. "It's okay. I'll figure something out.

Let's go see what Joe Edward has to say. Where are Luther and Nikko?"

"They're waiting in the parking garage. Luther thought I'd be okay with you for a while. We're all becoming very close."

"Wonderful."

Turns out, the first thing Joe Edward did was offer his condolences about losing my job. It was going to be one of those days. I thanked him for his concern and didn't bother to explain.

Katherine was not of the same mind. "John didn't lose his job. He took a leave of absence—a *voluntary* leave of absence. The paper got their facts wrong, as usual. We're thinking about filing suit."

"Is that so? Well that's good to hear. Ol'John seems like a decent sort. It'd be a shame to see him come up short because of this case. That aside, it raises my next question—what the heck are you doing here, Katherine?"

"John's asked me to assist him."

Joe Edward's eyes narrowed and he looked from her to me, then shrugged. "I guess that's fine. Everyone's entitled to the counsel of their choice. Why don't we go into my office and talk in private? I don't know if you're aware of it, but Kathy here is one tough lady. We've had some real Donnybrooks in the past."

I mentally winced at his use of "Kathy" because I knew Katherine hates the name.

Joe Edward ploughed on without waiting for a reply. "Oh, these are for you," he said, handing me a half-inch-thick sheaf of papers. "They're the discovery forms we talked about. Have your boy fill them out when he gets a chance. It's all pretty boilerplate."

"And these are for you," Katherine said, handing him an equally thick set of papers.

"What's this?"

She replied, "*Our* standard discovery forms."

Joe Edward hefted them in his hand a few times. "Looks like y'all are girding for battle. If I have to go through these it'll impact my fee."

Katherine commented on the subject, "I doubt it, Joe. Actually, your office generated them. I simply asked my secretary to copy the requests you sent us in the Franklin case, then we changed the name."

Joe Edward started to say something, but apparently thought better of it. Instead, he motioned us toward two chairs in front of his desk. I did my best to keep a straight face.

He said, "All right, let's get down to brass tacks. From what I can see Ted Jordan's in some deep trouble right now. My client recognizes this and understands his future may be uncertain. Given the circumstances we feel, and I'd hope y'all would agree, that temporary custody of the children should go to his wife. She'd also like to stay in the marital residence while the details are being sorted out. That way it will be less disruptive for the children. I understand the third boy is off at college, but the two younger ones still live at home."

I replied, "Use of the house is fine. I've already discussed that with my client and he's agreeable provided custody is joint."

Joe Edward replied, "Maureen's pretty upset at the moment, but I'll raise the subject with her. And by the way, it didn't help you throwing her friend in the Central City Fountain the other day."

Katherine's mouth opened slightly and she turned to me. "You threw someone in a fountain?"

"He started it," I mumbled, not meeting her eyes.

She blinked and turned back to Joe Edward. "John has a unique style of negotiating. After you talk with Maureen, get back with us and let us know what she says. I assume there's no question about Ted's qualifications as a father. He coaches the boys' little league teams, goes to PTA meetings, Boy Scout meetings, and church on Sundays. Once his legal problems are behind him he intends to continue those activities. The parties may wind up living in separate homes, but they'll still be a family. All Ted wants is to be part of his sons' lives."

Joe Edward thought about this for a few seconds. "That's not unreasonable. Let me make a few notes." He paused to scratch something down on his pad. "Now what about some support for these children?"

"Support isn't a problem," I said. "Ted has retained the services of Atlanta Federated Bank to act as trustee. We've already provided them copies of his financial records. Whatever the court's guidelines say he has to pay, he will. I've brought copies of his W-2 forms and his tax returns for the last five years, as you requested."

"That sounds fine. Do you happen to know how much he makes off the top of your head?"

I told him.

Joe Edward took a calculator from the corner of his desk and did some quick math. When he was finished, he turned the display around so we could see it. It was in accordance with established parameters and I nodded my agreement.

He said, "Great. Now what about—"

"College?" I asked.

"Right."

"My client is also willing to set up a fund for his sons' education, which the bank will also administer."

Joe Edward asked me, "Would you mind telling me why we need a bank? It's normal for the custodial parent to control the children's investments."

I informed him, "Mr. Jordan feels more comfortable with a professional institution watching his sons' money. If Maureen doesn't agree to joint custody it's a deal breaker."

The pleasant smile on Joe Edward's face faded and then reappeared. "Let me tell you a little bit about me. I'm the type of lawyer who would rather settle a case than fight. In fact, I consider it a personal failure if all parties don't walk away from the table happy. However, we won't be pushed into any hasty decisions. I've said I'll talk with my client, and I will."

"That's fine," I replied.

Joe Edward continued, "All right, it looks like we're making progress here. Now there's the little matter of my fee. I suppose we should get that out of the way now, particularly since y'all are paying for it.

"Your client's abrupt departure from the family residence, along with his legal difficulties obviously took Ms. Jordan by surprise. She's devastated, as you can probably imagine. What are you willing to do?"

"Mr. Jordan will deliver a check for $7,500 to you tomorrow morning. That should be more than enough to draft an agreement and take your lady to court for a final decree."

Joe Edward seemed to find that amusing. "Well now, that's a reasonable start and I appreciate your client's flexibility. A lot of husbands dig their heels in on this point. But Kathy here'll tell you it won't make much of a dent. I was thinking of something more along the lines of $25,000.

"The fact is Maureen needs to conserve her money. She's planning to expand her business. The poor woman has to now, as a matter of survival. Once we get things hammered out regarding alimony and dividing his retirement and profit-sharing plans we can fuss about the rest. Do you think you can sell him on that sum?"

My wife informed him, "My name's Katherine, and there won't be any alimony."

"I suppose this is what we have the courts for," Joe Edward said. "How about if I set up a temporary hearing on the alimony issue and we let the chips fall where they may? In the meantime, I'll have my girl make a draft of what we've agreed to. Does that suit you?"

"Not really," I said.

Joe Edward gave me a sour look and turned to Katherine. "Maybe you should take a moment and educate your associate here on what a Fulton County domestic relations judge is likely to do. This case is assigned to Cynthia Roberts and she ain't gonna cut this woman loose without support."

"John doesn't need educating and Maureen's not getting alimony," Katherine said. "As I recall, Judge Roberts has a low tolerance for adultery."

Before Joe Edward could respond, Katherine took out the package of photos and slid them across the desk. Earlier, we removed the two showing Maureen coming out of the bank in Decatur.

Whatever else you might say about Joe Edward Fanning, you'd have to admire his flexibility. He must have been a great poker player because his face showed no reaction at all. After examining them he handed them back.

He asked, "Is that supposed to be Maureen Jordan? You can't hardly make out her face."

Katherine remarked, "I don't think a jury will have any problem with that. The faces seem clear enough to me . . . hers, and her friend's. The man's name is Frank Nardelli, in case you didn't know. According to our investigator he and Maureen have been dating off and on since high school. That's why there won't be any alimony."

Joe Edward was silent for several seconds as he considered how to respond. "I'll discuss this with my client and get back to you."

THIRTY-SEVEN

Y OU *threw Nardelli in a fountain!*" Katherine exclaimed when we got to the elevators. "And don't tell me he started it. What in the world happened?"

"I was just coming from a meeting with Maury Katz and Rena Bailey at Hamilton's home. When I left, I noticed he was following me. I mean I didn't know it was Nardelli; I just knew I was being followed."

"So you threw him in a fountain?"

"Of course not. He came at me around a corner. I just reacted."

"You're a lawyer," she said, keeping her voice down. "He could file a complaint against you."

"That's possible."

"Oh my God. What happened after you threw him in? Did you have a fight?"

"Uh . . . no, a cop came over and arrested him for trespass."

Katherine's mouth opened slightly.

"I swear to God," I said, holding up my right hand.

I got the feeling she was having difficulty keeping a straight face. She finally shook her head and slipped an arm through mine. When the elevator arrived we got on and rode to the lobby.

As the doors opened, I inquired, "Would you like to take Luther and Nikko to lunch?"

"Of course. I go nowhere without my bodyguards."

We called them. They declined. Luther informed me he had already eaten a yoghurt and fruit salad; Nikko was just finishing a meatball sub. I told them to meet us at Katherine's office in two hours.

"How much time do we have before your plane?" Katherine asked.

"A little more than four hours."

"Are you taking Mr. Jag to the airport?"

"No, I'll use MARTA."

"There's no need," Katherine said. "I'll drop you off. We have some time to kill. Would you like to take a walk?"

"Sure. But don't you need to get back to work?"

"The office will survive. How about the botanical gardens? They're not far," she said. "We could cut through the Prado."

"Fine."

"How long will you be in Miami?"

"Not more than two days."

"Umm."

"Is something wrong?" I asked.

"John, do you think you're really looking at this case objectively? I know Ted is your friend, but I'm concerned . . . so is Luther."

"What about Nikko?"

Katherine shook her head. "I don't think Nikko is concerned with anything. This isn't funny."

"No it isn't. A man's life is at stake."

"The bee stings and a forgotten medical bracelet don't add up to a conspiracy. Neither does the accident at Lake Lanier. They're interesting, but explainable."

"Which is why I'm going to Miami," I said.

"And if you don't find anything there?"

"I may have to rethink my defense strategy. I'm not blind to how far-fetched the conspiracy theory is. I just owe Ted my best shot."

"Charlie Evans called me last night. He's worried about you, too," Katherine said.

"Charlie's a good man. I'll phone him before I leave. Right now I'm just chasing down leads. That's the way these things work. I don't expect to find a smoking gun. You build a case one layer at a time."

We turned right on 18th Street and began walking through the Prado, a winding old neighborhood with stately homes. I usually get lost each time I enter it. Katherine, however, seemed to know where she was going.

"Do you see that house on the right?" she asked.

I followed the direction she was pointing and said, "Sure."

"Alley's friend, Sherri Davis, lives there now. After she graduated

Emory, she went to work for the IRS in their legal department. Did you know they went to middle school together? I can't believe how quickly the children have grown up."

"Alley has a friend named Cherry?"

"Sherri. Her name is Sherri, with an 'S'."

"Right. Got it."

The entrance to the botanical gardens was just in front of us. I paid for our tickets and we went in. I don't know why I wasn't surprised to see Stan Coleman sitting in the café. His legs were crossed and he was sipping from a tiny espresso cup. He waved. There was no sign of his partner, but I was sure he wasn't far.

I started walking toward him, but Katherine tightened her grip on my arm and tugged me in the opposite direction. I let myself be led.

"There's the reason I haven't pled Ted out yet," I said. "The amount of energy Britton and Coleman are spending to intimidate must be huge."

"You think they have something to hide?"

"I do."

Katherine nodded slowly. "It's possible. It's also possible they told you the truth when you first met."

By unspoken agreement, we decided to change the subject and enjoy the grounds. After an hour we headed back toward Katherine's car. I phoned Luther to let him know Katherine was driving me to the airport. He said he would meet us there.

Coleman was gone by the time we left the garden, which was just as well.

THIRTY-EIGHT

THE humidity hit me as soon as I stepped off the plane. You could cut it with a knife. Miami is not one of my favorite places nor is its sibling, Miami Beach. I'm not sure what the difference between the two is. Food, clothing, and home prices are ridiculously high and people don't say "good morning" when you pass them on the street. New Yorkers don't do that either, but no one expects them to.

Several years earlier a rash of killings along I-95 had put a damper on the tourist business and Miami's economy had taken a hit. The last time I visited was the day I left for my cruise on the *Majestic*.

As I got in the cab I saw two advertisements on the back of the driver's seat. Apparently, the powers that be were intent on getting back those tourist dollars. One showed Miami's skyline at night and referred to it as the "New Riviera." The other announced the Hard Rock Casino was now offering blackjack.

Come back to Miami . . . we weren't shooting at you, seemed more to the point.

On the way to my hotel I called Luther. He assured me that all was quiet. He was sitting at a bar in a restaurant watching Katherine have dinner with three other women.

"What could be more fun than that?" I asked.

"Not much," he said. "Some good-looking ladies here tonight."

"How's Katherine look?"

"Better than you."

"Any sign of our friends?" I asked.

"Maybe. There are three in the corner that fit the description you gave me." Nikko's outside checkin' license plates. Won't do much good though. The feds ain't dumb."

"You need additional help?"

There was a pause. I could almost see the amusement on Luther's face.

"I don't think so," he said.

"You get the message about where I'm staying?"

"Got it. You really goin' to a cemetery to dig a man up?"

"That's where they keep the bodies," I said.

"Then I'm glad I'm here watchin Katherine's and not the one you be seein' tomorrow."

THE sky was dark when I awoke at 6:30 A.M. That's another thing about Miami. I always seem to get less sleep when I'm there. The "Garden of the Palms Cemetery" is located in Coral Gables, an inner city suburb. I looked around for the palm trees and spotted one near the back fence.

A lieutenant from CID got out of an unmarked cruiser as my cab pulled up to the entrance.

"Delaney?"

"In the flesh."

"I'm Dan Dougherty with the Coral Springs Sheriff's office."

"Great alliteration."

"Excuse me?"

"Nothing. It looks like it's going to rain," I said. Sometimes my humor falls on deaf ears.

"It looks like that every day," Dougherty said, glancing up at the sky. "You must have friends in high places. The U.S. Attorney called my captain at home. What's this all about?"

"Maybe something . . . maybe nothing. It's too soon to tell yet," I said.

"Former cop?" he asked.

"Fourteen years . . . eight in homicide."

Dougherty nodded. "I've got a backhoe and two men waiting, as requested. A tech from the county ME's office is also standing by."

"Sounds good."

"You might want to take your jacket off and leave it on the backseat. It's going to be hot as hell in a little while. The grave is just a short walk."

To the east, through a break in the trees, I could just see a tiny strip of blue that was the Atlantic Ocean. The backhoe bit into the earth and removed a chunk of black soil mixed with sand. After about four feet, two men took over. I watched their shovels slide into the earth. As the sun rose higher, sweat began to flow freely down my arms and back. I followed Dougherty's example, opened my shirt collar and rolled up my sleeves. To the south was Miami's skyline. The progress was slow and taking longer than I thought. All the while, the sky continued to darken as clouds rolled in from the sea. Within an hour there was a noticeable drop in the temperature.

A single raindrop splattered on my shirt sleeve. Dougherty and the ME both looked up at the darkening clouds, as did the men with the shovels. They paused momentarily in their task, exchanged glances, and continued digging. The breeze continued to freshen. A storm was approaching.

Thirty minutes passed and then an hour. Dougherty left the grave site, went to his car and returned with a lantern and an umbrella. Though it was still light out, he held the lantern over the workers. Another hour dragged by before one of them struck something solid. The sound immediately drew everyone's attention. The man from the ME's office stepped forward and looked into the grave, then took out a small digital camera and snapped a photo. He made eye contact with me and motioned for the workers to continue.

Using ropes, it took all of us to lift the coffin out of the ground and onto a gurney. The rain had begun falling steadily by then. We were covered in mud and sweating profusely. Dougherty held his umbrella over the ME, who carefully brushed some dirt off the top of the coffin. We read the name engraved on a small plaque. Another photo was taken before the workers wheeled the coffin to a waiting hearse parked a short distance away. As if by agreement, no one spoke during this time.

I watched the scene with a mixture of emotions. The smell of freshly dug earth filled my nostrils. It occurred to me few residents of that place ever got to ride a hearse *away* from the cemetery.

Dougherty and I walked back to his car. The rain was coming down harder now, angled by the wind. Headstones and monuments became silhouettes against the fading light. Water ran along gravel paths to form large pools on the main road. The angels and cherubim perched atop stone mausoleums took a foreboding aspect rather than anything comforting.

The living had no business in a cemetery.

Dougherty and the ME were waiting.

THIRTY-NINE

THE laboratory had an antiseptic odor that reminded me of visits to the doctor when I was young. Including myself there were eight people in the room. Two uniform officers and the assistant DA had joined us, along with a man who was operating a video camera. The ME had changed into surgeon's scrubs. He was joined by a forensic toxicologist from the University of Miami's medical school. We were all issued green face masks and rubber gloves. Five minutes earlier the ME passed out dabs of ointment and instructed everyone to place it directly under their nostrils. He warned us the smell of death could be overpowering. The videographer looked pale. It was cold and I was still damp from the rain.

At the end of the room were two machines on a metal table, a gas chromatograph and a something called a spectrometer. I'd attended autopsies before and had a reasonable idea how they work. The doctor's explanation helped, though it was more for the camera than anyone present. The coffin was still sitting on the gurney. Alongside it was a metal examining table.

Both doctors spent a great deal of time brushing and vacuuming as much dirt off the coffin as they could. Above their heads was a microphone. When they were through, the toxicologist took over and explained they were trying to ensure no contaminants from the earth were introduced into the procedure. Once he was satisfied, he stepped back and motioned for the officers to unlatch the coffin and open it.

Despite the ointment, the smell was overpowering. One of the men placed a hand over his mouth and stepped back. The doctor glanced at him and waited. It took a second before he composed himself. At a signal from the doctor, both officers lifted the body from the coffin and placed it on the table.

After nearly a year in the ground the corpse was badly decomposed. Its skin had shrunken in and the hands resting on the man's chest barely covered the bones beneath them. The rest of the body was equally skeletal and grotesque to look at. I had to force myself to watch, grateful his eyes were closed.

According to the medical records, Jean Gillet went to meet his maker following an extended illness. His cause of death, as I told Phil Thurman, had been listed as kidney and heart failure due to pulmonary edema. Interestingly, Monsieur Gillet had been admitted to Piedmont Hospital four times in the previous six months before his final trip there.

Gillet's clothing was removed and placed in plastic bags for further examination. Once again, the toxicologist went through the procedure of vacuuming the man's body. He then emptied the contents into another plastic bag. Using long tweezers the doctor carefully picked pieces of wood from the skin and set them aside. Presumably they would also be examined. Bits of Monsieur Gillet's hair and nails were snipped away and also bagged.

The doctor continued his narrative as he made the first incision. Four hours passed before his work was complete. With the exception of the prosecutor, everyone, including myself, were asked to wait outside while tissue samples were examined in the spectrometer.

Another hour ticked by before the door opened. The toxicologist stepped into the hallway and nodded to us.

FORTY

I was sitting in Dan Dougherty's office sipping coffee from a thick white mug. He had a similar one. There was a bottle of Maker's Mark between us. I hefted my mug a couple of times and examined it.

"The wife got them for me a couple of years ago," he said. "She thought they suited my personality."

I frowned at the mug. "White porcelain?"

Dougherty shrugged. "Who knows with women. I just said thank you and took her to dinner."

"Wise man," I said, raising my mug to him.

"You married, Delaney?"

I nodded.

Dougherty added a little more whiskey to his cup and took a swallow.

"Get along good?" he asked.

"Real good," I said.

He raised his mug back to me. "That where it's at. Did you expect to find arsenic when you came down here?"

"Not really. I was just covering my bases."

"So will this help your guy?"

"It will, but we still have a long way to go."

"What's your next move?"

"Pick up some knishes tomorrow, then meet with Gil Mechlen at the university."

"Knishes?"

"Part of Thurman's price for helping. The Atlanta detective who took over the case also put in an order."

Dougherty laughed to himself. "The South Beach Deli or Mo's have the best ones."

"In your professional opinion?" I said.

"I'm married to a Jewish girl," he said. "Mechlen's the best. He's working with Atlanta PD to identify the murder weapon right?"

"According to the memo Maury Katz sent me this morning. As long as I'm here I thought I'd stop out and see him. We've met a number of times before."

Dougherty nodded and took another sip of coffee. "I read the file Thurman forwarded. Something odd is definitely going on. But do you honestly think a company like Tissinger would commit multiple murders, and then conspire to frame someone just to prevent a screw-up? It doesn't sound reasonable."

"No, it sounds excessive," I said, pushing myself out of the chair. I walked to the window and looked out. "Where's the ocean?"

"About twelve miles to the northeast off Miami Beach," he said.

"What's the difference?"

"They're Miami Beach; we're Miami. Two totally different cities. You want a lift out to the school?"

I told him I did.

GILBERT Mechlen was well into his seventies and showed little signs of slowing down. He was a bearded sprite of a man who stood just shy of 5'5". He was considered one of the foremost authorities in the world in forensic science. One of his talents was identifying murder weapons. Mechlen had authored three books and regularly consulted with law enforcement agencies around the world. His most recent work dealt with reconstructing facial features on centuries-old skulls to determine their cause of death. It received a half-page write-up in *The New York Times* and was the subject of a PBS special. We spoke by phone the night before and he agreed to see me after his morning class.

I arrived at the school a little after 11:00 A.M. Mechlen was in the middle of a lecture in the teaching amphitheater, or "the pit," as the students referred to it. On a table in front of him was the cadaver of an obese man. Twenty students lined the first three rows, writing furiously as he spoke. I took a seat in the back and waited.

"Ladies and gentlemen, as you can see, the injury to this skull occurred in the temporal region and is what we refer to as a crush-type trauma. It was inflicted as a result of a fall. Until recently, this man was a guest of the State at our prison facility in Jacksonville. He was found dead in the prison laundry by one of the guards. Another inmate was initially charged with his murder. Both men had been seen fighting only a day earlier.

"I say *initially*, because through the use of forensic science we were able to determine the cause of death was not from the blow, but from an ischemic episode. To put it simply, this man died of a stroke. The head injury happened *after* he fell and struck his head on the floor.

"The damage is widely dispersed across the bony structure of the skull casing, as you can see from the photograph to my right. Had this been a blunt object, like a pipe or a baseball bat, commonly used in prisons to settle arguments, the pattern would have revealed itself in the form of shattered skull fragments. But here there is no bruising of the meninges, nor do we see evidence of a bleed.

"I've taken the liberty of removing the brain and cutting it into tomographic slices for you to examine."

Mechlen reached down and picked up two slabs of gray material from a metal tray. A few students in the front row grimaced and at least one fellow went pale. I'd seen other professors do this from time to time and the results were always the same. Someone either threw up or passed out. From the expressions and general appearance of the class my guess was that they were freshmen. For reasons I have never been able to explain, doctors think getting first-year students to throw up is a rite of passage. It's like the hazing sailors go through when they pass the equator for the first time.

Mechlen was speaking again. "Now, if you will all draw closer you can observe how restricted the cerebral artery is. *This* is the reason our friend died. Excuse me . . ."

Lying near the brain slices was what looked like a submarine sandwich. When he reached out and took a bite, I saw the pale fellow's color drop another shade.

"The section of brain we are examining has been hardened in a soaking solution, otherwise it would literally drip through my fingers. Isn't that right, Professor Delaney?"

"Correct," I called back.

Several heads turned in my direction.

"Class, one of my colleagues is visiting us today. The eminent John Delaney, professor of law and, like myself, a forensics teacher of some skill."

He pointed his sandwich in my general direction and I acknowledged the students with a nod. If nothing else, Gil was entertaining. With a half-bow to me, he returned his attention to the cadaver and moved the table so the man's feet were facing the back of the stage. The head was now pointed directly toward the audience. Then he removed the towel covering the man's face.

"A little earlier I cut through the skull casing. Please observe carefully as I lift off the top of the head. Here are the bony ridges of the interior cavity. In cases where the head snaps forward and then backward, these ridges account for a great deal of trauma, but it's important to remember the injury happens *opposite* the point of impact, which is exactly what occurred here."

Mechlen took another bite of his sandwich, which turned out to be the final straw for the fellow in the front row. He got up and literally sprinted out of the amphitheater. Two girls followed him with hands over their mouths.

Mechlen blinked and looked around in surprise at the few remaining students. "Humph," he said. "Well, I suppose this is as good a time as any to take a break. Class is dismissed. Would anyone care to help me with the body?"

I won't say there was a stampede for the door, but the students certainly wasted no time in exiting the room. Needless to say, there were no volunteers. I got up and walked to the podium as Mechlen covered our cold friend.

"My dear fellow, how are you?" he said, extending his hand.

"Well enough, Gil. Thanks for seeing me. How have you been?"

"Better, if I didn't have to teach four classes. By the way, I heard about your leave of absence. Ridiculous—absolutely ridiculous. I called Ben Chambers and made it clear what I thought of his decision. In my opinion it demonstrates a lack of character."

I commented, "I don't know that Ben had a choice."

"That's very generous of you."

"If you have a moment, I'd like to discuss my case."

"The late Sanford Hamilton. Yes, I know. I've been consulting with Maury Katz for the last week."

"To lock down the real murder weapon?"

"Precisely."

"And?"

A look of annoyance crossed Gil Mechlen's face and he punctuated it with a hand gesture as if he were brushing a fly away. "Very frustrating . . . so far. Walk with me a bit."

"Aren't you forgetting something?" I asked, motioning to the cadaver.

"What? Oh, he's not going anywhere. Someone will be along to see to him shortly. Perhaps the janitors."

FORTY-ONE

'D seen pictures of Gil's laboratory in magazines and it never failed
to impress me. It was more so in real life. Hanging on every spare
inch of wall was the largest collection of weapons I had ever been
around. They ranged from guns, pikes, and stilettos, to broadswords
and halberds. A halberd, in case you're taking notes, is an evil-
looking weapon, half pike and half curved axe. Normally, I couldn't
have put a name to it, but Katherine's son once made me sit through
Lord of the Rings with him. Apparently, halberds were big in Middle
Earth.

In addition to the weapons collection, Gil also maintained a catalog
on his computer of every type of wound he had ever photographed.
He could literally bring up three-dimensional images of them in a
matter of seconds.

He continued, "When Detective Katz called several days ago and
sent me his file, it included the crime scene photographs, an MRI
study, as well as the Medical Examiner's findings. The ME did a
good job with the measurements, but as I'm sure you've already figured out, we're dealing with a most unusual wound to the back of
this victim's skull.

"At my request, the body was disinterred yesterday so I could ob-
tain a mold of Mr. Hamilton's head. My assistant flew to Atlanta to
supervize the procedure. Lately, I've been using a rubber-based cement that can be poured directly into the wound itself. See here."

"They dug up Sanford Hamilton?"

"Actually, he was buried in a mausoleum so it was more a matter
of opening the crypt and sliding him out."

Gil motioned for me to join him at his workbench. On it was a
life-size model of Sanford Hamilton's head staring back at me. I

found it disconcerting because the eyes appeared to be looking directly at me.

He turned the head sideways and carefully lifted the left side of the skull off revealing the brain, ocular nerves, and interior structures of the cranial cavity. It reminded me of those see-through plastic models we used in science class when I was a kid. The only difference was this one contained an ugly gash at the top back portion of the skull. It started where the parietal and occipital lobes meet, passed through them, and ended just above the midbrain.

Gil informed me, "You can tell the blow was delivered with a great deal of force. If you look closely, you can see bone splinters have been driven forward and down."

"Any guess as to what caused it?"

"Not yet. The closest I can come is a single-bladed axe from Renaissance Germany. It dates from the late fourteenth century, but even that's not exact. Honestly, I've never seen a weapon with a triangular shape. The underside is smooth while the top is serrated. It's fascinating."

"So Hamilton was either killed by a museum curator or a six-hundred-year-old German soldier."

Gil peered at me over the top of his glasses. "These things take time, John. I'll continue trying to match the weapon to the wound. Unfortunately, there are about 23,000 samples to go through."

"Why is it unfortunate?"

"Because if you were back at your school where you belong, you could assist and help and speed the process. You have too much talent to waste it—"

"On a man like Ted Jordan?"

Gil replied calmly, "I wasn't going to say that. I was going to say *pursuing a lost cause*. My dear fellow, the television and newspapers paint a very dismal picture of your client. I don't want to see him drag you down."

I took a breath and looked up at the wall at a two-handed broadsword. There was some type of scrollwork on the blade, or maybe they were script words. I couldn't tell which. I gave up after a few seconds when I realized Gil was watching me.

I said, "Sometimes the lost causes are the ones worth fighting for."

"Perhaps I was wrong to speak out of turn. I only know what I've seen on the news and what I have been told. Follow your conscience of course. Just don't do it with blinders on.

"As far as the weapon is concerned, I'll identify it sooner or later. When I do I'll let you know. I assume you're here because you feel Theodore Jordan is innocent. If you wish to prove that, you might consider narrowing your search to the *type* of person who wielded it."

"Meaning?"

"Think, my friend, think."

A long time ago Paul Simon wrote a song called "50 Ways To Leave Your Lover." There are a lot more ways to commit a murder. People are endlessly creative. When psychologists attempt to profile a killer they often look at the method that was used. The sad fact is, most murders are committed by people who know each other. Guns and poison are considered impersonal because the instrument that causes death *leaves* the murderer's hand. Knives and axes are a different story. Using a knife to kill someone is highly personal. In other words, there's no distance between you and the victim. An axe would indicate rage.

According to Gil, the blow that ended Sanford Hamilton's life was delivered with tremendous force. I agreed. It was done by someone who knew and hated him. An image of Ted Jordan's reaction to the deputy's taunting at the courthouse chose that moment to pop into my head. Neither thought gave me any comfort.

FORTY-TWO

LUTHER'S Escalade was waiting for me outside baggage claim. I rated the SUV; Katherine got his Mercedes. I got in and tossed my overnight bag on the backseat. I put the cardboard box I was carrying beside it.

"Been waiting long?" I asked.

"Maybe twenty minutes," he said.

"How'd you manage that? The cops always make me leave."

"Got friends in high places," he said, nodding to a lady officer. She was in the process of writing someone a ticket.

"Reverse discrimination," I said.

" 'Course it is," he smiled. "Now that Obama's in we gonna correct all abuses of the past."

"Your people were abused at the airport?"

"Maybe. What's in the box?"

"Knishes for Phil Thurman and Maury Katz," I informed him.

"Potato?" Luther asked, examining the box closer.

"Yep. Brought back six for you, too."

Luther's smile widened. "No lox?"

"Sorry."

"There you go. Another abuse that needs to be set right," he said.

"I didn't get any for Nikko," I said. "I can't see him eating them."

"I don't believe he would," Luther said, "Nikko can surprise you though. Got him to try sushi the other day."

"Nikko?"

"The same."

"Where are we going?" I asked, noting we had just driven by the Camp Creek Parkway exit.

"Gotta drop off them knishes, don't you? Katz wants to see you."

"About what?" I said.

"I suspect he has some information on your man."

WE did not go to the downtown precinct as I had thought. Instead Luther drove to High Museum. We found Maury on the third floor in one of the impressionist galleries. He was seated on a wooden bench looking at a painting by John Singer Sargent. Luther and I sat on either side of him.

"I feel like a partial Oreo," he said, glancing at us.

"Delaney can't help it," Luther replied. "We working on his tan. Is that Venice?"

"It is," Maury said, turning back to the painting. "Have you ever been there?"

Luther shook his head slowly and looked at the painting closer. "That bridge the boatman is going under, does it have a name?"

"It's called the Bridge of Sighs."

"How come?"

"When people went to prison that was the way they took them," Maury said.

"The prison still there?" Luther asked.

"Not for many years."

Luther leaned forward and looked around Maury at me. "You been to Venice?"

"About five years ago with Katherine," I said. "You were occupied with that problem in Detroit."

Luther nodded, then turned to study another painting of a gondola on the Grand Canal. "I prefer this one," he said after a moment.

Maury said, "I wanted to share a few things with you." Maury tapped a large yellow envelope lying beside him on the bench. "As you know, I was asked to take a second look at this case by Rena Bailey. The original detective who worked it was Harry Eberhart. His phone number and address are on the second page. I mentioned when we first met that Eberhart left the department shortly after the investigation. He now works for a company in North Atlanta called Delta Electronics. They make security systems.

"The timing of his departure didn't bother me so much as the quality of the investigation Eberhart and his partner did. Both men were fifteen-year veterans in robbery-homicide.

"Some of these oversights you and I have already discussed."

I nodded. I had reached the same conclusion after observing the crime scene and reading Eberhart's report. I was curious, however, to see where Maury was going with this. Granted, we were using hindsight, but if I had to grade the cops' performance, I wouldn't have given them better than a "C."

"And you're sharing this, why?" I asked.

"I think it would be a good idea for you to speak with him."

"Won't he talk to you?" I said.

"We . . . ah, don't get along."

"Professional disagreement?" I said.

"Only in that I'm Jewish and he's a dyed-in-the-wool Aryan bigot."

Luther broke off his study of Sargent's painting and looked at Maury.

"Criminals were not the only people passing over that bridge," Maury explained. "There were thirteen concentration camps in Italy during World War II."

Luther and I exchanged glances.

"Any of your people die in the war?" Luther asked.

Maury closed his eyes for a long moment and then drew a deep breath into his lungs.

FORTY-THREE

WHEN Maury opened his eyes again there was a change in his expression.

He said, "Yes, I lost people in the war. My uncle was arrested in Venice. He was a watchmaker. They sent him to an internment camp on Rab, a small island north of there.

"The rest of my family is from Germany. As in Italy, during the war they kept Jews in prison camps. One was called *Dachau*. You've heard of it?" he asked us.

"Of course," I said.

Luther nodded.

"My grandfather, grandmother, and two older brothers went to the gas chambers at Dachau. My father, the youngest member of the family, saw this happen. Toward the end of the war, when things began to go badly for Germany, an order came down from the *Reichstag* to eliminate all remaining Jews in Dachau and destroy any records they ever existed. It was called the Final Solution. An interesting choice of words, wouldn't you say?

"During this time, a German captain took a liking to my father and kept him out of the ovens. He put him to work in the commandant's office because he knew how to type.

"Strange, no . . . ? For typing to save someone's life? According to the history books, over 500,000 people were processed through Dachau in three years. *Processed* is another way to say murdered. The actual number was probably quite a bit higher. Can you imagine killing every man, woman, and child in a city the size of Cleveland? That's what happened in Dachau and it was only one of several camps.

"When the allies began to close in, the Germans abandoned their ovens in favor of faster, more expedient methods. The Jews and most of the Soviet POWs who could still work were led out of the camp and forced to dig a series of trenches. The officers told them it was for defensive purposes. When the trenches were finished, they were lined up and ordered to stand in front of them. That's when the machine guns opened up. Moments later, the trenches became a mass grave. Bodies were pushed or thrown in. It made no difference if the prisoners were still alive. To erase the evidence, the Germans poured thousands of gallons of kerosene over them then lit it.

"Sixty years later, my father would still wake with dreams of what he had seen. He told me he was never able to get the smell of burning flesh out of his nostrils. Next came the bulldozers to seal up the holes in the earth. The last one shut its engine only two hours before the allies liberated the camp.

"My father never forgot what happened in Dachau, and he passed the story on to me. As a young man it was just words and events I couldn't relate to. Why should I? A decade had passed since Dachau and I was safe and sound in the United States, thousands of miles from what happened. I had nothing to relate it to.

"When I was sixteen, my family took a trip to Germany and I finally got the see the infamous death camp for myself. It's a bleak, gray place. The barbed wire is still intact, as is the crematorium. Interestingly, if you look at the old pictures, nothing has changed much. It's as if time remains frozen there. The *Arbeit Macht Frei* Gate my father had told me about still stands guarding the camp's entrance.

"I saw all these things through the eyes of a sixteen year old who knows he will live forever, and the impression it made on me was only a small one, until I read a poem by a man named Martin Niemöller. Niemöller was a pastor who originally supported the Nazis and eventually wound up in Dachau after he opposed what they were doing. Would you like to hear what he wrote?"

Luther and I both nodded.

"First they came for the Communists, and I did not speak out—
because I was not a Communist;
Then they came for the Socialists, and I did not speak out—
because I was not a Socialist;

Then they came for the trade unionists, and I did not speak out—
because I was not a trade unionist;
Then they came for the Jews, and I did not speak out—
because I was not a Jew;
Then they came for me—
and there was no one left to speak out for me.

"I've never forgotten this. I'm sure psychologists have a name for it, but those words changed my life. Not in any major way. The change was more subtle. What I'm saying is, my father's story was no longer just words to me."

Maury continued, "When we came back to the States I finished school. My grades were good, so I went to college, met Emma, and got married. I sold life insurance for a few months, but it wasn't for me. Then a friend told me the Atlanta Police Department was hiring, so I applied. We were living in Columbus then.

"I became a police officer because I thought I could make a difference. There was more prejudice in the South in those days. For the most part it was directed toward blacks, but there was no shortage of hate when it came to the Jews. As times changed, so did the prejudice. It became less fashionable to speak openly of your feelings. Still, it was there . . . in the jokes, in the sidelong glances, in the jobs that were offered to others, and in whispered comments men made behind their hands.

"When I was promoted to detective, my belief that police served the law never wavered. I still believe that to this day."

Maury got up and went across the room to look at another painting. I noticed he didn't take the envelope. From my standpoint, something didn't fit. Eberhart probably was a bigot, as he said, and incompetent as well. The investigation he and his partner had done was substandard, but that could have been handled internally. Police departments bury secrets every day.

I asked, "Did you ever work any cases with them?"

"A few times. Let's stay in touch."

Maury pulled his overcoat around him and headed down the hall, leaving Luther and me sitting there. I glanced around the gallery. Except for the oil paintings and us, it was deserted.

Luther glanced down at the envelope, then at me. He raised his eyebrows and waited. I opened it. Inside were several pages. The first two were a report from internal affairs criticizing the way the Hamilton investigation had been handled. The last was a petition to exhume the body of Charlotte Jordan.

FORTY-FOUR

I LAY in bed with Katherine that night unable to sleep. From the rhythm of her breathing I knew she was awake, too. The bedroom was illuminated only by moonlight filtering through the trees. A spider-work of shadows moved across the window. Peeka entered the room and jumped up on the bed just the way we taught him not to. I moved my feet to accommodate him.

"I don't understand," Katherine said. "Why would Ted want to dig up his mother's body?"

I answered, "I don't know. Charlotte's been dead for almost nineteen years. . . ."

The rest of my words trailed away as the image of my genetics book in Ted's study entered my mind.

"What?" Katherine asked.

I told her about the book.

"Maybe he was just curious."

"I may have said the same thing when I was at his house. It's possible to satisfy your curiosity without exhuming your mother's body."

"It's sick, John."

Peeka, hearing Katherine's tone, opened an eye and looked at her. He closed it a moment later and curled himself into a ball.

"I need to take a look at Charlotte's police file tomorrow," I said.

Katherine commented, "I'm beginning to think Ted really is crazy. Why don't you just call and ask him about it?"

"For a couple of reasons—"

"I understand," Katherine said. "You want it to be his idea."

I slid an arm around her shoulder and pulled her closer. She rested her head on my chest. After a moment her head came up. So did Peeka's. The cat looked annoyed.

"He didn't tell you about buying a gun either or that he was having an affair with that woman until you brought it up."

"No."

Katherine made a derisive noise and put her head back down. "What did Luther say?"

"That everyone in this case seems to have an agenda."

"Great point."

"Luther can be quite insightful when he wants. Have you had any more visits from Coleman and Britton?"

"They came back yesterday to ask a few more questions about Coleman's brother-in-law. But it was more a show of ego, or maybe arrogance."

"How so?"

"After we were through, I walked them to the lobby. Nikko was there. No one said anything to anybody, but while I was talking to Coleman, he and Britton basically locked eyes. I don't know how else to describe it. Nikko didn't move and Britton didn't look away. He just smiled at him on the way out. Of the two I'd say Britton is the more dangerous."

I kissed the top of Katherine's head.

"Ever feel you're following a trail of bread crumbs? You know it's going someplace, but you don't know where until you arrive?"

Katherine asked, "Would they still have it after all these years?"

"Have what?"

"Charlotte's file?"

"The murder was never solved."

"We can both go," Katherine said. "My day is clear, besides I want to check the court records on Maureen. I have an idea."

"What sort of idea?"

"Everything has a price, Delaney," Katherine said, trailing her fingers up the inside of my leg.

WE slept in the following morning. Not surprising, we were both a bit more tired than usual. At least I was.

Katherine leaned across me for a bottle of water on the nightstand. She took a sip, put the bottle back, and stretched her arms above her head. Her eyes were closed. The sheet fell away from her breasts.

After a moment or two she asked, "Are you looking at me?"

"Yes."

"Have I changed much?"

"You haven't changed at all. I told you that in the restaurant the other day."

"I wasn't naked then."

"True. But you look wonderful."

"So do you."

"John?"

"Yes."

"Do you love me?"

I turned on my side to face her and she did the same. "Always and forever."

"I had a dream the other night that you and Julia Levy were out together on a date."

I nearly laughed, but that would have been dangerous. Instead I told her, "I'd never look at another woman. I mean I might look, but that's all."

"I got really angry,' Katherine said. "I had this urge to drive my car up on the sidewalk and run you both over."

"Well, I'm glad you didn't." *But let's keep working on those coping skills.*

My cell phone interrupted the rest of what I had to say. I picked it up from the nightstand, looked at the caller ID, and mouthed the name, "Ted" to her. Katherine motioned for me to take the call.

Ted informed me, "Maureen called me a little while ago."

"Really?"

"I guess your meeting with her lawyer must have gone well, because she called me every name in the book."

"I have that effect on people sometimes. Katherine did most of the work. I just tagged along."

"Good. I'll send her some flowers later."

"Tell me what she said."

"I'm not sure you want to hear it."

"I'll risk it."

I heard the sound of paper rustling in the background.

"I made some notes . . . oh, here they are. Okay, let's see . . . she said she was reporting you to the bar. I'm not sure why. I guess for representing me; that Katherine is a slut; and she'll see us in court."

"There's a novel expression. I'll have to remember it."

"She also said she didn't give a damn about alimony and that I would spend the rest of my life in jail. Oh, and . . ."

"What?"

"Oh, this is great. Do you have the TV on?"

"No."

"Go turn on Channel Two. I don't believe this. Some reporter is interviewing Maureen."

I took a mental breath, reached for the remote, and flipped on the set. Katherine sat up in bed as the picture came on. I found Channel 2 and turned up the volume just in time to hear Maureen say, "I was as shocked as anyone when the news about Ted came out. My whole family's just devastated."

The reporter asked, "I understand you and Mr. Jordan have filed for divorce."

"That's true. It's not what I want, but as a mother I have to consider the welfare of my children."

The reporter, a woman named Bebe Sanchez, according to the caption beneath her, nodded sympathetically. "Did you ask your husband to leave the house because you were afraid for your safety?"

Maureen started to speak, then stopped to dab the corner of her eye with a handkerchief. "I probably shouldn't say anything else. I still love my husband and don't want to get him into trouble. I only hope he can get some help quickly."

Bebe placed a sympathetic hand on Maureen's shoulder—brave girl, then turned to the camera as it zoomed in for a tight headshot. "More troubles for Ted Jordan and his family. This is Bebe Sanchez reporting from the Jordan home in Brookhaven."

"Nice performance," I commented.

Ted expanded on the subject, "That's just fucking great. Can't we get an injunction against her?"

I glanced at Katherine who shook her head in the negative. She was close enough to hear both ends of the conversation.

"Probably not. I'll see if the judge is willing to issue a restraining order."

Ted informed me, "I have a couple of errands this afternoon. Can we get together tomorrow? There are some things I need to discuss with you."

Katherine gave me a thumbs up sign.

"Tomorrow will be fine."

"Around noon?"

"Also fine."

"How did it go in Miami?" he asked.

"Pretty well. The autopsy confirmed Monsieur Gillet died of arsenic poisoning."

"John, that's unbelievable! I knew you would do it. Forget tomorrow. What are you up to now? We should celebrate."

"Let's do it tomorrow. I'm just taking care of some old business at the moment."

That earned me a jab in the ribs from Katherine. She got out of bed and slowly bent from the waist to pick up her nightgown, then made her way toward the bathroom. Just before she entered, she looked back at me over her shoulder. Her expression left no doubt as to what she was thinking. I don't remember if I ever said good-bye to Ted, but I heard the shower come on a moment later. I've always believed in multitasking whenever possible. I may have sprinted down the hallway.

FORTY-FIVE

AFTER Katherine and I dressed, we took Mr. Jag downtown. Luther and Nikko had the day off. I felt relieved when Ted suggested that we meet. It's fine to play your cards close to the vest, but not with someone who's trying to save your life.

The Fulton County Courthouse was a very different place from the last time I was there. Gone were the mobile television trucks with their cameras and space-age antennas. No reporters were shouting questions now. There were only people with apprehensive expressions passing through the large bronze doors at the entrance. For reasons I've never been able to explain, most of the people you see in court look like they belong there, particularly if the case is criminal. I know this is a generalization, like crime going up every time there's a full moon, but you can ask any cop about it. Nine times out of ten, they can pick out the guilty ones sitting in the gallery. And for the record, the number of arrests practically doubles when the moon is full.

Katherine was in her working clothes: a pair of chocolate brown tailored slacks and a tan camel hair jacket. She added a strand of pearls, which set the outfit off nicely. Even dressed down she looked spectacular.

On the ride I asked several times why we were going to the record room, but she refused to tell me. "I'd rather show you" was all she would say.

The fact is, I hate surprises. But her tone of voice and expression were familiar. Few people enjoy being right as much as Katherine does, so I decided to go with the flow. After my physical exertions last evening and again this morning, I was feeling particularly mellow.

We took the staircase to the basement and made our way to a

room filled with large books on long gray metal tables. Katherine went straight to the GRANTEE INDEX. I waited while she looked up Maureen Jordan's name. To my surprise, there were several entries. She glanced at me over her shoulder to see if I was paying attention, and then jotted down the reference numbers on her legal pad.

The first two had been made a few months before Sanford Hamilton's death and bore the code "WD" next to them, which meant the documents were warranty deeds. Once we finished with the index we went to a second book containing photocopies of the actual deeds themselves. Another lawyer was in the process of looking up some information and we had to wait until he finished.

When he was gone, Katherine informed me, "I figured it wouldn't hurt to start a news clipping file. While you were in Miami *without* me, my paralegal came across an article about a real estate deal Tissinger is involved in. I didn't pay much attention at the time. But when I was driving home last night, I got to thinking how out of place it seemed for a drug company. I mean, it doesn't fit their profile, so I checked some more on the computer."

"What are we talking about?"

"They're building a planned community in Dunwoody called St. Andrews. It will include a commercial development called Fashion Avenue." Katherine pointed to the second entry on the page. "This deed is for one of those spaces.

"According to the newspaper, Tissinger is one of twenty-five limited partners in the project. Plans call for the developer to build two hundred homes in the million-dollar range, a golf course, and a shopping center. From what I read, it will be pretty exclusive."

"Sounds impressive."

"There's big money involved, John. I have the list of the partners."

Katherine took a folded sheet of paper out of her handbag and laid it on the counter.

I said, "I don't see Maureen's name here."

Katherine turned around and leaned against the desk, giving me one of her smug smiles.

"Southern Federal Bank is funding the project. By the way, your friend Charles Evans is also listed as a limited partner—he's about halfway down the page. Is any of this starting to make sense yet?"

Southern Federal was where Ted was supposed to have opened his account, but I still didn't get the tie-in to Maureen.

I raised my shoulders indicating I didn't know. Katherine sighed and pointed to the eighteenth name on the list.

"*CDPG* Designs, Inc.?" I said, reading it aloud.

"Exactly. Maureen is supposed to have set Ted up, right?"

"Yes, but—"

"The newspaper said each limited partner put up $500,000. Where would she get that kind of money? Certainly not from her dress shop. You told me Ted was always complaining about having to support her business."

"Sure, but—"

"I did some quick math on the homes. Assuming they make a twenty percent profit, which is on the conservative side, Maureen and the other partners stand to gain upwards of five million dollars *each* on their investment. And that doesn't take into account selling country club memberships or the commercial real estate leases."

I was still lost. "All right, tell me again how you came up with Maureen's name?"

"Do you remember when we met with Joe Edward Fanning? He said Maureen needed to conserve her money because she's expanding the store?"

"Sure."

"I picked this handbag up when I was there yesterday." She held her purse up up for my inspection.

"Very nice."

"It's an imitation, like the rest of her stuff. I paid less than two hundred dollars. The real one would have cost closer to three thousand dollars."

"Okay."

"Afterward, I went back to the list and checked the companies who had signed up for the retail space at Fashion Avenue. One of them was CDPG Designs. The name got me thinking . . . *CDPG* . . . *CDPG*. That's when I came up with it."

"Came up with what?" I asked.

"The name CDPG, silly. It stands for Chanel, Dior, Prada, and Gucci. I mean it's a weird combination of letters, right? But those are the knockoff bags Maureen sells. I checked with the Secretary of State and found the company was formed eight months ago. Guess who the president is?"

"Maureen?"

She gave me another smile. "Anyone could have figured it out."

I stared at my wife in disbelief. "K.J., *no one* could have figured that out. It's completely mental."

"That's because you're a man."

It took a few seconds to recover from this peculiar brand of logic. However Katherine had come up with it, I now had another link in the chain. My next thought was somewhat more practical—get as many women on the jury as I could.

"You're astonishing," I said.

"That's what I keep telling you," she said, slipping her arm through mine.

FORTY-SIX

ON our way out of the courthouse Katherine suggested, "Let's get Mr. Jag and I'll buy you lunch. I found the cutest place a few weeks ago. We should celebrate."

I wasn't quite as effusive. The connection between Maureen and Tissinger could be explained away. I never expected to find a smoking gun. But what we had were the beginnings of a defense to place in front of a jury. If they bought the concept, it would go a long way to knocking down a motive on Ted's part and pointing a finger at Tissinger.

"Oh, Ms. Adams. May I have a word with you?" The voice came from a parked car.

Stan Coleman got out of the backseat of a black Chrysler 300, a friendly smile on his face. Behind the wheel was a man I had never seen before. He eyed me but stayed where he was. Another man was seated next to him on the passenger side. The car was parked in front of the courthouse in space reserved for the police.

"Excuse the interruption, Professor. If Ms. Adams can spare me a moment, I'll be brief. It's about my brother-in-law again."

"I'm a little busy, Stan," Katherine said. "Why don't you call my office and make an appointment?"

When Katherine turned to go Coleman reached for her arm. His hand never made it. I slapped it away and stepped between them. He responded by taking a step backward and holding his hands up defensively.

"Relax, Delaney. This is strictly business. I really do have a brother-in-law and he really is going through a divorce. Your wife has been trying to help me. Why don't you get your car? While we're talking? We'll only be a minute. I promise."

"My wife has a generous nature," I said. " I don't. Take a hike, Stan."

The man behind the steering wheel opened the door and got out. He was large and heavily muscled with a deep chest. I figured him for a bodybuilder. He stayed where he was.

"Tough guy, huh," Coleman said.

"Common knowledge."

"Maybe you don't count so good," he said, glancing back at his companion.

I stared at Coleman's driver for a second or two. The bulge under his jacket might have been a gun. For all I knew Coleman was carrying, too. I simply didn't think they were going to shoot us in front of the courthouse. Their goal was intimidation. Nothing more.

"I don't think so," I said, keeping my eyes on the bodybuilder.

"What are you looking at?" he asked, coming toward us.

"I ain't lookin' at nothin," I said.

"How about we step around the corner and discuss it some more?" he asked.

"John," Katherine said, putting her hand on my shoulder.

"Tell steroid boy to back off before he gets hurt," I said to Coleman.

The bodybuilder took another step toward me and reached for my jacket. It was an amateur thing to do. I sidestepped him and placed the top of my foot across his instep. Unable to keep his balance he continued forward, colliding with a trash can. Amused, Coleman moved out of the way.

The bodybuilder didn't go down. He regained his balance at the last moment, spun around, and came at me again. I ducked under his arms, landed a roundhouse punch to his solar plexus, then clubbed him behind the left ear, putting all my weight into the blow. This time he went to his knees. The guy was strong, but not experienced. He also wasn't used to getting hit.

"Hold still and I'll rip your fucking head off," he said, staggering to his feet.

"That doesn't give me much incentive to stand here."

My next blow was a left to the bridge of his nose. I felt the cartilage collapse. I moved to my right as he grabbed for me again.

"You fight like your wife," he said.

"You think?"

This time he put down his head and charged like a bull. A right hook I'd been saving forever landed squarely to the side of his jaw and snapped his head sideways. I followed it with another and he went down in a heap.

Somewhere behind me a woman screamed. A number of people on the street had stopped walking and were trying to see what the commotion was about. I caught a glimpse of Coleman as he got back into his car, the smile gone from his face. Agent Britton was now in the driver's seat.

Katherine's tug on my sleeve brought me back to the moment.

"Let's go, Muhammad . . . fight's over," she said.

I straightened my tie and watched their Chrysler disappear around the corner.

FORTY-SEVEN

M Y car was where we left it.

"Hello Mr. Jag," Katherine said. "John and I were just in a fight. Well . . . he was. I managed the corner."

Mr. Jag didn't respond. He's quite nonjudgmental.

"Does your hand hurt?" Katherine asked, seeing me stretch my fingers back.

I smiled at her and shook my head no, as I reached in to release the roof's side latches. There's no point in owning a convertible if you ride around with the top up.

From somewhere at the bottom of her new knockoff handbag, Katherine produced a tiny barrette and tied her hair back. Women can be endlessly resourceful. I went around to the driver's side to repeat the process. Perhaps a little celebrating was in order . . . or at least some ice for my knuckles.

Katherine tossed her purse between Mr. Jag's seats and was about to get in when I noticed a tiny wire lying on the ground near to my front wheel. It couldn't have been more than three inches in length. Both ends were bare where the green insulation had been stripped away. An alarm immediately went off in my head. Maybe it was due to our encounter a moment ago and maybe it was because the ends of the wire weren't oxidized, indicating it had recently been dropped there.

"*Stop*," I snapped, pointing at her.

Katherine froze. "What?"

"K.J., I want you to back away from the car slowly." I spoke the words as calmly as I could so as not to frighten her.

"John—"

I started coming around the hood toward her. Whatever else

might be said of my wife, she is not wasteful. Nor was she about to leave her new purse behind, knockoff or not. The second I saw her reach for the stupid handbag I broke into a run and grabbed her around the waist. We crashed into the rear quarter panel of a car parked two spaces away, our momentum carrying us over the trunk. A second later the air was shattered by a deafening explosion.

A flash of orange light lit the inside of the garage followed by a tremendous bang. Instinctively I threw myself across Katherine's body trying to protect her as we hit the cement floor. Bits of glass and metal stung my arms and legs. A second explosion followed. Out of my peripheral vision I saw the Jag lift off the ground and felt a blast of hot air rushing past my face.

It took several moments to get my bearings again. My head was spinning and an acrid smell filled my nostrils. I rose to my feet, half-pulling half-dragging Katherine with me. We got to the far end of the garage. Flames and black smoke were pouring out of what was left of Mr. Jag. I stood there and watched it burn for a moment.

I felt neither anger nor sadness at the sight. I don't know what I felt. I had taken years to restore that car and now it was gone. Neither of us spoke. In the distance I thought I could hear the sound of sirens, but my ears were still ringing from the explosion. The elbow of Katherine's suit was ripped and there was a dark smudge on her left leg.

"Are you okay?" I asked.

She nodded numbly. "Someone just blew up Mr. Jag and my purse."

Sixty feet away I could feel the fire's heat. The smoke was making it difficult to see. Supporting each other, we made our way to the street.

Police and fire engines began to arrive within minutes. A crowd had gathered as bilious black clouds poured out of the building. A fireman approached us and asked if we were all right. I said we were. He draped a coat around Katherine's shoulders. We both must have looked like hell.

For some reason I wasn't surprised when an unmarked cruiser pulled up and Maury Katz got out. The man with him was Gordon Bonham, Atlanta's Chief of Police. Bonham was a throwback; a cigar-chewing hulk of a man who had risen through the ranks to the high-est position on Atlanta's police force, a post he had held for the past eighteen years. Three or four administrations had come and gone yet he remained.

Bonham came directly up to me. "Were you in there?"

"Chief, this is Katherine Adams," I said, introducing him to Katherine. "We were both in there. Someone planted a bomb under my car."

"This better not be a joke, Delaney. I've had a hell of a morning and my prostate is killing me."

Katherine informed him, "John's telling the truth. We were on the fourth floor when the bomb went off."

Bonham stared at her for a long moment. "I'll be a son of a bitch," he said, pulling a walkie-talkie from his back pocket. He keyed the SEND button a few times. "Darlow, this is Chief Bonham. I'm at the entrance to the municipal garage across from the court-house. Someone just set off an explosive device on the fourth floor. The whole place is a goddamn mess. I want the courthouse evacuated and a perimeter set up for ten blocks in every direction. No one gets in—no one gets out. You have that? We have a Code One here. Repeat, a Code One."

A voice on the speaker responded, "Understood, Chief. Special Ops is rolling."

"I'm sorry about Mr. Jag," Katherine said.

The chief asked, "Who the hell is Mr. Jag?"

"John's car," Katherine explained, rubbing my arm. "Someone blew it up."

Bonham put his hands on his hips. "Mr. Jag, huh? Well, right now I'd like to speak to Mr. Explanation. Delaney, you may not be the most popular guy in town at the moment, but why the hell would someone want to blow you up? Ted Jordan will just get another lawyer, won't he?"

"That's generally the way it works."

It took me nearly fifteen minutes to lay out what we had found out about Maureen and her involvement with Tissinger. Then I told him about the bee sting victim and the husband and wife who had died at Lake Lanier. I ended with the arsenic-poisoned scientist in Miami.

Bonham listened without comment. He continued to chew on his cigar, nodding every now and then thoughtfully. At one point he glanced over his shoulder at Maury, who was standing off to one side watching the firemen. I had the impression much of what I was saying wasn't new to him.

He said, "I don't know about this conspiracy theory of yours, but it's intriguing. Keep me posted."

"I—"

"Make no mistake, Delaney. If I wake up at night with a bad feeling, or I come to find you're dicking me around to build a defense for your client, I'll cut you dead. You've helped us in the past so I'm returning the favor. You need something from us, you go through Katz to get it. He'll be your point man. The DA's already having a fucking cow over Sanford Hamilton, so watch your step around him."

"Kind of you to tell me."

"Kind has nothing to do with it. The last thing this city needs is a self-centered prick for its mayor."

I was just beginning to understand why Gordon Bonham had outlasted so many administrations. He was a power broker and Atlanta was his city.

"I hear you, Chief."

"Great."

Then he turned to Katherine. "Ms. Adams, I'll be blunt. If what Delaney is saying is true, I'm not crazy about a woman being in a situation like this."

Katherine started to respond, but he held up a hand.

"Don't get me wrong. I know you're a competent attorney and this has nothing to do with gender. My wife is competent, too. My comment relates to training. Whoever the players are, they've just raised the stakes considerably. You might want to take a backseat until this situation is resolved."

"Thank you, Chief. I'm not ignoring your advice, but I think I'll continue to help John for a while. I don't like what's going on here either. Besides, some bastard just blew up my new purse."

Bonham chuckled to himself, then took what was left of his cigar and flicked it at a nearby garbage can. It bounced off the rim and hit the ground. He muttered an obscenity under his breath, then walked back to his car. On his way he stopped to speak with Maury for a moment. Katherine moved closer and lowered her voice.

"That was interesting," she said. "What do you suppose they're talking about?"

I answered. "We'll find out in a minute."

Katherine asked, "What do we do next?"

"Update Ted on what just happened. If Tissinger really has set him up and they think their plan is falling apart, they'll move to cut losses. I'd like to get him to a safe place as quickly as possible. Afterward, we need to have a talk with Sanford Hamilton's housekeeper and his cook."

"Because?"

"According to Maury's investigative report, neither of them were home the night of the murder, and that bothers me."

Katherine digested this for a several seconds. "You think they're involved?"

"No idea. We're playing catch up. The two detectives who handled the case cleared them. I'd still like to speak with them, as well as with Eberhart. He was the lead detective."

"Here comes Maury," Katherine said.

FORTY-EIGHT

ESPITE all that dirt and grime you're still an attractive couple," Maury said. "What happened?" He took a handkerchief from his pocket, reached out, and wiped a smudge off Katherine's cheek.

"John knocked me down, officer. Arrest him."

Maury wagged a finger at me. "It's not nice to abuse women, young man—even if they're lawyers. You should buy us lunch to make up for it. Will that satisfy you, madam?" he asked, turning back to Katherine.

"Only if it's expensive. I need to go home and change clothes first."

Maury's face turned serious. "I'm very sorry about your car, John. Thank God neither of you were hurt. Do you have any idea who did this?"

"Don't you?" I asked.

"I'd rather hear your thoughts first."

I told him.

He said, "I've already met Agent Britton and Mr. Coleman. They're an interesting pair."

"Where was that?" I asked.

"At your client's townhome a few hours ago. I've been trying to reach you. Is your cell phone turned off?"

I fished my phone out of my pocket and saw the screen had been smashed when I hit the ground. I held it out for Maury to see.

"Pity," he said. "Maybe you can use this one."

I thought I recognized Ted's cell phone, but said nothing.

He continued, "I found it sitting on your client's desk and didn't want it to accidentally disappear."

I asked, "What were you doing at Ted Jordan's house?"

"One of the neighbors reported a gas leak and called central dispatch. They called the utility company and the message was passed along to me."

"Is Ted all right?"

"I wouldn't know. No one was home when I arrived. In fact, it looked like the place has been empty for several days. There was trash in the container and dishes were piled up in the sink. What disturbed me most, however, was Frank Nardelli's body in the living room."

"*What?*" Katherine exclaimed.

"I believe Mr. Nardelli was the gentleman who has been doing uh . . . Maureen Jordan's tile," Maury said.

I asked, "Is this on the level?"

Maury nodded soberly. "An all-points bulletin was issued earlier to pick up Mr. Jordan. When Thornton Schiff found out, he called a press conference to announce the new developments. I imagine the news trucks will be arriving soon."

"I think I'll skip lunch," Katherine said.

Maury pointed to his car and we all started walking.

I inquired, "Have you determined the cause of death?"

"It appears to be a gunshot wound to the head."

"Murder weapon?"

"Not recovered at this time. Whoever killed Nardelli also took three souvenirs from his right hand."

I stopped walking. "You're kidding?"

"I wish I were, John. Nardelli's murder may be a different case, but Mr. Schiff believes they're both tied together. Why wouldn't he? He's going to tell the press there's a deranged man on the loose. The public will also see it that way."

I felt my stomach drop several inches. Schiff would have a field day.

We started walking again. Maury's car was parked near the garage entrance. The police were already setting up the barricades. As predicted, news trucks were rolling in right behind them. The last thing I wanted was to speak to a bunch of reporters. We almost made it.

A white Channel Two van with the words MOBILE NEWS TEAM pulled in behind us and a reporter named Gayle Barron got out. She immediately spotted me and broke into a trot, waving her microphone to attract my attention.

"Professor Delaney, Professor Delaney, may I have a word with you?"

When she was close enough to see the condition of my clothes, she exclaimed, "Oh, my God. What happened to you?"

"Police brutality."

"What?"

Maury muttered "Oy" under his breath and stepped back into the shadows, taking Katherine with him.

Ms. Barron said, "You look like you've been in a fight. We were a block away on another story when the police scanner said there was an explosion here."

"That's correct. Someone set off a bomb under my car."

Gayle's eyes went wide for a moment before she regained her composure. "Are you certain it was a bomb?"

"Reasonably certain. The loud bang and flying shrapnel gave it away."

"Was anyone hurt? I mean, are you all right?"

"I'm fine. Mr. Jag was the only fatality—that's my car."

Gayle was having trouble deciding if I was playing with a full deck or not. She finally flipped her microphone off and signaled the cameraman to stop filming.

"C'mon, Delaney, give me a break. Is this legit or not? Off the record."

"Off the record, that's exactly what happened. No exaggeration."

"Someone tried to kill you? Why?"

"They probably weren't crazy about my jokes."

She gave me a flat look and folded her arms across her chest.

"All right. I've been proceeding on a theory that Ted Jordan has been framed for the murder of Sanford Hamilton. Apparently, there are some people who don't want that to come out."

Gayle started to ask another question, but I continued before she could.

"I'm not prepared to name names yet, but when the time is right the evidence will point to who is really behind the murders and the explosion."

"You said *murders* as in more than one?"

I nodded. "In a little while, the District Attorney will tell the press another body with three missing fingers has been found in Ted Jordan's home. Mr. Jordan is also missing. I don't know where he is."

"*Another* body?" she repeated incredulously. "Who?"

"His name is Frank Nardelli, the same gentleman who has been having an affair with Maureen Jordan."

Gayle's jaw dropped further, but again she recovered quickly. "If you're pulling my leg, you won't have to worry about a bomb killing you."

"I'm not and I'm also being straight with you. I really don't know where Ted Jordan is or what happened at his home. Do your job and report the news. I'm just hoping you'll report it fairly."

Gayle took a deep breath and ran a hand through her hair. "I need a moment to think. You just dropped a real . . ." She caught herself before she could say, *bomb on me* and regrouped. "You know Thornton Schiff will crucify you. No one's better at it than he is. I liked what you said in court that day and I'll report whatever I find down the middle."

"That's all I'm asking, Gayle."

"Would you consider giving me an exclusive when you're ready?"

I replied, "Within the bounds of the judge's gag order."

"I promise I'll be fair with you and your client. Whatever the story is it is."

"Then I guess everything's fine."

She commented, "Yeah, for some of us."

FORTY-NINE

ORDON Bonham's Special Ops team responded quickly. They may not have set roadblocks up in fifteen minutes, as the chief ordered, but they weren't far behind it. As a result, we were stopped twice on our way out of town. Maury's ID got us through without a problem. It had been a long time since I'd ridden in an unmarked police car. The seats were worn and there was a vague tobacco smell mingled with air freshener. The car conjured up memories of a time gone by. It wasn't that I was nostalgic for the good old days. They weren't that good, but they were simpler.

Katherine's cell phone rang. She glanced at the caller ID, then handed it to me. It was Luther.

"Still have all of your body parts?" he asked.

"As far as I can tell. I'm with Katherine and Maury at the moment. My phone's out of commission."

"Why you think I'm calling you on this one? Nikko and I heard what happened. Is Katherine all right?"

"She's fine. She lost a purse and tore her suit."

There was a pause and some whispering in the background. "Nikko wants to know which one."

"Which one what?"

"Which purse she lose?"

I asked Katherine. "Nikko wants to know which purse was blown up."

"The Gucci knockoff we bought at Maureen's store yesterday," she said.

Another pause. "Nikko expresses his relief," Luther said. "He thought the leather lacked quality."

"Tell him not to be a fashion snob," Katherine called from the front seat.

"We're on our way home," I told them.

"Figured. We behind you."

I twisted around in my seat and saw Luther's Escalade about fifty feet back. He wiggled his fingers at me and I wiggled back. I didn't ask how he found us or had gotten past the roadblocks.

"Can you meet us at the house?" I said. "Our friends have just upped the ante. I don't want Katherine alone."

"Meanin' you goin' out someplace?" Luther said.

"I'm considering it."

"We'll meet you."

Maury, who was following the conversation, made eye contact with me in the rearview mirror and shook his head. "You have interesting friends, Professor."

I don't remember much about the ride. My mind was elsewhere. When I finally looked up I was surprised to find we were at the front gate.

Along the way, Katherine phoned her office and asked her paralegal to record Thornton Schiff's press conference. At least one of us was thinking like a lawyer. Ted's problems aside, I was having trouble dealing with a variety of emotions competing for my attention.

Katherine excused herself to change clothes. I was pretty grungy, too, but decided to wait. Maury, Luther, Nikko, and I went out to the patio. We were joined by Peeka, who went from person to person looking for a head scratch.

I took a seat near the fountain while Maury wandered the grounds looking at the flowers and shrubs. Luther settled into a chair and stretched out his long legs. Nikko selected the glider, took out a set of earbuds, and turned on his iPod. Peeka watched him for a moment, then jumped up next to him and stretched out. Nikko made a sour face, but gave in and petted him. Eventually Maury returned and took a seat next to Luther. He nodded. Luther nodded back. Maury then took out one of his Turkish cigarettes and lit it.

I commented, "Those things'll kill you."

Maury's eyebrows rose. He contemplated the cigarette's glowing end for a few seconds and took another puff.

"In the car you said, 'they upped the ante,'" he said. "You were referring to—"

"Britton and Coleman. Just before we went into the garage they had one of their guys pick a fight with me. Coleman stopped us on the street on the pretext of talking with Katherine about his brother's divorce."

"And the reason for that?" Maury asked.

"So Delaney go in and get his pale ass blown in the next county while they speakin' with Katherine," Luther said.

I glanced at Nikko, who raised his eyebrows twice for a response.

"That sounds reasonable," Maury said. "I take it you're aware of what happened at Mr. Jordan's townhome?"

Luther smiled at him.

Maury turned to me. "If you have any way of getting in touch with your client I'd do so as soon as possible. He would be much safer in police custody than on the streets."

"You don't believe he murdered Frank Nardelli?" I said. "The setup is so obvious it screams."

"Let's say my mind is open. Right now Mr. Jordan is only a suspect. His fleeing the scene doesn't look good, but there may have been reasons for it."

"He might just as well have signed his name on Nardelli's head," I commented.

"That's occurred to me," Maury said. "We won't know until we speak with him."

"Assuming the man still alive," Luther said.

"That also occurred to me," Maury said. He turned to me. "Have you had a chance to speak with Harry Eberhart yet?"

"Tomorrow."

"Be cautious around him, John."

"I will."

"What did you think of Ted's petition to exhume his mother's body?" Katherine asked. I hadn't heard her walk up. She was wearing jeans, a cream-colored sweater, and carrying a silver serving tray with drinks on it.

"Very strange," Maury said, taking a glass from her. He took a sip. "Schnapps?"

"Peppermint flavored," Katherine informed him.

"Ah . . . a lovely girl, this," he said to me.

Katherine smiled and handed Luther a glass of orange juice. A bottle of Heineken went to Nikko, who winked at her. My drink was scotch.

"To answer your question," Maury said to Katherine, "I don't know. I'm as baffled by Jordan's request as you are. With all the craziness going on I haven't had time to check further, but I'm sure one of you will."

"Delaney check everything," Luther said.

"I know," said Maury.

"I made something to eat," Katherine said. "Give me a moment."

All three of us watched her disappear through the kitchen door. Maury shook his head and turned back to me, his face serious.

"What happened earlier was no laughing matter," he said, lowering his voice. "I'd talked to both Britton and Coleman a few days ago. For all their smiles and good cheer I think they're dangerous men, Mr. Britton in particular. A bomber didn't just pick your car at random to blow up. Maybe it would be a good idea for Katherine to leave town for a while."

"You ever try to tell Katherine something?" Nikko asked, pulling out one of his earbuds.

Maury looked at me. "But you're her husband."

"That don't mean shit," Nikko said. He glanced at me and added, "Sorry. The lady's got a mind of her own. Don't no one tell her anything. You ought to know that. She was your lawyer, man."

Maury stared at Nikko for a moment and then at Luther, who raised his glass in a small toast. He shook his head and turned back to me. "If you and Katherine have children, I would love to meet them."

"Me, too," Luther said, laughing to himself.

"Double here," Nikko said.

"Can we discuss someone else?" I asked.

" 'Course not," Luther said. "This is too much fun."

The conversation changed as Katherine reappeared. She was

carrying a plate of sandwiches. Until I saw them I didn't realize how hungry I was. After Maury finished, he got up, kissed Katherine on the cheek, and informed us he had to get back to work. Before he left he turned to me and mouthed the words, "Talk to her."

FIFTY

Later that day, I placed a call to Harry Eberhart and his secretary answered. She informed me he was in a meeting. I wasn't sure about giving her the real reason for wanting to see him, so I asked a few questions about the type of security systems Delta Electronics installed and how well they worked. She assured me they had the latest models and best prices. I made an appointment for the following morning.

For the record, I did speak with my wife that night and I did suggest she go to Boca Raton for a few days to visit her parents. I'm too polite to repeat her response. Maybe she felt the need for revenge against whoever had destroyed her purse. More likely she wanted answers and wasn't about to let the matter go until she had them. I suspect standing by her man figured prominently in her decision.

Our plan was for Luther to accompany her to Decatur and see if she could look at the file on Charlotte Jordan. Charlotte had been killed at Stone Mountain, which was in their jurisdiction.

I tried calling Ted on his home phone a couple of times and got no answer. I really didn't expect one, but I left a message anyway. I was now certain we were onto something where Tissinger was concerned; Britton and Coleman were also connected, otherwise their intimidation and the car bomb made no sense. Neither did the murder of Frank Nardelli. The man was a buffoon, but no one deserved to die that way. If their goal was to silence Ted, they had just enlisted cops' help. It was just a matter of seeing who got to him first.

The lead stories that evening were about the second murder. Thornton Schiff, of course seized the opportunity and was riding the publicity crest for all it was worth. A call from his secretary informed me they were filing a motion to revoke Ted's bond the following the day. Wonderful. That meant I would lose my condo in New York if he didn't show up for trial. If Britton and the cops didn't shoot him, I was considering it.

BEFORE leaving for my appointment at Delta Electronic Systems, I stopped at a tattoo parlor in Sandy Springs. According to Maury, Eberhart was a card-carrying member of a Neo-Nazi group. The few inquiries Nikko had made indicated that all they did was sit around drinking beer and discussing the glory days of the Third Reich. Their goal was to purify America. They might just as well start with themselves. The fact that idiots like these could even exist in the twenty-first century amazed me nearly as much as their admiration for Adolf Hitler, who they thought was a misunderstood guy.

The gentleman who greeted me at Psycho Tattoos was a thirty-year-old hippie named Moon. He had enough artwork and piercings on his arms, legs, and face to qualify for a museum exhibit. I counted at least fifteen metal rings before losing track. He was probably a riot at the airport metal detectors.

When I said I wanted a small temporary swastika on my ankle, he informed me, "We don't get a lot of requests for those, dude. They're kind of uncool, if you know what I mean."

"I do and I'm not a fan. That's why I only want it temporarily."

"You mean like as a joke?"

"Right. How long will it last?"

"Oh, about a week . . . maybe a little less if you scrub real good. Are you sure you wouldn't like something more artistic, like Sumerian lettering? I've got some. Take a look at this."

Moon pulled down the collar of his T-shirt and pointed to an area below his collarbone. There, next to a Zen-like scene of a temple, were several letters, which I supposed were Sumerian.

Curiosity compelled me to ask, "What do they say?"

"No idea, but they definitely draw attention. I tried looking them up once, but there aren't a lot of Sumerian dictionaries around, you know? The Internet was no help either."

"That sucks," I agreed. "Give me a call if you ever find out."

"Oh, definitely, dude."

The total cost for my artwork was fifteen dollars and I was definitely billing Ted for it.

THE cell phone rang just after I got on the highway. It was Charlie Evans.

He asked, "How's the war going, son?"

"Not so good, Charlie."

"Why?"

"Well, Maureen's boyfriend was found murdered in Ted's apartment and my client's missing."

"*Jesus H. Christ!* Nardelli was murdered? I'm in Chicago on deposition. When did this happen?"

"Yesterday."

"Oh my God. I don't know what to say. Delaney, this is horrible."

"Sorry to break the news to you this way," I said. "When are you coming back?"

"Two days. I was just calling to see if you needed anything."

"A live client would be nice. Schiff is moving to revoke Ted's bond today, which means they'll seize my home if he doesn't show."

"I don't know what to say. Would you like me to call Thornton and speak with him?"

"I don't think it will do any good."

"Maybe, but it's worth a shot. Are you going to withdraw from the case?"

"I don't know, Charlie. Everything is up in the air right now. If I don't hear from Ted soon, I won't have a choice"

There was a long pause. "You're in a tough spot, son. If there's anything I can do to help, let me know."

"Thanks, Charlie."

"I did want to mention one thing to you. When we met you asked if any feds were involved in Ted's case. Before I left I saw two men in Ted Jordan's office. Bill Doster was there with them. I've noticed them around the firm a couple of times in the last few days, but I never thought anything about it.

"Anyway, I decided to ask what they were doing. One of them, a man named Coleman, said he was Tissinger's head of security. I don't remember his first name, but I checked and he's legit. The man with him was from the NSA. He told me they were trying to recover some sensitive research materials they thought were in Ted's office.

"I put a stop to it and asked them to leave. I wasn't real happy with Bill Doster for allowing them in and told him so. It was done behind my back. Just thought you should know."

I asked, "Have either of them been back?"

"Not that I know of. That Britton gave me the creeps. What are you up to?"

I informed him, "I'm on my way to interview one of the detectives originally assigned to Hamilton's case. There are a ton of holes in the investigation."

"Like what?"

"Remember when the newspapers announced the cops had found Ted's gun at Hamilton's house?"

"Of course," Charlie said.

"I can tell you for a fact, that gun didn't kill Sanford Hamilton. He was killed by a blow to the back of his head. We're working to identify the weapon now."

"That's great news."

"It may be a little soon to celebrate."

We spoke for about fifteen minutes longer and I told him about the arsenic victim in Miami and the two people who had gone over Buford Dam. I even mentioned the bee sting victim. Charlie listened thoughtfully.

When I was finished, he informed me, "Before I left I ran into Thornton Schiff at my club and we spoke a little. He's still not a fan of yours, but he's willing to waive the death penalty if Ted enters a plea. The problem is, he's stuck his neck out so far with the press that's about all he can do without getting himself crucified. Politicians have excellent survival skills."

"Exactly," I said.

"Delaney . . . do you think Ted's alive?"

"I don't know, Charlie. You'd think he would have contacted his lawyer by now."

Charlie blew out a long breath. "Good luck with the interview, son. Keep me informed."

FIFTY-ONE

DELTA Electronic Systems occupies a modern glass building in Dunwoody, one of Atlanta's many suburbs. It sits on a hill and overlooks I-285, or the "perimeter" as locals call it, a ninety-nine mile stretch of highway that circles the city. As many businesses are spread out along I-285 as there are in the city itself, making traffic uniformly horrible during rush hour. A block from my destination I spotted an AT&T store, pulled over, and picked up a new cell phone.

Harry Eberhart greeted me in Delta's lobby and led me to his conference room. He was a beefy kind of guy with an old fashioned crew cut that seemed out of place in the ultramodern environment.

"What business are you in, Mr. Delaney?"

"Education mostly. I teach at Emory."

He smiled. "We've done a lot of work out there. It's a fine school. What subject, may I ask?"

"Evidence and forensics, but I'm on leave of absence right now."

"I understand. How can Delta be of service to you?"

"Actually, I just wanted to talk with you."

Eberhart's smile faded slightly and a hint of wariness crept into his eyes. "How's that?"

"You were with the Atlanta PD before you came to work here, right?"

"Twenty-year man. I took early retirement. You meet a lot nicer people in this line of work. Exactly what type of security system are you interested in?"

I said, "I guess there's some misunderstanding. I'm here on behalf of my client, Ted Jordan. I was told you and your partner originally worked the case."

The smile was completely gone now. "Yeah, I thought you looked familiar when you came in. Listen, I don't have to talk to you, Delaney. And I don't appreciate you wasting my time. You got a lot of nerve coming here under false pretenses."

"I don't think I've said anything false, but if I gave you the wrong impression I apologize."

"You did. You handed my receptionist a line of bull about being interested in a security system."

"Like I said, I'm sorry. Would you have agreed to speak with me if I told you I was investigating the Jordan case?"

Eberhart's chest rose and fell while he considered what to do. Nobody likes someone checking over their shoulder. He leaned back in his seat and glared. I maintained eye contact with him because I had to. I'm good at that sort of thing.

"Probably not," he finally said with a shrug. "What do you want to know?"

"From what I could see in the report, you and your partner went over the house and grounds pretty thoroughly, right?"

"To the extent we could. The place was a goddamn mess after the fire."

"Did you check the pool area?"

"What for? The corpse was inside the study. He wasn't taking any walks," he said.

"Maybe to see if the killer left footprints on the grass or something like that."

"If he did, he would have been a freakin' magician. The door to the patio was locked from inside."

"Really?"

"Yeah, really. You think you're dealing with amateurs? I checked the door myself. The only way in or out of that study was through the front door. The basement had a dead bolt on it, so that was no good either."

"Are you aware they found Ted Jordan's gun out by the pool the other day?"

"I read it in the papers. That little prick, Maury Katz, called me and started asking the same questions you are. Fuckin' kike thinks he's so smart."

My stomach tightened at his use of the word "kike." It's a derogatory term used to describe Jews. I've heard it before and never liked it.

"You and Katz didn't get along?"

"Let's just say he can stay with his people and I'll stay with mine. It's just as well we run in different circles now." Eberhart leaned forward and dropped his voice. "I'll tell you this, a lot of guys on the force feel the same way, I do."

I nodded slowly and commented, "All Jews think they're smart. I used to work homicide with NYPD. We had a few like that."

I then made a show of crossing my ankles. As I did my pant leg rode up slightly exposing my new tattoo. Eberhart spotted it and gave me a knowing smile. There's nothing like two bigots having a friendly chat. In response, he pulled back his shirtsleeves. On the back of his wrists were two little H's. They stood for *Heil Hitler*. I'd seen gang members with this symbol years ago when I worked homicide.

"You got that right," he said. "Katz will get his one day. Count on it."

I winked at him and asked, "So what about the fingers?"

"What about them?"

"I'm curious how you found them at Jordan's home."

"Okay . . . we were coming up with nothing, see? Baxley and I interviewed everyone we could think of and no one had a damn thing against Hamilton. The guy was a war hero and everybody liked him. We found lots of fingerprints at his house and started running them down. Two of them belonged to your boy, so we set up an interview. Of course we didn't let him know about the prints. Jordan told us he couldn't remember ever having been to Hamilton's home.

"Baxley thought it was an oversight and we wrote it off, but out of the blue Jordan's name pops up again. We received a tip about Hamilton and him having a fight a few days before the murder."

"A tip?"

"Yeah, someone called in anonymously. We were never able to trace the caller down, but the voice belonged to a male in case you were about to ask."

I was. The part about the about the tip was in Maury's book, but no gender was indicated.

I said, "Thanks, Harry. This is really helpful."

My new friend continued, "The investigation started to roll after that. A few days later, the State Bar got in touch with our white collar crimes unit and said they received a report about money missing from the trust account at Jordan's law firm, so his name comes up for a third time. That was enough for us. We took a trip out to his house to talk with him, but he was out of town. His wife explained he was in France."

"Did you go there planning to arrest him?"

Eberhart was sharp enough to recognize a courtroom question when he heard one. If they had gone there with that purpose then a search warrant would have been necessary. He sidestepped it neatly.

"Not really, we only wanted to talk. According to the State Bar, the law firm said they were handling the matter privately. They only reported it because of lawyer ethics or some shit like that."

I nodded again.

"Anyway, the wife was home. She's quite a looker, by the way. You ever see her?"

"I have. You were telling me about the fingers."

"Right, right. I'm getting there. We explained we were investigating Hamilton's murder and she invited us in with no fuss. She even fixed us coffee—a real nice lady. So we're sitting around her kitchen schmoozing and looking at her tits until Baxley finally remembers why we were there and asks if her husband owned a gun. She told us he did, but didn't know where he kept it."

I inquired, "Didn't she think that was an odd question?"

"Maybe. Who the fuck cares? I mean, she wanted to know why we were asking. That's only natural. We gave her the line about eliminating suspects and she was fine with it. That really wasn't far from the truth. We had Jordan in our sights, but there wasn't anything to tie him to the crime directly.

"It was my idea to ask if we could look around the house and maybe help her find the gun. She gave her permission with no problem."

I commented, "That was a break. She's a lawyer's wife and she lets you search her home with no warrant."

Eberhart shrugged. "Less paperwork for us. Anyway, she took us into Jordan's office and told us to look the place over, so we did. Of course, it was clean. Then she took us through the other rooms one by one. Same result. Finally, we got to the basement and that's where we found them."

"How? Were they sitting out on a work bench or something?"

He ignored the question. "This," Eberhart said, tapping the side of his nose. "I noticed a funny odor as soon as we walked down the steps. They were stuck up on top of an air-conditioning return near the ceiling.

"I don't envy you, Delaney. This guy is bad news. He bashes the poor fucker's head in, shoots him, then burns the place down. I mean, Hamilton was a goddamn cripple. How fucked up does a person have to be to do something like that?"

I shook my head.

Eberhart asked, "Jordan . . . isn't that a yid name?"

"I don't know."

We talked for a while longer. After finding the fingers, Eberhart and his partner finally decided it was time to get a search warrant. Why, I didn't know, since there weren't any other missing body parts, but search warrants always looks good in court. He said nothing about looking for whatever was used to sever Sanford Hamilton's fingers. This was an important point. According to the ME the skin around the wounds was pushed inward in a uniform manner. Knives don't do that. It was another fact lost in the shuffle. They had motive and hard evidence to tie Ted Jordan to the crime scene. End of story. Almost.

I thanked Harry Eberhart for his time and left.

When I got to the lobby I phoned Katherine's secretary to ask a favor.

"Galena, would you punch up the Secretary of State records and see who owns a company called Delta Electronics?"

"Sure. Give me a second. Here we go. It's a limited liability company out of Delaware called Sky City Investment Corporation." Fifteen minutes of digging and six state databases later revealed what I wanted to know. Approximately a year earlier an attorney in Alaska had formed a company called Areva Investment Group. Their registered agent was a gentleman in New York named Laurent Malliard. Also no big deal, except Mr. Malliard's address was listed as: Tissinger Corporation, Legal Department, 1683 Third Avenue, New York, New York.

FIFTY-TWO

On my way to the car, my thoughts turned to Messers Coleman and Britton. I half-expected them to find them waiting for me. They weren't. My next call was to Mike Franklin, my former partner. Mike had been with NYPD's anti-terrorism task force since 9/11 and it wasn't uncommon for them to work with the feds. This usually meant they did the footwork and the feds took the credit. He answered his phone on the first ring.

"Delaney? How the hell are you, buddy? It's been a while."

"Too long. How are you?"

"I'm all right. How's your better half?"

"Great. Where are you?" I asked. There was a lot of noise in the background.

"I'm at One Hung Low's. It's lunchtime—gimme a second."

One Hung Low is a hole-in-the-wall on Mott Street in New York's Chinatown. Mostly cops and locals eat there. The real name is *Wan Lo*, but at some point in the past it acquired its nickname. Mr. Lo writes the daily menu on a chalkboard he places near the front door and the food is whatever Mrs. Lo decides to cook that day. The place has no tablecloths and all the napkins are paper. At most, it holds thirty-five people. If they're in danger of exceeding that number Wan Lo will push you back out the door and say, "No room, no room. You come back later." The man is all about marketing.

Mike said, "Okay, I'm outside now. What's up?"

"You ever run into a fed named Brad Britton?"

"Britton . . . Britton," he repeated. "Let me think . . . yeah, he's with the NTSB. I met him about a year ago. We were keeping an eye on some rag-heads over in Rego Park who were up to no good."

I described Britton for him. "Early forties, about my height, light blond hair, slender. Reminds you of a tennis pro."

"Yeah, that's the guy. When did you run into him?"

"A couple of times over the last few days, except his ID says he works for the NSA not the NTSB. Is there any way of checking him out?"

Mike was silent for a few moments. "Maybe. What's the story?"

"I'm handling a murder case involving a friend of mine. Britton and his partner, a guy named Stan Coleman, have been trying hard to push me off it. By the sheerest coincidence someone blew up Mr. Jag the other day."

"*Holy shit.* You must be pissed. You loved that car. Are you all right?"

"Fine," I said. "Just offended."

"What do the feds want with a murder case? Your guy kill a congressman or something?"

"Good question, Mike." I related Britton's story about the government and Tissinger having common interests.

My former partner put his opinion succinctly. "Sounds like a crock of shit. You think you're dealing with spooks?"

"That would be my guess."

"Then you'd better watch your ass. Those guys don't fuck around."

"Yeah, someone else told me the same thing a few days ago."

"It's good advice. I'll start checking. How fast do you need this?"

"Yesterday."

"Figures. Hey, when are you coming up to New York? I'm dating this little stripper who works at Flashers. She's got all kinds of cute friends. We'll have a couple of brews and some laughs."

"I don't know right now . . . maybe after the holidays. I'll keep the strippers in mind if things don't work out with Katherine."

His last words were, "Good point. Watch your back."

FIFTY-THREE

I CALLED Katherine and was surprised when Luther answered her phone. "The Missus is inside talking to some police officer right now," he said.

"Where are you?"

"Outside, waiting on her. She been in there about an hour."

I told Luther about my conversation with Eberhart.

"Spoke with two cop friends I know," he said. "They didn't think much of him."

"How's K.J. holding up?" I asked.

"We bonding. That's a strong lady you got."

"You don't know the half of it," I said.

"Yes, I do."

He was probably right. "Any sign of the feds?" I asked.

"Not so I can see. I asked Nikko to join us. Two pair of eyes are better than one. He didn't go in neither."

"I would be surprised if he did," I said.

"Nikko don't like cops."

"Who does he like?" I said.

"Maybe you and me . . . definitely Katherine, and now that little Asian girl he's dating."

"Asian girl? You mean Tikumi's daughter?"

"One and the same," Luther said.

I tried to picture Nikko on a date with anyone and couldn't. I gave up after a moment. "Guess there's no accounting for personal taste."

"That's what people say about us, but I still your friend. What you up to now?"

"I'm going to touch base with Rena Bailey and Phil Thurman and bring them up to speed on what we've found, then I'll interview

Hamilton's housekeeper and cook. Both were supposed to be working the night he was killed."

"They weren't?" Luther said.

"No, both were off."

"Interesting coincidence. We don't like coincidences, do we?"

"No we don't."

I REACHED Rena Bailey at her office and told her I thought we should meet. She agreed right away, but never asked my reason. She suggested I drop by her home for dinner.

"Won't the neighbors talk?"

She replied, "I hope so. My husband's out of town. It'll make him jealous."

"Okay. What time and where?"

"How about six-thirty? My address is 441 Lakeview Close in Roswell."

"Sounds good."

"Do you need directions?"

Obviously she didn't know that real men never ask for directions. I told her I would find it.

"Is barbecue okay?"

"Wonderful. What can I bring?"

"Just yourself and those questions you've been saving up. Phil Thurman will also be here."

Now that *was* interesting. "See you later."

On the way to her home my sense of etiquette got the better of me and I stopped at a shopping center to pick something up. Katherine always gets on me about forgetting to do so. I knew Rena was pregnant so wine was out. My first wife once explained that when a woman is pregnant all they really want is for someone to massage their feet. That was a possibility, but suggesting a foot massage to opposing counsel might set the Canons of Legal Ethics back a hundred years. Even well-intentioned bribes are frowned upon in most circles. This rule did not however apply to the unborn.

I wandered around the local Target store for fifteen minutes trying to remember what babies liked, other than clean diapers and interesting mobiles. It had been a long time since I had bought anything for a child. Then I passed the lava lamps and a bulb went off, so to speak.

My son had one in his room when he was young and eventually took it with him to Penn State. I still thought they were kind of cool . . . dated maybe, but cool. I picked out a purple one along with a copy of *Green Eggs and Ham* by Dr. Seuss and proceeded to the checkout. You can never go wrong with Sam-I-am.

TURNS out real men should have asked for directions. In my haste, I had scrawled Rena's address down as 441 Lakeview, Roswell. There were at least ten streets that started with the name Lakeview. I tried Lakeview Court, Lakeview Road, Lakeview Trace, and Lakeview Circle with no luck. I was almost ready to give up and call Rena when a flash of insight struck. Reasoning that a house on Lakeview might actually be near a lake, I stopped a lady walking her dog and asked for help. She told me there was a small lake not too far from where we were. John Delaney, detective extraordinaire.

Katherine and I spoke and I explained I couldn't make dinner because of my appointment with Rena Bailey. She was fine with it, but thought meeting at Rena's house was a little odd. I promised to be home early. In return she promised to tell me what she had found at the police station.

FIFTY-FOUR

Rena came to the door wearing a loose-fitting housedress. Her hair was down around her shoulders, different from the way she had worn it in court. I noticed she had added a touch of makeup. There was a second car in the driveway which I assumed was Phil Thurman's.

"I was beginning to worry," she said. "Did you have trouble finding me?"

"Piece of cake. There was a lot of traffic. These are for Junior," I said, handing her the gifts. Her face broke into a smile.

"*Green Eggs and Ham*! I love this book! Thank you, John. That was very thoughtful. What's in the box?"

"A lava lamp."

"A what?"

"A lava lamp."

"What does it do?"

I shrugged. "Not much. It just makes interesting shapes that go up and down. Children really like it."

She gave me a funny look. Obviously, Rena was from a different generation.

"How nice. Why don't we go out on the patio? Phil's already here. I've got chicken on the grill. Do you like chicken?"

"Love it."

"There's beer in the fridge, unless you want ice tea. I'm on the wagon," she added, patting her stomach.

The house was contemporary with high ceilings. The furniture was also modern. There were abstract pieces of art scattered around the living room and in the hallway. Most of them looked a bit bizarre. In the corner of the breakfast room was an object that appeared to be

part chair and part guitar. There was a sign on it that said DON T SIT
ON ME.

"That belongs to Brian," Rena explained.

"It's, uh . . . different."

She looked at the piece for a moment and shook her head. "He
collects this stuff. It's too bad you can't meet him. He's attending a
medical conference in Houston at the moment."

"What kind of doctor is Brian?"

"He's a butt doctor."

"I beg your pardon?"

"A proctologist."

My eyes widened slightly.

"Someone's got to do it," Rena said, a little indignantly.

"Of course."

Personally, I've never understood what might possess a person
to go into that field. I mean, do they line the students up in medical school and show them a chart of the human body? *Say, that's
where I want to be.* If they learn by doing, I would have skipped class
that day.

Rena's patio looked out over a well-manicured lawn and swimming pool. The outdoor furniture had a matching umbrella and the
largest grill I'd ever seen. Apparently, proctology was looking up . . .
if you'll pardon the expression. Phil Thurman was seated in a
lounge chair drinking beer from a bottle. He waved when he saw us.

"Expecting more company?" I asked, noticing there was a fourth
place setting on the table.

"I've asked a friend to join us. I hope you don't mind. He should
be here shortly." She lifted the lid of the grill and used a wooden
spoon to taste whatever was simmering in a pot. "Hmm . . . a little
more salt I think."

It was becoming obvious a number of people had more information about the case than I did. I conjectured Rena's mystery guest
was probably one of them. We'd see. For the moment, all I could do
was to wait and find out how the scenario played out. If she wanted
to keep things close, that was fine. Ted's situation reminded me of
an iceberg. There was more below the surface than above it.

My observation was based partly on intuition and partly on how quickly Rena had accepted my suggestion that we meet. Defense lawyers and prosecutors get together all the time to negotiate settlements and exchange documents. She hadn't been surprised by my call. She simply agreed and deflected the meeting away from her office. What all of this added up to, I didn't know—something.

While she was stirring the pot, I asked. "Do you have a personal interest in the Jordan case?"

"I'm the prosecutor John, remember? We met at the court."

"Yeah, I recall . . . you were pregnant."

She glanced at me over her shoulder, then turned her attention to a chicken that was slowly rotating on a spit, basting it a few times with a brush.

She continued, "Justice and truth always interest me. Isn't that enough?"

"Try again."

"Okay. Are you having problems with the case?" she asked.

"Apart from getting blown up, you mean?"

"I heard. I'm sorry about that. Is Katherine all right?"

"She's fine. I'm confused about two gentlemen who have been nosing around. One of whom is supposed to be with the NSA."

"You mean the Bobbsey Twins?"

"Excuse me?"

"That's what we call them around the office. You're talking about Britton and Coleman, right?"

"They told me the U.S. government is interested in how I plan to defend Ted Jordan."

"That would be accurate," a voice in the doorway said.

I turned to see a man in his late fifties standing there. Rena left the chicken to fend for itself and went over to give him a hug.

"John Delaney . . . this is Sam Talmadge," she said.

"Senator Talmadge?" I asked, shaking his hand.

"In the flesh," he replied. "Good to meet you, Mr. Delaney. I enjoyed your impromptu news conference at the court last week. It was very creative."

"Delaney's always creative," Phil Thurman said, coming over to join us. He handed the senator a bottle of beer. There was one for me as well.

I said, "I wasn't trying to be. Which conference were you referring to?"

"Actually, both. I thought the second one might have been prompted because the judge ordered you to apologize. Am I right?"

"That he did."

Talmadge commented, "McKenzie runs a tight ship. I was in front of him twenty-five years ago and he nearly tore my head off. It was a contract case and opposing counsel wanted to put my client in jail for not paying. I stood up and announced we don't do that in the United States. Pretty obvious, right? To my surprise McKenzie asked if I had any cases to support my point. When I said I didn't, he lit into me in front of about a hundred people and told me not to appear in his court again in such an abysmal state of ignorance.

"I took his advice and went into politics."

I suppressed a smile, recalling my encounter with the judge. The senator was an easy fellow to like, but then so are most politicians.

He continued, "I'm trying to remember exactly what you said at the second press conference."

I started to answer, but Rena did it for me. "His apology consisted of 'I regret the incident occurred.' Thornton went ballistic and started yelling that John was a lying son-of-a-bitch and his statement didn't constitute an apology."

"Right, right. That was it. Hey, something smells good," Talmadge said to Rena. "What's for dinner?"

She led him over to the grill to see. Thurman and I looked at each other.

"And you're here for what?" I asked.

"Dinner and to learn about the world," Thurman said. "This should be interesting."

The senior senator from Georgia was dressed in a green Izod golf shirt, a sport jacket, dark slacks, and loafers. Sam Talmadge was in either his fourth or fifth term and had been around the political scene for quite a while. He was extremely popular with the voters. His last two elections hadn't even been close. I also recalled he was the ranking member of the Senate Foreign Relations Committee. A bit more of the iceberg poked its head above the surface.

The evening was pleasant and Rena was more than competent as a cook. Our conversation at the table remained innocuous and centered on everything but Ted Jordan's case. We had just started on our desserts when it dawned on me they were waiting for me to broach the subject.

I said, "Senator, you're one of the last people I expected to meet tonight. A little earlier you asked me about the Jordan case; does your office have some interest in it?"

Talmadge answered through a mouthful of cake, "I don't know about my office, John, but I do."

"And why is that?"

"I just hate losing one of my voters."

I smiled politely at his joke. "Is your interest official or personal?"

Talmadge put down his fork and took a sip of coffee before answering. "It's hard to separate the two, John . . . at least where I'm concerned. Senator Benson and I were discussing the same thing just last week."

"Before you arrived, I was telling Rena about two individuals who keep popping up in my investigation. One is a fellow named Britton who claims to be with the NSA. He's working with a man named Stan Coleman, who's Tissinger's head of security. They're both concerned I'll try and pull the company into a scandal."

Talmadge and Rena exchanged looks. Thurman leaned back in his seat.

"Very interesting," said Talmadge. "How would you accomplish that?"

"By alleging Tissinger is attempting to frame my client for murder."

Talmadge asked, "Do you have some proof they are?"

"I haven't completed my work yet, but let's say a number of facts are pointing in that direction."

"Did you share this with them?"

"Not in so many words."

"What exactly you did say?"

"I told them to fuck off. Excuse me, Rena," I added to her.

The senator chuckled. "I assume they were less than thrilled."

"That's one way to put it."

Talmadge went silent for a few seconds. It appeared he was searching for the right words. "Are you aware that Tissinger contributed heavily to the president's last election campaign?"

"Not really."

"Well, they did. They've also contributed heavily to the campaigns of a number of senators and congressmen. What I'm saying, John, is that Tissinger is a player in Washington, a very powerful player. Its interests reach into a great many areas.

"If you think back to high school political science, every senator is required by our house rules to serve on a number of different committees. That's where most legislative problems are hammered out before they're passed along to a joint committee made up of members from both the Senate and the House of Representatives.

"Some time ago, a bill came before Foreign Relations to cut the U.S. funding on a drug testing program Tissinger has been conducting in third world countries."

"Muslim countries?"

Talmadge's smile was tight-lipped. "It might not be obvious to the general public, but in view of our present economic situation, my colleagues and I have been trying to tighten our belts. When the bill came before us, I thought it was a pretty good idea. That's when the phone started ringing."

I asked, "Who was calling?"

"Different people. The names aren't relevant. Suffice to say, members of my own party and the administration wanted the bill defeated. That sort of thing happens all the time in Washington.

"One of the more interesting calls I got was from Jacque Flamont, the French ambassador. He invited me to dinner at his residence. It's a lovely place. Have you ever been there?"

"All the time. We're having brunch on Sunday."

Talmadge opened his mouth and closed it again. "Sorry. At any rate, when we met he put on a full-court press. Not only does our government want the bill quashed, he made it clear the government of France is equally intent on defeating it."

"I assume you asked him why . . . being a senator and all."

"I did. But his story about mutual cooperation between our countries and the greater welfare was a bunch of crap. I may have been born at night, but it wasn't last night. In other words, I know when I'm being played. Eventually, my own party started putting pressure on me."

"So what happened to the bill?"

He answered, "It's buried in subcommittee. As chairman, I can keep it there for the time being, but not forever. Sooner or later, it will come up again. In the last week the pressure from the Administration has increased."

"Why don't you just go to the newspapers and tell them what's happening?"

"Because I'm a loyal American. My goal isn't to embarrass the president because I think something might not be kosher. There's also the matter of an oath I took. There may be perfectly legitimate reasons why he doesn't want Tissinger's program killed. Personally, I'd like to know what those reasons are before I make a decision."

"So what am I supposed to do?"

"You, my dear Professor, are supposed to find out those reasons."

FIFTY-FIVE

I SAT back in my chair and considered Samuel L. Talmadge. Over the years I'd interviewed hundreds of witnesses, suspects, and clients. Sooner or later you get a sense of who's pulling your chain and who isn't. I didn't think he was.

I said, "Maybe I'll call the White House and ask them directly."

Talmadge smiled. "That might not be very practical."

"It's at least as practical as what you're suggesting. If *you* can't find out what's going on, how am I supposed to? You're a United States senator."

Rena offered, "From what I've heard from Maury and Phil, you're off to a good start."

"I'm glad you think so. I could use a little help in that department now that you mention it."

Rena remained silent. So did Talmadge. Phil Thurman merely stared back at me. There was a message beneath the surface. I just wasn't seeing it.

Talmadge informed me, "Washington's particularly lovely this time of year. If you get up my way, stop in and say hello." Then he turned to Rena. "My dear that was an elegant dinner. I've got to be running."

The senator got up from the table, stretched, and glanced at the lava lamp that was just now beginning to bubble.

"I love those things," he said. "Had one just like it when I was a kid."

I spent the next ten minutes telling Thurman what I learned in Miami, and about Coleman and company showing up just before the bombing.

"Sounds like he was trying to keep Ms. Adams from going inside," he said.

"That was my take."

"And you've heard nothing from your client since then?"

I shook my head slowly.

"You're in a tough spot, Professor," he said. "You think Ted Jordan's still alive or just running?"

"I don't know. If he is he would have contacted me by now."

Thurman patted me on the shoulder. "Let's stay in touch."

After we were alone Rena began tidying up. I brought the dishes and remaining food inside. Neither of us spoke for a time.

I finally asked her, "What did you mean before, when you said I was off to a good start?"

"There are some things you'll have to figure out for yourself. That's all I can say."

"Marvelous."

"You remember Sam mentioning that oath he took? Well, he's not the only one. If I ever find myself on a polygraph or testifying in front of a subcommittee, I'd like to answer all the questions truthfully, understand? Officially, I've told you nothing."

I nodded. "Any suggestions would be welcome." I was curious as to how far she was willing to go.

She shook her head. "Not really. You might take the senator up on his invitation though. My husband and I visited the National Archives on our last trip. It's a fascinating place. In fact—"

Rena's expression suddenly changed.

"Is something wrong?" I asked.

"The baby just moved."

"Oh . . . uh, that's great, I—"

"Quick, give me your hand."

Without waiting for a reply, Rena took my hand and placed it on her stomach. Women love doing this. Nothing happened. After several seconds standing there with my hand on an assistant district attorney's stomach, I began to feel awkward.

Then I felt it.

When something under her blouse moved, I pulled my hand away in surprise. By rights, I should have told her how amazing it was, but I'm not good at that sort of thing. To be perfectly blunt, it reminded me of *Alien*, where the creature bursts out of the man's chest and starts killing people.

"What's the matter?" Rena asked.

"Nothing. It just startled me. Have you, ah . . . picked out a name yet?"

I kept one eye on her stomach in case whatever was in there decided to make a break for it.

"We're still working on the names—just like you are, John. I hope you enjoyed dinner."

FIFTY-SIX

My cell phone chirped as I was pulling out of Rena's neighbor-hood. Mike Franklin had left a message asking me to call him.

"What's up, Mike?"

"Who is this?" he practically shouted.

"It's Delaney. Jesus, where are you?" There was so much music and background noise I was having trouble hearing him.

"At Bridgett's strip club. Hang on a sec."

It took a minute for the noise level to drop. "Okay, I'm in the can now. You should see the broads here. They're having amateur night."

"Really?"

"You remember Barbara Scapperelli from over in burglary?"

"Sure."

"We were always wondering if her boobs were real or not."

"Barbara's there? She's got to be at least fifty."

"Not her—her daughter, Diane. She's doing an internship with us this summer. Buddy, I'm here to tell you if there's anything to ge-netics, big boobs definitely run in that family."

The thought that Barbara Scapperelli had a daughter old enough to dance at a strip club was depressing. I changed the topic. "Any luck on what we talked about?"

"A little. The story on this guy Britton is he recently transferred to New York from Dallas, like he said. The problem is when he was there he was supposedly with the ATF. Of course he told me he was NTSB."

"Gets around, doesn't he?"

"Seems to. This comes from Dave Sturkey. Dave was working with the feds keeping watch on a terrorist cell. The bad guys were supposedly targeting the Dallas water supply and someone here in the metro area was funneling money to them. Anyway, Dave said he worked with Britton for six months and described the guy as squirrelly. I don't even know if you can use that word anymore, but that's what he said."

"Did he mention anything about Britton having a partner?"

"No, but there was another guy on their team who fit the description you gave me. But he was with Interpol, not Tissinger security."

I asked, "Did you get a name?"

"This is me, remember? The Interpol guy's name was LeDoux. According to Dave, he was only around for a short time and disappeared after they shut down the cell. He tried locating him to sign off on their final report but ran into a dead end. Britton transferred out later and also dropped off the radar. If this is the same pair, something's definitely not right here."

"I agree."

"Out of curiosity, I called a couple of friends with the Bureau and dug a little deeper. Same result. Officially these guys don't exist. Sounds to me like you're dealing with a couple of spooks."

Mike might be rough around the edges, but he was a good detective and didn't miss much.

"Any chance of a photo?"

"You mean like from a security badge they might have used?"

I smiled. "Yeah, just like that."

"Sent it to you a few hours ago. Check your e-mail."

FIFTY-SEVEN

I ARRIVED home around nine o'clock and Katherine met me at the front door wearing a see-through negligee and holding a scotch. That didn't happen. Actually, I let myself in and she was in a jogging suit.

"How did your meetings go?" she asked.

"Not bad. It was an odd sort of day."

"How so?"

I told her about my dinner with Rena Bailey, Thurman, and Senator Talmadge.

"Sam Talmadge wants us to go to Washington and look in the National Archives?"

"That part came from Rena and she was referring to my going there," I said.

Katherine was quiet for a while as she digested my last statement. We sat on the couch and she put her feet in my lap.

"Am I your partner?" she finally asked.

"Of course."

"Just some of the time?"

I knew where this was heading. "K.J., you're my partner in everything. But I can't risk losing you or you getting hurt. We're dealing with some very bad people. This isn't a game."

"I'm aware of that."

"Then you know why it's best that you to stay here. Luther and Nikko can protect you."

"And who's watching out for you?"

"I'll be fine. If Britton and Coleman get their hands on you, they can use you as leverage against me. We almost have enough information to put a conspiracy defense in front of a jury now."

Katherine withdrew her feet and sat up. "Have you considered the possibility there won't be a case?"

I nodded slowly.

Katherine continued. "Luther and I spoke about it earlier and he thinks Ted isn't just running. There a good chance he's dead."

"Luther is a bright fellow."

"Then wouldn't it be smart to let the police take over? I don't want to lose you, either."

"Possibly."

"But you won't."

"K.J.—"

"Delaney gonna feel like the man died on his watch," Katherine said, doing a reasonable imitation of Luther's voice.

I opened my mouth to reply, then closed it again.

She continued, "He speak for the dead. It's hard to explain. Don't make no difference whether it's the mama or the son . . . or a person in some county he don't even know that killed himself cause of a bad drug. . . ."

"Is that about right?" Katherine asked me.

"I need a drink."

"I'll get it. Scotch?"

"That would be great."

"Ice?"

"Straight."

Katherine crossed the room to our liquor cabinet and took out a bottle of Macallans 12, then broke her own rule by pouring me a healthy triple instead of a double. "You and Luther have known each other a long time," she said.

"Yes."

"As long as you and Ted?"

"Not quite, but long enough."

"And you won't let this go, will you?"

"I can't, K.J."

"Until the scales are balanced," she said.

"Something like that. Did you learn anything at the police station?"

Katherine sat again and returned her feet to my lap. Peeka appeared and jumped up on the couch, wedging himself into the space

between the back cushion and her legs. I received a slight protest in
cat language when I didn't pet him. I raised my eyebrows, inviting
my wife to continue.

"We have an appointment tomorrow afternoon with Jackie Cyzck."

"Who?"

"The detective assigned to Charlotte Jordan's case," Katherine
said.

"What kind of name is that—Cyzck?"

"Uh . . . Polish, I think," Katherine said.

"How do you spell it?"

"C-Y-Z-C-K. You'll like her. She was really helpful."

"Sounds like someone needs to buy her a vowel."

"Be nice."

"I'm always nice. Why are we going to see her?"

"Because Charlotte Jordan wasn't raped. Murdered, yes . . . but
not raped. According to Jackie, it was staged."

"*What?*" I said, nearly spilling my drink on Peeka.

Katherine informed me, "That's what they believe now. The State
Crime Lab recently got a cold hit on semen stains taken from the
crime scene and matched them to someone named Hector Grace. "I
don't understand it either. That's why we're going to see her."

It was turning out to be a red-letter day. Before turning in for the
night, I checked my e-mail. There were two messages waiting for
me: One was from Mike. The photo of Charles LeDoux was the
same man I knew as Stan Coleman. The other was from Maury Katz
telling me a few hours earlier a boater at Lake Lanier had fished a
man's wallet out of the water belonging to Ted Jordan. The police
were sending divers down in the morning to search for his body.

FIFTY-EIGHT

I DIDN'T sleep much that night. An early shower helped. At 7:00 A.M. Nikko and Luther showed up to take Katherine to her office. I told them about LeDoux and Ted's wallet. Nikko shrugged and poured himself a cup of coffee from a carafe on the kitchen counter. Luther had a bottle of water with him. He listened thoughtfully, then took a sip.

I turned on the radio to see if there was any news from Lake Lanier about the search. My plan that day was to interview Sanford Hamilton's cook and housekeeper, then meet Katherine at the police station. According to Maury's file they both worked in Cabbagetown. After saying good-bye to everyone, I went to get dressed.

I picked out a pair of jeans, a black T-shirt, and a herringbone sport jacket. I hadn't carried a gun in a long time, but it was time for an exception. My Bersa .380 was in my sock drawer. The Bersa is a short 9mm that resembles a Walther PPK, the gun James Bond used to carry. It works just as well and costs half as much. I briefly considered wearing it on my ankle where it would be less conspicuous, but went with a hip holster instead. Speed can mean the difference in life or death situations. If nothing else it would provide peace of mind.

To my surprise, Luther was waiting for me when I walked out the front door.

"What are you doing here?" I asked.

"Your orders been countermanded by higher authority."

"Really?"

"Katherine said for me to stay with you today."

"Goddamnit," I said, taking my cell phone out.

"Won't do no good," Luther said. "She shut hers off when she left. Won't take your call at the office neither."

"Why didn't you come and get me?"

"Like I said, orders come from a higher authority. She'll be fine with Nikko."

I gave him a sour look and got in the passenger side of his Escalade. It was an overcast gray morning with light rain. The windshield wipers beat steadily on the glass. As we drove, images of a tiny Bronx garden drifted into my mind. Growing up, I was at the Jordan home almost as much as my own. It's funny how the mind works. For some reason I thought of the roses Charlotte Jordan used to grow in her backyard, no small feat in the midst of a concrete landscape. Even now I could remember their smell. They were heavy, ponderous things she would cut and bring into the house. As boys, Ted and I spent a lot of time in her garden lying on our backs, looking up at the night sky and the constellations. We caught fireflies and put them in glass jars.

My memories of Charlotte Jordan were equally vivid. She was a beautiful woman with a kind heart and a gentle soul. She had moved to Atlanta to be near her sister after her husband died. The day she was killed she had been walking one of the nature trails at Stone Mountain Park when a mugger decided to single her out. According to the police, Charlotte was raped then shot to death. She was working for Charles Evans' firm at the time. If Katherine was right about the rape being staged, history was about to change.

Ted's bizarre request to exhume his mother's body made sense now. It was clear he knew about the DNA hit, though what he expected to prove I didn't know. Luther agreed. Whenever I worked a case in the past, a small adrenaline drip would start in my stomach as it neared a breaking point. That was how I was feeling. But until we spoke to the police all we could do was speculate.

On the seat beside me was my copy of Maury's file. Sanford Hamilton's cook was a man named Reggie Washington. He was now working at a restaurant called Elizabeth's Drawing Room. Elizabeth's is a noisy place with white vinyl tablecloths. It's been at the same location for a half-century. My one and only visit had been years earlier. The food is decent, especially if you're into Southern cooking. I'm not. I've never been able to develop a taste for collard greens, grits, or redeye gravy. Give me a good old-fashioned steak any day of the week.

Maury had included in the file a photo of Washington from his driver's license. It was less than three years old.

Luther took Boulevard Avenue east, passed over a set of railroad tracks, and made a sharp turn onto Carroll Street. We found a parking spot near the entrance to Oakland Cemetery, where Bobby Jones and Margaret Mitchell are buried.

A few young mothers were out pushing baby strollers. According to a lady friend who teaches with me at Emory, one circuit around the cemetery is a great workout if you're into jogging. I decided to take her word for it.

CABBAGETOWN had changed since my last visit. It was no longer an inner-city slum. Those derelict homes the federal government had been selling for one dollar all had undergone substantial renovations. Many now had neat front yards and flower boxes under the windows.

Elizabeth's, on the other hand, hadn't changed at all. The white vinyl tablecloths were still there, as were the waitresses with beehive hairdos. A hostess at the door seated us.

"Do you have a man working here named Reggie?" I asked.

"Sure. He came on a little while ago. You want me to send him out?"

"That would be great."

I noticed she didn't ask who I was or why I wanted to see him. Cabbagetown may have been a neighborhood in transition, but the unwritten rules still applied: Keep to your own business. She handed us menus and disappeared through a set of double doors lending to the kitchen.

Reggie came out a moment later, wiping his hands on a white towel. There was no sign of apprehension on his face. He was a black man, between sixty and sixty-five, whose hair was thinning. It looked like he enjoyed being a chef, because he probably weighed close to three hundred pounds. He was wearing black cotton pants and a typical white chef's jacket.

"Lila said you wanted to see me."

I got up and held out my hand. "My name's John Delaney. This is Luther Campbell. I represent a man named Theodore Jordan and I was wondering if I could ask you a few questions."

Reggie hesitated before taking my hand. "This is about Mr. Hamilton's murder, right?"

"Yes, it is."

"And your man's the one who's supposed to have killed him?"

"That's also true, except he didn't do it."

The skin around Reggie's eyes tightened. "The police said I don't have to talk to you."

"No, you don't. When did they tell you that?"

"Yesterday afternoon. They come in here and called me out of the kitchen just like you done."

"Did they leave a business card?"

"Didn't catch no names and they didn't leave no cards either."

"You said 'they,' Mr. Washington. I take it there was more than one?"

"Yes, sir. There was two of them that stopped by. They didn't have no uniforms; they was dressed in suits."

"Could you could describe them for me?"

Reggie's brows came together and he rubbed his cheek. "Well, they was both about the same height and slim-like. One of them had blond curly hair . . . good-looking boy with real white teeth. He smiled a lot and did most of the talking. Reminded me of a car salesman. His partner was bald like, uh . . ."

"Michael Jordan?" I prompted.

"Yeah, like Michael."

I nodded. "I think I know who you're talking about. Did they say why you shouldn't speak with me?"

Reggie frowned again. "They was afraid you was going to mess up their investigation."

"Is that so?"

"Yes it is. Now it occurred to me that was a strange thing to say, 'cause after they arrested your man I figured the investigation was pretty much over. What do you think?"

"I think some people get ideas into their heads and don't want to be confused by the facts, Mr. Washington. The truth is you're under no obligation to talk to me, but it might save the life of an innocent man."

Reggie nodded slowly in what I thought was agreement. "That's what they said you'd say. Let me ask you a question, counselor, straight out-like. Did Jordan kill Mr. Hamilton?"

I looked him straight in the eye when I answered. "No, he didn't. I've known Ted Jordan since we were boys. If I thought he did it, I wouldn't be here now, friend or no friend, and that's the truth. The men you saw weren't with the Atlanta Police. I'm not sure who they work for; a branch of the government I suspect, but they're definitely not Atlanta PD."

"Is that a fact?" Reggie said, leaning backward in his seat. I could hear the chair creak under his weight.

"Yes, it is."

A long moment passed while he considered what I was saying. "You know who did kill Mr. Hamilton?"

"Not yet. But I'm getting close. There are people involved in this case who want me to stop asking questions. I think you met two of them yesterday."

"How about you?" Reggie asked, turning to Luther. "I seen you in here a few times. You don't play ball no more?"

"Not for ten years," Luther said. "And I don't know who killed Hamilton neither. But for what it's worth I don't believe it was Jordan. Mighta been, but I don't think so."

"You were with the Jets and then Detroit," Reggie said.

"That's right."

"You a lawyer, too?" Reggie asked.

Luther stuck his lower lip out. "Coulda been a lawyer. Didn't want to. I'm just here to help Delaney. The boy can't go anywhere without his car being blown up."

Reggie folded his hands across his stomach and looked at Luther, then at me.

He said, "We saw that on the news the other day. Looked like one hell of a mess." He motioned to a television mounted on the wall in a corner of the restaurant. "You gentlemen want something to eat? I got some chicken and biscuits that are out of this world. Picked up fresh vegetables at the farmer's market, too, before I came in work today."

I told him, "I could do with a bite, but hold off on the collard greens, okay?"

A chuckle rippled through Reggie's body. "Haven't met a white boy yet partial to collards," he said. "The problem is y'all don't know how to cook 'em right. What about you?" he asked Luther.

Luther smiled, "Just a plate of vegetables be fine. Thank you."

Reggie heaved himself to his feet and lumbered off to the kitchen.

FIFTY-NINE

WHAT do you think?" I said to Luther.

"I ain't being paid to think."

"You're not being paid at all."

"True. There's another example of white exploitation."

"We made a connection with him," I said.

Luther shook his head. "We not home free. That's a smart man. He just wanted time to collect his thoughts."

I agreed. There was intelligence behind Reggie's eyes—maybe not the Ph.D. variety, but common sense and a lifetime of experience. Reggie returned in less than ten minutes carrying two plates of food. I took a bite of the chicken.

"This is good," I told him.

"Obviously a gentleman of refined tastes, counselor. What was it you wanted to ask me?"

"Do you remember talking to the original detective who worked the case?"

"I only spoke to one of them . . . a man name of Eberhart."

"According to the police report, Eberhart indicated you weren't home the night of the murder. Is that true?"

"True enough. I went to visit my son and his wife down in Buck-head. He works for IBM."

"Really?" I said, impressed.

Reggie nodded. "Terrance, that's my oldest boy, write software programs for them. His younger brother, Gerald, is assistant curator at the High Museum."

"You must be proud."

"My wife and I done the best we could. We raised 'em right, took them to church regular, and they turned out okay. They're good boys and that's all a parent can ask. Married nice girls, too."

I thought of my own son for a moment. Reggie was right; it really was all a parent could ask. As much as you might wish otherwise, you can't be there to protect them from the predators. You just hope they can hear you whispering in their ear when some lowlife tries to entice them through the wrong door.

I said, "The murder occurred on a Wednesday. Was that your normal night off?"

"Generally, it was Mondays and Tuesdays, unless Mr. Hamilton had something special happenin'. But ever since his wife died he didn't go in for a lot of entertaining."

This was an interesting point, because the report made no mention about Reggie's work schedule. Eberhart had simply cleared him as a suspect, saying his alibi had checked out."

"Can you recall when Mr. Hamilton told you to take off?"

"He didn't. His secretary called the house around lunchtime that day and gave me the message."

I made a note in my book. "Mr. Washington, do you remember anything about the secretary?"

"You can call me Reggie. Everybody does. When you say Mr. Washington, it makes me think of my daddy. I believe the lady's name was Martha . . . Martha Ludlow."

I frowned. I'd heard that name before, and recently. It came to me a moment later. "Wait . . . isn't Martha Ludow, Charles Evans's secretary?"

"Could be. Mr. Evans and Mr. Hamilton shared a secretary as far back as I can remember. They shared lots of things."

I stared at Reggie trying to read between the lines. There was something under the surface of his words, but whatever it was, wasn't clear to me yet, so I pushed on.

"Did you think it unusual to get a night off in the middle of the week?"

He shrugged. "Not really. It happened that way sometimes. But I wasn't looking no gift horse in the mouth, so I prepared his dinner—roast beef, taters, and cornbread and put it in the refrigerator. I left him a note just like I always did. Never saw the man again."

I inquired, "How long did you work for Sanford Hamilton?"

"Would have been thirty years this May."

"Out of curiosity, did you ever meet a woman named Charlotte Jordan? She worked for Hamilton's law firm."

"I knew Ms. Charlotte. She come out the house a couple of times to help set up parties and such. Fine lady. Everybody was real upset by what happened to her. It was just a shame."

"Wait a minute. Are you saying Charlotte Jordan was Hamilton's secretary? I thought she worked for Charlie Evans."

"Like I said, Mr. Evans and Mr. Hamilton shared a lot of things."

Luther and I glanced at each other. This was the second time Reggie had used that expression. I began to wonder if it was deliberate or just his manner of speaking. I searched my memory, trying to recall if Ted had ever mentioned that Charlotte working for Sanford Hamilton, too.

Outside the restaurant's window I watched a young mother pushing a stroller along the street while she chatted with a friend walking with her. The mother had one hand on a four-year-old little boy and the other on the stroller's handle. Floating above the boy's head on a string was a red Spider-Man balloon.

My son stopped playing with balloons a long time ago. The memory called up a happier time. The world was very clear to me then, just as it is to Peter Parker, Spider-Man's alter ego. There have always been good guys and bad guys. It's harder to know which side is which now. People tend to straddle the fence. I thought Reggie was one of the good guys. I wasn't sure what to make of this latest wrinkle, so for the moment I filed it away, conscious the adrenaline drip in my stomach had kicked up another notch.

We thanked Reggie for his cooperation and asked if he thought I would have any trouble speaking with Thelma Bowen, Hamilton's housekeeper.

"Thelma? Don't see why you would. She's working at the homeless shelter down on Edgewood Avenue. You need to hustle if you want to catch her, though. This is a half day for her. She get off at two o'clock. One word of advice . . . don't be standin' in the doorway come quitin' time. Thelma don't wait for no one."

"Would you give her a call and tell her we're on the way and maybe put in a good word for us?"

"Yes, sir, I believe could do that."

SIXTY

SOMETIME in the late seventies the mile-and-a-half section between Courtland Street and I-75 was renamed Sweet Auburn by an Atlanta resident named John Wesley Dobbs. It's now on the National Historic Register. Most city travel guides mention Peachtree Street, but few mention Sweet Auburn. It's a diverse neighborhood, and home to dozens of mom-and-pop businesses as well as the place where Martin Luther King was born. Though not strictly on Auburn Avenue, Coca Cola actually got its start about a block away. The National Park Service would have you believe Sweet Auburn is a fine place to start your walking tour of the city, but the truth is it's also a good place to get mugged when the sun goes down. Much of Atlanta's homeless community congregates there and they have their own rules.

This time we put Luther's car in a lot rather than leave it on the street. The attendant didn't look like much, but he was better than nothing. The Mission Homeless Center is located in a red brick building that was probably built around the turn of the century. All the residents are required to leave during the day, presumably to look for work. They're allowed to return at 5:00 P.M.

By the time we arrived there was a line stretching from the entrance to around the corner. A number of women with children stood patiently waiting their turn to enter the building. Some stared straight ahead, others had the look of apprehension mixed with fear that comes from living on the streets. The face of the little boy with the Spider-Man balloon came back to me as I walked to the front door. All children should have superheroes protecting them.

My cell phone chirped, pulling me out of my reverie.

"Hey," Katherine said.

"Hey. What's up?"

"My meeting finished early so I decided to take another look at Charlotte Jordan's file. I'm at the Public Safety Building on Memorial Drive. Nikko is waiting outside. Where are you?"

"At the Mission Homeless Center."

"Be careful, John. That's a rough neighborhood."

"I have Luther here to protect me, in case you forgot."

Katherine ignored the sarcasm. "Want to hear something interesting?"

"Always."

"It turns out the detective I spoke with yesterday actually contacted Ted Jordan and asked if he ever heard his mother mention the name Hector Grace. He was the cold hit I told you about."

"And did he?"

"No."

"What does Hector Grace have to do with Charlotte Jordan?"

"Nothing. He's a two-bit hood and a member of a gang called the Night Saints. According to the police, he has a string of arrests going back to middle school. Most of them are minor, like criminal trespass and malicious mischief. He also has two DUI's. More recently, Grace spent eighteen months in Arrendale for stealing a car. His lawyer pled diminished capacity due to intoxication and the judge went along with it."

"Mr. Grace sounds like a delightful guy."

"He is. At the time he and his friends were picked up, the arresting officer noticed bloodstains on the backseat and mentioned it to one of the detectives. I'm sitting here with Jackie Cyzck, the lady I told you about. She's the one who sent the samples to the State Crime Lab for analysis."

It took me a moment to parse through that.

Katherine informed me, "There's more you'll be interested in. Remember we have an appointment later."

"I'll be there. I'm about to interview Hamilton's housekeeper."

"Did the cook have anything worthwhile to say?"

"Possibly. But I can't talk right now," I said, glancing at my watch.

"That's not fair. I told you what I found."

"K.J., I only have a few minutes before this woman leaves. I'll call you when I'm through."

Katherine was in the middle of saying something that is probably best not repeated when I clicked off. I pocketed the phone and went to find Thelma Bowen. Luther elected to wait outside.

From my conversation with Reggie I had formed a mental picture of her that looked more like a female version of . . . well, him. I was wrong. An attendant pointed her out to me in the lobby. Miss Bowen was barely 5' 1" and wore an old-fashioned pair of rimless spectacles. She had a head of pure white hair that reminded me of someone in a Norman Rockwell painting. She was wearing a full-length black coat that ended just below her knees. A clock over the lobby door read 1:58 P.M.

"Ms. Bowen, I'm John Delaney. I believe Reggie Washington phoned to say I was coming. May I have a few minutes?"

"Reggie did call, Mr. Delaney. We'll have to talk as we walk. I'm on my way to church."

"That will be fine."

"Reggie said you were very polite. I like that in a man. So many men today forget their manners."

"Thank you."

"I take it you're not a police officer?"

"No, ma'am. I'm an attorney. I represent Theodore Jordan."

My answer didn't surprise her, but neither did she respond. I waited while she went to a time clock near the reception desk and punched herself out. Miss Bowen was an attractive woman with high cheekbones and eyes that were vaguely almond shaped. Maury's report indicated she was sixty-three years old. She didn't look it.

When she returned, I said, "Reggie told me two men had been out to see him. They said they were Atlanta police officers and advised him not to speak with me. I was wondering if you received a similar visit?"

"I did. They also told me they were officers, but I didn't believe them."

"Why is that?"

"Because I can't imagine an officer of the law threatening someone . . . or needing to."

"They threatened you?"

"Not in so many words, but their message was clear enough. They said if I got involved in a trial, it could go on for weeks, and I would be pulled in as a witness and probably lose my job."

Miss Bowen paused to allow me to open the front door for her. A few people, adults and children, said good-bye to her on the way out. I took her elbow as we descended the steps. I hadn't been in this part of town for many years and the number of homeless now populating the streets came as a surprise. In a small city park directly across the way, a man and woman shambled along pushing a shopping cart filled with what looked like all of their worldly possessions. They were wearing worn overcoats. Miss Bowen followed my glance.

"There's not enough room in the shelter to house everyone," she explained. "We usually start turning people away by five P.M., but with the weather turning cool like this . . . It's very sad."

I spotted Luther and mouthed, "Meet me at the car."

"Yes it is," I said. "Do you remember what the men said to you?"

"They talked a great deal, but mostly it was about not trusting lawyers and losing my job if I was called on to testify. That upset me."

"I understand."

"It wasn't the threat that upset me, Mr. Delaney. I'm always bothered by people who are so sure they're right they refuse to consider any other possibilities. You'd think the police might want the real facts to come out. Do you consider yourself a trustworthy man?"

The directness of her question took me by surprise. Miss Bowen was no fool and the only way to answer her was in the same manner. "I'm not saying I've never told a lie. I have, but I generally try and stick with the truth."

Miss Bowen nodded and we kept walking. At the corner we turned left and proceeded along Auburn Avenue. A woman coming down the street saw us and smiled a greeting. A moment later an elderly man tipped his hat to her.

He said, "Good day, Miss Thelma."

Miss Bowen inclined her head and smiled. "Good day, Deacon."

When we were out of earshot she explained, "That was Deacon Reece. He used to attend services five days a week, but he's been slowing down some over the last year. The congregation makes allowances. I've known him forever."

"I take it you attend church regularly?"

"Oh, yes. I've been coming to Ebenezer Church since I was a little girl. I grew up three blocks from here."

We came to a halt in front of a nondescript red brick building. Above the door was a cross and a blue sign with white lettering that proclaimed it to be the Ebenezer Baptist Church. The name was familiar, but I couldn't place it.

"This was Dr. King's church before his son took over," she told me. "Dr. King, senior, that is."

Now I remembered. Martin Luther King, Jr. had preached here in the early days of the civil rights movement. Many of his famous speeches had been delivered from the pulpit.

"Would you like to come in and sit with me, Mr. Delaney? Visitors are always welcome and the new pastor is a fine man."

The extent of my churchgoing generally involves Christmas, Easter, and a wedding now and then, so my first instinct was to decline. That would have been a mistake.

"Miss Bowen, I'd be delighted."

SIXTY-ONE

L ATE afternoon sunlight streamed into the church through stained-glass windows bathing the interior in yellow and red. The windows had an opalescent quality that diffused the light and softened it. A few other people had already arrived. I took a seat next to Miss Bowen in the third row. The pews were made of dark polished wood that had been worn smooth over the years.

I remarked, "This is lovely."

Miss Bowen gave me a satisfied smile. "I've been to the new Ebenezer Church at the King Center and the big church on Wheat Street, but they don't feel quite the same to me. It's hard to explain, but somehow this is more like home. I was baptized here."

"I understand."

"Mr. Delaney, you asked about the men who came to see me earlier. Are you quite certain they weren't police officers?"

"No, I'm not. But I think I'm correct. I believe they work for the government. For reasons I can't explain they seem to have an interest in Ted Jordan's case. They're not happy with me because I've been digging into the matter. I also I think they were responsible for blowing up my car two days ago. You may have seen it on the news."

Miss Bowen twisted around in her seat and looked at me over the top of her glasses for a moment. "Reggie mentioned that as well. What is it you wish to know?"

I asked about how she was told to take the night off and she repeated virtually the same story Reggie had—Martha Ludlow had called her as well. Another red flag went up. A single phone call to Hamilton's house made sense. Either Reggie or Miss Bowen could have passed the message along to the other. Two phone calls were overkill. Could have been Martha was just being efficient. She was certainly good at walking. It might also mean someone wanted to make certain the house was empty that night.

Since viewing the crime scene with Maury and reading his report, I was of the opinion Sanford Hamilton's murder had been planned, as opposed to a spontaneous crime of passion. Innocuous or not, Martha's phone calls made her a suspect in my book.

Here again, the police work had been sloppy. Eberhart and his partner both interviewed Reggie and Ms. Bowen and cleared them. But nowhere in the report was there any reference to Martha Ludlow. Slipshod work always scared the hell out of me when I was a cop and my attitude has remained the same.

"Miss Bowen, did the men say anything else?"

"They told me the investigation into Mr. Hamilton's death was still ongoing. I remember that phrase specifically. They said until the trial was over anyone who interfered with it could be put in jail themselves."

"That's not generally how it works."

"Yes, I know."

I raised my eyebrows and looked at her.

"Being an elderly black woman doesn't mean I checked my brain at the door."

I smiled. "No, ma'am, it doesn't."

"Our shelter feeds and houses two hundred and fifty people a day, Mr. Delaney, and I've heard just about every story in the book, some from real experts. After sixty years, you learn to read between the lines."

"Reggie also mentioned something about Charlotte Jordan that struck me as odd. I take it you also knew her?"

There was a pause before she answered. "Yes, I did. Charlotte was a fine woman . . . so alone, so frightened after her husband died."

"He said Charlotte visited Mr. Hamilton's house a number of times. Do you recall that as well?"

For the first time in our conversation, Miss Bowen broke eye contact with me. She looked toward the pulpit. A few more people had entered the church, though no one was sitting near us. She appeared to be struggling with something.

"Yes . . . Charlotte was a *guest* in the house," she finally said.

I knew I had just struck a chord. It was as much from her expression as her choice of words. The word "guest" spoke volumes and conveyed more than simply dropping off legal papers or running errands for the boss. I decided to press the issue.

"Do you know what Reggie meant when he said Charles Evans and Sanford Hamilton shared a great many things?"

This time Miss Bowen's silence was profound. After several seconds she closed her eyes and took a long breath before turning back to face me.

"I don't like to speak of the dead, Mr. Delaney. They should be allowed to rest in peace. No good will come of questions like this."

I told her quietly, "I think you're wrong. Ted Jordan is not just my client; he's also my friend. So was his mother. I knew her from the time I was little. I can't bring Charlotte Jordan back, but I can make sure her son isn't convicted for a murder he didn't commit. I think this is important and I'm hoping you'll help me understand."

Another silence followed, longer than any of the previous ones, and I began to fear she was not going to answer. I was relieved when she did.

"I've always prided myself on staying away from gossip. It's a vile trait and I don't believe in it, but I'll tell you what I know. Sometimes in the old days, I would go to Mr. Hamilton's law office to bring him lunch. He was on a special diet you see. I didn't mind because it gave me a chance to get out of the house and to visit with my sister, Louise. She worked in the law firm's copy room until a few years ago when she retired. Reggie prepared the meals and I brought them. At the time, Charlotte was working for Mr. Evans. That was before . . ."

"Before what, Miss Bowen?"

"Before he and she became socially involved. Do you understand what I'm saying?"

I understood and it felt like someone had just spilled a cup of water down my back. *Charlotte Jordan and Charles Evans?* I couldn't believe what I was hearing.

"Ms. Charlotte wasn't the first secretary Mr. Evans saw. She and

I talked a good bit when she came to the house. He was a handsome man with money and power and she was a widow without many friends. All of her relatives were New York people, I believe.

"The situation with Mr. Evans fell apart after several months. None of his relationships ever lasted very long. I've never understood why men are like that. Most of the time the secretaries merely quit or the firm found them jobs elsewhere. But it wasn't that way with Charlotte. I've always felt the reason she didn't leave was because she had no place else to go.

"One evening she came to the house and told Mr. Hamilton that Mr. Evans wasn't treating her right. He said he would look into it and see what he could do. I wasn't trying to eavesdrop, but their voices carried. After Charlotte left, Mr. Hamilton told me she had gone off the deep end . . . I remember those words to this day. She was threatening to sue the law firm.

"Now I knew Charlotte and I didn't believe that was true of her, but it wasn't my place to say anything."

As Thelma Bowen talked, the shock gradually wore off. It was replaced by anger.

She continued, "I don't know a great deal about what happened after her visit or what the lawyers worked out, but a change was made. A short time later, Charlotte became Mr. Hamilton's personal secretary.

"At first, she might come out to the house to bring him a file. Sometimes she stayed for dinner, particularly if they had work to do. Later, she began to accompany him on business trips and eventually . . . well, you know."

An alarm went off in my head. If Ted was still alive and learned his mother had been taken advantage of, it would cast him in a different light with respect to motive. Charlotte was still working at the firm when he did his first summer internship there.

I said, "I know this is difficult for you, but it clears up a number of questions I've had. Unfortunately, it raises others. Do you know if Charlotte and Mr. Hamilton were still seeing each other when she was killed?"

She nodded slowly. "I believe they were."

I'm good at reading people and there was something in Ms.

Bowen's tone that prompted my next question. "Did you and Charlotte ever discuss her relationship with Mr. Hamilton?"

"Some. Charlotte was very upset about something else."

"What?"

"The rumors."

"I'm sorry, I don't understand. What rumors?"

"It seems a sum of money had been taken from the law firm's
petty cash drawer. I don't know how much was involved . . . a little
over a hundred dollars, I believe. My sister told me the lawyers believed Charlotte had taken it and were thinking of prosecuting her."

"Which lawyers?"

"The partners: Mr. Hamilton, Mr. Evans, Mr. Doster, and Mr.
Stanley. There was no truth in what they were saying, Mr. Delaney.
When her husband passed Charlotte received a settlement from the
insurance company and wasn't in need of money. I consider myself
a good judge of character and stealing was not in hers."

Silence descended on the congregation as the pastor entered the
room. He was younger than I expected, perhaps in his early forties.
He greeted everyone and acknowledged me with a nod. I'd like to
say I heard his sermon. The truth is, I didn't. I was far too distracted
by what Miss Bowen had just told me. My heart was beating quickly
now and it continued to do so throughout the sermon. The case was
taking shape, moving with a life of its own.

I once had a partner who was fond of saying, "leopards don't
change their spots," meaning that criminals tend to repeat the pat-
terns that work for them. This was the case here. The reasons were
still not clear; I just knew I was getting closer to the truth.

The coincidence that both she and her son had been accused of
stealing money from the same law firm was too much to write off. As
a trial lawyer you learn there are two ways to impeach a witness: Pile
up enough facts so the jury sides with you, or destroy their credibil-
ity. In other words, make them unworthy of belief.

I snuck a glance at Miss Bowen as the congregation was singing
a psalm. Her face was serene. We sang a slightly different version
when I was young, but the words were the same. Usually, my mother
had to hold my hand to keep me from fidgeting. An image of her
hoisting me up onto one hip while she exchanged pleasantries with

the priest after services worked its way into my mind. I was probably no more than five or six at the time.

Charlotte Jordan was dead and if whoever was trying to frame her son succeeded, no one would be left to speak for them. I was not about to let that happen. That was my religion.

SIXTY-TWO

WO messages were waiting on my cell phone when I left the church. I recognized Nikko's number; the other was from Katherine. I had thirty minutes to make my meeting with her and that cop with the unpronounceable last name. I dialed Nikko's number first.

"Where have you been? I'm leaving messages for you all over town."

"In church."

There was a pause.

"You're kidding?"

"What's the matter, don't I look like the churchgoing type?" When he didn't answer, I added, "I had to speak with a witness. Where's Katherine?"

"Still inside talking to the cops. Wasn't my kind of atmosphere. I'm in the lot across the street."

"There's a shocker," I said.

Nikko informed me, "I did some poking around like you asked and picked up some more information on Eberhart."

"What do you have?"

"Something's definitely not right with him. Six months after leaving the department, he and his wife bought a house on a golf course in Peachtree City. You been there?"

"I know the name."

"There's not a home in their subdivision under eight hundred grand. Out of curiosity, I did a drive-by yesterday. His house has gotta be worth at least a million bucks, maybe more."

I gave a low whistle.

"Exactly. Interesting how a former cop can afford a home like that. Maybe he won the lottery, but something definitely don't smell right."

"Because?"

"Because the mortgage Mr. and Mrs. Eberhart took out is for $400,000, which means—"

"They had to come up with the difference. Jesus. That would be around $600,000 if you're right."

"It ain't just guesswork. I called that little Realtor I used to date and asked her about it. I can't even imagine what the monthly payments are like. When you add the new car he's driving and Mrs. Eberhart's BMW X5 I'd say they have a sugar daddy someplace. There's more."

"I can hardly wait."

"Word around the department is that Eberhart was known to have sticky fingers. Koslowski told me about a robbery suspect Eberhart and his partner busted. The guy screamed holy hell over a gold Rolex Eberhart took off him when he was arrested. The charge got kicked at a preliminary hearing, but the watch was never found, see? Likewise the ten grand he claimed he had on him. According to the property room cop no money and no watch were ever logged in. Eberhart and Baxley denied seeing them. Internal Affairs investigated and cleared them, but the whispers are still there."

It's not uncommon for suspects to accuse cops of planting evidence or stealing their property. It goes on all the time, usually from criminals trying to gain a bargaining chip to use against the department. What struck me as unusual was for other cops to give credence to such accusations.

Before I could comment Nikko continued, "I also talked to a bookie friend of mine and mentioned Eberhart's name to see if anything would shake out. Turns out our Mr. E is a regular at a place called Platinum Dolls."

"The strip club?"

"You know it?"

"A bunch of friends once took one of our buddies there for his bachelor party a few years ago. Unfortunately we didn't know he was a born-again Christian. The celebration didn't go over as well as we expected."

Nikko chuckled. "I can imagine. Anyway, the bookie told me Eberhart likes to hang out with a stripper named Krissy Kat. He put me in touch with her and we spoke. That's not her real name, by the way. According to Krissy, Eberhart always acts like he's a big wheel, flashing rolls of hundreds and spending a lot of time in their Champagne Lounge. The dances there cost two-hundred and fifty a pop, you should pardon the expression. She also told me she's seen him place bets over the phone on college games. Until recently, most of them were low end—twenty-five or thirty dollars, that kind of stuff, but in the last year they suddenly jumped up to well over a grand each."

"Great work, Nikko."

"Want to hear what I found out about Maureen Jordan?"

Nikko never got an answer to his question. I knew something was wrong a block from the car. There was an ambulance parked alongside Luther's SUV. Its lights were flashing. I clicked the cell phone off and began to run. A crowd had gathered and stood there watching as two paramedics worked feverously over a man lying on the sidewalk. Without being told, I knew it was Luther. I pushed through them and got to his side, dropping to one knee.

"Please stand back, sir. This man has been shot," one of the paramedics said.

Luther's eyes were unfocused. He had gone into shock. Blood was coming from the corner of his mouth.

"I'm a friend," I told the man.

"Yes, sir. I understand. Please move away now."

I got up and stepped back a few feet, nearly bumping into two teenage boys holding skateboards. Their faces looked ashen.

I asked, "Do you know what happened?"

The taller of the two shook his head. "We were down the street and heard three loud bangs."

His friend added, "Then a black car drove by us real fast. It nearly hit me."

"Did you see the license plate or who was driving?"

"Uh uh. I just jumped out of the way."

A third paramedic removed a mobile stretcher from the ambulance, collapsed the legs, and rolled it alongside Luther. It took all three of them to lift him.

"Can I ride with you?" I asked. "I'm his friend."

"You'll have to follow us. We're taking him to Grady."

"I think these belong to him," the tall boy said to me. He was holding a set of car keys. "They were on the ground by the curb."

The paramedics loaded Luther into the ambulance and closed the doors. I caught a glimpse of three bullet holes in his back when they lifted him. A second later the siren went on. People stepped away.

"Did anyone see what happened?" I asked.

All I got were blank looks and headshakes. The crowd slowly began to disperse. I stood there helplessly and watched them, my mind reeling. In less than a minute I was alone on the street. I pointed the key fob at Luther's car and was about to hit the OPEN button when I caught a movement in the shadows of a doorway across the street. I don't know why I wasn't surprised to see Agent Britton.

"Professor, we seem to run into each other in the strangest places. I'm sorry about your friend."

I took a step toward Britton, but he held up his hands.

"We didn't have anything to do with this . . . or with your car being blown up. I hope you believe me, because it's the truth. What are you doing at a cemetery?"

"Looking for spooks. That's what you are, aren't you Britton—a spook?"

I got a broad smile for an answer. "How's your investigation going?"

I said, "You'd better hope I don't find you or your playmate were involved in this, because if I do, I'm going to fuck you up."

Britton wasn't fazed by my threat. He asked, "Still chasing the old conspiracy theory with Tissinger?"

"Read about it in the papers, asshole."

I turned my back on him and pointed the fob at the car again. If it was wired to explode, I figured Mr. Britton would have already made himself scarce. I didn't hear Coleman until it was too late. His punch hit me in the kidney, buckling my legs. Pain shot through my back and up into my shoulder blades. I tried to turn, but he grabbed a handful of my hair and smashed my head into the hood of the SUV. Everything went dark for a moment. A second kick behind my right knee sent me to the ground.

I felt my arms being pulled behind me and cuffs snapping into place. Britton and Coleman hauled me to my feet and half-dragged me to a black sedan that had just driven up. They shoved me inside.

"I don't think you'll be needing this," Coleman said, removing the gun from my holster. "Do you have a license for it? Yes? No? It doesn't really matter. Threatening a federal officer is a felony, Mr. Delaney."

He got in next to me and Britton got in on the opposite side. There was a third man in the driver's seat.

"Fuck you," I said.

That earned me an elbow to the sternum that took my breath away. I was in pain, but more angry with myself for having let my guard down. It was a rookie thing to do. Fact is, I was rusty and they caught me unprepared. At the moment I needed the anger. It was all I had.

Britton said, "Now that I have your attention. I need to ask you a few questions. You met with Senator Talmadge and that pregnant bitch from the DA's office the other day. Why?"

"She was having a dinner party and wanted our opinion on the bordelaise sauce."

A punch to my jaw snapped my head sideways and I felt my mouth fill with blood. I responded by spitting in Britton's face. He backhanded me, then took a handkerchief out of his pocket and slowly wiped the spit off.

He said, "You're a funny guy, Delaney. Do you know what happens to funny guys?"

"Yeah, they get their fingers cut off and murdered."

Britton chuckled. "No, that was your client's handiwork. You have a vivid imagination. It must keep your students entertained. Why don't you wake up and smell the roses? We told you before, we don't care what happens to him. Our interest is in protecting the United States government."

"And who protects them from you?"

Britton shook his head and turned his palms up in a what-can-you-do gesture.

His partner said, "We're the good guys. Why is that so hard for you to grasp? Your stupidity is really wearing thin. Maybe if you have some time to reflect it would help you to see things clearly. What do you think, Brad?"

Britton winked at me then turned to the driver and nodded.

SIXTY-THREE

I RECOGNIZED the Richard Russell Federal Building as we pulled into the basement parking garage. It has the same bleached architecture many government buildings do. The cement barricades erected after 9/11 were still in place, preventing street traffic from getting too close. The driver slowed long enough for a security guard to check his ID before we were waved through. By then I couldn't feel my fingers because the cuffs were biting into my flesh.

Agent Britton got out first and with the driver's help hauled me out after him. I was half-pushed, half-led to an elevator at the rear of the garage. They used a key card to access it. No one said anything on the ride up.

I expected them to make good on their threat and book me for assaulting a federal agent. The charge was bullshit since I never had the chance to assault anyone, a fact I intended to remedy if the opportunity presented itself again. Their act was a show of muscle. Still, finding yourself handcuffed and in custody is hard to ignore no matter how tough you think you are. The weight of the federal building alone is sufficient to get your attention. As far as criminal charges were concerned, I would handle them if it came to that. The last thing Britton and Coleman wanted was notoriety. Their kind operate in the shadows.

There was no booking nor was there a mug shot or fingerprints. Instead they took my belt and shoelaces and shoved me into a holding cell. The last thing I saw was Britton's smirking face as the door slammed shut. Frustrated, I sat on a vinyl cot and waited. Gradually my anger subsided and anxiety set in. To make matters worse I was worried sick about Luther.

Time passed.

They had also taken my watch, so I had no idea how long I was there. I only knew the hours were crawling by. I tried to sleep and couldn't. The room was cold and smelled of antiseptic. It was lit by a single bulb in the ceiling.

At some point I noticed the sky beginning to show signs of light. The gray predawn gradually gave way to a reddish glow in the east and turned blue as the sun rose. I was tired and sore and my eyes felt scratchy.

Before they locked me up I asked to call an attorney.

Britton responded by laughing in my face, "Been nice knowing you, Delaney. You'll probably be an old man by the time you get out. Too bad . . . you could have had a decent life."

The noise from commuter traffic drifted up to my cell. A sheet of unbreakable glass and a wire mesh outside the window muffled the sounds. The glass and mesh were there to prevent anyone breaking out, a needless expenditure. We were on the seventeenth floor and any escape would only be to the afterlife. A key being inserted into the door lock pulled my attention back to the cell. I expected Britton or Coleman again and was surprised to see Jimmy d'Taglia standing there. A Federal security guard was with him.

"I'm sorry, John. I just found out."

I shielded my eyes against the light in the corridor and didn't respond.

"Let's get you out of here," he said. Jimmy turned to the security guard and added, "We'll be fine. Thanks, Lou."

Lou responded with a slight nod and left. I stayed where I was.

"I promise I didn't know you were here until I came to work this morning," Jimmy informed me. "There was a message waiting for me on my phone from Katherine. She's been trying to find you. Britton showed up five minutes later and told me you had been arrested for threatening him."

"Then go ahead and charge me."

"No one's charging you with anything." Jimmy glanced around the cell with a look of distaste. "I haven't had breakfast yet. Let's get a bite to eat and talk."

I remained where I was.

He asked, "Do you want to stand here eyeballing each other or get out of here? This isn't getting us anywhere and Katherine's worried to death."

The use of Katherine's name put me in motion.

SIXTY-FOUR

THE cafeteria wasn't crowded. Jimmy picked out a spot in the corner and asked me to wait while he went to the serving line. The tables were all made of laminated wood and the chairs were brightly colored plastic, our government's idea of cheerful decor. A clock above the entrance indicated it was a quarter past ten. I had been locked up nearly nineteen hours.

Jimmy returned with two plates of scrambled eggs, bacon, toast, and coffee. Another man I'd never seen before was with him.

"Mr. Delaney, I'm Ray Rosen, assistant U.S. Attorney for the Northern District of Georgia."

I recognized the name. At one time Rosen had been Katherine's boss.

Rosen said, "I understand you've had a rough night."

"It fit the rest of my day."

Rosen was wearing a pale blue shirt and maroon striped tie, but no jacket. His sleeves were rolled up. I guessed his age to be about fifty-five.

He said, "I heard about the explosion. Is Katherine all right?"

I supposed this was his way of building rapport. "She's fine, except for a few bruises. Do you know how my friend Luther Campbell is?"

"No, but I'll check. Would you mind if I join you?"

I used my leg to push a chair toward him. This meeting was clearly not by chance. I was also in no mood to be accommodating.

"Thanks for the breakfast," I told them. "If I'm not being charged with anything, I'll be running along."

Rosen remained seated. "I understand you haven't been treated very well. Jimmy's already discussed what happened with me and

I've talked to Mr. Britton. If I thought there was a legitimate reason to prosecute, I would."

"Good for you."

"You're not that tough, Delaney. How 'bout you sit down and finish your meal? We might be able to help each other. I'd even venture to say hearing me out would be in your client's best interest."

I glanced at Jimmy and read nothing in his face. As much as I wanted to tell them what they could do with their breakfast, Rosen had just used the magic words—*in your client's best interest*, assuming he wasn't at the bottom of Lake Lanier.

I took my seat again. Until someone showed me otherwise I intended to proceed as if Ted Jordan was alive.

"Those eggs any good?" Rosen asked, eyeing Jimmy's plate.

Jimmy shrugged. "They're okay. You want some?"

Rosen shook his head. "The doctor says I need to cut down on my cholesterol. Sheila's had me eating egg-white omelets for the past two months. Fucking things are like rubber."

"They're an acquired taste," Jimmy pointed out. "My girlfriend eats them three times a week."

"Wonderful," Rosen replied glumly. "I get to spend the next six months acquiring a taste for food that tastes like shit." He turned back to me. "If you're not going to finish your breakfast, it seems a shame to waste it."

I pushed the plate toward him. "Be my guest."

Rosen commented, "You ever notice no one has to acquire a taste for stuff like apple pie and chocolate ice cream?"

"You were about to tell me why I'm not that tough and how we can help each other."

Rosen reached for a jar of Tabasco sauce and shook a few drops over the eggs. "Can we agree our conversation will be off the record?"

"Meaning?"

"Meaning, you can't use it in court or go public, unless I give you the okay."

"And how will that help Ted Jordan?"

Rosen took a bite of his eggs. "We're about to wind up an investigation that's been ongoing for eleven months. I don't want you screwing it up at the last minute."

"And I can't agree to withhold anything that involves his welfare. In case you haven't heard, he's facing a murder charge."

"*If* he's still alive. The cops found a shoe they think belonged to him on the shoreline of Lake Lanier last night in addition to the wallet that was recovered. I'm sorry to tell you there was blood on it. They're trying to get a match now."

Rosen chewed some more and thought for a moment. "Thornton Schiff can't go to trial without a live body. In a month we'll have our investigation wrapped up and you can use what I'm going to tell you any way you see fit. I assume by then you'll know if Jordan is still with us. All I know is what I've read in the papers about him supposedly killing Sanford Hamilton and whoever that other fellow in his apartment was."

"Frank Nardelli."

"Nardelli, right. As far as I'm concerned, proving that is up to the State of Georgia, not the United States government. If your client did it, he'll go to jail. If not, they'll catch the right person sooner or later. Do we have an agreement?"

I looked into Rosen's eyes, trying to get some sense of whether he was on the level or this was some kind of act. From past conversations with Katherine I knew he was no fool. She told me he had graduated Yale Law at the top of his class and had headed the U.S. Attorney's office in North Georgia since he was twenty-nine. They had worked with each other for seven years before she left to go into private practice. The description that stuck in my mind was that he was brilliant, sometimes erratic, but someone who kept his word. At that moment, he could do more for me than I could for him.

We shook hands.

"Good," Rosen said, helping himself to my coffee. "As I was saying, for nearly a year now our office has been conducting a probe into offshore bank accounts and where the money in them has been going. That's why we were interested in your case."

"Mine is a murder trial. What does Ted Jordan have to do with offshore accounts?"

"Jordan made a number of trips outside the country over the last six months. We think there's a good chance he used that time to establish a number of different foreign accounts."

I asked, "And this information comes from who?"

"That's not relevant."

"I thought we were sharing."

Rosen tapped his finger on the table for a few seconds. "The investigation was initiated by Homeland Security. They assigned Brad Britton to track down the funds. He brought in Stan Coleman, the other gentleman you met. Coleman is Tissinger's head of security. I don't know what cover story they told you, but the reason Tissinger is involved is because they want to show us they're not involved in funneling money."

"You're right. That's not what they told me."

"Two accounts we located in the Cayman Islands are owned by Evans, Stanley, Doster & Young."

"I'm a little fuzzy on how Tissinger became a player," I said. "Maybe you could clarify that for me."

"Early in the case we identified a number of checks made out to Evans, Stanley, Doster & Young from them. The funds were withdrawn a few days later. We've never been able to determine exactly where they went. That's why were so interested in Jordan's activities while he was abroad. Ultimately, we contacted Tissinger and asked them to clarify their relationship with Evans, Stanley. They explained they were in the process of launching a new depression medication and the money was for legal fees. The Evans firm is handling their FDA application."

"So your investigation is about tax evasion?"

"Right," Rosen replied, taking a sip of the coffee. He made a face and emptied two packets of sugar substitute into the mug.

I informed him, "Charlie Evans is a wealthy man. Why would he risk jail to evade taxes? It doesn't follow."

"People do strange things. And it's not just Evans. Legally, all the partners are involved. One particular account we've been watching is controlled by Bill Doster. It was established years ago. As the law firm's senior partner, Evans had to know what was happening.

"So far, the Caymans' privacy laws have made getting information difficult. It's like pulling teeth, but we're within twenty . . . maybe thirty days from closing down the operation. When we do, I'll present indictments to the grand jury."

"Ted Jordan is also a partner in the firm. Will he be indicted as well?"

Rosen used my toast to clean up the remainder of his eggs. "Probably, but it's not definite. If he's alive and you're still in contact with him, we might be willing to work out a deal. There's a good chance we could put him in a witness protection program, say in Mexico or some country like that."

I glanced at Jimmy. "It's a good deal, John," he commented.

"But Ted Jordan's a mad killer," I pointed out. "He shoots people, then cuts off their fingers, and keeps them around his house for souvenirs. Why would the Mexican government want someone like that in their country?"

Rosen answered, "The government of Mexico is more concerned with our looking the other way at the border. In return, they trade us favors."

Big surprise. The security at Borders bookstores is better than our security at the U.S. border. Whatever Rosen was angling for, I couldn't see our government allowing a killer to go free just to nail a few tax-evading lawyers.

"Did your information reveal anything about Tissinger's connection to a NeoNazi group here in Atlanta?"

Rosen's coffee mug paused halfway to his lips. He sat back in his seat and put it down again.

"No, why?"

"One of the detectives who originally worked Sanford Hamilton's murder is a big fan of *der Führer*. His name is Harry Eberhart. Eberhart left the force a while back and now works for a security company owned by Tissinger.

"That hardly—"

"In my first meeting with Britton and Coleman they warned me against involving Tissinger in Ted Jordan's case. Actually, threatened is a better word. There's a good chance they also posed as police officers and tried to intimidate two witnesses into not speaking with me."

"Tell me how you would involve Tissinger?"

"By alleging the company was trying to frame Jordan for Hamilton's murder. No one said anything about the Cayman Islands or offshore bank accounts."

Rosen frowned. "They were probably making up a cover story to protect their investigation."

I informed him, "Anything is possible. Did either of them mention that critical data had been omitted from Tissinger's FDA application?"

"What are you talking about?"

"The initial tests Tissinger ran on their new depression drug revealed a number of suicides occurred in the control group. The head of their research team found out and went to management over it. He was fired. Now here's the good part." I lowered my voice and leaned forward. "The team consisted of five members. Four of whom are dead. Two drove off Buford Dam a few months ago, one died of arsenic poisoning in Miami, and one died of anaphylactic shock due to a bee sting. The medical alert bracelet he wore every day has yet to be found."

Rosen and Jimmy exchanged glances. Either they were both excellent actors or I had just hit them with something they didn't expect.

"Tell me more," Rosen said.

I spent the next half hour going over what I knew about the odd deaths and how Ted's son and roommate had discovered the FDA report had been altered. I also related some of Harry Eberhart's anti-Semitic comments, which couldn't hurt since Rosen was Jewish.

The crease between his eyes deepened. From his expression it was obvious Britton and Coleman had held back a good deal of information from him. To his credit, Rosen didn't go off the deep end. He simply listened and scratched a few notes on a paper napkin. When I finished, he folded it and stuck it in the pocket of his shirt.

"It's been a pleasure meeting you, Mr. Delaney," he said, standing up. "I need to check on a few things. Why don't we touch base in a couple of days? Will you need a lift back to your car?"

"That would be nice. Oh, by the way, the first time I met Britton he told me he was with the NSA, not Homeland Security. He needs to get his story straight." Coleman's real name is LeDoux and he's an Interpol Agent. He doesn't work for Tissinger.

Rosen nodded slowly. "I'll try to get word to you about your friend's condition. Please give K.J. my regards."

"I will."

Then he turned to Jimmy. "Call me after you drop him off and get a message to Agent Britton and Mr. Coleman, or whoever he is. I'd like a word with them."

SIXTY-FIVE

THE ride to Luther's car was unnecessary because Katherine was waiting in Jimmy's office. As soon as she saw us she ran forward and hugged me.

"Can't let you out of my sight for a minute, can I?" she said. "Are you all right?"

"I'm fine."

She turned to Jimmy, "Your secretary called me a little while ago and I decided to come over."

"No problem. I couldn't let our boy languish in jail."

Though she didn't show it, I could tell Katherine was fuming. She smiled back at him, but the smile never touched her eyes. It was a look I was familiar with.

She said, "What is John being charged with and how much bond will we have to post?"

"There won't be any charges. John can fill you in on the details."

Katherine's eyebrows rose. "No charges? I'm confused. Then maybe you can explain what he was doing here all night and why your office denied him the right to make a call. The last time I checked the system doesn't work that way."

"Katherine—"

"Or does the U.S. Attorney's office endorse pulling people off the street whenever it suits them?"

Jimmy took a breath and let it out slowly. "We don't *endorse* anything like that and you know it. For the record, I argued my ass off with Rosen not to press charges. Both men said John assaulted them and one of them is a federal agent. It might be nice if you thanked me instead of jumping down my throat."

Katherine replied, "I'll let you know about thanks *after* I hear what happened. And you better hope I'm impressed. I've had all the game playing I can stand. You can tell Ray I said that."

Katherine is my hero. It was neat to watch her in action. I didn't have to say a word, just stand there and look offended. The sad part is we probably did owe Jimmy our thanks. Unfortunately, he was in the line of fire. Maybe he guessed Katherine was posturing. I did. She was being proactive, as they say. If Ray Rosen decided to play tit-for-tat, she was setting up a false arrest suit to bargain with. I love my wife.

Jimmy shook his head sadly, turned, and walked down the hall to his office.

In the elevator I explained what occurred with Britton and Coleman. Katherine already knew most of this from the secretaries. It pays to have friends in high places.

"So you never actually hit anyone?" she asked, as we walked to her car.

"Never had a chance. Where's Nikko?"

"He dropped me off and headed to the hospital. Luther is in the intensive care unit. They operated on him last night. John, he was shot three times in the back."

"I know. Is there a prognosis?"

"Nikko will call us as soon as he hears anything. We can go there and wait or we can meet with Jackie Cyzck. It's your call."

I was torn. If Luther pulled through, he would probably be unconscious or so doped up on drugs he wouldn't know we were there."

"Let's go to Decatur," I said.

At the car Katherine used her remote to open the doors and got in on the passenger side. By unspoken agreement driving duties were usually ceded to me. It's like men taking out the garbage.

I headed across town and found the entrance to I-20. Traffic was light at that time of day. Fifteen minutes later we merged onto I-285 and got off at Memorial Drive, where the DeKalb County police department is headquartered. It's a modern cream-colored building that practically shouts "government." Adjacent to the complex is the Adult Detention Center, a lasting tribute to euphemism. Whoever dreamed up the name obviously thought calling the two-acre barbed-wire enclosure a "detention center" was somehow more genteel than referring to it as a jail. I've never been clear about who's supposed to feel better, the neighbors living across the way, or the inmates. "Hey man, I wasn't in no jail. They just detained me for a year." Big difference.

We announced ourselves to the receptionist and waited in the lobby for Detective Cyzck. Near the building's entrance, a group of people congregated on the lawn and sat on the steps. They smoked or talked quietly on cell phones while waiting for a bondsman to arrive. I'd been to jails before and it seemed to me the crowd was always the same. The majority were black, Hispanic, and poorly dressed. Most avoided eye contact. A few had bored expressions, as if they had gone through the process before.

Jackie Cyzck turned out to be an attractive brunette. She was dressed in a black pants suit and a button-down white shirt. A gold detective's badge was pinned to her belt.

"So you're Katherine's better half?" she asked, giving me an appraising look.

"Grubby, but in the flesh."

"Cute," she said to Katherine. "Mine was cute, too . . . when he was sober. I need to stop at Magistrate's Court and pick up a warrant. You guys can tag along. It might even help."

I asked, "Are we going somewhere?"

"You want to meet Hector Grace, don't you?"

"You bet," I said.

SIXTY-SIX

"EVERYTHING depends on the judge giving us a warrant," Jackie said. "It won't be a cakewalk because of how old this case is. All we know is the crime lab tied Grace's DNA to Charlotte Jordan's crime scene based on the semen samples they recovered back then. But the problem is—"

"Charlotte wasn't raped, like I told you yesterday," Katherine said, finishing the sentence for her. "Someone set it up to look that way."

Jackie handed me a manila folder. "This is our case file," she said. "The lab report is at the back. Ballistics identified the murder weapon as a .38 caliber revolver. I'm asking for a warrant to search Grace's home for it."

I don't remember which of us opened the door to the Magistrate Court or even entering the room and taking a seat in the gallery. I was completely engrossed in what I was reading. It was a thick file complete with photos. Despite all that I had seen over the years, I wasn't prepared for them. Crime scene pictures are always graphic, but they usually don't involve people you know. Charlotte Jordan was naked from the waist down. Her hands had been tied behind her back and her face was swollen and bruised. After studying them for several seconds, I averted my eyes and stared out the window. I tried to recall what I knew about that horrible episode until something else surfaced in my mind, a thought that made my blood run cold. If Ted was alive and knew what I was looking at, Hector Grace's life wouldn't be worth two cents.

My training eventually took over and I forced myself to examine the photos again. The first thing that struck me was a close-up of the semen stains. They were on a rock next to Charlotte's body and no effort had been made to conceal them. The crescent shape indicated they had been deliberately splattered. A normal ejaculation pattern is different. We've learned enough from forensics over the years to cull out the phonies from the real thing. That wasn't the case in 1988. At the bottom of the page, someone had written the word, "fake," so it appeared the detectives had reached the same conclusion.

"The judge wants to see you," Jackie said, touching me on the shoulder.

"What?"

"I said, the judge wants to see you in chambers," she repeated. "Actually, he wants to see all of us. I don't know what's going on. Technically, this is a police matter, but I thought since your client—"

A flame had been slowly building inside me since I began reading the report and the heat had now worked its way into my face. I felt outrage at Charlotte's death and outrage because Luther had nearly been murdered. Another man was being framed for a crime he didn't commit. A number of unrelated facts were suddenly beginning to make sense.

I didn't know what the judge wanted either, and I wasn't going to find out sitting where I was.

"Let's go," I said, getting to my feet.

Judge Milton Foster was not what I expected. As a result of a grenade exploding in his foxhole toward the end of the Vietnam War, he had a pair of metal prosthetics instead of hands. I made his age to be somewhere in his early sixties. He was a man of middle height with sharp brown eyes. He entered his chambers through a side door and invited us all to be seated. He addressed Jackie first.

"Detective, I've read your affidavit and there are some points I need to clear up. This murder took place almost nineteen years ago, is that correct?"

"Yes, sir."

"You state here the crime lab recently identified a DNA sample taken from semen stains at the murder scene as belonging to a man named Hector Grace."

"Correct, Judge."

"The woman was raped and then killed at Stone Mountain park?"

"That was our original conclusion, but we now have reason to believe the rape was staged."

"Really?"

"Yes, sir. The scene was set up to look that way. If you'll glance at the bottom of the report, the medical examiner indicated evidence of penetration wasn't definite. What's not in question though is the cause of her death. The victim was killed by a gunshot to her head from a .38 caliber Smith & Wesson."

The judge frowned as he scanned Jackie's affidavit. "And this is the weapon you're asking me to issue a search warrant for?"

"Yes, your honor."

Judge Foster grew pensive, tapping the two metal pincers that were his hands together for several seconds. "I'll be frank, I'm having difficulty with probable cause. Is there anything to connect Hector Grace to the gun?"

Jackie answered, "Not at this time, your honor. We only know he was definitely at the crime scene—"

"Of a woman who might not have been raped at all from what you're telling me. I gather you can't even state the semen stains were made at the time the crime was committed."

"No, Judge. Due to the sample's age our lab can't pin down a specific time."

"So they could have been present before it happened?"

"Possibly."

"Or Hector Grace might be a pervert who just happened along afterward, viewed the scene, and got off on it. Help me out, Detective. How do I make this work?"

"According to Detective Cyzck, Hector Grace is a known member of the Night Saints," Katherine said, speaking for the first time. "They're a group—"

"I'm familiar with the Night Saints. Ms. Adams, isn't it?" Foster said, swiveling around in his chair to face her. May I ask what your interest in this case is?"

"I'm assisting Mr. Delaney—"

"Who represents Theodore Jordan. Yes, I already know that."

For a moment it appeared Foster was going say something else, but he changed his mind. Katherine had on her I-dare-you-to-challenge-me expression, which generally forestalls further comments. At least it does in my case.

The judge cleared his throat and continued, "The newspapers have been very diligent in chronicling Mr. Jordan's adventures of late, including his recent disappearance. I may be going out on a limb here, but is there a connection between Charlotte Jordan and Theodore Jordan, their having the last name and all?"

I informed him, "Charlotte was Ted Jordan's mother."

Foster nodded slowly and rested his chin on his metal pincers. "Interesting. Is the presence of semen the extent of your connection between Grace and this gun?"

I answered, "We don't know at this point. But it's safe to say Ted Jordan believes there is more. A few weeks after Detective Cyzck got in touch with him regarding the new DNA evidence, he filed a petition to exhume his mother's body."

"Yes, he filed that with me."

I exchanged a glance with Katherine.

Foster continued, "This is all very interesting—spooky even. But I need to know *why* I should issue a search warrant for a gun with no connection to the suspect. They haven't changed the constitution lately and we still need probable cause."

I replied, "Judge, last year the Night Saints desecrated a Jewish synagogue. You may remember the news reports. While we were waiting I had a chance to go through Charlotte Jordan's file. The detective who originally worked that case is a man named Harry Eberhart. Detective Eberhart also headed the investigation into Sanford Hamilton's murder. I met him a couple of days ago and he has an odd taste in tattoos."

The judge's eyebrows lifted and he gestured for me to continue.

"Eberhart left the police department earlier this year and is working for a private security firm in Atlanta now. While we were speaking I noticed a small letter "H" tattooed on the back of each of his wrists. If you put them together they stand for Heil Hitler. I know this because I used to be a cop.

"According to the file, it appears Grace has a string of priors going back to middle school. Before we were called in to see you, I was about to ask Detective Cyzck if Grace and Eberhart ever ran into each other. There are too many coincidences involving hate crimes for my comfort level."

The judge studied my face for a moment before turning to Jackie Cyzck. "Detective, would you be good enough to check this out? Mr. Delaney piqued my curiosity."

Jackie looked from one of us to the other, muttered something under her breath, and left his chambers. She was back in less than twenty minutes with Hector Grace's rap sheet. She gave me a thumbs-up sign as she came through the door.

Jackie informed us, "Your honor, Hector Grace and three friends were arrested for spray painting Nazi slogans on mausoleums at the Edgemont Cemetery when he was in ninth grade. The detectives who made the arrest were Ray Cummins and Harry Eberhart."

Judge Foster stuck his lower lip out, but didn't respond.

I asked, "Is Cummins still around?"

Jackie shook her head. "He was before my time. I asked our captain and he said Cummins retired five years ago. He's living in Charleston, South Carolina now."

"All right," the judge said. "We have something unusual, but we're talking about issuing a search warrant for Hector Grace, not Harry Eberhart. You're still coming up short."

Jackie suggested, "Maybe not. Grace's latest arrest was eighteen months ago, and it was for damaging property at a convenience store off Covington Highway. Mr. Nyguen Kim and his wife own the store. According to the report, there was an argument between Grace, his buddies, and Mr. Kim over a racial slur Grace supposedly made. When Mr. Kim ordered them out of the store, Grace responded by knocking over several candy racks. The Kims called 911. Grace and his buddies were long gone by the time our uniforms arrived on the scene.

"Here's the good part—in her original statement, Mrs. Kim reported seeing Grace brandish a .38 caliber revolver and point it at her husband. Unfortunately, when he was picked up the gun was nowhere to be found. The Kims own an identical handgun they bought for protection, which is how Mrs. Kim recognized it. We charged Grace with terroristic threats and criminal damage.

"Sometime later, Mrs. Kim came down with a case of selective amnesia and recanted her testimony. As a result, the threat charge was dropped."

Foster said, "You've lost me . . . selective amnesia?"

"The Kims have an eleven-year-old daughter. Prior to the incident, the girl walked to school every day with her friends. Shortly thereafter, Mrs. Kim started driving her to and from class. The detective who arrested Grace added a note to his report saying he thought she got cold feet because the Night Saints had threatened to harm the girl. It's the way they operate."

Judge Foster asked, "And you feel her original statement is enough for me to issue a warrant?"

Before Jackie could respond I posed a question of my own. "Do you have any way of knowing if Ted Jordan ever found out about what happened to the Kims?"

She frowned and flipped to the front of the file. "The only person who requested access to either of the files is . . . oh, shit—"

"Ted Jordan," I said, finishing the sentence for her.

The judge asked, "Do you think there's any chance Hector Grace is carrying around the same murder weapon after nineteen years? That would be quite a stretch, Detective. Wouldn't you agree, Mr. Delaney?"

I considered his question for a moment and nodded. "It is, your honor. But the search warrant will accomplish two things. Even if we don't have a perfect fit, the DNA definitely connects Grace to the scene. As far as the gun is concerned, we might get lucky. I think there's enough here for probable cause."

"And the second?"

"I don't know if Ted Jordan is still alive, your honor, but if he is, taking Hector Grace into custody might save his life."

The judge got the message at the same time. Keeping his eyes fixed on me he reached for his pen.

SIXTY-SEVEN

I THOUGHT Buford Highway was a strange place for a white supremacist to live. In recent years the population had gone from working class white to a mixture of Asian and Hispanic.

Katherine and I rode in the back of Jackie's vehicle. Her partner, Elvis Taylor, a twenty-year veteran of robbery-homicide, had joined us. A second unmarked car with two detectives was following behind.

Elvis's real name, as I learned, was Vernon. He acquired the nickname early in his career because of the way he wore his hair and sideburns.

On our way to the Perry Housing Projects, Elvis explained that Grace had been an on-again-off-again customer of his for at least ten years. He was also familiar with Harry Eberhart and had a low opinion of his police skills.

He said of Eberhart, "Basically, the guy couldn't get out of his own way. When he transferred to Atlanta PD, there was a collective sigh of relief from the other guys in the department."

Katherine asked, "Why was he allowed to work Charlotte Jordan's murder if he was so inept?"

Elvis turned his palms up. "Things change. There wasn't as much accountability back then. I actually to remember the Jordan case. It came in as a rape-murder, and forensics more or less confirmed it, so there weren't a lot of reasons to second-guess him."

"Do you think Grace will talk when you confront him with the DNA evidence?" Katherine said.

Elvis started to reply and then abruptly changed his mind. He shifted back around in his seat and stared straight ahead for several seconds without speaking. Jackie glanced at her partner, then made eye contact with me in the rearview mirror. I knew what was going through their minds.

I said, "This type of crime really doesn't fit Grace's pattern, does it?"

Elvis shook his head. "No . . . Hector is a maggot, but he's strictly small time. I can see him trashing someone's house or busting out a store window, but not this. Something ain't right, but I'm a sonofabitch if I know what it is. Sorry ma'am," he added to Katherine.

Jackie elbowed him in the ribs.

"What?"

"Say you're sorry to me, too."

"How come?"

"Because I'm a lady, too, you ape."

"Jesus, Cyzck, you're my partner," Elvis said, rubbing the spot where she jabbed him.

The look he received reminded me of that unspoken communication married couples engage in from time to time. It wasn't lost on Elvis, who displayed his wisdom and made a gentlemanly retreat.

"Sorry," he mumbled.

Jackie nodded to Katherine in the rearview mirror and Katherine nodded back.

Then she asked, "John, you think Jordan will go after Grace, don't you? I mean I would if it were my mother. Christ, what a mess this is."

"I do," I answered quietly.

Jackie guessed my next thought and informed me, "You understand, I'll to have to let Atlanta PD know about this?"

Before I could respond, Elvis suddenly pointed at a figure walking down the street toward us. "That's our boy," he said. "Hit it."

Katherine and I were thrown back in our seats as Jackie floored the vehicle. The car trailing us reacted a moment later. The moment Grace spotted us he reversed direction, and headed straight for the entrance to an apartment building. Elvis was out of the car before it came to a complete stop. For a man in his early fifties he moved quickly and was on Grace before he could get a key in the lock. Slamming him forward into the door, he yanked one of Grace's arms behind his back, kicked his legs apart, and began patting him down. The second car pulled in behind us.

A mother coming up the street took her child by the arm and crossed to the opposite side. Apparently, cops arresting someone wasn't that unusual in this part of town.

Elvis said, "Hello, Hector. Long time no see."

"What the fuck's the matter with you, man? I didn't do anything."

Grace's words carried the slight hint of an accent.

"Now what kind of language is that?" Elvis asked, tapping Hector lightly on the head. "Don't you see there are ladies present?"

"Fuck off, Taylor. I'm clean. You can ask my probation officer."

Elvis snapped a pair of handcuffs on Grace's wrists then spun him around so they faced each other.

"Is that so? Well, we're not interested in drugs today, Hector. Detective Cyzck and I only want to have a little chat with you."

"I'm not answering any questions. If I'm under arrest, I want a lawyer. I know my rights."

Elvis turned to me and said, "Ain't it great? He knows his rights. What a country. Maybe you can get Mr. Delaney here or maybe Ms. Adams to represent you. They're lawyers. In fact, they want to talk to you, too. Seems you're a real popular guy."

Grace finally noticed me standing there and his expression grew wary. Having a pair of attorneys present for an arrest isn't exactly standard procedure. His eyes then shifted from me to Katherine and slid up and down her figure with a look that was scarcely less than obvious.

"Who the fuck are they?" he asked Elvis

"Just interested parties, Mr. Grace," Katherine told him. "We're here to make sure you're treated well. You know, police brutality."

"Bullshit. I want my own lawyer . . . unless you want to wait till I get out. I could rock your world, mama."

Katherine replied. "I bet you say that to all the ladies. I bet you even said that to Charlotte Jordan, didn't you?"

There was no hint of recognition at the mention of Charlotte's name—nothing.

"I'm not saying a goddamn thing until I talk to my attorney. How come I'm being arrested? I have a right to know that."

Jackie nodded sympathetically and turned to her partner, "He's got a point, Elvis."

"Damn," Elvis said, "I knew I was forgetting something. That's what happens when you get old. Let's see . . . why did we stop you? Oh, yeah . . . now I remember. Hector, you're under arrest for the murder of Charlotte Jordan."

Elvis took a card from his jacket pocket and read Grace his rights. Again, there was no reaction to Charlotte's name.

Jackie suggested, "What do you say we all take a little ride? Maybe it will help Hector with his memory."

Grace started to protest, but the other detectives grabbed him under the arms and escorted him back to their car. His complaints stopped when they shut the door in his face.

SIXTY-EIGHT

I WATCHED the gray mass of Georgia's Stone Mountain grow larger as we drew near to it. It's a whale-shaped rock with a massive carving of Robert E. Lee, Stonewall Jackson, and Jefferson Davis majestically mounted atop their horses. Once again, Katherine and I rode in the backseat. Grace was in the car behind us with the other detectives. We pulled into the parking lot at the base of the mountain and took the tram to the top.

As we began our ascent I looked out over the countryside. The day was windy and the sky overcast, but Atlanta's skyline was still visible in the distance. A white church with a steeple stood out against the rolling green hills that surrounded the state park. Other buildings and a network of roads came into view the higher we went. They reminded me of toy models. In the distance, a railroad whistle, carried by the wind, drifted up to us. After scanning the countryside for several seconds I caught sight of a train moving slowly through the Georgia pines. On the other side of the tram car, standing sullenly between the two detectives, was Hector Grace. He was staring straight ahead. But there was a difference in his expression now. It was not quite as arrogant as before. I thought I could detect a touch of apprehension.

The train's whistle died away, replaced by the sound of bells. From previous visits, I knew the bells were part of a giant carillon by the lake that played on the hour. Although I'd been to the park before, this was the first time I was actually going to see the top of the mountain. The ride took about twelve minutes.

The summit of Stone Mountain is over a hundred yards wide and practically barren. Not far from us a group of teenagers were talking loudly and laughing at some joke. Oblivious to our presence, they snapped digital photos of each other then moved to the mountain's edge for a better view of the landscape.

Below the summit, a few trees had pushed their way up through solid rock and between boulders. We were almost nine hundred feet above the valley floor. The mountain itself and the surrounding land had been acquired by the state many years earlier and now served as a tourist attraction. People came to play golf, ride boats on the lake, and walk the nature trails. It was the last place Charlotte Jordan had visited.

From Jackie's report, I knew two boys had discovered her body about a hundred yards off the main trail. I glanced at Grace to see his reaction. The street bravado was gone now and his breathing was noticeably quicker. His eyes darted back and forth at the surroundings. With the other detectives supporting him under the arms, we followed Elvis down the mountainside to the upper walking trail. Katherine removed her high heels and went barefoot.

Elvis asked, "Any of this look familiar, Hector?"

"I don't know what you're talking about. I've never been—"

"Save it," Jackie cut in. "We know you were here. The State Crime Lab identified the DNA in your semen. We just wanted to give you a chance to tell us what really happened."

Elvis put an arm around Hector's shoulders. "C'mon, son, talk to us. Confession's good for the soul."

Fear began to show in Grace's eyes. "I'm not saying anything until I speak with my lawyer."

"That's where they found her," I said, pointing at the trees.

Everyone turned toward me.

"Over there, Mr. Grace." I reached out, grabbed him by the chin, turning his head and forcing him to look. "That's where they found her and that's where they found samples of your semen after you raped her. For a smart guy like you that was an incredibly dumb move. I teach forensics at Emory and it's a funny thing about DNA—it can remain intact for years and years. I read someplace recently they were able to identify Thomas Jefferson's descendants based on his DNA. Imagine that."

"Good for you," Grace said, jerking his head away. "And good for your fuckin' DNA. I don't know what you're talking about. I want my goddamn lawyer."

"And you'll get one," I said, bringing my face closer to his. "Your lawyer will defend as best he can and he'll lose, because DNA doesn't lie. You'll file an appeal—maybe lots of appeals—and you'll lose them, too. And with each passing year you'll grow older as you rot away behind bars. Eventually even your friends will forget your name. But the state won't. And one day the guards will come for you. They'll shave your head and fit you with a rubber diaper, then they'll lead you down a long hall to the electric chair. You'll probably piss on yourself and they'll have to help you walk, or maybe they'll drag you to what's waiting in that room at the end of the hall. You might even think about the DNA then because the mind does funny things at a time like that.

"I don't—"

"Have you ever seen someone electrocuted, Mr. Grace? I have. They put a wet sponge on top of your head so the current can pass through your brain easier. Then they put a leather hood over your face. I'm told it's hard to breathe.

"I've attended three executions. The last one was a real tough guy, just like you. He didn't want the hood. When they threw the switch, fire shot out of his mouth and eyes and everyone in the audience jerked back in their seats . . . including me. I'm not ashamed to admit that. Do you know what part has always stayed with me . . . the smell. We were behind an inch-thick sheet of glass and it got to us anyway. You have to wonder what it's like, smelling your own flesh burning. But I guess you'll find out after they strap you in.

"You raped and killed an innocent woman and you're going to die for it."

Jackie took the packet of crime scene photos out of the file and held one in front of him to look at. "Maybe this will refresh your memory, Hector. Take a good look. Her name was Charlotte Jordan and those stains on the rock next to her body come from you."

"*I didn't kill anyone,*" he screamed. "*I want my lawyer.*"

"Fine, Hector," I said. "We'll contact your lawyer. Who would you like us to call?"

"Charles Evans. You get me Charles Evans and stay the fuck away from me."

SIXTY-NINE

To say I was stunned at hearing Charlie Evans' name would have been an understatement. It took an effort to keep the surprise off my face.

After the detectives carted Grace off to the jail, Katherine and I sat down with Jackie and Elvis and told them what we knew. Like Rosen, they were skeptical, but they listened, particularly to the details of the research team deaths. En route, I also placed calls to Maury, Jimmy, and Phil Thurman and asked them to meet us at the detention center. Thurman was out of town, but his secretary said she would get a message to him. Katherine phoned the hospital and learned there was no change in Luther's condition. He had still not regained consciousness.

One of the peculiarities of DeKalb County's jail is that until a prisoner is actually checked in, they don't officially exist at least insofar far as the system is concerned. The holding cells, which are usually full, act as a kind of limbo. Elvis spoke with the watch commander and bought us some time. It would be hours before they got around to booking Hector Grace.

In the interim, he arranged for an undercover officer to be in the holding tank with him. While we couldn't eavesdrop on attorney-client communications there was no law that prevented us from noting what numbers Grace called.

At the station, I spoke with Katherine privately and made a request. There was something in Hector Grace's file I wanted to see again. She nodded and asked Jackie if she could borrow her computer for a few minutes. Everyone made small talk until she returned carrying a sheaf of papers. Several sections were marked with paper clips and highlighted in yellow. I glanced through them and found what I was looking for. My chest suddenly felt like someone was sitting on it. I made eye contact with Katherine, who shook her head sadly.

MAURY was the first to arrive, followed by Jimmy d'Taglia. Each of the people in the room were there for reasons which had nothing to do with Ted's case. I, on the other hand, felt everything was connected. As quickly as I was able, I brought them up to speed on my conversations with Reggie and Thelma Bowen. Katherine then took over and supplemented my comments with what she had found out about Ted's wife and the Fashion Avenue development. She concluded by mentioning Charles Evans and Tissinger were also listed as partners in the project.

She added, "We don't think Maureen came by her money legitimately. We just don't know how Tissinger funneled it to her yet."

"Maybe I can help," Jimmy said. "When our office began looking into Evans, Stanley, Doster & Young our interest was based strictly on tax evasion. That changed in the last few hours after our discussion with John.

"The four deaths we learned of this morning are disturbing enough. If Tissinger was involved in orchestrating them, we have a whole new ballgame. After John left I got curious about his conspiracy theory and started checking some things on my own. One, was who actually owns Southern Federal Bank. It turns out, over forty percent of their stock is held by a French company. Anyone want to take a guess who?"

"Tissinger?" Katherine asked.

"Actually, it's *Fiduciaire Tissinger, SA*. They're a subsidiary controls. Maureen Jordan received her business loan from them."

"Southern Federal also holds the mortgage on Harry Eberhart's house," Katherine said. "A friend of our checked the court records. What's more—"

A uniformed officer interrupted the balance of her statement when he stuck his head in the room and announced, "Elvis, Harry Eberhart is on the line. He's looking for Hector Grace. Says he got a call from Grace's wife about two detectives picking him up earlier."

Elvis said, "Tell him I'm in a meeting and I'll call him back."

The officer nodded and shut the door.

"What do you make of that?" Elvis asked. "What does Eberhart have to do with Grace?"

I said, "A few minutes ago I asked Katherine to check the State Court records on Hector Grace. We know Charles Evans represents Grace now. Apparently he took over from Sanford Hamilton several years ago."

I slid the papers across to Jimmy, who took a moment to read them and passed them around the room.

He inquired, "Are you trying to connect Evans with these murders?"

Before I could answer, Jackie commented, "I'm not seeing it. So Evans represented him? That doesn't prove anything. I can't imagine a man like Charles Evans being involved in this. I mean, why would he?"

"I'll start with Jimmy's question first. No, I'm not trying to connect Charles Evans with anything. I agreed to keep everyone in the loop and that's what I'm doing.

"Jackie's absolutely right. Charlie Evans could have been appointed by the court or he could have decided to do pro bono work.

There were nods of agreement all around.

"My interest is in Ted Jordan. At this point I don't think he killed anybody, though I think someone has gone to a lot of trouble to make it look that way. I'm also certain the death of his mother is related. Two separate murder scenes have deliberately been staged to mislead. We also have . . ."

I broke off what I was saying as I saw the expression on Maury's face.

He said, "I haven't had an opportunity to tell you this yet, John, but on the way here I received a phone call from Gil Mechlen at the University of Miami. He finally identified the weapon used to kill Sanford Hamilton. It was an ice axe, the kind mountaineers use. I believe climbing is one of your client's hobbies.

"Our copies of Mr. Jordan's bank records indicate he purchased just such an axe earlier this year. I'm very sorry, my friend."

And the hits just keep on coming. One step forward, two backward.

SEVENTY

KATHERINE put her hand on my arm. Jimmy shook his head and decided to look out the window at the cars in the parking lot, while Maury scratched a design on his legal pad with more attention than was strictly necessary. Generally, I felt like shit. The conspiracy defense had just exploded in my face.

It took a long moment to regroup. Charlotte Jordan had an affair. Maybe she had two: one with Hamilton and one with Evans. It certainly seemed that way. But no matter where I went, the bottom line was that her death had been made to look like a mugging and rape gone wrong. Why kill her and why the cover-up? And why would men of Evans and Hamilton's stature ever get involved with scum like Hector Grace?

Possibly Ted had asked himself these same questions. His response depended on the answers he came up with. One of them seemed pretty obvious now, at least where Sanford Hamilton was concerned. Still . . .

"I want another crack at Grace," I announced.

Elvis shook his head in the negative. "We can't do that. He's already asked for his attorney. If we keep hammering him we could lose the case. You're a lawyer—"

"That's right. I'm a lawyer, not a cop. I have no connection to the justice system, except as a private individual."

"And you think Hector will start talking just because you ask him a few more questions? I hate to say this, but it's pretty obvious your guy's got some serious mental issues. I know you have to defend him, but it all fits."

"Let me tell you what doesn't.

"From what I saw of Hector's rap sheet it indicates he's strictly small time. Murder isn't his MO nor is staging a rape. You had the same thought earlier in the car on the way to pick him up. Even if he killed Charlotte Jordan, the staged rape makes no sense at all.

"Next, we have Eberhart. Do you really believe Grace's wife called him? You phone a lawyer when you're arrested. It's unlikely Eberhart and Grace run in the same circles. He's a dyed-in-the-wool bigot and Grace is Hispanic. The last I heard the Nazis weren't recruiting Mexicans.

I turned to Maury. "Evans is out of town at the moment. But my guess is he already knows what happened and he can't afford to leave Grace sitting in jail, the one person who can connect him with Charlotte Jordan's murder. So who does he send? Eberhart, our accommodating Neo-Nazi."

Jimmy informed me, "That's quite a stretch, John."

"Maybe. Do I get the chance?" I looked at Jackie then at Elvis.

They exchanged glances. After a few seconds Jackie shrugged.

It took several minutes to locate Hector Grace. The deputies had put him in a cell well away from the general population. The interrogation room they took me to had a table and four chairs. On the nearest wall was a two-way mirror. Hector was waiting for me. As soon as he saw me he said, "I told you I got nothing to say. I ain't talkin' to no one until my lawyer gets here."

I smiled at him and walked to the mirror to adjust my tie. "That's right, Hector. You told us your lawyer is Charles Evans."

"So what?"

"And before that, it was Sanford Hamilton, except Hamilton's not coming because he's dead."

"Fuck off, man. You're not even a cop. I don't have to say shit to you."

I continued to look at Grace in the mirror. "Correct again. I'm not a cop. You may find this hard to get this through that little pea brain of yours, but I'm actually here to do you a favor. Charlie Evans is out of town at the moment. But not to worry, he's sending someone else to take care of you, a fellow named Harry Eberhart. That name ring a bell?

"No? Well, it doesn't matter because Harry Eberhart knows you."

My mention of Eberhart's name was just a way of keeping the conversation going. I didn't expect a street-wise guy like Grace to react, but he did. Sometimes you catch a break in a case and sometimes you don't. The reaction was slight, but there was no question about it. His eyes widened, and he tried to cover it with a nervous laugh. I could tell I had just struck a nerve.

I continued speaking to Grace's reflection. "Now Eberhart will be here in a little while. Your wife saw the detectives pick you up and she called your lawyer. Unfortunately, Evans is too smart to come out in the open yet. He likes to operate in the background, but you already know that, don't you, Hector? I'll let you in on a little secret. This is the *last* place Evans wants you, but not for the reasons you think.

"Pay attention because I'm about to tell your future. This is an old case and even though we have the DNA, we don't have an eyewitness to the crime or a confession, so the judge will set a bond. You won't have the money for it, but your pal Evans will see that it's posted, and do you know why?

Grace made eye contact with me in the glass and I returned a mirthless smile. "Good, I see you're curious. It won't take long before someone, maybe a friend, approaches you and asks you to help them. It doesn't matter why. All you'll have to do is take a little ride together. The problem is you won't be coming back. If that doesn't work, they'll snatch you off the street, or right out of your home if they have to.

"They'll take you to a basement where no one can hear you scream. It will be dark and the smell will remind you of a grave. Basements all smell alike, don't they? Eberhart will be there; so will Charles Evans. Then they'll begin asking questions because they'll want to know what you told the police. The sad part is, whatever you say won't make a difference."

Grace's chest was rising and falling more quickly and the color of his face was noticeably paler. I turned around and moved toward him. He watched round-eyed as I opened my loose-leaf and turned to the photos of Sanford Hamilton. The first picture was of Hamilton's charred body.

"Oh, Jesus," Grace said. He started to turn away.

I reached out, grabbed the back of his neck, and slammed his head into the book. After a second I let him go and flipped to the next photograph. It was a close up of Hamilton's hand showing where his fingers had been severed. Even my stomach tightened at the sight.

I brought my lips close to his ear and whispered, "This is what they'll do to you, Hector . . . because they need to be sure."

"Jesus, Mary, Mother of God," he swore under his breath.

"You recognize who this is, don't you?"

"It's Mr. Hamilton. Oh God, it's Mr. Hamilton. Man, I'm gonna be sick."

Still, I wouldn't let him turn away. Next, I showed him the photographs of Frank Nardelli. Maury had sent them to me for my file. Grace really did look like he was about to throw up.

"Charlotte Jordan, Frank Nardelli, Sanford Hamilton . . . Evans had no problem taking them out. How long do you think he'll keep a piece of shit like you alive? You won't last ten minutes on the street."

"You don't understand. It wasn't . . . I was just a kid."

"Detective Cyzck told me you have a little girl. They're going to bring pieces of you back to her in a bag, Hector."

"You don't know anything."

"Maybe you're right, Hector. I'll tell you what I do know for sure. If you're real lucky, you might live long enough to have a trial, but there's be something waiting for you at the end of it. It woke up and started looking for you in the dark the moment the state fixed your DNA at Charlotte Jordan's crime scene."

He shouted, "You get the fuck away from me. This ain't right. I'm gonna—"

I lunged across the table, grabbed him by the front of his shirt, and threw him against the back wall. My face was inches from his.

"Gonna what, Hector? Tell your lawyer?" I reached back, grabbed a photo of Charlotte Jordan, and held it up. "Take a good look. Her name was Charlotte Jordan and those marks on the rock next to her body come from you.

"You're going to die for what you did to her."

Tears were streaming down Hector's face now. "I was only a kid at the time," he repeated. "I didn't kill her. I swear to Christ. It was Eberhart. They just wanted me to jerk off on her body, but I never touched her. I swear on my mother's soul I never laid a hand on her."

"And what about Charles Evans?"

"Watching. He was there watching the whole time. Oh, Jesus."

"Who else was there, Hector? Who else killed Charlotte Jordan?"

"Just Mr. Hamilton, but he didn't kill her. He stayed in the bushes like Mr. Evans did."

I finally released him and sank against the table's edge. It felt like the energy had been drained out of my body. Hector must have felt the same way. There was a puddle of urine at his feet.

SEVENTY-ONE

Maury spoke to Thornton Schiff by phone to let him know the latest developments. Schiff informed him he would arrive at the jail within the hour. The gist of their conversation centered on offering Grace a plea bargain in return for his testifying against Evans. The revelations had been startling. Where that left me now I didn't know. Finding out you've been used by your friend isn't easy to swallow. It was impossible to explain away the ice axe. The sad fact was, in coercing Grace's confession, all I had done was make Schiff's case even stronger. If Ted lacked a reason to kill Sanford Hamilton before, that certainly did the trick.

While we were waiting, Katherine motioned for me to follow her outside. I had a pretty good idea what was coming. We exited the building and walked to the far end of the lawn.

"John, we need to talk."

"Okay."

"You know what I'm going to say, don't you?"

"I think so."

"And?"

"I need to give some thought to withdrawing from Ted's case and letting the police deal with it. Is that what you were about to suggest?"

"It was. It's about time you came to your senses. If he's dead it makes no difference, if he's not he's been playing you from the start."

"That's possible."

"When Schiff gets here, I'll talk with him and ask him to release you from the bond. I think he'll listen to me."

"K.J., all we really know is that Ted found out about Grace and his connection to the Evans law firm. We don't—"

"And as soon as he did he went after Sanford Hamilton. Why can't you see that? Grace and Evans would have been next on his list. We can add Eberhart, too. It's as plain as day."

"What about Frank Nardelli?" I asked.

"Someone who was in his way . . . revenge for screwing his wife. Take your pick."

I shook my head. "No, it's too simple."

"*Why?* After Hamilton and Evans got what they wanted from Charlotte, they set it up to look like she was stealing from their firm to get rid of her. They didn't want a sexual harassment suit floating around, did they? God, I hate lawyers. When that didn't work, they upped the stakes. Her son found out about what happened and sought revenge. It all fits."

"Too well. We're missing something."

"Like what? That's why Evans has been keeping tabs on you. It's not because he wants to help. He wants to make sure all the loose ends are tied up."

I asked, "And his motive for killing Charlotte?"

"Maybe she decided to cause problems, or maybe she just wouldn't go away quietly. Both men were married, right?"

"Yes, but—"

Katherine moved closer and touched her forehead to mine, "John, let's drop this loser and drive to Savannah for the weekend. I need a vacation. So do you. I'll model some new sexy lingerie I bought. You can relax on the couch with a scotch and soda and watch."

The last part didn't happen either. What she really said was, "There's a great little bed and breakfast I want to take you to."

I smiled back at her. Unfortunately, Katherine was making sense and I was running out of arguments.

"Let's say you're right. How do Tissinger and the feds figure into this? Someone tried to blow us into the next county two days ago, remember? They also shot Luther."

"Ted could have planted that bomb himself or hired someone to do it. What makes more sense: a government plot to frame him to protect an evil drug company, or someone who has already killed twice and is planting phony clues to deflect suspicion?"

As I saw it, there were two possibilities: Ted was using me as

Katherine was suggesting, or Charlie Evans had killed his partner. Motive and the recent purchase of an ice axe went on Ted's side of the board. Covering his ass, on Charlie's side—*if* Hector was telling the truth. I thought he was.

I explained, "You understand I'm still Ted's lawyer until the judge lets me out?"

"I know. A man's gotta do what a man's gotta do," she said glumly.

"It's more like a lawyer's gotta do what the state bar says."

"But you will withdraw, won't you?"

I took a deep breath and let it out. "Yes. It will take ten days under the rules. Until then—"

"We're stuck representing that bastard."

"I'm stuck," I corrected.

"*We're* stuck. I'm in for as long as you are."

WE stopped talking as Thornton Schiff's car pulled up to the curb. He got out, followed by a very pregnant-looking Rena Bailey. She waved. He didn't. Our meeting lasted an hour and it wasn't pleasant. Schiff was no longer interested in a plea bargain where Ted was concerned. Hector's story and what I shared of my conversations with Thelma Bowen only reinforced his view of Ted as deranged. If Ted was captured, he promised the only thing he would consider was the death penalty. Though he listened to Katherine's explanation of the Maureen-Tissinger connection and the Eberhart-Tissinger connection, he dismissed them as unworthy of serious consideration. It was the same for the research team deaths.

"Pure fantasy, Delaney. You're molding facts to fit your theory and I'm not buying."

"Then how do you explain a man being poisoned by arsenic?" I asked.

"I don't have to. Miami is outside my jurisdiction."

"Thank God everyone isn't endowed with your burning curiosity for the truth."

"Make all the fun you want, wiseass. Your client is going to the electric chair when I find him. The ice axe will turn up sooner or later. Even if it doesn't—"

Katherine interrupted by asking, "Thornton, would you at least consider the possibility that Charles Evans killed Sanford Hamilton and Frank Nardelli?"

"I would if there was a shred of credible evidence to connect him. All you have is smoke and the word of some slimeball trying to cut a deal for himself. Charlie Evans has been a respected member of this community for years and I'll have nothing to do with destroying the man's reputation. He'll be thrilled to hear what you people think of him."

Literally translated—I'm not risking my neck unless I know I can win.

I pointed out, "Grace also named Harry Eberhart."

"And what's your plan? Wait until he stops in and ask him to confess? People accuse cops of all kinds of things. You know that better than anyone. I've viewed the interrogation tape of you and Grace and, frankly, I'm appalled. It was you who mentioned Eberhart's name first. You virtually planted it in Grace's mind. When that didn't work you slammed the poor bastard into a wall. First-rate stuff, Delaney. Really first-rate. I'm not taking that crap anywhere near a jury."

Rena said, "I agree with Thornton about the confession. A defense lawyer would have a field day with it. But what if we get Eberhart to talk voluntarily? If there is anything to what Grace said, this could be the case of the century."

Meaning it will help your election campaign.

I started to add my two cents, but stopped when Katherine and Rena both kicked me under the table at the same time. Maybe women are more perceptive than men. Schiff looked from Elvis to Jackie and then at Maury while he weighed what to do.

Seconds passed before he spoke. "All right, I'm open to suggestions."

SEVENTY-TWO

It had been a crazy twenty-four hours. Jimmy said good-bye and left, presumably to report to Ray Rosen. I felt drained and wanted a hot shower. When Hector finally got his phone call it wasn't to Charlie Evans, but to his wife. She confirmed she had called Evans after seeing him being loaded into the detectives' car. Schiff, who was listening in on the conversation, looked at me and cocked an eyebrow. He said something to Maury. They both departed five minutes later, leaving Rena Bailey behind to work with us.

Elvis then returned Eberhart's phone call and informed him Hector had been arrested and was being charged with the murder of Charlotte Jordan.

"He asked if Hector was our only suspect. I told him, thus far. The son-of-a-bitch went on to say that Evans had called and asked him to look into the matter. He was simply returning a favor."

Maury observed, "Mr. Eberhart is a very accommodating man."

"Seems so," Elvis agreed. "I never liked that prick. Anyhow, he let me know Evans would probably represent Grace as part of his pro bono work. I told him that was fine with me. I let him know the bond hearing would be later this afternoon and the court was appointing Hector a lawyer to handle it."

"What else did he say?" Rena asked.

"He started digging around to see how strong our case was. I explained we'd take what we could after all this time. I figured that would make it sound more credible."

Jackie's eyebrows went up in surprise and she commented, "That was smart, Elvis." She patted her partner on the back.

He shrugged. "It's been known to happen."

So far, so good. Two hours later bond for Hector was set at $50,000. The judge even helped our cause by expressing his doubt about State's case from the bench. I thought Rena did a good job in holding back just enough facts to accomplish what we wanted. It's amazing how quickly the criminal justice system can move when it wants to.

When the hearing ended, Hector phoned his wife to let her know the amount. According to Jackie, when he wasn't busy vandalizing convenience stores, Hector worked as a window washer. Things must have been going well, because Mrs. Grace appeared at the jail with a certified check by the end of that afternoon. Twenty minutes later Eberhart showed up to drive them home. It was my turn.

The moment Eberhart caught sight of me coming out of the building his expression grew cautious.

"What are you doing here, Delaney?"

As I passed him on the steps I said under my breath, "Turn around and walk back to your car."

"What?"

"You heard me. I'm trying to help you."

Without another word I headed for the parking deck. Eberhart stood there for several seconds, uncertain what to do, before he followed me.

When we were alone he asked, "What the fuck was that about?"

I put a finger over my lips, then pointed to the farthest corner of the garage.

"One of the detectives, a Jackie something, called my office to let me know they had just made an arrest in Charlotte Jordan's case. Charlotte was Ted Jordan's mother. I'm here because I wanted to see who it was."

"So what?"

"The guy's name is Hector Grace. He's a spic—probably here illegally." I didn't like the term, but it was a reasonable way to build rapport with a fellow racist.

Eberhart folded his arms across his chest and leaned back against the nearest car. "What does this have to do with me?"

"I think you already know that, Harry. The detectives allowed me interview Grace for fifteen minutes before he clammed up and started yelling for his lawyer. I leaned on him pretty hard and told him he was going to the chair. That didn't sit very well with him."

"Great. If he killed someone then he ought to fry. We need to get all those worthless bastards out of our country. I'm just here doing a lawyer-friend a favor."

Eberhart was a good actor and he wasn't going to shake easily. I was better. Plus I was prepared. I took my cell phone out and pressed a button. It has a neat little recording device built into it. A second later my voice came on describing how the electric chair worked for Hector Grace.

"Those marks on the rock are from your semen, Hector. You raped and killed an innocent woman and you're going to die for it."

"I was only a kid at the time. I didn't kill her. I swear to Christ. It was Eberhart. They just wanted me to jerk off on her body, but I never touched her, man. I swear to Christ I never laid a hand on her."

I pushed the button again and waited.

"Big fuckin' deal," Eberhart said. "He's looking to work a plea for himself, so he names a former cop. That shit happens every day of the week and you know it."

I informed him, "You're right. But I don't have two detectives looking to make brownie points on my back. You do. Cyzck has a partner named Elvis who listened to what Hector was saying real close. I don't think he likes you."

"Well, I don't like—"

"They went into conference after they heard Grace's story and called the DA. He showed up here with Maury Katz an hour later."

"Katz?"

"Right."

"That fuckin' yid is always sticking his nose in where it doesn't belong."

Eberhart's breathing was more rapid now and a drop of perspiration slowly rolled down the side of his forehead. He was trying to appear calm, but his hands were clenching and unclenching. I could tell he was working out his next move and I didn't want to give him time. I continued, "The good news for you is this is the only record-ing. After Grace asked for his lawyer, I had to stop."

"So how come you're suddenly my best friend?"

"I don't like being used. Katz told me they finally identified the murder weapon that was used on Sanford Hamilton. It is an ice axe Ted Jordan purchased a few months ago. If you read the papers to-morrow you'll find I'm quitting the case."

"No shit? An ice axe? My partner and I saw the wound, but we figured it was gunshot. We made a note for the ME about it. I never got to see the final report."

"Doesn't make any difference, does it? Either way I'm out. I'm just telling you this so you can protect yourself. I was a cop for a long time and I know the drill with scum like Hector Grace. My guess is Elvis and his partner are going to arrest you the second you show up."

Eberhart eyes narrowed and he stared at me.

I continued, "Out of curiosity, did Elvis encourage you to come down here?"

"Yeah, he did," Eberhardt answered slowly. He looked back at the police station through the opening in the deck and nodded slowly. "He called to let me know that bond had been posted, the prick. This is total bullshit. I need to talk to a lawyer."

"I would."

I turned the cell phone around so the screen was facing him and pressed the button erasing Hector's voice. Eberhart searched my face for a few seconds, then turned and started for the exit. I headed in the opposite direction toward the stairwell. His voice stopped me.

"Hey, Delaney . . . thanks," he called back.

I put a fist over my heart and acknowledged him with a small salute. The Führer would have been proud.

SEVENTY-THREE

I HOPED Luther's SUV was still where I left it before Coleman and Britton jumped me. I still wanted a few minutes alone with each of them, federal agents or not. I'm not the forgiving kind.

Katherine wasn't happy about putting myself in harm's way. Eberhart might not be the sharpest tool in the shed, but he was clever as well as dangerous. You don't spend twenty years as a homicide detective without taking something away from the experience. We'd made a connection earlier, but that was all. Bigotry can be a great common ground, nevertheless there was still a long way to go before he trusted me.

Part of our plan called for me to announce my resignation as Ted's lawyer the following morning. At my insistence, Katherine returned home with Nikko. I promised to call as soon as I was on the way. Jackie gave me a lift to the Oakland Cemetery and then called it a day. It was nearly dark by the time we arrived.

Except for a pair of homeless people, the street was practically deserted. For all I knew they could have been the same couple I'd seen day before. I watched them for several seconds as they moved slowly along the broken sidewalk pushing a shopping cart packed with their possessions. Eventually I turned away, conscious I was intruding. There was a certain poignancy in the way they held one another's hands. I hoped there would be enough room at the shelter that evening.

Before inserting my key in the lock, I checked for signs of tampering and saw nothing. Out of an abundance of caution, I even got down on my back and looked under the car. It was an odd thing to do on a public street, but after what happened to Mr. Jag, I had no desire to increase the cemetery's population.

Everything seemed normal, so I put my key in the lock and turned it, holding my breath.

"No one's been near it all night," a man said behind me.

I knew that voice. I looked up to see the homeless couple about twenty feet away from me. The woman with Ted Jordan was Gabriele Severin.

I started to come around the car, but a slight headshake from Ted stopped me. He glanced away and stared down the street checking it. "Meet us at the end of the block in ten minutes. You'll see an alley just after you turn the corner."

It took a great deal of self-control not to react. A kaleidoscope of feelings were running through me. Fuming, I forced myself to get in the car and start the engine. Ted and Gabriele continued along the street at the same pace. Neither looked back. I watched them in my rearview mirror for nearly a minute before I put the Escalade in gear.

The alley came up so quickly I nearly missed it. He had chosen carefully. Because of the angle of the buildings there was no direct line of sight from the street. Luther's SUV barely cleared the brick walls on either side as I pulled in. Ted and Gabriele were waiting for me.

Our reunion was not filled with hugs and pats on the back. My expression conveyed how I was feeling. Ted held his hands up in a placating gesture as I approached him.

He spoke before I did. "I panicked. There was blood everywhere and I panicked, John. I just came back from the supermarket and was carrying in the groceries when I noticed a stain under the door. At first I thought maybe a pipe had burst, so I put the bags down and pushed the door open. That's when I saw Frank lying there. The stain wasn't water,—it was blood. His mouth was open and his eyes—Jesus, I can still see his eyes. A second later I saw the fingers on his right hand had been cut off, just like Sandy Hamilton's were. That's when I lost it. I left everything and ran. We've been in hiding ever since."

I didn't reply.

"I wanted to call you, but I didn't know if it was safe. When you came to the shelter the other day to speak with Miss Bowen, I tried to get to you, but I couldn't because of the men.

"You have every right to hate me. I just wanted you to understand why I did what I did. It was never my intention to pull you into this mess. If you think I should turn myself in, that's what I'll do."

Gabriele placed a hand on his arm. She was not looking at Ted, but was watching me, trying to gauge my reaction. The anger I was holding in check suddenly erupted and I grabbed Ted and threw him up against the wall.

"You are so full of shit."

"John, I swear to God—"

"Don't—because I don't want to hear your lies anymore. Find someone else to jerk around. I'm through. And for the record, I think it's a great idea to turn yourself in. It might stop you from catching a bullet."

Ted pressed his lips together and stared down at his feet. "I know you're angry. I didn't have time to plan anything out. Gabriele and I decided to stay underground until it was safe to get in touch with you again. I didn't kill Frank Nardelli and I didn't kill Sandy Hamilton and you goddamn well know it."

"I don't know anything of the sort. Why didn't you tell me about exhuming your mother's body?"

"I was going to, but I needed to be certain first."

"About what?"

"That I can identify the man who raped her."

"Save yourself the trouble. Charlotte wasn't raped. The scene was set up to make it look that way. The police picked up Hector Grace this morning, so you can forget about going after him."

"What?"

"Right. Sooner or later they'll figure out that Charlie Evans is more than just his attorney. But you already know that, don't you, Ted?"

Gabriele decided it was time for her to speak. "Don't be angry with Theo, John. He's telling you the truth."

"That would be a real novelty."

"After he learned about the DNA, Theo called me. I flew back to be with him. He couldn't sleep at night, so we called the police and spoke with a female detective, a woman with an odd name. All she would tell us was that Hector Grace had been in trouble with the law before and they were checking into the matter. Afterward, we went to the court and read about the cases ourselves. Can you imagine what it was like to see this information after so many years?"

"No, I can't imagine that, Gabriele."

"We were in shock when we learned Grace's lawyers were Hamilton and Evans. It was my idea to exhume his mother's body. That was the only way we could know for certain."

"And when did you find out about Charlotte's relationship with them?"

"Miss Bowen told us," Gabriele continued. "She wouldn't come right out and say it, but the implications were clear enough. She and Theo's mother had been close."

I let Ted go and stepped back. "So you decided to take revenge on Sandy Hamilton."

Ted leaned his head back against the brick wall and looked up at the sky. "Revenge for what? Having an affair with my mother?" he asked, in a weary voice. "You don't kill someone for that. Our plan was to confront Charlie with what we found out and see his reaction. Somehow he's involved in all this. I can't prove it yet, but I'm certain about it. We were on our way to meet him when those apes jumped you."

It just so happened I agreed with Ted, at least where Evans was concerned, but I was too pissed off to say it out loud.

"All the facts point to it, John. Don't you see? With Hamilton dead, Charlie's the only connection between Grace and my mother. If you add everything up you—"

"Come up with squat. Grace is a vandal and a petty crook. Murder is outside his pattern."

"He's also a known sex offender—"

"I just told you your mother wasn't raped. The scene was made to look that way for some bizarre reason. Stop me if I'm boring you. I'm sure you already know most of this. You also checked out Grace's file, remember?"

"Go on."

"When you and Gabriele found out your mentor was Grace's lawyer, I'm sure it came as a shock. It usually does when friends betray you. But this is what really happened: While Evans was trying to plead Grace to a charge of public indecency, the cops sent a blood sample they took from the back of his car to the State Crime Lab. The match they got was for the semen samples taken at the scene of your mother's death, *not* from her tissue samples, so exhuming her body wouldn't have proved a thing, because the rape was a phony.

"Evans' representation of Grace also doesn't prove anything either. What did you plan to do? Go to Grace's home and beat a confession out of him?"

"No . . . yes, I . . . I don't know—something."

"Brilliant—just brilliant. Fortunately, the cops got to Grace first. I spent most of the morning and half this afternoon with him."

I wasn't about to tell them Grace had implicated Charlie in Charlotte's murder and that he was now cooperating with the cops. We talked for several minutes and I slowly calmed down. Ted explained how he and Gabriele had eluded the police and about the leads they had been pursuing. Against my better judgment I listened. He still clung to his theory that Tissinger had set him up, only now he added Evans, Maureen, and the United States government to the mix.

I said, "If you had bothered to stay in touch you could have saved yourself a lot of trouble. Katherine figured out Maureen's scheme. It involves a business loan for a shop at Fashion Avenue. And since we're being so candid now, do you remember a detective named Harry Eberhart?"

"Certainly."

I went on to explain about the financial arrangements on Eberhart's home.

Ted asked, "So you do believe me?"

"I believe something's fishy. Possibly Evans, Maureen, and Eberhart are all in this together. Possibly not. I'll keep representing you until the court relieves me in ten days."

"What do you mean?"

"I mean, I'm out, Ted. Find another lawyer. I would have stuck with you till the end if you had leveled with me. We could have worked out a plea bargain with Schiff, but you decided to play me. I've been standing here waiting for you to tell me about the ice axe you bought, but you didn't . . ."

I broke off what I was saying as a police cruiser slowly pulled across the alley entrance, blocking it. At the opposite end another car was just rolling to a stop. Maury Katz got out. Ted and Gabriele saw them at the same time. Two uniformed officers exited the first vehicle and leveled a pair of shotguns in our direction.

When Ted realized what was happening, a look of panic crossed his face. He started to reach inside his coat. I reacted instinctively and hit him with a right cross to the jaw. Sending him to the ground in a heap. Gabriele screamed.

Maury started running toward us, moving with surprising speed for a man his age.

"Hold your fire!" he yelled at the uniforms.

Both cops raised their weapons and came around the vehicle.

Ted was dazed but unhurt. They put him onto his stomach and snapped a pair of cuffs in place, then hauled him to his feet. As they were taking him away he looked over his shoulder at me and said, "Find the fifth name, John."

SEVENTY-FOUR

MAURY said, "I'm sorry. When you went missing yesterday, Katherine called to see if I knew anything. I didn't, of course, but I began making inquiries. She gave me a description of Luther's SUV. One of our men spotted it this morning. He ran the plate and confirmed it was his. In view of what happened to your car the other day, I asked them to keep an eye on it."

"Thank you."

Maury massaged his lower back. "I'm getting too old for this. Are you okay?"

"I'm fine."

"That's a relief. Perhaps you'll introduce me to your companion."

I had to admire Gabriele. She had regained her composure and extended a hand to him as if they were meeting in a restaurant. "I'm Gabriele Severin, Detective, a friend of Theo Jordan's."

"I see."

"I'm also an attorney and I understand my rights."

"Your accent is French, no?"

"Correct. I live in Paris."

Gabriele removed her passport from the pocket of her coat and offered it to Maury, who examined it for a moment and surprised me by handing it back. I half-expected him to arrest her as an accessory.

He asked, "You're here in the United States on vacation, I assume?"

"No, I came here to help Theo with his problem. He did not commit those crimes."

"That is possible. Regretfully, our prosecutor doesn't share my view. If I may be frank, mademoiselle—Theo, as you call him, has done very little to help his cause. And if I might make an avuncular observation, as attractive as your outfit is, you might wish to change into something a little less trendy. One could get the impression you were attempting to aid an escapee from justice, which would constitute a crime. And by the way, manicured fingernails are also out of place with the homeless these days."

Gabriele glanced down at her shabby coat and smiled. "Thank you," she said quietly.

Maury responded with one of his shrugs. "For what?" Then he turned to me and commented, "You've had an interesting day, my friend. We didn't get a chance to talk earlier in all the excitement."

"No, we didn't."

"After I left the police station I spent some time with Ray Rosen and learned some interesting things." He glanced back at Gabriele. "This is not the time or place, but if you call or drop by tomorrow, I'll share them with you."

I told him I would and went on to describe my meeting with Eberhart in the parking garage.

When I was done, he informed me, "Be very careful, John. This is a dangerous man."

"I know. Right now, I'm concerned with Hector Grace. If we don't confirm his story, Eberhart walks. Now that everything is falling apart, he has no choice but to make a move. That's why he showed up earlier. The story about giving Grace a lift was a crock. The moment he gets him alone, that will be the end of it."

"We can monitor Grace through an ankle bracelet."

I informed him, "It's not enough. A sniper's bullet will do the trick. In my opinion we don't have much time. Our friends aren't going to let Grace run loose."

Gabriele and I exchanged glances, but she didn't comment.

I continued, "I need to figure out a way to get close to Eberhart."

Maury thought for a second. "Every other Tuesday he and his Aryan friends meet at a bar called the Silver Saddle in Little Five Points." He moved closer to me so Gabriele could not hear and dropped his voice. "We have a man on the inside."

STING operations never go quite the way you anticipate they will. This one was no exception. Ted and Gabriele's sudden reappearance had complicated matters. Neither Maury nor I thought leaving Gabriele on her own was a good idea, particularly with Britton and Coleman, or whatever his real name was, lurking about. I phoned Katherine from the car and let her know Ted had been arrested, then I explained the situation with Gabriele. She suggested I bring her home to stay with us for a few days until we saw our plan through. I didn't believe Ted had blown up Mr. Jag, but I was still disturbed by the ice axe and questioned Gabriele about it on our ride home.

"I heard you mention that earlier," she said. "Theo's been looking for it for months. Has it turned up?"

"You might say that."

She twisted in her seat and looked at me, waiting for an explanation.

I explained, "The axe was used to kill Sanford Hamilton. The police withheld that information from the public."

"Theo didn't lie to you before, John. Much of what he did was at my urging. He really did try to get in touch with you after that Nardelli man was killed."

"That makes me feel loads better. He should have tried a little harder. Unfortunately, the district attorney doesn't see it that way. He's only going along with our plan to see if there are bigger fish out there."

She asked, "What is your plan?"

"Did you find it odd that you weren't arrested earlier?"

"Yes, but—"

"I managed to persuade Thornton Schiff that there might be a connection between Harry Eberhart and Charles Evans. He wasn't totally convinced, but he listened. Whether the connection extends to Tissinger remains to be seen. At any rate, the next forty-eight hours are crucial. Assuming we're correct, we think Evans will send Eberhart to eliminate Hector Grace very shortly."

She was silent for a few moments before she informed me, "I may be able to help."

SEVENTY-FIVE

To my surprise, Katherine and Gabriele hit it off immediately. Sharing a house with one attorney can be daunting, two . . . well, you get the picture. Our home is decorated with a mixture of antique French and traditional furniture . . . Katherine's taste, not mine. Many of the pieces have gold leaf or ornate scrollwork down the legs. I suppose there's a certain charm to them that goes beyond my level of sophistication. Apparently, Louis XV thought so. At one time the furnishings reminded me of a museum, but I've grown accustomed to them over the years, or maybe it's numb. It's better to pick your battles. Lest you think I'm a complete wimp, I did stand firm on the subject of my overstuffed leather chair, which moved from New York when I did. Always one to compromise, Katherine relegated it to a corner of the family room and out of her general line of sight.

Gabriele received the grand tour and spent the first fifteen minutes ooing and aahing over the Austrian draperies and various bedspreads. I went to the kitchen to make a roast beef sandwich.

No sooner had I sat down than the phone rang. The caller ID indicated it was Charlie Evans. I wasn't surprised—disappointed maybe, but not surprised.

"Hello, Charlie. How are you?"

"Fine. More important, how are you?"

"No worse for wear. I got into a disagreement with that federal agent and his partner who were at your office the other day."

"What are you talking about? I was referring to the police arresting Hector Grace and charging him with Charlotte Jordan's murder. The news floored me. What happened with the federal agent?"

I took a mental breath and told him.

Charlie informed me, "You should have called if you needed help."

"I will the next time."

"What do you think of this situation with Grace?"

So much for his concern over me. "It shocked me, too, Charlie. Getting that call from detective Cyzck about a DNA match to Charlotte Jordan's killer was last thing I expected."

"It's amazing, just amazing."

"Tell you what else is amazing: Grace said you were his lawyer. Talk about being floored."

I placed a finger over my lips as Katherine and Gabriele entered the kitchen. I showed them my cell phone. Both moved closer in time to hear Evans reply, "We've represented that little bastard for years. He's always in and out of trouble. Sandy Hamilton was originally appointed by the court. I inherited him as a client after Sandy was paralyzed. He's been up to this office several times. I hope to God Ted never finds out. If he does, Grace's life won't be worth a plug nickel."

I ignored the obvious opening and told him Grace had implicated Eberhardt in the murder. I figured Eberhart had probably briefed him anyway, so there was no harm in confirming the news. Charlie was skeptical, if not downright contemptuous.

He informed me, "Grace is full of crap. I'm the one who sent Eberhart to the jail to drive him home. I've known Harry a hell of a lot longer than I've known Hector Grace. He's clearly trying to cut a deal, so he pulls a decent cop like Harry Eberhart into his mess. It just makes me sick. He can find another goddamn lawyer to represent him, 'cause I sure as hell won't do it anymore. I can just imagine how Ted will feel when he finds out. Shit . . . this is just horrible."

Charlie was definitely good. He was giving out just enough facts to support Eberhart's story and cover himself at the same time. Katherine shook her head in disbelief, then touched Gabriele on the shoulder. Using hand gestures, she pointed to my roast beef sandwich, to ask her if she wanted one. Gabriele nodded.

I told Charlie, "I'm sure Ted will understand; unfortunately, he has bigger problems to deal with at the moment. The police picked him up about an hour ago."

"*What*? Is he all right?"

"Just some bumps and bruises. We didn't have a chance to talk for more than a few seconds."

"What did he say?"

"Same old crap about Tissinger setting him up. Charlie, I need to tell you I've decided to withdraw from his case."

A silence before he commented. "I understand. He's put you in a pretty bad position. I told you in the beginning there are some clients that can drag a lawyer down with them."

"It's not that he ran away. Forensics recently identified the real murder weapon. It turns out to be an ice axe Ted bought a few months ago. The truth I can deal with, but not a client lying to me."

This time the silence was even more profound. I had a vision of Charlie sitting in his office, feet up on the desk, clipping the end off his cigar. He had probably used the cigar cutter on Hamilton and Nardelli. He took a breath, then told me, "All right, John, I understand. No one will blame you."

"I appreciate that. I'll put your check back in the mail tomorrow."

"Take your time. There's certainly no rush. Do you mind if I ask one more question?"

"Go ahead."

"Harry Eberhart told me bond for Grace was set at $50,000. Don't you think that's kind of low, given the charges?"

"Not under the circumstances. Personally, I'd like to see Grace in jail until he rots. Unfortunately there are problems with the DNA and the integrity of the tissue samples. I happened to be in court when they arraigned him and the judge was skeptical openly. I think the State was lucky to get any bond issued. There was one odd thing, though."

"What?"

"When it was over the prosecutor and Grace's attorney spoke. According to the prosecutor, the lawyer asked if a deal was possible. Apparently, he hinted there were other accomplices."

"*What?*"

"Speak to her yourself. Her name is Rena Bailey. She wouldn't say anything more. I'm assuming she wants to talk to her boss and the cops now. Between you and me, I don't believe Eberhart was involved either. Scum like Grace are always try to lay the blame on a cop. The accomplices are probably his friends. That makes more sense than Eberhart killing a woman he didn't know just for the fun of it."

Charlie commented, "That's right. It's interesting that you raise this point because now that I think of it, Grace probably did know Charlotte. He was at our office a number of times to discuss his cases. There's a good chance he ran into her. She was Sandy's secretary back then."

The cadence of Charlie's speech had grown quicker as the conversation progressed. His volume also went up. Often, these are tells that someone is lying. He was trying hard to explain his involvement with Eberhart and Grace. All of it fell short. The more I listened, the more depressed I found myself getting. One glance at my wife told me she had picked up on this as well.

She had forgotten to make Gabriele's sandwich. Absently, she reached out and slid mine over to her. When the conversation ended she shook her head in disbelief.

"I feel like a need a shower," Katherine said.

SEVENTY-SIX

I CALLED Maury to let him know how the conversation had gone. If Hector Grace wasn't previously in Charlie Evans's sights, he was now. Frankly, I didn't care. We agreed I would meet an undercover officer named Ed Mazurek the following day.

While Gabriele was finishing my sandwich, Katherine fixed another for me, half the height of the original and minus the potato chips. It was served with a glass of sparkling water rather than the beer I had in mind.

She informed me, "Water's healthier for you before bedtime. It nourishes the body."

Gabriele nodded in agreement. When I was in France I visited Villa Vergèze, where Perrier is produced and saw their famous spring firsthand. The villa is located outside of Nimès in the southwest part of the country. Perrier turns out about a grillion bottles of the stuff a day, so I was dubious all of it originated there despite what their advertising claims. My personal opinion is that they have the world fooled. There's probably a guy in Philadelphia filling the bottles from his bathtub. Outnumbered two to one, I gave in.

I asked Gabriele, "Earlier you said you might be able to help with the connection to Tissinger. What did you mean?"

She said, "There is a man living in Baltimore who used to work for the company. I think you should speak with him. His real name is Phillipe Brumot, but he goes by the name Arthur Burnside now. This is his phone number and address."

Gabriele picked up a pen from the counter and wrote the information on a napkin. For the first time I noticed she had changed her outfit, apparently borrowing a pair of slacks and a blouse from

Katherine. It was an improvement over the shabby coat and dress she had been wearing.

Katherine asked, "Why is he important? We know about four of the dead scientists. Does he know who the fifth is?"

"Phillipe *is* the fifth," Gabriele said.

"I'm confused," Katherine said. "How can this man be the fifth if he's still alive?"

"Phillipe is dying of radiation sickness. They've taken him to a hospital near Washington, D.C. for treatment. How long he will last, we do not know. Theo and I were going there to take his statement when the tile man was murdered. Obviously that complicated the situation."

"Obviously," I said.

Gabriele ignored my remark and continued. "We were trying to help."

Katherine asked, "How did he contract the illness?"

"Phillipe was Tissinger's financial comptroller for eighteen years. To answer your question, the doctors do not know how he was exposed. They only know is that he is dying. One would think an accountant is not a very dangerous occupation, however it became so after he sided with my father."

"In what way?" asked Katherine.

"Two years ago my father began to complain the Torapam tests were flawed. He discovered the missing suicides and found this information had also been left out of the FDA application. Believing it was a clerical error, he brought the matter to the attention of his superiors and was assured the problem would be corrected. He later learned, quite by accident mind you, that it was not. Again he complained. Only this time he was told to keep quiet if he wanted to keep his job. My father, unfortunately, is not the quiet type and told Philippe what had happened.

"Philippe asked him to place his concerns in writing. He then took the report directly to the president of the company. A month passed and then another and still nothing was done, so my father threatened to contact the FDA directly."

Gabriele paused to take a bite of my former sandwich and told Katherine, "This is wonderful. I didn't realize I was hungry until you asked if I wanted something to eat. Where was I? Oh, yes. He discussed what to do with me and I told him to phone Philippe again and insist the application be corrected. He did.

"That same week, two men came to his home and threatened him. One was Tissinger's head of security. The other he did not know. An argument ensued when my father would not relent. The next day, he was removed as head of the project and transferred to our plant in Germany. He quit. Philippe took up his cause, threatening to go to the newspapers."

Katherine said, "But he didn't."

"No . . . he didn't"

"When did Philippe become ill?" she asked.

"Less than a month later."

I inquired, "Is there any proof that Tissinger is involved?"

Gabriele put down her sandwich and looked first at me, then at Katherine, before replying. "The same two men who came to my father also visited Philippe. They explained the nature of his illness and told him his wife and children would be next if he didn't cease his complaints. He called my father and told him.

"It took month and quite a lot of money for us to arrange new identity papers. Philippe and his wife fled to the United States. So did my father and mother. I do not know where Philippe's son and daughter are now."

I asked, "Have you ever met these men? I mean would you know them again if you saw them?"

Gabriele nodded. "Twice. They appeared at my office one day to ask for my father's new address. I told them we were estranged and hadn't spoken for a long time."

I already knew the answer to my next question before I asked it. "Can you describe them?"

"One was bald. The other mentioned his name but I don't remember it. He was about your height, slender, blond hair and, perhaps in his mid-thirties."

SEVENTY-SEVEN

Aᴼᴛᴇʀ Gabriele turned in for the night, Katherine and I stayed up until three in the morning talking. We both agreed Ted was safer in jail than running around. Whatever Tissinger's resources, I doubted if they could reach him there. Regarding Messers Coleman and Britton, I wasn't so certain. As a cautionary matter, I sent Maury a text message asking him to assign Ted additional security.

Katherine conceded she might have been too quick to judge my friend. The operative word here is "might." She's not one to surrender her opinion easily. Well, neither am I. She still wanted me off the case, but accepted my need to finish what I had begun. Neither of us pushed the subject. We both agreed a vacation was in order once it ended. She was in favor of someplace with sand and water. I was ambivalent, but didn't voice it aloud. I told her it would be ladies' choice. Apparently, this was also not the right response. She wanted my input, so I suggested a week in New York with theaters and museums and maybe a Circle Line cruise around Manhattan would be great. We're going to St. Barts.

In the morning, it was decided Katherine and Gabriele would visit with Jimmy d'Taglia and bring him up to date on the situation with Philippe Brumot, now known as Arthur Burnside. I phoned Nikko and asked him he accompany them. After they were gone I went to Grady Hospital to visit Luther. He had recovered consciousness, but was still in ICU. The nurse would only allow me ten minutes.

"How are you doing?" I asked.

"Doctor says I won't dance again."

"You don't dance now."

"I know. But I didn't want to hurt the man's feelings."

"Do you have any recollection about what happened?" I asked.

"Got careless. Must be getting old like you."

The tube in his mouth made it difficult for him to speak. At best his voice was little more than a croak.

"They tell you how long you'll be here?" I asked.

Luther shook his head. "No way to know. Thurman came by just before you. Asked me the same questions."

"And what did you tell him?"

"That I'd settle affairs myself."

I looked at Luther for a long moment and nodded. "Did you see the shooter?"

"Didn't have to. Britton drove up to me in his black Chrysler and asked if you were around. Never got a chance to answer. They had a man waitin' in the cemetery."

"We'll set it right together," I told him.

Luther met my eyes and then looked away and stared out the window. After several seconds his eyes closed. Beside his bed on a metal stand was an IV bag of clear liquid. It dripped medicine down a long tube running into his forearm. I studied his face. It was grim and devoid of emotion. It's odd, but I had the feeling Luther was embarrassed by what happened. I patted him gently on the hand and turned to leave.

Phil Thurman was waiting for me in the corridor. In his hand was a paper bag from Starbucks. He took out a cup of coffee and handed it to me. He had another cup for himself.

"Clairvoyant?" I asked.

"Luther said you were on the way. I wanted to give you sometime alone."

I took a sip. "This is good, thanks."

We both moved to one side of the hallway to allow an orderly pushing a gurney to pass.

"Chocolate chip cookie?" he asked, holding the bag open for me.

"Our government spares no expense," I said, taking one.

Thurman smiled. "I'm sorry about your friend," he said.

"Me, too."

"Did he share anything useful with you?"

It was my turn to nod. "That federal agent I told you about, Brad

Britton, pulled up to him on the street. Britton wanted to know if I was around." He had a shooter hiding in the cemetery.

"If you were, you'd probably be sharing a room with Luther now. You do realize that, don't you?"

"I realize that this can't go on," I said. "If this is the way our government operates—"

"You know better than that," Thurman said. "I've spoken to my boss and he's spoken to the NSA. They don't have anyone by the name of Brad Britton with them or Stan Coleman either. Most likely this is a CIA operation, which makes it illegal."

"I'll make sure and tell Britton that when I see him," I said. "Maybe he didn't get the memo."

Thurman said, "I'll be in Washington later today. I received calls from both Rosen and Senator Talmadge. We have a meeting set up at Quantico with the CIA's director. It's about time for the right hand to let the left know what's going on."

"Agreed," I said, taking a bite of cookie.

"We'd very much like to talk to Britton and Coleman in person. You understand what I'm saying?"

"I do."

"So what are your plans?" Thurman asked.

"I have to finish up a few loose ends here and then speak to a man in Washington."

"And he would be?"

I related what Gabriele had told me.

"Have you let Rosen know?"

"Katherine is at his office now, briefing him," I said.

Thurman took a brownie out of the bag and broke off a piece.

"How come you got the brownie?" I asked.

"Agent-in-Charge," he said, taking a bite. "I could put a man on Luther's door if you like, but I don't think that will be necessary. Your call, though."

I turned to face him. "Because I was the target?"

Thurman's response was to lift his eyebrows. He took another bite.

SEVENTY-EIGHT

M Y meeting with Maury's undercover man wasn't for two hours. In preparation for what I had in mind regarding the Tissinger Corporation, I placed a call to a lady named Bonnie Cochran. Bonnie is a reporter with *The New York Times*. Three years earlier, she had written a story regarding a man named Warren Blendel and a case I was involved in. She did a credible job and reported the facts without trying to sensationalize anything.

When I was through summarizing for her, she said, "Jesus Christ, Delaney, if this is on the level the implications are staggering. You understand I'll have to verify the facts, but if it checks out, I'll have your baby. By the way, are you and Katherine still together? I remember you were going to get married."

I said we were.

"Great, you were a nice couple. How can I reach you?"

I gave her my cell number as well as Katherine's and cautioned her not to call the house directly. She understood.

Bonnie inquired, "What's your next move?"

"To withdraw as Ted Jordan's attorney. After that I need to meet some people. I'll keep you posted."

She said, "I have a friend at the ABC affiliate in Atlanta who could use a good story. Would you mind if I tell her about you withdrawing as Jordan's lawyer?"

"As long as you don't discuss anything else we've talked about."

"Scout's honor."

"Deal. I'll be at the courthouse in about two hours. If she happens to be there, I might be available for a quote."

"You, Professor, are too cool for school. Let me know if anything else develops."

A LITTLE over two hours later, I found myself standing at the clerk's office with my motion to withdraw as legal counsel for Theodore Jordan. The grounds were "irreconcilable differences," which made it sound like we were getting divorced. The process is about the same, except you don't lose half your stuff.

As I exited the lobby, I was met by an attractive woman in her early thirties. She introduced herself as Bitsy Daniels and said she was with Channel 2. It was the sheerest good luck her cameraman happened to be with her.

"Professor Delaney, there's a rumor you've asked the court to release you as Ted Jordan's attorney. Is that true?"

"Yes, it is."

"Has something happened to affect your decision?"

"Obviously, I can't reveal any communications with Mr. Jordan, Bitsy. All I can say is, we've come to view the nature of his defense very differently. A lawyer has an obligation to do what is ethically correct."

Bitsy's jaw dropped slightly at my statement, but she recovered quickly. For the record, I knew exactly what I was saying and exactly what point I wanted to get across. My hope was that the membership of the New Aryan Nation watched the news.

"Will your client be charged with the murder of Frank Nardelli?"

"I only represent Mr. Jordan in the matter of Sanford Hamilton. Should the district attorney decide to charge him, he'll be free to seek new counsel. You'll have to forgive me, but that's all I can say at this time."

SEVENTY-NINE

CANDLER Park has become trendy over the last twenty years. It's convenient to downtown and home to a number of young upwardly mobile types. As a result, housing prices have tripled there. Many of the homes are old, dated, and worth more for their teardown value than their ambience. The residents are quick to point out Candler's location and chic restaurants are what make the area so attractive. Apparently they don't mind having no closet space and squeezing into their kitchens. One has to make certain sacrifices to be trendy.

I used to frequent Dunphy's when I first moved to town. Back then it was just an old bar and grill. I was relieved to see it was still in business, though the name had now been changed to Chez Dunphy. With the exception of a few sidewalk tables, it looked the same to me. I went inside and selected a booth in the corner to wait for Mr. Mazurek.

The menus had also changed. They now offered a variety of continental dishes that had names I wasn't familiar with and items I had never heard of. I consider myself moderately sophisticated, but when you need a thesaurus to order your meal, something is definitely wrong. I selected the daily special, a chicken potpie, which seemed safe enough. It came with a side haricot verts.

"What's a *vert*?" I asked the waitress.

"Oh, they're green beans. A lot of people ask that."

"Why don't they just call them green beans?"

The girl shrugged. "I think Chef George has been watching The Food Channel."

"Chef George? As in George Dunphy, the owner?"

"Um hm, except he wants us to call him Chef George now."

I glanced at the kitchen and saw a man in checkered pants and a chef's jacket. He waved to me and I waved back. After placing my order I was offered a choice of sparkling or imported bottled water to go with my meal.

I asked, "Do you still have Atlanta water?"

"Oh, sure. I'll be right back with some brioche."

See what I mean? Apparently bread isn't trendy anymore, either. A short while later my waitress returned carrying a chicken potpie. At least that's what I thought it was. Basically, it looked like a bowl of soup. Instead of a pie shell, there were two thin strips of phyllo dough lying across the top.

"Didn't you forget something?" I asked.

"Like what?"

"The pie."

She gave me a weak smile. "This is how Chef George makes it. It's nouvelle cuisine."

"Let me guess . . . The Food Channel, right?"

"Yeah, sorry."

The rest of our discussion was interrupted by a bearded man who had just entered the restaurant. He was carrying a motorcycle helmet and dressed completely in black leather. We made eye contact and he headed toward my table.

"Delaney?"

"That's me."

"Ed Mazurek," he replied, offering his hand.

Mr. Mazurek took a seat and surprised me by ordering a bottle of Pellegrino. Maybe he lived in the neighborhood.

The waitress asked, "Would you care for something to eat?"

"Yeah, how bout a . . ." Mazurek frowned as he glanced down at my plate. "What is that?"

"Chicken *not* pie," I informed him.

Puzzled, Mazurek looked at the waitress for confirmation, but she only lifted her shoulders. "Right," he said. "I'll have a burger and fries."

"One hamburger with a side of *pommes frits*," she repeated, writing his order down on her pad.

"Huh?"

"Don't ask."

Once we were alone, he said, "Katz tells me you were with NYPD homicide for fifteen years."

"Thirteen. How long for you?"

"Nine this May. I caught your act on the tube a little while ago. Very convincing. Are you really withdrawing from the case?"

"It is part of the game plan. Talk to me about the New Aryan Nation."

Mazurek took a sip of his water first. "I've been working undercover for about three years now. Mostly they're a mixture of skinheads looking for someone to blame for their being losers. They also have a few older, more intelligent guys, but they rarely attend any of the meetings. Those are the dangerous ones in my opinion."

"Like Eberhart?"

"I wouldn't call him intelligent, but you definitely need to keep an eye on him. I've always had the feeling he takes his orders from someone else, someone who stays in the background. It's strictly a gut thing. The man higher up is the one we want."

"And you're now working with the feds on this?"

"How did you know?"

"I had a long talk with Ray Rosen a few days ago and he let me in on some of the background. Have you ever heard the name Tissinger come up in any of your meetings?"

"As in the drug company?"

"The same."

Mazurek shook his head. "Never. Why?"

"Rosen and his group have been trying to track down how money is being funneled out of the States to banks in the Cayman Islands. Maury Katz is checking with the Department of State to see if Eberhart made any trips abroad."

Mazurek nodded slowly. "He's gone a lot, so there might be something to it. I've never heard one way or the other."

I asked, "Are you familiar with Hector Grace?"

"I know the name, but he doesn't attend the meetings. Being Hispanic, he wouldn't pass the fitness committee. Katz filled me in on the murder of that lady nineteen years ago. You think there's a connection?"

"Not so much a connection as a loose end. Grace recently fingered Eberhart as one of the participants in Charlotte Jordan's murder. He also implicated Charles Evans and Sanford Hamilton."

"The lawyers?"

"Right."

"Brother, this is some fuckin' world we live in. So what want do you want me to do?"

"I need to attend your next meeting. I've already done Eberhart a favor by erasing a statement Grace made implicating him."

"You destroyed evidence of a crime?"

"Only my copy. Jackie Cyzck and Elvis Taylor have their own."

Mazurek stared at me for a second, then laughed to himself. "Eberhart's a stupid bastard, but like I told you, watch yourself. I'll cover your back as best I can, but—"

"You've got an assignment and you can't blow your cover. I understand."

We spent another hour talking. I showed him my tattoo and he agreed it would pass a casual inspection. He particularly liked the double lightning bolts.

EIGHTY

KATHERINE and Gabriele were still out when I returned to the house, so I left them a note saying I would be home late. I changed into a pair of jeans, boots, a dark blue T-shirt, and a sport jacket. I added an ankle holster and my second gun, a Glock 23. As Katherine says, it's all about the accessories. The Glock is compact, accurate as hell, and generally trouble free. I had no idea what to expect at the Silver Saddle, but it pays to be prepared. According to Mazurek, the meetings were mostly drinking and complaining about the state of the world. No one sat around plotting the government's overthrow, at least not openly. Most of the New Aryan Nation's shenanigans came down to threats and vandalism, but even those were infrequent. They reminded me of cockroaches that come out at night and scurry back into their holes when it's light.

I placed a call to Maury Katz and let him know I was en route to the meeting. We were both convinced Eberhart would make a move on Hector Grace fairly soon. Good for us; bad for Hector. The only question was when. Stakeouts and undercover work generally involve more waiting than action. You just have to bide your time.

I arrived at the Silver Saddle around seven o'clock and met Mazurek in the parking lot. We went in together. Not many people were there. Of those that were, a few were eating—most were drinking. Over a set of loudspeakers someone was singing about losing his truck and his wife, or maybe it was the other way around. On the opposite side of the bar was a smaller room where two skinheads and a third man, dressed like a plumber, were sitting. They were all watching a basketball game on a flat screen television. Mazurek entered, shook hands with everyone, and introduced me as an old friend. To be sociable, I ordered a beer and took part in the conversation. Mostly it centered on the game, basketball in general, and how sorry the Atlanta Hawks were that year. Eberhart and another man showed up about an hour after we did.

"I didn't expect to see you again," Eberhart said.

"I didn't expect to see you either, Harry."

"So what brings you here?"

"Him," I said, motioning to Mazurek with my head.

Eberhart and his friend turned to Mazurek for an explanation.

"John helped me out with a problem a few years back, then he dropped off the face of the earth. I saw him on TV this morning, so I decided to give him a call and see what he was up to."

"You were on TV?" the plumber asked.

"Unfortunately."

Eberhart informed them, "Delaney represented that yid cock-sucker who killed Sanford Hamilton. I saw the interview, too. He withdrew from the case today."

"No kidding?" the plumber remarked. "You find out the Jew did it?"

"Let's just say I learned some things I didn't know when I agreed to represent him."

Skinhead One commented, "I hope they fry the bastard. That'll make it six million and one."

The remark drew a laugh around the table, with the exception of Eberhart's friend. He simply smiled. Eberhart had yet to introduce him.

Skinhead One asked, "Did you know Harry was the cop who arrested your guy? What the hell was his name?"

"Theodore Jordan and yes, I knew. Harry and I have met before."

"No kidding. Small world, huh?"

"Certainly is," I replied.

"Delaney's okay," Eberhart announced, giving my shoulder a squeeze. "I gotta hit the can. Someone order some nachos—my treat." He tossed twenty bucks on the table and got up, leaving his friend there.

"I didn't catch your name," I said.

"I didn't throw it."

"So you just gonna sit there and be a mystery man or what?" Mazurek said.

The new arrival eyed him for a moment. "The name's Greg . . . Greg Mueller."

"Good German name," the plumber commented. "I'm Deiter Kuntz, but my friends call me DK."

"Actually, it's Austrian," Mueller replied, shaking his hand.

"You mean like Arnold Schwarzenegger?" Skinhead One asked.

"Yeah, like Arnold."

Introductions were made and Mazurek offered to buy the new arrival a beer, but he declined. Eberhart stayed gone a long time. Mueller was affable, but gave away nothing about himself. As the conversations around the table progressed, I occasionally caught him looking at me. I turned and stared back until he broke eye contact. I'm good at that sort of thing.

Skinhead Two finally got around to asking what he did for a living. He replied, "This and that."

From the way he carried himself I made Mueller as either a cop or a hired leg-breaker. Having run into this type before, my leaning was toward the latter. Either way, Mr. Mueller could be a problem if trouble started. He wasn't physically large, but looked solid enough, and I thought the bulge under his coat was more than just muscle. Mazurek glanced at me, and if I read his mind correctly we were both on the same page in our impressions of him. The fact that he was there caused the adrenaline drip in my stomach to tick up a notch.

When Eberhart finally emerged from the restroom, he went to the end of the bar and started talking on his cell phone. Using hand gestures, he signaled the bartender for something to write on. She handed him an order pad.

Once his conversation ended Eberhart returned to the table, but didn't sit down. He motioned with his head for Mueller to follow him.

"Gotta run," Eberhart informed us. "Sorry I can't stay longer. Something just came up at work."

"Take care of yourself, Harry," I said. "Nice to meet you, Greg."

Mueller indicated his distress at leaving by saying, "Yeah."

"Thanks again, Delaney," Eberhart said. "Don't play poker with these guys. They'll rob you blind." He gave everyone a cheery wave and headed for the door.

I waited for a minute to make sure they were gone, then left the table and went to the bar. The order pad was where Eberhart had left it.

"Do you have a pencil?" I asked the bartender. She was an attractive girl in her late twenties.

"Sure."

She reached behind her head and pulled one out of her hair. My eyebrows lifted in surprise and she giggled in response, then shook her head and let her hair fall loose.

"You don't happen to have a sharpener in there, do you?"

She smiled again, took back her pencil, and reached under the bar. A second later I heard the electric whir of a sharpener.

"First time here?" she asked.

"Yep."

"I thought so. I'm Elaine. Can I get you a drink?"

"How about a Killian's Red?" I didn't really want a beer. It was just an excuse to tip her.

Elaine reached into a cooler and produced a bottle for me. "Whatcha doin'?" she asked.

"A little artwork."

I continued to rub the side of the pencil back and forth across the pad, shading it in. After a few seconds the impressions Eberhart had left began to emerge. I was able to make out the letters G, C, and E on the first line and the numbers 3 5 2 and 8 on the second line, along with S R I N. Mazurek came over to join me and saw what I was doing.

"Great time for doodling," he said. "Your guy and his buddy just drove off."

"I'm not doodling. Eberhart was talking on his cell phone and writing on this pad a minute ago. I'm trying to make out what he wrote."

Mazurek peered over my shoulder for several seconds and commented, "Those numbers could be a street address."

"Exactly. I just can't make out the next part. He didn't press hard enough for everything to come through."

"Spring Street," Elaine said, looking closer at the pad. "See, there's a space between the S and the R. If you add a P and put G at the end it spells 'spring.'"

We both looked at her.

"I watch *Wheel of Fortune*. A lot of guys tell me I look like Vanna."

Mazurek and I looked back at the pad, then at her. "You're a genius," I said, squeezing her hand. I hadn't seen the quiz show in years, but added, "You're a lot prettier than Vanna White."

She rewarded us with a smile and went down the bar to help another customer. Suddenly the other letters made sense. The message Eberhart had been writing said:

Grace
3528 Spring.

"Call Maury and tell him to get to 3528 Spring Street on the double. Eberhart and his friend are going to kill Hector Grace tonight."

Mazurek's brows came together. "I know that area. 3528 is an office building. It has to be closed for the night."

"Not to a window washer."

EIGHTY-ONE

I SPED through the streets, pushing Katherine's Explorer hard. It's an ungainly beast and I was sorry not to have Mr. Jag with me. 3528 Spring Street was a twenty-minute drive from the bar. I figured I would do it in ten at the rate I was going. Along the way I tried Maury again and got his voice mail. For a fleeting second, I thought of calling Katherine, but dismissed the idea. I knew what she would say. At the moment I didn't need an argument or, worse, her rushing there to help.

After weaving my way through traffic and nearly hitting several startled pedestrians when I veered onto the sidewalk to get around a bus, I saw the building ahead of me. It was a modern glass and steel structure about fifty stories high. Two thirds of the way up a scaffold was suspended from the roof. I guided the Explorer toward the back and made for the service entrance. There was still no sign of Maury and I couldn't wait on him.

A beat-up looking white panel van bearing the name SUNSHINE WINDOW CLEANERS was parked at the rear entrance. So was a black Chrysler.

There were two service elevators in the hallway. One was already at the roof. The other was open. I got in, hit the UP button, and drew my gun. The amount of time it took to reach the top was maddening. The doors hadn't opened completely when the first bullet struck. I immediately dropped to one knee and fired three shots in succession at the muzzle flash. In the confines of the elevator the noise was deafening. About thirty yards away someone screamed.

At the opposite end of the roof were Harry Eberhart and Hector Grace. Eberhart had his gun pointed at Grace's head.

"Let him go, Harry. It's over. The cops will be here in a few minutes."

My eyes were still adjusting to the darkness. A quick glance to my right told me I had hit Greg Mueller. He was lying on the floor, one leg bent under him. The Glock fires a .40 caliber bullet and has an impact like a brick through a plateglass window. I didn't know if Mueller was alive or dead. I moved out of the elevator and began moving toward him. Problem was there were two of them and one of me. Wounded or not, a downed man can still be dangerous.

Eberhart called back, "I'm not letting this son of a bitch ruin my life."

"You did that to yourself, Harry. Don't make it worse. There's no way off this roof."

I spared another glance at Mueller. He was moving, though just barely. He had landed on his right side with his arm tucked under him. There was no sign of his gun. He was about twenty feet away now.

Eberhart said, "We can make a deal. What do you care about this stupid spic?"

"Actually, I don't . . . sorry, Hector."

"Delaney, I work for people who can take care of whatever you need. They'll help Jordan and set you up for life. You'll never have to worry about anything again."

"How about Charlie Evans?"

"He's just part of it. These people are big and they're into everything. You don't know what you're dealing with."

"You're right, Harry, but it doesn't make a difference. Killing Hector won't solve your problems."

I had nearly reached Mueller now and could see where my shots had struck. In the dark and firing rapidly most of it had been pure luck. Blood bubbled from a hole in his chest and a portion of his jaw had been blown away. Using my toe I lifted his body and saw the gun. I kicked it away. Mueller's eyes were open, but they were glazed over. He wasn't going anywhere. I left him and began moving toward Eberhart, keeping the Glock trained at his head. Hector was too close to risk a shot. Even in the cool night air, I could see Eberhart was sweating. They both were. The muzzle of Eberhart's gun was under Grace's chin and he was holding him by the back of his shirt collar.

"Tell me about Charlotte Jordan," I said.

"What's there to tell? The nosy bitch started poking around where she wasn't supposed to."

"In what?"

"The company books. She even stole a confidential memo about a new drug. Evans and Hamilton were treating her well, but that wasn't enough, so she tried to shake them down. It's always that way with Jews and money. You know that."

It wasn't a great time to bond, even for fellow bigots. "So they killed her?"

"That was an accident. Hector will tell you."

Hector never had a chance to respond. Three muted pops from behind me cut his reply short. One minute he was standing there. The next a third eye appeared in the middle of his forehead. He crashed backward into a metal safety rail and was dead before he hit the ground. Two more bullets caught Eberhart in the stomach and shoulder, spinning him around. A look of surprise appeared on his face as he crumbled to the floor. I reacted instinctively and dove to my left, rolling. I came up behind a cinder-block structure that housed the building's air-conditioning units. Another shot hit just above my head, sending cement chips flying. Someone was firing at me with a silenced weapon.

It took a moment to regain my wits. The Glock has a total of twelve shots in the magazine and I had already spent three. Five feet to my left was a service ladder attached to the side of the cinder-block housing. Fighting from an elevated position is always preferable. I scrambled to the top and looked back in time to see a red laser beam sweep the area I was just in. A moment later a crouching figure holding a semiautomatic pistol stepped into the light and began moving toward me. He was dressed completely in black, right down to his ski cap. He was still searching the ground level. The laser continued to sweep across the floor and along the edge of the tiny building I was now on top of. At fifty feet, I thought I could make the shot. Twenty-five was better.

To this day I don't know what possessed me to do it. I learned a long time ago there aren't any rules in a gunfight. My assailant was almost directly under me and it would have been a simple matter to blow his head off. Instead, I found myself dropping through the air. I hit him with the side of my body and we both went to the ground.

As I came up in a crouch and started to level my gun he it kicked out of my hand. A second kick caught me in the chest and put me on my back.

Tissinger's head of security tried to stomp my head as I was rising. I caught his leg and landed a punch to his groin. Actually it was two punches. I didn't particularly like Stan Coleman. He doubled over in pain and couldn't get out of the way in time when I rushed him. My shoulder caught Coleman squarely in the stomach, leveling him. Three punches in a row found his nose and chin. He responded by digging his thumbs into my eyes. A heavy knee to the middle of my back knocked me off his chest.

Coleman slowly got to his feet and looked around, trying to find his weapon. I didn't know where it was. I didn't know where mine was.

"You're dead, asshole," he said, spitting out a mouth full of blood.

We both saw my Glock at the same time and went for it. The race was a tie. As we were struggling to gain control, I drove my forehead into his nose and felt it break. Coleman grunted and swung an elbow at my head. The blow glanced off my chin and hurt like hell.

When your nose is broken, the eyes start to water which is exactly what happened to Coleman. I took advantage of the situation. I can't say how many times I hit him before he went down again. He was tiring and starting to panic. Eventually he dropped to one knee and held up a hand for me to stop. Like an idiot, I did.

The moment I reached out to pull him to his feet, he charged. The momentum carried us backward toward the roof's retaining wall. This time I felt, rather than saw it, as my sense of self-preservation kicked in. Twisting my body sideways, Coleman hurtled past me, arms flailing as he tried to stop himself. I grabbed for his tie and caught it. My hand was now the only thing keeping him from plummeting into oblivion. He was back on his heels and half way over the edge.

"What's Tissinger so afraid of?" I asked.

"Fuck off, Delaney. You're a dead man. You just don't know it yet."

"I asked you a question."

"If it's not me it will be someone else. We'll find your wife, then your kids. We'll finish what we started with that nigger in the hospital. You're up against more than you can handle. Why don't you get wise?"

The sound of an elevator arriving caught my attention. Somewhere behind me Maury Katz yelled, "John, don't—"

If Coleman was bluffing, it was the wrong time, the wrong place, and the wrong person to do it with. In the end he might have realized that when our eyes met. His expression changed from of one of belligerence to terror as my fingers relaxed their grip.

"Oops."

I leaned over the edge and watched him tumble through the air end over end until he smashed into the hood of a passing automobile. The back end of the car rose abruptly and its horn started blaring.

EIGHTY-TWO

AURY and the two uniforms with him. They were probably in time to see Coleman leave.

"*Holy shit,*" one of the officers exclaimed. He immediately drew his service revolver and pointed it at me.

"He's with us," Maury said. "See to the others."

Maury joined me. "Are you hurt, John?"

I shook my head and bent over, putting my hands on my knees. In a moment my breathing returned to normal.

Maury moved to the roof's edge and peered over it. "Who was that?" he asked.

There was now a great deal of commotion below. Somewhere off in the distance the sound of a siren could be heard.

"Coleman or Ledoux. Take your pick."

"This one's dead," one of the officers called out. He was kneeling over Hector's body.

His companion moved to where Eberhart lay. He bent down for a closer look. "This guy's still breathing. I don't know for how long though. I've called for two ambulances. Jeez, what a freakin' mess. Hey wait a minute, he's trying to say something."

The officer brought his ear to Eberhart's lips. We all moved closer. The only word I could make out clearly was "Evans." Maury took out a notepad and asked the officer to write down everything he had heard. His partner read it and signed the statement afterward. He then showed it to me.

"I'll make one copy for you and Rena Bailey," Maury said. "Mr. Jordan is a lucky man."

I looked at the carnage on the rooftop and took a deep breath.

LATER that evening a Maury phoned to let me know that Harry Eberhart had died on the way to the hospital. His family was notified and his funeral was scheduled for the following day. Rena Bailey also left a message on our answering service saying that after reading Eberhart's confession the district attorney had ordered Ted's release. And that all charges were being dropped. Katherine and I watched Schiff's press conference on the eleven o'clock news.

Before retiring for the night, I went into the kitchen and played Rena's message one more time. There was something in it I had missed earlier.

"John, Rena Bailey here. Just thought I'd let you know I had a meeting with Thornton and Maury Katz. He showed us Eberhart's confession. That should pretty much do it for your client. I know you'll be happy about the way most things have turned out."

The news for Charlie Evans wasn't quite as good. According to Maury, who called again the following morning, Evans was at his office when the cops arrived to arrest him. After his secretary announced their presence on the intercom, a single gunshot rang out. They rushed back to his office, but it was too late.

Evans had put a revolver in his mouth and pulled the trigger. I conveyed this news to Katherine, who shrugged and continued packing for our weekend in Savannah.

She inquired, "How do you feel about this dress?"

"Deeply emotional."

"John."

"I like it," I told her. I walked over to the bar and fixed myself a Bloody Mary.

"That's your second one," Katherine commented.

"Am I being punished?"

"Of course not, but we should set a limit."

"I didn't realize we were drinking."

"We're not. I'm trying to get you to eat healthy. Actually one glass of red wine a day isn't a bad idea."

"All wine tastes the same to me. How about if I just have the tomato juice?"

Katherine drew a long-suffering breath as she folded a sweater. "I love you," she said.

"I love you, too."

She asked, "What time would you like to leave? Savannah is about a four-hour drive."

"Right after the funeral."

"I still think it's weird."

"It's something I have to do, K.J. We can stay at that bed and breakfast of yours."

Katherine shook her head. "My father always said you were a bit odd."

"If anyone would know about odd, it's your father."

The arched eyebrow I got effectively terminated that conversation.

THE Bethlehem Evangelical Church is located in the little town of Lithonia, about a mile off I-20. I spotted Maury's unmarked cruiser in the parking lot. He was already inside. Katherine and I entered and took seats next to him. Our timing had been good. The minister was just finishing his remarks about the deceased. Friends and family stood and began filing past Harry Eberhart's casket to pay their final respects. I noticed Ed Mazurek near the front of the line. He had combed his hair and put on a sport jacket in honor of the occasion. Two members of the New Aryan Nation were behind him.

After shaking Maury's hand, I stood and took my place among the mourners. Katherine and Maury remained seated. When I reached the casket I paused. Harry was dressed in a gray suit and looked at peace. The morticians had done a fine job. I reached out and took his hand, then bent my knee to touch my head to the side of the casket.

Once I finished his wife stopped me and asked, "Were you a friend of Harry's?"

"We only knew each other a short time, but we were close at the end."

She nodded and hugged me. On my way back up the aisle a few people touched my sleeve in sympathy. It was a genteel thing to do, but unnecessary . . . for I had already drawn a good deal of comfort knowing that Harry Eberhart would spend the rest of eternity clutching a Jewish Star of David in his hands.

Hopefully St. Peter had a good sense of humor.

EIGHTY-THREE

SAVANNAH is an old city on Georgia's east coast. It has numerous interconnecting squares and fine homes with intricate wrought-iron balconies. Farther south than Atlanta, autumn comes later to this part of the state. The leaves were still vibrant and blew down the street past twisted old oaks with Spanish moss hanging from them.

Our bed and breakfast was at a place called the Wentworth Inn, a brown antebellum mansion not far from the Bonaventure Cemetery. This wasn't a great recommendation in my opinion. The owner, a pleasant lady named Sue Karsten, met us at the front door with two glasses of champagne and a plate of homemade cookies. Cute. Katherine was in seventh heaven. I was happy, too, but more for the pleasure she was getting than from the ambience. The inn was nice enough, but early American quilts and doilies aren't my thing. After the last few days I could have fallen asleep standing. I held that opinion, and made all the appropriate noises as Mrs. Karsten gave us a tour of the place. She informed us the house was on the National Ghost Register. Ghosts have to register? I definitely should have brought my gun.

The rest of our day was spent shopping and strolling along Factor's Walk. We watched ships in the harbor gliding silently past us.

That evening we dined at a restaurant Katherine had found in a travel guide. She called her daughter and told her we had arrived safely and how romantic the atmosphere was. I ordered a whiskey sour and listened politely as they engaged in rapid girl-talk.

When my wife finally came up for air, she told me, "Alley says to have a good time."

I smiled and sent her my love.

Like the Wentworth Inn, our restaurant was also located in an historic mansion. A plaque at the front door proudly proclaimed, or warned visitors, that it's also listed on the National Ghost Register. Apparently ghosts are big in Savannah. If my wife suggested we take the midnight tour of the cemetery she read about in her guidebook, I was putting my foot down. I had enough problems trying to get our waiter to reappear. Ghosts I didn't need. When he finally showed, I ordered another drink and got a look from Katherine. I canceled it and went with an ice tea. She told the waiter to make it unsweetened.

The evening was languid and the food good. The highlight of it took place in an oversized bathtub back at the inn.

In the morning, we mopped up as much water as we could and thanked Sue Karsten for the stay. We assured her no ghosts had visited our room during the night, not that we would have noticed.

Sue informed me, "A courier delivered this letter for you a little while ago."

I opened the envelope and read it.

Professor, congratulations on a job well done. It would seem your work is nearly at an end. May I say again, Washington is particularly lovely this time of year. Stop by and say hello if you're in the area.

With kind regards,
Sam Talmadge

I showed Katherine the senator's note on our way to the car.

"What does he mean, 'your work is nearly at an end?' "

"He's referring to the Tissinger Corporation. Now that I think of it, Rena Bailey implied pretty much the same thing."

"What did she say?"

"It was something about my being pleased at the way *most* things had turned out. I didn't get her reference at the time. I thought she meant Ted's case."

"Haven't you done enough?" Katherine asked.

I considered that for a second. "They want me to finish what I started."

Katherine moved closer to me and lowered her voice. "Why don't we let Ray Rosen and the authorities handle this now? We have our own lives to live."

She had a point. Ted was out of danger and the people who murdered his mother were dead. Maybe Charlotte would rest easier. Sooner or later the authorities would get around to Maureen. The tie-in between her and Tissinger might not be a lock, but there was enough to torpedo her alimony claim and prosecute her as a coconspirator.

And then I thought back to what started it all. Two kids doing a college paper looked at a bunch of statistics that didn't add up. It would be nice to say the matter was closed, except those statistics represented people. Like Charlotte Jordan, there was no one to speak for them. I could look the other way and pretend they didn't matter, but they did.

As I wrestled with the problem, I was aware Katherine was watching me. When our eyes met she searched my face for a moment, then muttered "oh, shit," under her breath.

I started to speak but she put her finger on my lips. "That's why I love you. How long will it take us to drive to Washington?"

EIGHTY-FOUR

IN Richmond, Virginia I stopped at a service station to get gas and placed a phone call to Bonnie Cochran at *The New York Times*.

"Bonnie . . . John Delaney here. I thought I'd touch base and see how your story is coming."

To my surprise she responded, "Just a moment please," and placed me on hold.

Nearly thirty seconds passed before she came back on the line. This time there was an echo when she spoke. "Delaney? Sorry about that. I wanted to move to where we could talk privately. I'm in the stairwell. Where are you?"

"In Richmond just off I-95. What's up?"

"What's up? Two hours after I started checking the facts I got called into my editor's office. He was there along with our company attorney, a lawyer from the Department of Justice, and a friend of yours from the FBI. They informed me I was delving into matters involving national security and delivered a request from the administration asking that we hold off reporting anything for at least sixty days."

"Did you happen to catch my friend's name?"

"Sure . . . it was Mike Franklin."

"Interesting. What did he look like?"

"I'd say he was about thirty-five, blond hair, and athletic-looking. He was dressed well."

"Like a tennis pro in a business suit?"

"Yeah, that's a good way to describe him."

"I hate to break this to you, Bonnie, but I've known Mike Franklin for twenty years and he's closer to fifty than thirty. He's also about twenty pounds overweight and has thinning brown hair."

"That can't be. I saw his identification. I also saw the Justice guy's ID. Maybe they have the same name."

"Maybe, but I doubt it. I've run into the person you've described several times in the last few days. His name is Brad Britton. The first time we met told me he worked for the NSA. A few months earlier he told the real Mike Franklin that he was with ATF's terrorism task force in Dallas. The smart money says he's a spook."

"A what?"

"A spook. It's another name for a CIA operative. Did you verify the Justice Department lawyer's credentials?"

"Uh . . . no. He had a photo ID. I saw that myself."

"It might be a good idea to check with the D.C. bar and see if he's registered."

"So these guys lied to us? They know we always check our facts. Sooner or later we'd find out their story was bull. It doesn't make sense."

I informed her, "It does, if something critical is about to happen. I just don't know what that is yet."

Bonnie took a moment to digest what I had said. "All right, I'll look into our guests. What are you doing in Richmond?"

"Katherine and I are on our way to Washington. There's a man I need to see. His real name is Phillipe Brumot, but he goes under the name Arthur Burnside now. At one time he was Tissinger's financial comptroller. When he found out about the situation with their Torapam medication he complained to his superiors and was told to shut up. At the moment he's in a hospital dying of radiation poisoning."

"Oh my God."

"The information is secondhand, but I trust it. I'll call once I speak with him. After that Katherine and I will be at the National Archives."

"Why?"

"I want to review any agreements between Tissinger and our government."

Bonnie informed me, "I can access them online. What are you looking for?"

"Anything that's time critical."

"Okay, I'm on it," Bonnie said. "Where can I reach you?"

"We don't have reservations yet, so use my cell phone. I'll let you know where we are once the dust settles. Is the story still on?"

"I'll need to speak with my editor again. When your friends approached us we agreed to wait for a green light from the administration in the spirit of being patriotic. If he finds out it was a snow job, he'll blow his top. Tom's old school when it comes to reporting.

"Great."

"We also hired a math professor from Georgetown University to go over the statistics you provided."

"Sounds good, Bonnie. I'll call you back after we finish interviewing Mr. Brumot."

Katherine was just returning as I clicked off. I told her I had just spoken with Bonnie Cochran.

She nodded, then informed me, "Gabriele is meeting us at the hospital. I thought Brumot would be more likely to talk if someone he knows is present. Her plane should arrive in about two hours. Jimmy and Ray Rosen land around the same time."

I kissed her on the forehead. "That's pretty fast work. I'm sorry about cutting our weekend short, but I'll make it up to you, Ms. Adams. That's a promise."

Katherine reached for the lapels of my jacket and pulled me to her. "The name's Delaney—Mrs. John Delaney. And don't think this gets you out of taking me to the beach."

EIGHTY-FIVE

WE saw Gabriele as she came through the airport security area. She kissed Katherine on both cheeks. I got a one-cheek peck. Jimmy and Ray Rosen settled for handshakes. The French, I suppose, have rules governing such things. I was a little surprised Ted wasn't with her. Gabriele explained he wanted to spend some time with his sons and sent his regards.

A court reporter met us at the hospital, along with Gabriele's father and her mother. She informed us both had been in the United States for the last two months. They were watching her car the day I first appeared in court for Ted. Madame Severin was a woman of middle height and fine features. The resemblance to her daughter was obvious. Her father was tall with a prominent nose and a bit shabby-looking.

Because of Brumot's deteriorating condition, the doctor would only permit a few people in the room at a time. Jeanne and Noel Severin went in first to pave the way. When they came out her eyes were red and Noel's face was ashen.

"He's so thin. I didn't recognize him at first," Jeanne told her daughter. "All of his hair is gone and his fingers have turned black."

Noel's eyes met mine. He shook his head and put an arm around his wife's shoulders.

Gabriele went in next and was out five minutes later. She was also crying. Katherine and Jimmy, who had been speaking with the doctor, came over to join us.

"He'll only give us thirty minutes," Jimmy said, "and maybe not even that much. It depends on how well Brumot tolerates the questions. Apparently he's taken a turn for the worse over the last forty-eight hours. They don't expect him to last long."

Rosen asked, "What about that subpoena for his medical records?"

"I'll see to it while you and the court reporter go in," Jimmy said. "According to the doctor, they found traces of polonium-210 in Brumot's urine."

"Which is?" Rosen asked.

"A radioactive isotope. Basically, it's a death sentence."

Rosen nodded soberly and turned to the doctor, who was standing a few feet away. "I'll be as quick as I can."

Katherine elected to wait outside with Gabriele and her family. Rosen, the court reporter, and I went inside. The smell of death hit me as soon as I walked in the room. That's the only way I can describe it. What little I knew about radiation sickness came from movies and television.

Lying on the bed in front of me was a man who looked more like a holocaust survivor than someone in his early sixties. On a nightstand next to him was a photograph of Brumot and a woman I assumed was his wife. They were standing in front of the *Arc de Triomphe* in Paris, their arms around each other's shoulders. They were both smiling. I had no idea when the photo was taken, but the deterioration in Brumot was remarkable. His eyes seemed to have sunken into his skull and there were dark circles under them. The rest of his skin was sallow. His arms were covered in lesions.

The sight caused my stomach to revolt. I wanted to look away . . . to be someplace else. It took an effort not to show any reaction and force a pleasant smile to my face.

Rosen began, "Mr. Brumot, I'm Ray Rosen with the U.S. Attorney's office in Atlanta. This is Professor John Delaney. He's been assisting us and the Severin family. I appreciate you seeing me, sir."

"Noel explained the situation. How can I help you, counselor?"

"I understand you were Tissinger's financial comptroller."

"That is true."

"And you recently left them and came here to the United States."

"It would be more accurate to say I *fled* to this country."

"May I ask why?"

"Because I am going to die of radiation poisoning—very shortly, they tell me. I did not wish to see my family suffer the same fate, so we left France and came here."

"Did you have any reason to believe they would also become sick?"

Rosen already knew the answers to most of these questions. His purpose in asking them was to make a record of Brumot's responses. I stood at the end of the bed listening. The metal on the frame felt cold under my fingers. At one point Brumot and I made eye contact. I looked away before he did. I think he sensed how I was feeling.

Over the next half hour he confirmed what Gabriele had told us and explained how he had brought the Torapam problem to the attention of Tissinger's management. Brumot had even spoken to the company president. He went on to describe the men who came to him after he had fallen ill, the ones who told him the real reason for his sickness. One of them had to be the late Stan Coleman, whose real name was Charles LeDoux. The other sounded very much like Brad Britton.

I asked, "Monsieur, did you ever tell the authorities in your country what happened?"

Brumot's lips pulled back into a skeletal smile.

"Twice . . . I went to them and twice and was told there was nothing they could do without proof. The last time, a police inspector I spoke with came to our office and met with Èdith Legard. Madame Legard is Tissinger's president. I was fired the next day. That was the night Le Doux and his companion came to my home and told me I had been poisoned. They were very calm, even apologetic. They said it was nothing personal. An interesting expression, wouldn't you say? I, however, did take it personally. Tissinger is a very powerful company. They control a great many things . . . politicians, banks, and alas, our police."

Ray Rosen and I exchanged glances.

I inquired, "What exactly did Madame Legard say when you told her that Torapam might be causing suicides among the test subjects?"

"She said, 'A few less Muslims in the world would be an improvement' and 'no one cares about what happens in third world countries.' It might have been in jest, but I had the feeling she was not joking. She went on to explain that millions had been invested in the project."

Rosen asked, "During the time you were with Tissinger, did you ever see any contracts or documents between them and our government?"

"There were several. Most involved tax incentives if we agreed to build our plants here and employ a certain number of people."

"Is there anything significant that might be happening in the next sixty days?" I inquired.

Brumot's brows came together and he pondered that for a moment. "There is one. When I left, our largest facility was still under construction in the state of North Carolina. They are to employ nearly six hundred people. The plant will produce Torapam and forty other medications. There will also be a research center associated with large medical school. I don't remember the name, but it is near the city of Raleigh."

"Duke University?"

"I believe that is it, yes."

"Both your state and federal governments reduced property and revenue taxes to a fraction of what they would have been, for a period of ten years, because the center will operate under a United Nations charter."

Rosen asked, "Why is the time frame important?"

"If the North Carolina plant is not operational by December thirty-first of this year, the charter passes to our competitor, Warwick Reed. The loss of revenue would probably approach nearly a billion dollars."

The questions lasted another five minutes before the doctor stepped in and called a halt. The court reporter packed up his equipment and promised to have a transcript ready within the next twenty-four hours.

EIGHTY-SIX

WHEN I stepped into the hallway, Katherine wasn't there. Jimmy told me she had gone to the cafeteria to get a Diet Coke. I informed him of my conversation with Bonnie Cochran and about the story she was working on.

Rosen said, "I have no complaint with that. You held up your end of our deal. Give me twenty-four hours to get the indictments drawn, then you and the reporter can go to town. There's no place for this shit in our society. You did a good job, Delaney."

He extended his hand and we shook.

"Will the indictments make a difference?" I asked.

"They'd better or I'm in the wrong business. Just so you know, we've been in touch with the FDA. They're going to pull the plug on Torapam, new and old. When I get to the car I'll call North Carolina's attorney general and let him know that Tissinger might not be moving into their new plant just yet."

I expanded on my previous question and asked, "Aren't you worried about interference from your employer? I haven't heard from Phil Thurman yet, but there's a good bet one of the gentlemen I've met in this case works for the CIA."

Rosen stretched his neck first one way and then the other. "It doesn't matter. My job is to prosecute people who break the law. I would hope whoever's behind this isn't part of our government, but if they are it won't make a difference. Mind if I ask you a question now?"

"Sure."

"I spoke with Maury Katz and he told me what happened on the roof."

"Okay."

"Did your fingers really slip?"

I stared at Rosén and didn't respond. After a moment he shook his head, then turned to Jimmy, and took a ten-dollar bill out of his pocket. He handed it to him. "You, Professor are an interesting fellow. I'll call if there are any new developments."

It's true. I am an interesting fellow. Truth is, I would rather be a dull fellow and lead a quiet life and let the problems find someone else. I said good-bye to everyone and went to look for my wife.

Katherine was not in the cafeteria nor was she in the gift shop. After twenty minutes I gave up and went back to the third floor, thinking we had missed each other. No dice. Gabriele and her parents were already gone. As a rule, Katherine is not fond of hospitals and has a tendency to wander when she's bored. I didn't recall seeing any shoe stores as we drove in, but then I wasn't looking for them. I tried her cell phone and was transferred to voice mail.

I finally went to reception desk and asked the lady working there if she had seen anyone fitting Katherine's description. She didn't. At that point I was more irritated that she wandered off without telling me than concerned. I decided to check outside the building. No sooner had I cleared the front doors than my cell phone rang. I didn't recognize the number.

"You're really getting quite annoying, you know."

"Britton?"

"That's right."

"What do you want, asshole. I'm busy."

"You don't look very busy to me. In fact, it looks like you're standing in front of the hospital with nothing much to do."

"Fuck off, Britton. We've got nothing to talk about."

"Actually, we do. You asked what I want. That's the wrong question, Professor. It's more what you want. How's your wife, by the way?"

As soon as I heard the words a sick feeling took hold of my stomach. I now knew why Katherine was missing.

Britton continued, "What, no snappy comeback this time? I'll tell you this, your missus is a hell of a fighter. She bit the crap out of one of my guys. You like that kind? I don't. Personally, I prefer my women more compliant. One guy to another, you can level with me."

I forced my anger down. Britton was obviously nearby or he couldn't have described my location. I scanned the parking lot for him.

"You're cold, Professor. Ah, getting better . . . warmer . . . warmer still. Bingo."

Britton was standing next to a blue van at the opposite end of the parking lot.

As soon as I was close enough he asked, "Did you have a nice visit with Mr. Burnside or maybe I should say Brumot? Pity about him it?"

"Where's my wife?"

Britton smiled. "Not far. By the way, here's a souvenir for you." He reached into his coat pocket, pulled out a pair of women's panties and tossed them to me. They were Katherine's.

I started for him, but stopped as a gun materialized in his hand. Britton was fast. He pressed the barrel to my forehead.

"Don't you remember I told you threatening a federal agent is a crime?" He tapped the barrel against my forehead for emphasis. "Maybe you're not as smart as I gave you credit for. What do you think, Dave?"

My eyes shifted to a man seated behind the steering wheel.

Dave said, "Let's get this over. You're standing out here in broad daylight with a gun to someone's head."

Britton replied, "True. Unfortunately, some people are like mules. You have to get their attention before you can explain things properly." He turned back to me. "Here's the deal, John. Mind if I call you that? Wonderful. I want you to go back inside and get the recording disk from the court reporter. That's right, we know all about him, too, and what you were doing.

"If he's gone, find him. I don't really give a shit what story you make up. Just get it."

"And if I can't?"

"That would be bad for you and the little lady—really bad. But just to show my heart's in the right place, I'll give you until five o'clock. You have my phone number. When you call I'll provide further instructions. If I don't hear from you or I find out you've spoken to anyone else, I *promise* you'll regret it."

Anger surged inside me. I wanted to smash the smug look off his face. Reading my mind, Britton took a step backward to put some distance between us. Even if I could reach him, he was armed and I wasn't. Katherine was clearly my first concern. There was little doubt in my mind that Britton would make good his threat. You get a sense of people and he was a cold, lying bastard. When you peel back the phony smile you'd find a genuine psycho under the surface. Despite the boyish charm, it was there in his eyes.

I stood in the parking lot and watched them drive away, my chest rising and falling as I fought to gain control of my emotions. For all the good it would do me I made a note of the license plate. The CIA might not be perfect but they weren't fools. The tag was probably stolen.

After a few minutes I was calm enough to think logically. My problem was I didn't know who in the government was involved besides Brad Britton. I also knew no one on the D.C. police force. Calling them in was the smart thing to do. Their resources exceeded anything I could muster on short notice, but time was a luxury Katherine and I didn't have.

EIGHTY-SEVEN

IF Britton was being careful he probably had me under surveillance to see how I would respond. Making phone calls in the street wasn't smart. He would know I was calling the cops. I went back inside to give myself some privacy.

A nurse on the third floor told me the court reporter had left thirty minutes earlier. I thanked her and headed for the stairwell, taking out my cell phone out as I went. I had just started dialing Phil Thurman's number when I felt a hand on my shoulder. I reacted without thinking, spun, and knocked the arm away. My left hand grabbed the front of a man's jacket and my right went back to pummel whoever was there.

I found myself looking into Ted Jordan's face.

"John, if you hit me again, I swear to God I'll kick you in the balls this time."

I blinked and let go of him. "What are you doing here? I thought you were in Atlanta with your sons."

"I was. Gabriele doesn't even know I'm here yet."

"Then why are you?"

"Did you really think Tissinger would let this go without a fight? I spotted the blond guy you were just speaking with watching my house late last night. He left, but one of his buddies is still there. I snuck out through the basement window. They have Katherine."

"How do you know—"

"Because I followed them. I was across the street waiting for you when she came out of the building. Two men grabbed her by the arms and forced her into a car. I was too far away to reach her. I followed them, then came back here to find you. I'm so sorry. I never meant to bring this down on your heads."

Ted's words were coming out in a rush. I held up a hand to slow him down. "You know where they've taken her?"

"They're on a boat called *Devon Dream*. It's at the James Creek Marina. It's about twenty minutes away. We need to call the police."

"We will—or rather you will. First, I want you to call a man named Phillip Thurman and explain what happened. He's with the FBI and he'll know what to do. This is his number. Tell him to get in touch with Ray Rosen at the U.S. Attorney's office. Got that?"

"Sure, but—"

"After, you're to call a lady named Bonnie Cochran. Bonnie's a reporter with *The New York Times* who's been working on this story. This might not bury Tissinger, but it will put a dent in their precious image." I gave him her number as well.

"What are you going to do?"

"I don't know, but I can't wait for the cops. There's no way Britton will leave Katherine alive even if I get what he wants. He'll eliminate any source that can hurt him."

"Who's Britton?"

"The blond guy you saw. I was just speaking with him. Are you sure no one spotted you?"

"Positive, but there are three of them and one of you. I'll come with you."

"Right now it's more important to notify the authorities. You're not trained for this. I am."

"You were trained fifteen years ago. It's too dangerous."

"She's my wife, Ted."

Ted searched my face for a moment and shook his head. "You're the most stubborn son-of-a-bitch I've ever met. If you're going after them you'll need this."

Ted removed a .357 caliber revolver from his pocket and handed it to me. My eyebrows lifted in a silent question.

"I bought it on the street a few weeks ago from some kids," he said. "I thought I could force Charlie Evans into confessing."

I took the gun and flipped the cylinder open. There were six hollow-point bullets in the chambers.

"Change coats with me," I told him.

"Why?"

"We're about the same size and I don't think this will fool anyone for long. I want you to go down to the lobby and stand with your back to the window for about fifteen minutes. Check your watch every once in a while, like you're waiting for someone."

"I don't get it. What good will changing coats do?"

"Maybe nothing. But I need to buy as much time as I can. Britton told me to get the court reporter's disc. It contains Brumot's statement. If he has someone watching, I want them to think I'm waiting for him."

EIGHTY-EIGHT

THE James Creek Marina sits below the National War College at
Fort McNair. The College is a massive red-and-white structure
with columns, a rotunda, and an American eagle above the entrance. I read somewhere their mission is to educate senior military
personnel and State Department officials on our national capabili-
ties and strategies. They don't have a football team and if they did,
you wouldn't want to play them. Whatever those strategies were I
doubted they included poisoning people in third world countries.
We're better than that. I've believed this ever since I was a boy and I
believe it now. Rosen was right when he said there's no place for
what Tissinger was doing in our society.

The *Devon Dream* turned out to be a sixty-four-foot Hatteras. It
was moored at the end of the marina. There were enough trees on
the War College campus to provide cover for me until the last sixty
yards. After that I had two choices, enter the water or approach the
ship by way of the pier. The water afforded an element of surprise.
On the way to the marina I stopped at a sporting goods shop and
picked up a pair of binoculars. Ted's revolver was now wrapped in
the plastic bag it had come in.

From my vantage point I could see two men at the ship's stern.
Both were seated at a small table. One was Britton—the other his
friend Dave. Every now and then Britton's head would swivel toward
the companionway. He seemed to be talking to someone in the cabin.
Whether that was Katherine or another member of his team I didn't
know.

The temperature was in the low fifties and I had no illusions about
how cold the water was at this time of year. At most I'd have a few
minutes before hypothermia set in. There was no sign of the cops yet

and I couldn't wait any longer. The moment Britton tired of his game he'd put an end to Katherine's life.

Along with the binoculars I had also bought a golf hat. I pulled it low on my head and walked casually along the grounds of the War College campus, moving closer to the pier. Three things were working in my favor. There were quite a few people out that day and the *Devon Dream*'s cabin blocked any direct line of sight toward me. The last was the element of surprise. Brad Britton was not just a control freak, he was arrogant. He expected everyone to fold. Thus far, he'd been right.

The last tree before the pier was on a point of land that jutted out into the Anacostia River. It was perhaps twenty feet from the water. I had to wait for a young couple to pass. They were strolling, hand in hand, looking at the boats. For all I knew they were thinking about their future. Britton's future was also clear to me—he didn't have one.

Once the couple was gone I stripped down to my boxers and slipped into the water. It was frighteningly cold, so cold it felt like my skin was burning. Shock set in and I began to hyperventilate. I knew I had to move. In the back of my mind I remembered reading about an airliner that went down in New York's Hudson River. The article said a person could survive in forty-one-degree water for ten, fifteen, or even twenty minutes before losing control of their muscles. The *Devon Dream* was about sixty yards away. Holding the bag with Ted's revolver in my teeth, I started forward.

Through the binoculars I noted there was a swim platform at the rear of the Hatteras. If I could reach it in time and unnoticed there was a good chance I could climb aboard. My muscles began to feel sluggish after thirty yards. Rage pushed me forward. At the same time fear set in. Fear that Britton would hurt Katherine or that I would spend my life without her built inside me until it was all I could do to stop myself from screaming. What progress I made felt like it was coming in inches, still I forced myself to move . . . quietly, silently. The platform was now about twenty yards in front of me. Breathing was becoming difficult. With ten yards to go, my vision began to blur. Above, I could hear two men speaking. After what seemed like an eternity my hand found the ladder and I pulled myself up, partially out of the water. I clung there for a moment until my head cleared. Even the wind on my shoulders was painful. After another minute I felt like I had enough strength to try for the deck. I flexed my fingers several times, trying to restore some feeling to them.

Britton had his back to me. Dave saw me first, his expression changing to one of shock. He started to rise, reaching under his jacket at the same time. He never made it. Two shots from the gun struck him in the chest and sent him crashing backward into the cabin's glass sliding door. Britton dove sideways and came up in a crouch only to find himself looking down the barrel of my revolver.

"Drop it and tell whoever's in there to come out."

Britton's upper lip curled into a snarl and I saw his shoulders tense. I fired another shot into the transom just past his left ear. "The next one takes your head off."

His eyes flicked to the revolver's chamber and then back to me. I could almost hear his mind working as he calculated the number of bullets I had left. The gun was leveled at his face and I was ten feet away. It was unlikely I would miss at this distance.

"Nice knowing you, motherfucker," I said.

A smile appeared on Britton's face as his gun clattered to the deck. He raised his hands. "Marco, c'mon out and meet the professor."

There was no response from the inside of the cabin. Because of the bulkhead whoever was in there had no clear shot at me and I had no intention of letting the situation remain stagnant. A sharp breeze was blowing in off the water and I was beginning to shiver. I pulled the hammer back.

"*Now!*" Britton screamed at the cabin. "We got a situation out here."

A second or two passed before the door slid open and a man stepped out. His hands were raised and he was holding an automatic rifle in one of them.

"Toss it over the side," I told him,

The rifle hit the water with a splash.

"Now both of you move backward."

Britton's gun was still within his reach. I kicked it away and asked, "Where's my wife?"

"Inside and unharmed," Britton replied.

I glanced through the doors and saw Katherine lying on the bed. Her hands, ankles, and mouth were bound with gray duct tape. She was naked.

"Let's stay calm, Delaney. No one touched her. This was strictly business. We're not monsters. We only took her clothes to make sure she didn't—"

The rest of Britton's words were lost as I fired another shot directly into his companion's head. Britton flinched hard. Guns can be incredibly loud in close quarters. Marco, or whoever he was, arched back and tumbled over the railing in what looked like slow motion. Britton's mouth opened in shock. He had no time to recover his wits. I moved quickly and clubbed him over the head with the butt end of the revolver. He hit the deck unconscious.

Until that moment I had no clear idea of what I would do. He said they weren't monsters, but monsters come in all shapes and sizes. Some have horns and breathe fire and some wear suits and sit in ivory towers. I prefer the first kind. You know what they are and there's no pretense.

There are certain lines when crossed you don't get to come back from. Maybe I had crossed one myself. I knew for certain Britton had. Soon, Philippe Brumot would be dead and his family would go on without him. Luther was wounded and would take months to recover. Five scientists had been killed. Even Frank the tile man deserved better. The people in faraway countries deserved better. They thought they were taking medicine to help them. And why not? An American company manufactured the pills.

The wind across my back almost hurt. I went inside to see about my wife.

EIGHTY-NINE

I SECURED Britton using his own roll of duct tape, then freed Katherine. There were welts across her back, buttocks, and legs from where he had hit her with a belt, trying to learn our plans. She put her arms around my neck and buried her face in my chest. She was shaking uncontrollably. There were no tears. In point of fact, I had never seen her cry . . . not at movies, weddings, funerals, or anyplace else. Katherine is quite possibly, the toughest person I know. What happened to her as a young coed at Ohio State may have had something to do with this. I wasn't sure. Nevertheless, it took a long while for her to stop trembling.

I sat there holding her and trying to comfort her as the anger that sustained me over the last few hours began to fade away. I had been afraid in the water and afraid when I climbed the ship's ladder. It wasn't because I might have been shot or killed. It was the thought of not seeing Katherine again. That was unacceptable. Living my life without her was unacceptable. An odd way to put it, I know, but that's the truth. Once again, my stomach tightened at the thought. I wanted to take Britton's head and pound it against the deck until there was nothing left to pound. Unfortunately, there are disadvantages to being a civilized man.

Katherine eventually calmed down and we separated. She dressed quickly, not looking at me. I wanted to know what she was feeling. I found a towel in the cabin and dried off while my wife disappeared below deck. She returned after a few minutes carrying some foul weather gear for me to wear. The outfit consisted of a bright yellow pair of pants and a jacket. There was also a matching floppy hat, which I declined. I already looked ridiculous enough. It took nearly a half hour before I stopped shivering.

Britton was still lying where I had left him. The low hum of the *Devon Dream*'s engines drifted through the decking as we passed out of the Anacostia River and into the Potomac. We entered Chesapeake Bay and made our way south past Cape Charles. According to a navigation chart I found on the bridge, Fisherman's Island lay to the southeast of us. Beyond that was the Atlantic Ocean.

We had been traveling for more than an hour and I was hungry. Katherine located coffee and enough food for sandwiches. The hot liquid warmed my insides going down.

Eventually Britton regained consciousness and maneuvered himself into a sitting position. He looked at his surroundings, noted the land passing by, and said nothing for quite a while. He was probably thinking of his next move.

"You've already killed two of my men, Delaney. Don't make it worse on yourself. One of them was unarmed."

"Then I guess he should have armed himself," I answered from the bridge, not turning. Katherine was next to me, a blanket wrapped around her shoulders.

"If I don't report in my people will come looking for me."

"I trust they'll have better success than you've had." I swiveled the captain's chair to face him. "Who the hell are your people anyway?"

"You already know the answer to that. We're the United States government."

I shook my head slowly. "No . . . you're not the government. I don't know what branch the CIA works for, judicial maybe, but you're not the government. There's a real problem when you guys start believing that."

Agent Britton said, "You are *so* naïve. We can still work this out and no one gets hurt. You made a mistake with Marco and Dave. Cut me loose and I'll write it up so it comes off as self-defense. If you play along, I'll see to it you and the lady are fixed for life."

Katherine stiffened and started to rise, but I put a hand on her forearm. "Like you fixed the tile man in Atlanta? Like you fixed Phillipe Brumot and the other members of Severin's research team? Like you tried to fix Ted Jordan? I'm losing count of the number of people you've fixed, pal."

"Our government has invested a great deal of money with Tissinger to make sure their plant gets up and running. It will employ hundreds of people. What do you care if a some rag-heads in another country have a few side effects from a drug?"

"Suicide isn't a side effect, Brad. It's an effect."

"Torapam helps millions. Our situation in Muslim nations is very complicated. We don't need another black eye. Tissinger will work out the kinks in time. You have to look to the greater good."

I stared at him. It's hard to say whether he believed his own bullshit or not.

Britton continued to press the point. "Come on, Delaney, you're no murderer. What are you going to do? Kill a federal agent in cold blood?"

"You're probably right."

We had been traveling for nearly three hours and were now about twelve miles off shore. The coastline of the United States had long since disappeared in the haze. I handed Katherine the gun, then went to Britton and pulled him to his feet. I cut the bonds with a knife I had found in the galley.

Britton smiled at me and I smiled back. I was a civilized man—to an extent.

Without another word I grabbed the front of his shirt and heaved him over the side. He hit the water cursing. Katherine displayed no reaction. We made eye contact and a silent communication passed between us. She nodded, turned the ship's wheel over, and pushed the throttles forward.

The day was overcast and the water reflected the white clouds overhead. I looked toward the horizon where they seemed to blend into the ocean making it hard to tell where one left off and the other began. Whatever Britton was yelling was swallowed by the sound of the engines, the wind, and the void of white that enveloped him. Soon there would be one less monster in the world.

NINETY

SENATOR Talmadge looked at me across his desk. I had a feeling he was trying to reconcile our version of what happened with what the authorities had reported to him. It had been three days since we returned from our cruise with Brad Britton. Frankly, I had lost my taste for cruises. In that time the Washington D.C. police had taken our statements, as had one Special Agent Ron Turco with the FBI. Agent Turco was accompanied by a young woman named Andrea Warren from the U.S. Attorney's office. Ms. Warren looked to be about the same age as Katherine's daughter Alley. Their appearance didn't surprise me, nor was I shocked to find we were subjects of a murder investigation. The authorities had fished two dead bodies out of a marina, both of whom had clearly not died of natural causes. Certain procedures needed to be followed. Death, no matter how much we see it in the movies or on the news, still has the power to shock.

Ted's statement was also taken by the D.C. police. He confirmed witnessing Katherine's abduction. He told them the gun used to end Dave and Marco's lives was owned by him and said he had called the authorities on my instructions. At the time we were both convinced Katherine was in deadly peril. The detectives listened carefully, their faces sober. His statement effectively eliminated premeditation on my part and reinforced the notion that I had acted in self defense—or defense of my wife, to be more precise. Lawyers can be very supportive when you come right down to it.

The cop who interviewed us said he thought the grand jury would see what happened as justifiable homicide. The sticking point was Brad Britton, which accounted for our second visit from Agent Turco and Ms. Warren. Earlier that morning, both had come to our hotel room again to clarify some facts. This time they wanted to question Katherine and me separately and I refused. Agent Turco was polite but insistent, explaining it was only a formality. As yet, they had been unable to recover Britton's body from the sea.

I really had no reason to worry because Katherine is a more astute trial lawyer than I am and we had already rehearsed what we would say. My refusal was more for show than substance. She and Andrea adjourned to the bedroom to talk while Turco and I stayed in the living room.

He began, "If I understand correctly, Britton got the drop on you after you boarded the boat and shot his men."

"Correct."

"And he forced you to take the boat downriver and into the open sea."

"Also true."

"How come he didn't he just shoot you on the spot?"

"No idea. I suppose he wanted to get rid of our bodies."

Turco shook his head. "That doesn't make sense. Two of them were floating in the marina."

"It's hard to say what was going through his mind. He wasn't exactly in a sharing mood."

"Yeah, I guess. So once you were clear of the land there was a struggle, you got the gun away from him, and he fell overboard. Am I correct?"

"That's pretty much the way it happened."

I walked over to the wet bar, poured myself a scotch and offered one to him. He declined.

"How did you manage that against a trained agent twelve years your junior?" Turco inquired.

"I have a forceful personality."

Turco locked eyes with me. "Look, I'm just trying to understand what happened. It's my job."

"And I'm getting tired of these bullshit questions. We answered them yesterday. If you have something to say, say it. If you're going to charge us with a crime, do it, but let's quit dancing, okay?"

Turco flipped his notepad shut. "All right, here's my problem. I can buy the struggle and your getting hold of the gun. I can even buy that

Britton went overboard in the process. According to what you and your wife told us yesterday, she was operating the boat when the fight started. When she realized he had fallen overboard, she turned the *Devon Dream* around and went back to look for him. After an hour you gave up the search, returned to shore, and notified the police."

"That's exactly right."

"Did you know Britton went to college on a swimming scholarship?"

"No, I didn't. We didn't discuss his college athletics or what fraternity he was in or what his favorite colors were. The only thing I know for a fact is that we went back for him and came up empty. To be perfectly blunt, I wasn't all that upset."

"Why didn't you call the Coast Guard from where you were?"

"Because we were twelve miles out and our cell phones had no reception."

"There was a marine radio on board. You could have used that."

"Was there? I had no idea. Katherine and I have no experience with boats."

Turco took a deep breath and was about to say something else when Andrea Warren and Katherine reentered the room. Andrea's face seemed a little pale, I thought.

She said, "Ron, I don't think we need to bother these people anymore."

"But—"

"Ms. Adams . . . excuse me, Mrs. Delaney was sexually abused by those men and I'm of the opinion that whatever steps her husband took were justified under the circumstances.

"I'm so sorry you went through this trauma. Mr. Britton's actions and those of his friends were not authorized by our government in any way. They acted completely on their own."

"Thank you," Katherine said.

"I want you to know my office will investigate and get to the bottom of this. If other people are involved, I promise they'll be prosecuted."

I glanced at Katherine and read nothing in her expression. She was wearing her trial lawyer face. When Britton said she hadn't been touched I believed him. Maybe wanted to believe is more accurate.

It was obvious Turco wasn't happy with the situation, but he was older and more jaded than the young Ms. Warren. He nodded to me, then Katherine, and wished us both luck, which I thought showed class. He then stepped into the hallway. Andrea also said good-bye and followed him, touching Katherine sympathetically on the shoulder as she left. When they were gone Katherine started to reveal what had really happened. I saw no reason to put her through that again. In candor, I didn't want to know the details. I crossed the room and hugged her.

SENATOR Talmadge closed the file he was reading and tossed it onto the corner of his desk, bringing me back to the moment.

He remarked, "This entire episode has been pretty traumatic for you both. I'd like to share a few things that aren't public yet because I feel you're entitled to know them.

"Late last night, Mr. Britton's immediate supervisor was arrested along with another member of his department. The agency's assistant director also tendered his resignation this morning as has his executive assistant. They've both been cooperating with the authorities.

"Shortly before you came in, Andrea Warren phoned to let me know she would be presenting her case to the grand jury on Thursday. She's asking for the arrest of three of Tissinger's executive officers.

"As head of the Senate's oversight committee I'll be speaking with the State Department later today to ask that Èdith Legard's travel outside this country be restricted until the grand jury concludes its deliberations. Last, the Vice President and I have a meeting set up next week with our French counterparts to inform them of these events.

"I wish there was more I could do for you given what happened, but you have the gratitude of your government."

Katherine and I shook Sam Talmadge's hand. Neither us were surprised when he pulled another paper from the top drawer of his desk and pushed it toward us. It bore the letterhead of the Justice Department and basically asked us to say we wouldn't sue the United States over the incident. The *quid pro quo* was their agreement that I had committed no crimes during my wife's rescue. I suppose the two bodies in James Creek harbor would be written off as flotsam.

Katherine read the document and scrawled her name at the bottom without hesitation, then handed the pen to me. I signed as well.

WE walked hand in hand down the National Mall past massive white buildings and the old Smithsonian. Eventually, we found ourselves at the Lincoln Memorial. You can't help but be impressed and somewhat awed. It's reassuring to know however slowly the wheels of justice turn eventually things are put right. Our detractors are quick to point out it's all about money. The system isn't perfect and there's no denying a mistake occurs every now and then, but the fact is we police ourselves. When a problem is discovered we fix it and move on. Americans have always set aside the flock to go looking for the one that's lost. *That* is evidence of our strength, not our weakness.

Katherine stared up at Lincoln's face for a time and slid an arm around my waist. "Tell me we'll be together always," she said.

"Always."

"John . . . what were you thinking when those men took me?"

"That I might never see you again and that life, my life, wouldn't be worth living without you."

When Katherine turned to me her eyes were bright with tears. "I wouldn't want to live without you either. From that first day on the *Majestic* I knew we would be together. You're part of me."

I smiled and pulled her close and we kissed with Abraham Lincoln looking down at us. I don't think Abe minded.

My wife continued in a voice that was not much more than a whisper. "When those men took me I was afraid, but I knew you would come. I knew it more than anything in the world. I knew you would rescue me."

A few seconds passed before I could answer her. The words nearly caught in my throat. "It's only fair . . . you rescued me first."

Katherine put her head on my shoulder and took a deep breath. "What do we do now?"

"Life."